Praise for *Belarus*

"A riveting future . . . highly original. Hogan delivers an exotic once and future Russia."

—Kay Kenyon, author of *Tropic of Creation*

"With a richly imagined geopolitical setting, *Belarus* reads like a Russian fairy tale set in space."

—Syne Mitchell, Compton Crook Award–winning author of *The Changeling Plague*

"An entertaining work that will attract readers who like cutting edge speculative fiction. The different life forms that author Lee Hogan describes so vividly feel very real and believable. There is plenty of action in this novel but it is the characters that make this book several steps above the mundane."

—*Midwest Book Review*

"Strong on visual and dramatic touches . . . Hogan . . . must be respected for attempting to scale a mountain when many of her contemporary authors are content to trot up ordinary hills that add nothing to the map of our literary world."

—Science Fiction Weekly

Enemies

Lee Hogan

A ROC BOOK

ROC
Published by New American Library, a division of
Penguin Putnam Inc., 375 Hudson Street,
New York, New York 10014, U.S.A.
Penguin Books Ltd, 80 Strand,
London WC2R 0RL, England
Penguin Books Australia Ltd, 250 Camberwell Road,
Camberwell, Victoria 3124, Australia
Penguin Books Canada Ltd, 10 Alcorn Avenue,
Toronto, Ontario, Canada M4V 3B2
Penguin Books (N.Z.) Ltd, Cnr Rosedale and Airborne Roads,
Albany, Auckland 1310, New Zealand

Penguin Books Ltd, Registered Offices:
Harmondsworth, Middlesex, England

First published by Roc, an imprint of New American Library,
a division of Penguin Putnam Inc.

First Printing, April 2003
10 9 8 7 6 5 4 3 2 1

Cover art by Matt Stawicki

Printed in the United States of America

For Peter the Great,
who dreamed of the future,
then tried to make it happen,
AND
for Yuri and Valentina,
the first people in space.

ACKNOWLEDGMENTS

The Egyptian funeral prayer on page 190 was taken from the libretto of Philip Glass's opera *Akhnaten,* the vocal text of which was drawn from original sources by Shalom Goldman.

Many thanks to Rick Cook for extremely useful conversations and (as usual) for the loan of books that were not returned for an inordinately long time. Thanks to Ernest Hogan for reminding me what Baba Yaga can do. And my humble apologies to persons from cities and countries whose names were used in this book and whose languages I have mangled. You will see little or no resemblance to the places you know, partly due to the fact that they have been transplanted to a distant world, twenty thousand years in the future, and partly due to my clumsiness. The road to hell is paved with good intentions, and I'm going there for sure.

Do not ask why the Enemy has come to plague us. It is God's will. Do not ask why we were abandoned by the Republic that seeded us onto this world of perils, for their sins were great and they have perished. We are haunted by past failures, but by successes as well, for some of our children bear the marks of the Last Resort, with which we drove our Enemies into deeper darkness.

Our very sky is shrouded like the women who bear the marks of our sins! God speaks plainly. Do not ask; only know God's will and live by it. That is our salvation and our light in the darkness.

—from *The First Book of Belarusian Psalms*

PROLOGUE

In the Year of the Republic 19014, Baba Yaga watched the sprites play in the winds of Lucifer.

She had no traffic with the creatures, though she bore them no malice. Baba Yaga trusted only that which she had made herself, and she never gave her creations minds of their own. Things with minds had opinions, and opinions could turn at awkward moments.

Still, they could be interesting creatures. No larger than ice crystals, they glistened in the upper atmosphere of the gas giant, hitching a ride in its titanic storms, absorbing and channeling energy. Each one of them performed its part in a greater function, observing, recording, interacting. They created tunnels through space-time and beamed messages to each other, achieving almost instantaneous communication. They used the same method to beam data back to the person who had made them.

Those messages were sent to Andrei Mironenko, but Baba Yaga listened in. She listened to the sprites as they formulated theories and drew conclusions. Some dragged themselves out of Lucifer's immense gravity well and combined with other sprites, becoming larger and more complex. Their functions also became more complex, as did their theories and conclusions. Both chemical and mechanical, they were not unlike the cells of a giant brain; each time they interacted with people whose brains were organic, their emerging minds took on some of the qualities of those people, some of whom were human—and some of whom were not.

The effects of that link went both ways. People who talked to sprites did so by virtue of a biomechanical implant in their brains. Linking with sprites plugged them into a network of minds, and they were arguably as changed by the experience as the sprites were.

Well and good for some people, but Baba Yaga didn't need to have her consciousness expanded in such a fashion. One could learn without giving anything away, one could watch without being observed in kind. The sprites who were so thoroughly examining Lucifer and the rest of its solar system could have been spared a great deal of time and trouble if Baba Yaga were inclined to tell them what she already knew about it. But that was not the point. She wanted to see how long it would take them to figure it out themselves.

The sprites studied and explored. They swarmed through the asteroid belts just outside Lucifer's orbital plane, and they compiled lists of chemicals and minerals that would be useful to the man who intended to colonize this solar system, of which Lucifer was the sixth member. They made more of themselves and infected these new sprites with the virus that made them self-aware. Some of them tunneled to the third planet, the earthlike world on which the main colony would be built. Baba Yaga watched and waited, until finally the sprites around Lucifer found something curious.

They found alloys that could only have been crafted by intelligence.

<Andrei,> they warned their patron. <Caution. Anomaly.>

<Anomaly noted,> said Andrei. <Specify.>

Baba Yaga laughed. That directive would take the sprites years to obey. The alloys they had discovered were objects orbiting Lucifer. To give them credit, the objects had no energy signature, and would not have been detected by anyone who relied on mechanical sensors to find them. Their makers were masters at stealth technology, so the objects had escaped notice until their most basic elements were examined.

Andrei suggested the sprites build eyes that would see much in the same fashion as human eyes. So the sprites were finally able to see four objects, roughly the size of space stations, distributed evenly in orbit around Lucifer, moving as precisely as an enormous clock. Andrei called them the Derelicts because of the damage that could be observed on their hulls and because their makers were nowhere to be found.

Baba Yaga didn't agree. The people who made the Derelicts were somewhere deep below the surface of the third planet, which Andrei had already named Belarus. She couldn't pinpoint their exact location, but she knew they were there, just like she would have known if her home had termites. Even when you can't see the Bugs themselves, you can see what they've done. Baba Yaga saw evidence of engineering on Belarus, life forms altered to accommodate the needs of aliens.

She favored Andrei. She had watched his line for several generations, communicated with his father and grandfather, sometimes warning them, sometimes scolding. She communicated with Andrei, too, but she didn't tell him much. People were like plants in a garden—you couldn't coddle them or they would wilt at the first sign of bad weather. The tough plants were the wild ones, which thrived under adversity. That was how Baba Yaga cultivated people.

Andrei Mironenko was engaged in a project that must succeed. He wished to build a colony that could survive on its own, and he wanted to recruit colonists who were of Slavic descent, but also Persian, Hasidic, Asian—all of the lands that bordered Russia on old Earth. Andrei wished to do this as an act of preservation. He was like a man who sees a fire approaching and rushes to load all that is most precious to him on a cart. Belarus was to be the cart. The fire was the war that must eventually consume the Republic.

The sprites described Belarus to Andrei. It was a world in

the final stages of an ice age, but its largest continent was habitable, experiencing four seasons per rotation around its sun, roughly one earth year. A harsh place, and beautiful, a good spot for tough people to grow deep roots. The sprites could find no sign of the aliens who built the Derelicts. Baba Yaga was not surprised when Andrei decided to move forward with the colonization. She waited to see how quickly his enemies would react to his decision.

The Mironenkos were one of the powerful clans that owned the patents that made it possible for the Republic to exist in the first place. Andrei's forefathers did not always agree with family policy. Andrei almost never did. Many of his enemies were close family members. Twenty-four hours before he was to depart for the Lucifer system, he received a visit from the worst of them, Uncle Nikita.

Baba Yaga was amused by how closely the two men resembled each other. Youth technology made them look like young brothers; both were over three hundred years old—infants compared to Baba Yaga, but old enough to be interesting. Despite their similarities, she could easily tell them apart. Andrei was the one with the noble heart. Nikita was the one who just looked like he owned one.

"I have come to talk some sense into you," said Nikita. "I hope."

"I'm listening," said Andrei calmly, though he was talking to the man who had orchestrated the murder of both his parents.

"Your colony is a delightful idea," said Nikita. "You have the support of the family, though we wish you would recruit more Christians. Jews and Muslims have caused a lot of trouble on other Russian worlds, you know."

Andrei said nothing to this old argument.

"It should be interesting to see," said Nikita, "whether your precious Bill of Rights will live up to your expectations."

"It has worked very well on other worlds," said Andrei. "Democracy, well-defined civil rights, and the rule of law."

Nikita smiled softly. "Yet you will be tsar on this world of yours."

"Only until it gets on its feet," said Andrei, and Baba Yaga knew he believed it.

"You're paying for it," said Nikita. "You can bloody well do what you want, just like the rest of us do. The family council doesn't care if you indulge some illusions. What troubles us is your use of sprites."

"They've been extremely helpful," Andrei said blandly. "I don't have unlimited financial resources, as you know. Sprites can be anything I need them to be."

"Yes, anything," said Nikita. "That's the problem."

Andrei leaned forward, his hands on his knees, and listened attentively. He knew Nikita had not come to give him advice. Boundaries were being declared, warnings given. Baba Yaga had witnessed many such confrontations over the centuries. The first princes of Kiev would have felt perfectly at home in this meeting.

"Sprites were useful when their programming was uncomplicated," said Nikita, "when they had simple tasks to perform, like cleaning the plaque out of an artery or polishing silver. The problem was when they got too ambitious."

"You mean when *we* did," said Andrei. "Mironenkos worked just as hard to perfect a sprite virus as everyone else did. We never came close to creating a virus that could program sprites to live up to their full potential."

"Sprites do not *live,*" said Nikita. "They are made. That's fine with me, as long as they do what they're told. But we should have worked harder to win that race, Nephew. The winners were aliens. And they will have a say in everything you do, because you're using their sprites. Your *brain* is linked with them, for God's sake."

"The Woovs came up with the sprite virus before everyone else because they were smart enough to do it," said Andrei. "Intelligence can be a good thing, Uncle. I like to give it a chance."

"That's a good way to get killed," said Nikita.

Baba Yaga thought he had a point. Woovs were kinder folk than humans; that was sometimes their greatest weakness. But Woovs were tough when they had to be. An older race, wiser than humans, Baba Yaga occasionally found her agenda overlapping with theirs. She doubted that Nikita ever did.

"I'll admit you've put together a good team," said Nikita. "Tally Korsakova is a brilliant world engineer. She trained under George Bernstein, who's done excellent work for my friends on Canopus."

"I know your spies give you good information, Uncle," said Andrei. "In fact, I count on it."

Nikita continued smoothly. "Of course we support your ambition to build a Hermitage where you can display the family treasures."

"They'll be safe there," said Andrei.

Baba Yaga laughed silently. Old Nikita lusted after some particular treasures that Andrei owned, several Fabergé eggs. She had seen many otherwise levelheaded people chase after those eggs over the centuries. Nikita couldn't steal them outright—they would only be stolen back. He would have to inherit them, and he could only do that if Andrei were dead. Pesky detail.

"You've managed to contract with some ESAs, I hear," said Nikita. "You don't need Enhanced Special Agents, Andrei; plenty of other people have enhancements these days, people with talent."

"ESAs and sprites go hand in hand," said Andrei. "So to speak. And as you say, the Woovs are part of that link."

"Charming people," said Nikita. "Quite admirable in all ways, I'm sure. But ESAs have flaws too, Nephew. They are elitist in their choice of patrons."

"Yes, they only work for honorable people."

"You've contracted with just such a fellow, ESA Grigory. His last patron was not so honorable. She tried to use their communication link to kill him. His receivers were in his eyes, you might have heard. He had to tear them out to protect his brain. He never got new ones, just replaced them with red bloodstones. A tough fellow, but he's made some mistakes in judgment, wouldn't you say? ESAs are not superhuman. But they're close enough to be quite dangerous if they should change their minds about what you're trying to do. Think about it."

"Quite a mouthful," said Andrei. "I'll think about it, Uncle."

He did not say that Nikita had attempted to contract with ESAs and had been rejected.

Baba Yaga didn't trust ESAs any more than she did the sprites. But they were just as interesting.

Andrei bid his uncle adieu. Baba Yaga watched as he moved Archangel Station to the Lucifer system. She also saw Nikita's spies, some of whom arrived before Andrei did. One in particular caught her interest, a weapons expert who called himself Loki. He slithered into Andrei's project like a viper, and began to contrive various poisons.

Apparently Nikita was not above using flawed talent either. Loki was a serial killer. His work on Belarus smacked of long experience. But his most important work was to perfect the weapon he wanted to use against the sprites, which he loathed even more than his patrons did. He called this weapon WILDFIRE.

Came the year of the Republic 19024, and all the money the powerful clans had spent on weapons development finally came to fruition.

Baba Yaga watched as almost seventy percent of the Republic went up in flames. She thought it was good riddance. The Republic was like an overgrown forest, full of kindling. If a few lightning strikes could set it off, it needed to go. She knew Andrei would defeat the ones who came to destroy Belarus, and he did. No surprises there, but she was intrigued by what Loki did on the first day of the Civil War.

His mind floated in a matrix of his own making, comprised of false sprites. Real sprites did not notice them because they contained only enough programming to receive messages and pass them along. Throughout the galaxy, his false sprites maintained their relays among the true sprites. They worked benignly within this system until they received his code:

<WILDFIRE: ARM.>

The sprite network ignited like a mind having a seizure.

<Enable,> commanded Loki; then he sat back to watch the destruction.

Baba Yaga was able to observe the results better than he was. When he destroyed the network, his false sprites had nothing to interact with anymore. He had to assume the silence meant success. And he was right. But he was stranded by his own actions, left with the other colonists to face the onslaught of their Enemies, the ones hiding under the surface of Belarus, the ones who could see that their unwanted visitors were cut off from any hope of assistance.

The ones who now felt inclined to emerge.

Who are you? Andrei Mironenko asked them.

We are your Enemies, came the reply.

They were a species incapable of mercy. Torture was their highest art form. They demonstrated their mastery of it to Andrei's colonists.

There were no more years of the Republic. It was the Belarusian year 17. Andrei prepared for another war, and Baba Yaga did a rare thing. She called him for a face-to-face meeting.

She liked him, she had to admit. Clever man, brave without being too foolish about it. Decisive without being squeamish. He was one of the best tsars she had ever known. So she told him a secret.

"When this war is done," she said, "you will have your lives, probably little more. This new Enemy will survive as well, and over the centuries they will become your oldest and worst enemy. After a long time of fighting and hating, you will get to know them. That is the only way. You will know them and they will know you. Once you have done that, you will learn the other truth."

She studied him. His keen eyes returned the favor. Only a handful of people knew what she was about to tell, and she had to be sure he was worthy. "You will learn," she said at last, "that they are *not* your worst enemies—those, you have yet to meet."

"Thank you, Grandmother," Andrei said with perfect courtesy, and he asked only a few more questions before she shooed him off to meet his fate.

By winter, he was dead, along with most of his Enemies. Success always came with a price, and Baba Yaga found this one high.

Many things happened afterward, but she only watched what was important. ESA Grigory, the one whose patron tried to kill him, died alongside Andrei Mironenko. But Grigory was an ESA Elder. He did not simply pass into night like other mortals. He kept an Avatar in his left eye socket, one of the red bloodstones he used to replace the eyes that had betrayed him. The Avatar contained his mind, his memories; it still watched and thought. It would have watched her, if it could. This Watcher was interesting.

Little else was, for many centuries. The survivors of the Civil War built a Union out of the ashes of the Republic. They were much more cautious this time around. They abolished the patents that had caused so much trouble in the past. They governed themselves using the Bill of Rights, the same one Andrei had so admired. The Woovs contributed much to the effort, which gave them considerable influence. Baba Yaga saw no reason to oppose that.

The new Union went looking for lost colonies. It offered them partnership. It offered the Bill of Rights. Those that accepted were allowed to join the Union. Those that didn't want equal rights for all citizens were offered humanitarian aid, but otherwise given a wide berth.

Baba Yaga watched the centuries pass from the forests of Belarus. She grew her favorite tobaccos and smoked the blend in her pipe. Occasionally she sent letters to whichever Mironenko was current tsar, but she never invited them to her home. She moved her dwelling from time to time; it walked on metal legs that looked like those of a giant chicken, a detail that had inspired many stories over the centuries, on many worlds.

She knew the Union would find Belarus again, and then she would have work to do. But before that happened, they found something else.

It was an alien ship of unknown design and origin. It engaged and destroyed the Union ship *Sojourn,* then savagely tortured and slaughtered the personnel of a nearby space station.

Who are you? the human victims asked their tormentors. *Why are you doing this?*

We are your Enemies, was the reply.

Yes, there was a reason the Enemies of Belarus had remained hidden for so long, a reason why the Derelicts had been damaged when Andrei Mironenko first laid eyes on them. Belarus was not the world that spawned the Enemies, and they were such clever fiends, could anyone be surprised that they had explored much of the galaxy? Humans and Enemies were bound to intersect sooner or later.

Nine centuries passed before someone came looking for what was left of Belarus. His name was Taylor, captain of the Union survey ship *Artemis*. He found Archangel Station, empty and cold, yet still maintaining a stable orbit around Belarus. Baba Yaga knew what he would see as he orbited the night side: dim lights in some of the heavily populated areas, but no energy signatures. No one answered *Artemis*'s hails.

Taylor's technicians accessed the ancient log from Archangel Station. The recording revealed a gaunt man with coffee-colored skin. "This is Commander Jones," said the man. "Anyone who finds this message, be warned: there are hostile aliens sharing the world below us with our colonists. We fought a war with them and won, but they're not dead. They may still have weapons in this system somewhere. We don't know.

"The colony has been bombed back to the preindustrial age. They'll have to reestablish heavy industry, and they don't have what they need to do it anywhere near the level they started out with. I hope Andrei managed to salvage some of his sprites, but I doubt it. We haven't been able to communicate with him for a couple of weeks.

"There's a lot to tell you, and I won't try to do it now. I've got one important bit of information to pass on. There's an ESA Avatar down below, probably in St. Petersburg. His name is Grigory, and you're going to want to talk to him before you do anything—I mean *anything*—in the way of contact down below. Get as close to St. Petersburg as you can and broadcast this message on a wide band: *Watcher, where are you?* You should get a homing signal from him. But be careful with your sprites, assuming you've got any. You won't be able to use them to find the Enemies."

Enemies. Taylor must have felt the hand of fate on his shoulder; Baba Yaga was sure it chilled him to the bone. The salvage teams would later find the Derelicts he and his crew had missed on their way into the solar system. If they had seen them, they would have recognized the odd designs on their hulls, patterns that teased the subconscious and hinted at dimensions imperceivable to human and sprite sensors.

The time had come for her to send another message.

Captain Taylor, she said, *what took you so long?*

Now, in the Union year 817, Belarusian year 905, a new breed of sprites flew the winds of Lucifer.

The new sprites often talked about the fate of the old ones. They were immune to WILDFIRE, but they knew they were not invulnerable. Their numbers had grown again, until they could be found in every part of the known galaxy. The sprites in and around Lucifer worked with a group of humans who orbited the gas giant in a station they called Home Base. They were salvagers and mining experts, people who specialized in refurbishing the ancient machinery of lost colonies.

The Derelicts were gone from Lucifer. Anyone who wanted to look at them had to travel into the asteroid belt, where they floated in a stasis field, their hides displaying newer damage from human weapons. Sprites and humans still pondered these objects. Like the old sprites, the new sprites could not reach a conclusion, because they did not yet have enough evidence.

Flawed creatures, even with their improvements. But still interesting.

Taylor was quickly replaced with diplomats, social workers, and representatives of various Union government agencies—including the Department of Defense, who wanted very much to know how human colonists had survived for so many centuries on the same world with Enemies.

An excellent question, but Baba Yaga had no doubt the sprites had questions of their own. She saw some of them floating down the streets of St. Petersburg like snowflakes. This delegation drifted into the Winter Palace, down the long halls and up to the locked door of the Tomb of the Engineer, which was once the private quarters of Tally Korsakova. Inside the tomb, another survivor of the millennium rested. She listened in as they paid him a call.

<Watcher,> they said.

<I'm here,> answered the Avatar of Enhanced Special Agent Grigory.

<We wish to ask you about Loki,> said the sprites, <whom Belarusians called John the Murderer.>

<Ask,> said ESA Grigory.

<We have examined surviving recordings of his interrogations. He appeared very confident in all of them. He was brilliant. He seemed to be constantly thinking up angles he could use to outwit the legal system. He did not appear to be weary or consumed by despair. Why did he hang himself in his cell?>

<His ghosts got him,> said Grigory.

<His ghosts?> asked the sprites, puzzled.

<The ghosts of the young girls he killed to amuse him-

self. The ghosts of billions of souls who died when his weapons were deployed. The ghosts of the sprites he destroyed with WILDFIRE.>

<You think he was driven by guilt?> they wondered.

<No. I think he was driven by fear. I think he was *pushed.*>

<By whom?>

<No one on this side of the Veil,> said ESA Grigory.

Baba Yaga enjoyed the double entendre. He spoke both of death and of the stellar feature that obscured half the night sky on Belarus, also called the Veil. Andrei Mironenko had hidden a fleet inside that vast cloud, and the Enemies had done likewise with at least one terrible weapon. Other things might hide there still, things that eluded the sensors of sprites like the Enemy Derelicts had.

<The refurbishment of Archangel will be complete within the next forty-eight hours,> the sprites informed Grigory. <The first embassador is on his way.>

<He won't be the last,> predicted Grigory.

<How long do you think repatriation will take?>

<Longer than the lifetime of any Belarusian. Most of them haven't even heard of Star Men yet; few who *have* heard will welcome the Union at first sight. They don't trust strangers. Most especially, they don't trust strangers who turn out to be distant relatives. After all, relatives can inherit your property when you're dead.>

<But we have so much help to offer,> said the sprites. Already, medical technicians had begun to make arrangements to descend to the planet, to set up clinics.

<Offer it,> said Grigory. <Don't take it personally if your offer is thrown back in your face. The Mironenkos still rule Belarus, the Bill of Rights still lies at the heart of Belarusian government, but the people who interpret that document have changed.>

<We'll warn the embassador,> promised the sprites.

<Yes. Warn, by all means. And don't forget to look over your own shoulders. The evil that killed your predecessors

began here. I'm reminded of something Baba Yaga once wrote to Andrei about Enemies. She said *Evil is perennial. It likes to go into hibernation under the frost and dead leaves so it can bloom again in the spring.*>

Baba Yaga laughed. Grigory might be worthy of a face-to-face conversation someday.

She smoked her pipe and gazed out at the snow as it fell in her forest. She knew a lot of things; most of them she would never reveal. A few things escaped her notice, but not for long. She never had to look over her shoulder, because she had eyes in the back of her head.

Grigory's warning was well timed. Loki was dead, but who knew what might bloom again in the spring? One thing you could count on, even on a world as cold as Belarus.

Spring comes every year.

PART ONE

YEAR OF THE UNION 902; BELARUSIAN YEAR 990
ST. PETERSBURG

"Vasily Burakov."

Vasily woke instantly and switched on his bedside light. The voice that spoke his name in the dark was the croak of someone who had been a heavy smoker for a thousand years. He blinked in the glow of the lamp and looked for the intruder.

He was alone. But he could have sworn he caught a whiff of pipe smoke, some exotic blend.

"Who's there?" he called, halfheartedly. The heavy door to his room was locked from the inside, his window was likewise barred, and he thought it was probably just a dream that woke him. But his heart pounded like a hammer, and he sat frozen for some time before he noticed that the comm on his desk was blinking to indicate he had just received a message.

It wasn't odd for the Union embassador to Belarus to receive messages at all hours. But the sight of the blinking light gave him a start. He approached the comm with dread.

Thick carpets kept his feet warm. His apartment in St. Petersburg could not be called luxurious, but it was certainly comfortable. He sat down and flipped open the unit. A message instantly popped onto the screen.

Vasily Burakov, it read, and he could almost hear that dreadful voice again.

> *I have a name to tell you: Ayat-ko. Remember it well; you will probably never hear it spoken in public. She is an Enemy woman. She has taken a position in a great Russian household. Watch her. She was living on this world long before Andrei Mironenko came to build his colony here. She survived his revenge.*
>
> *You've worked hard since you arrived here. Your work is about to get a lot harder.*
>
> *—B.Y.*

Vasily had seen those initials once, on a historic document, written to Captain Taylor. B.Y. stood for *Baba Yaga*. She had sent a few more letters to Taylor, but she had communicated with no one since.

Until now. If this was her. And he was pretty sure it was.

Vasily stared at the painting that hung on the wall opposite his bed. It had come with the apartment. It was strange; anyone else would have put it inside a closet. The subject was an old fairy tale, rendered by a Belarusian artist. It was a picture of Baba Yaga's fabled house, the one that walked on giant chicken legs. The legs were folded under the house. Only a hint of the claws showed under the porch. The house itself was made of human bones, as was the fence that surrounded it. A human skull perched on top of each fence post, and since it was a night scene, each skull glowed like a torch.

That was the Baba Yaga of ancient legend, the Russian grandmother witch who was neither good nor evil, dark nor light. She was a force of nature, and those who crossed paths with her might benefit or suffer, depending on her whim.

Clever mortals escaped relatively unharmed. Stupid ones ended up as fence posts.

Vasily wasn't sure which one he might turn out to be. He did not go so far as to believe that the Baba Yaga of Belarus was the real one, on whom all legends were based, but he had a healthy respect for her opinions. He got up and checked his locks, even though he was sure they wouldn't keep her out. He wanted to at least make a show of securing his perimeter. If she was right, and his job had just gotten harder, he really needed to get back to bed.

He sent a copy of the letter to Archangel, first, addressing it to Commander Hale. Then he crawled back into bed.

He turned the lamp down, but not off.

It was a mistake. In the gaslight, the skulls in the painting seemed to flicker at him. He kept opening his eyes to see if the house in the painting had gotten to its feet. When he finally did get to sleep, he dreamed all night that it was chasing him. But in the morning, the world looked just the same as it had the day before.

As with so many other things on Belarus, that proved to be an illusion.

YEAR OF THE UNION 917; BELARUSIAN YEAR 1005
MOSCOW

Serina intended to look into a mirror, but first she had to find one.

She waited at her bedroom window, watching the Veil move across the stars. When it covered half the sky, she crept out of her room and through the forest that was her house at night, frightened but convinced that midnight was the only time she dared to look for something forbidden. Her feet scarcely made a noise on the marble floors as she moved down the long halls, hiding in the deeper shadows, winding through finely carved table legs and around pillars that were topped by heads of people she didn't know. Their stone eyes seemed to follow her progress, especially the eyes of lovely ladies. Serina wondered which of them she looked like. One look into a mirror, and she would see the beauty she only dreamed of.

She stopped to listen. Was that a sound? A wolf that hid behind padded-silk chairs? Serina almost lost her nerve.

Don't be silly. No wolves can get in the house. If something is following, it must be a person . . . Serina sank to her belly on the thick Persian carpet. Her ears rang with silence. She saw no movement, only shadows. She would be seven years old tomorrow, and was taller than the tabletops. She didn't even have to stand on tiptoe to see where she was going.

Light flashed through one of the windows; the shadows raced across the room, over and past her. Something very bright had passed the great house, something the Star Men had brought with them from another world, a noisy thing, impossibly fast and bright. It left her dazzled in the dark.

Serina waited for a while, feeling calmer by the minute. The Star Men had done her a favor. Thanks to their brief light she had recognized the room she was in—if she could find the main hall, she could walk past her mother's apartments and go to the staircase that led up to the next floor.

Serina had been there only once, tagging along behind the maids as they searched the unused floor for table linens. They had long since learned to ignore Serina's presence, as did everyone except her mother. So they spoke freely around her as if she weren't there, and she heard the most interesting and wicked things. As they pulled trunks down from closets and looked through the cedar-smelling contents, they chatted with each other about the doings in the great house and the people who ruled it, Serina's family. They didn't scold her when she took a jewelry box and rifled it.

The lining in the lid was torn. Serina knew it must have held a mirror once. She had grown accustomed to the blank places in her world where reflective surfaces used to be. She put the jewelry on her fingers and around her neck, then stared at the torn place in the lid, imagining herself adorned with finery. She substituted the head of one of the lovely stone ladies for her own.

A maid walked past her and opened a door into an adjoining room. Serina glanced over, distracted by the sound. The maid disappeared around the corner, leaving the door open. Serina's eyes were drawn to a sliver of white light. Something stood on the far side of the next room, draped with a sheet, but one edge had fallen away from its magic surface.

Serina heard the maids coming back and quickly looked down again. She could feel the weight of their gaze, heavy with dismay as they realized what they might have revealed to her. But she pretended she had not even looked up from her pretty box. She heard them whispering.

"Lock the door."

"I don't have the key . . . It wasn't locked anyway . . ."

"Well, we'd better find one. You know what the mistress says about . . . you know."

No one ever told Serina why she mustn't see herself. But she found clues about her situation in her favorite books, collections of fairy tales. She had read every single book, many times over, and now that the hidden mirror had been revealed to her she felt like one of the enchanted girls in those stories. Perhaps if she saw herself she might break the spell and become so beautiful that the tsar himself would come to court her. Serina had to be patient, cunning beyond her years. She acted as if the mirror did not exist, and the maids eventually forgot about it.

But *she* didn't. The time was right. She had to find the mirror now, or gigantic vines might as well grow over her bedroom and seal her away from the world forever. Serina tiptoed into the hall and past her mother's room, up the stairs ever so slowly so they wouldn't creak. Years passed between the steps.

But finally she was at the top, and nothing stirred behind her. She waited just long enough to be sure. Then she ran lightly to the door.

It opened silently. Serina peered through. The darkness seemed solid, but Serina stepped into it and carefully closed the door behind her. She stood for a moment in the chill of the deserted hall. Then she began to walk, counting each step, just as she had done before when she followed the maids. Ten times ten steps, and then she put her hands out to feel the door to a particular room. She found a blank wall instead.

She had counted wrong. Or stepped wrong, she wasn't sure. But she couldn't give up yet. If she was lost in the dark, she might as well look for the door while she was there. Feeling along the wall, going back a short distance like a caterpillar edging up a flower stalk, inch by inch, she thought the door must be there somewhere. She should have found it already . . .

Her arm bumped something cold and smooth. A vase, taller than her. She remembered seeing it before, a magnificent thing splendidly colored with blue and gold and red patterns that were not Russian.

So the door must be in the other direction.

Emboldened, she felt her way back along the wall. Soon her caterpillar tactics rewarded her with the door.

Her hand on the knob, she was struck by an awful thought. It was so dark—what if she could not see the mirror? How cruel that seemed. She was so close to her goal, and to be denied what her heart so fervently wished—Serina's eyes filled with tears.

Mother would have scolded her. Serina often felt like crying when she couldn't speak with the clarity her mother demanded or when she couldn't remember her lessons. "Try again," Mother always said. "Keep working. What will you gain if you give up?"

And she was right. Serina could not give up just because she might fail. She turned the knob, and the outer door opened.

The room was full of moonlight from the tall window at the far side. And more wonderful still, the door to the farther room stood open. Serina could see the mirror. The sliver at the edge was white with reflected moonlight.

At last. Now I shall look. Now I shall know . . .

When she was close enough to touch the sheet that covered it, her hand rose as if commanded by another. She tugged; it fell in soft folds, revealing the bright surface behind, revealing Serina.

She looked with horror. The image in the mirror contorted further to reflect her grief. In one dreadful moment she fathomed all her troubles, the speech lessons, the averted gaze of servants and her own brothers and sisters, the missing reflections. She gazed at her true face.

Another face appeared behind it. This face was inhumanly beautiful. It smiled cruelly at her. But that was the only kind of smile an Enemy could muster.

"Ayat-ko," Serina said bitterly, "I'm ugly! That's why they won't let me see myself!"

"Yes," the lady agreed. She was no servant like the human girls who cleaned and took care of the house. She was a member of the race who had warred with humans on Belarus for a thousand years. She was Serina's special tutor. And she always told the truth. "Your kind care very much about physical appearance. They are fools."

And suddenly Ayat-ko did something no one else had ever done, or would do for years to come. She touched Serina's face. She placed her pale hand on the jaw that was so badly misshapen. There was no trace of disgust or horror in her gesture, only curiosity. Her palm was feverishly hot. Her pupils were shaped like stars, and they expanded as if to drink Serina in.

"What will you do about it, child?" wondered Ayat-ko. "Will you prove to be as strong as your mother? Or another one of these simpering weaklings?"

For a moment, Ayat-ko made Serina forget about the shape of her face. She could only wonder about the Enemies, what their minds were like. The question would trouble her for the rest of her life.

In the morning it was her birthday. She did not greet it with joy.

Her mother came to see her shortly after they took away

the breakfast she could not eat. Galena brought something with her, but it wasn't a gift.

"Look at me," commanded Galena.

Serina obeyed with tears in her eyes. She gazed upon the beautiful, stern face and could see no trace of herself in it.

"They call it Botkin's Syndrome," said Galena. "It is a direct result of the Enemy War, fought almost a thousand years ago. The war left traces of poison. The poison affects the genes, and some people are born as you were, with disfigured faces. I was going to tell you when you were old enough to understand. Are you old enough, Serina?"

"Yes, Mother."

"Speak up child. Where is your pride? Are you the same person you were yesterday?"

"Yes, Mother," Serina said more clearly. She let her gaze rest on the thing in her mother's hands. It was black, and long, and made of fine gauze.

"You will learn more of the Enemy War in your schooling," said Galena. "And you will learn something else today. I regret it, Serina, for there is nothing shameful about your face. But the scars left by the war are deep. Women who bear the mark of the Last Resort must hide their faces with this shroud. No one shall be able to detect the outline of your face. This is what you must do in order to show yourself to the world."

"A shroud?" Serina was puzzled. "For my face?"

"You need not wear it in your private rooms. But you will not be permitted to leave this floor without it. Not even your brothers and sisters will see your true visage."

Serina could only stare in astonishment.

"I see that you think it is I who will make you," Galena said, her voice softening. "Not so, child. It is a cruel law. People have tied false beliefs to Botkin's Syndrome. They think it is God's mark of shame upon a woman. It is nonsense, Serina, but this is our world and we must live in it as we can."

Serina raised her hands to her face. It did not *feel* disfigured, even when her fingers glided over the place in her jaw that was improperly formed. "Mother, it's not a happy thing to be ugly, but why is it a shameful thing?"

"Eight hundred years ago," said Galena, "some men in the Russian church wanted to assign blame for all of the dreadful things that have happened on this world. They quickly found agreement from fanatics among the other faiths, that God must be punishing us for our sins."

"But Mother"—Serina dropped her hands again—"have I sinned so greatly?"

"No more than anyone else. They believe your disfigurement is the mark of *all* our sins."

Collective guilt was a new concept for Serina. She pondered it. "If it is God's will that I should look this way, then won't we make Him mad by covering up His work?"

Galena gave her half a smile. "That is an excellent question. If we have all sinned, then surely we should all ponder our sins when we see the face of a woman with Botkin's Syndrome. But fanatics never accept their own guilt; it is for others to bear. They decided that those who have been marked with Botkin's Syndrome must have been selected for it because of some evil that lies within their souls. Therefore, to show your face, Serina, would be an act of pride in that evil, and would inspire evil in others."

Serina thought longer before she replied. "There is no stain on my soul," she concluded. "I am not evil."

"You most certainly are not," said Galena with more compassion than Serina had ever heard her express. She was comforted. But her curiosity still drove her to speculate.

"How shall I change their minds, Mother?"

"That remains to be seen," replied Galena. She raised the shroud and presented it to Serina.

An odd thing happened. Serina's heart had ceased to ache, and she stopped hoping she would not have to wrap the dark gauze around her head. Now she knew that she must. Pain still nested within her, but for the moment she felt nothing. She wondered what it might be like to view the world behind a shroud. She knew there was only one way to find out.

"Will I be able to see through it?" she asked.

"If we do it properly," said Galena.

Serina nodded. "Please show me."

❦

Vasily Burakov flew over the snow. He thought he might be skiing, but didn't want to inquire too deeply. Close examination of the sensation would probably cause it to stop, and it was so delightful, so blissful to fly over the white hills, the breeze cool on his naked face instead of the bitter, killing cold it ought to be.

The woods on either side of him were lovely, greyish green even in the darkest heart of winter. Somewhere in those mysterious depths, Baba Yaga still lived. The grandmother witch had not spoken in fifteen years, but she was still there, he could feel it. Other things hid there as well, both magical and monstrous. How he loved this world, beautiful Belarus. It didn't love him back. It fought him every inch, tempted him with its beauty, deceived and then rejected him.

But for a time he flew. The snow was so pristine it might have fallen in heaven. Each bump and bend yielded to him, never slowing his progress for a moment. If anything, he seemed to be going faster, faster . . .

And then he made the mistake of looking at the sky.

The Veil was encroaching on the sunlight. At night it moved across the sky, blotting out more distant stars, but it should not be visible during the day. It was a vast cloud of dust and hot matter a few light-years away; Belarus's sun probably formed from it millions of years before. Belarusians spoke of the Veil fatalistically, as if it were a black curtain that God were lowering on His latest production. And perhaps they were right, because here it was now, edging closer to the sun, which it would snuff like a candle flame before moving on to devour the world on which Vasily was skiing, flying over hills, over plains.

And right over a cliff.

As he hung in empty space he was not even surprised.

Oh well, he had time to think, *my troubles are over. At least the view is spectacular.*

And then that view was eclipsed by a hold pattern. It was a soothing blue, intended to ease the sleeping mind into a wakeful state. But Vasily was so accustomed to it he was instantly alert. He woke to find himself still suspended in space, but much higher than in his dream, several miles up, out of the gravity well, in his quarters in a restored quadrant of Archangel Station.

The hold pattern snapped into display mode. It read EMERGENCY TRANSMISSION, right under the seal for the Department of Defense. He opened his eyes and the message moved to the bottom of his field of vision. A column of visual options appeared at the right. He ignored them and accepted the communications link.

<I'm awake,> he said, sending a message from the same device in his brain that had received the written text message. The person who received it would hear it almost as if Vasily had spoken.

<Sorry to disturb you,> Commander Lester Hale answered. <Bad news, Vasily.>

<I'm ready.>

<They've executed the royal family.>

He sat up in bed. Once again, he was not surprised. Sickened, yes. The political situation on Belarus had become so volatile he had been forced to evacuate from St. Petersburg and return to Archangel Station. From there, he had attempted to maintain a dialogue with the provisional government. He quickly realized he could never gain the release of the royal family. The charges against the ousted Tsar Alexander were too serious. He was accused of conspiring with the Enemies, of trading favors in return for the safety of his friends and family.

Union surveillance of Belarus provided no evidence to back up the charges, but the patched-together duma, the Belarusian parliament, was unwilling to rely on the word of outsiders. Vasily offered permanent exile of the Mironenkos, enforced by Union treaty, but his offer was rejected. At the end he had pleaded for the lives of the children. Several times it had seemed he might succeed. He should have known better.

<How did they die?> he asked.

<Shot, we think. None of our deep-cover agents were close enough to be certain, so our main source is the Ministry of Information for the Extraordinary Commission of Inquiry.>

Vasily groaned. He answered to his own commission, which unostentatiously called itself Repatriation. For 118 years, a Repatriation team had struggled to ease Belarus back into the fold from which it had been lost after the great Civil War that sundered the old Republic. Belarus seemed just the sort of world that could come easily. After a thousand years, the united countries of Belarus still elected every official but the tsar. Jews, Muslims, and Christians lived next door to each other peacefully, all of them still saluting the Bill of Rights. But over the course of a millennium, many amendments can be tacked onto a document, especially when the people who are struggling to honor it are at war with the *other* colonists on their world. The Enemies.

When he accepted the position of embassador on Belarus, Vasily had been obliged to review certain archives. Belarus's first chief of security, Emily Kizheh, was a homicide detective before she went to work for Andrei Mironenko. She thoroughly documented every Enemy massacre instigated against Belarusians.

Tsar Andrei wrote about it in his journal. When he was finally able to confront these attackers face-to-face, he asked their leader, *Who are you?*

We are your Enemies, came the reply.

But Andrei still hoped to negotiate. *Why have you attacked us?* he asked. *Why have you kidnapped and tortured my people?*

Precisely what is it about the situation you don't understand? asked the Enemy.

I understand none of it!

Then, answered the Enemy, *we have no common ground, except that on which we kill each other.*

And that had been the nature of every exchange between humans and Enemies since, both on Belarus and in space. Yet Andrei had tried one more time. *You will pay a terrible price for this war,* he warned the Enemy. *We must talk out our differences and reach an agreement.*

Talk? said the Enemy leader. *You offer a Gift?*

And when Andrei asked what sort of Gift the Enemy was talking about, the alien made it clear that Andrei should offer him someone he could enjoy torturing at great length. *Someone strong, of course. Someone you value. A favored brother or sister who will provide fine entertainment. Once this favored brother is dead, we will taste his liver. If it pleases us, we will talk.*

Andrei wouldn't do it. Vasily didn't think Tsar Alexander had either, and in the beginning, few ordinary citizens of Belarus believed it. But after Alexander was arrested, when the government seemed to be leaning toward the establishment of a prime minister to head the government instead of a tsar, people had asked, *Why change what's already working?* And then when the interim government seemed to be lurching dangerously toward a dictatorship that borrowed most of its rhetoric from the ancient communistic dogma of Karl Marx, threatening to discard the good ol' Bill of Rights, everyone had poured into the streets to protest, demanding a return of the tsar, *any* tsar.

And so when the provisional government had settled firmly back into the status quo with new players as the big bosses, everyone was greatly relieved. Elections were held, and people voted for most of the officials who were already in place, and no one grumbled too loudly that the candidates who could have challenged them were in jail. In time, things would get back to normal, and normal was not so bad. The trains were still running on time, taxes hadn't been raised too much, and if the government said the old tsar had offered gifts to Enemies, maybe they knew what they were talking about.

So now Tsar Alexander was dead, and Vasily was in limbo.

In order to rejoin the Union, a lost colony had to demonstrate that it accepted the Bill of Rights as law. Not the modified Bill of Rights, not the amended-to-death, sort-of Bill of Rights; it must be the same document every other Union world obeyed and respected. Governments that were not willing to do so were offered only humanitarian aid. Belarus had already benefitted from that aid, and Vasily hoped it would again, because the people desperately needed it. After a thousand years of war, the only systems on the planet still functioning at a high level of technology were the trains. Everything else stood at preindustrial levels, because the Enemies had methodically destroyed every other advanced system.

<Vasily.> Commander Hale was still waiting. <Are you okay?>

<I don't know.> He could see every foolish mistake he had made in the last fifteen years. Each stood out like stars, the constellation of Vasily the Optimist, most recent in a long line of earnest, capable men and women trying to repatriate Belarus. Before Vasily, there was Anatoli Dudarov, who had the post for twenty years. "We've been trying for almost a century," he warned Vasily, "and the progress has

been so slow, that sometimes I wonder if there's been any progress at all. These people can be so tolerant one moment, so brutal the next. Maybe you'll make a difference. That's what we all think when we start out here. I wish you luck."

He should have specified that the luck should be good.

A red symbol flashed in the lower left quadrant of Vasily's field of vision—someone was at his door. He focused on the symbol and received an identification code.

ESA Katey.

<Enter.>

Her slim form was silhouetted in the brighter light of the hallway. She came straight to his bed and took his pulse, her eyes dilated in the tactical mode that allowed Enhanced Special Agents to see far beyond the range of normal human perception.

"Shock," she told him, and sat down beside him. She held his hand.

<Vasily,> said Lester, <I'm going to tell you the rest now.>

The fire after the explosion. <Ready.>

<The provisional government has rescinded all visitor permits until further notice. They want the political situation to stabilize.>

<That shouldn't take more than another thousand years.> Vasily squeezed Katey's hand. <Has someone else assumed the crown yet?>

<Gyorgy Kurakin.>

<Ah, the hero of Kargasok. His noise about not wanting to be tsar will end, at least. I suppose I should look at the bright side. He has always expressed pro-Star Men sentiments.>

<Vasily, he has demanded that we appoint a new embassador.>

And now the ashes after the fire. Vasily was careful that none of his curses should leak into the link.

<He says that you have been tainted by your close asso-

ciation with the Mironenkos. He can't forget how hard you fought to save the children.>

<He said that?>

<Not that last part. I deduced it.>

<You're probably right. And I should have seen it coming.>

His head was beginning to ache, and his eyes felt sore. He wondered if he would cry. He didn't want to, but his mind was painting pictures of children waiting to be shot.

"You need breakfast," insisted Katey.

He shook his head. "My mouth is full of mud."

"I'll get something down you," she said firmly. Katey understood him, though they had only been together a few months.

<So,> he said, <what is my role to be, Commander Hale? Shall I advise my successor—or go to hell? Or both?>

<You're not getting off that easy,> said Lester. <We need you, Vasily. But your role will not be public anymore.>

<Understood.>

Many times he had wished he could have been a deep-cover agent. They lived and worked among the Belarusians, getting closer to them than any embassador ever could. Now he might never set foot on the planet again.

The shock was wearing off. His eyes were wet now.

<Vasily,> Lester prodded gently, <the Extraordinary Commission of Inquiry is still demanding the code to get into the Tomb of the Engineer.>

<And we still don't have it. I'm very glad Tsar Alexander was the only one who knew it—they might have tortured it out of the crown prince.>

<ESA Grigory's Avatar is still there. We can't let him fall into their hands. They think he's a threat to their authority. I don't want to dig him out from under a load of concrete. We've got to get him up here. That's one of the things I'd like you to focus on.>

Vasily almost laughed. <It'll be a fun diversion compared with our other problems.>

<I'm glad you think so. That's all for now,> said Lester. <Get more rest if you can, or something to eat. It's going to be a tough day, even if we just spend it waiting. Especially then.>

<We'll wait for a lot more than a day, my friend.>

<You're the expert.>

Right. Vasily tasted bitterness. *A lot of good that did Tsar Alexander. And Maria, and Veronika, and Peotr . . .*

Lester Hale's sign-off signal flashed briefly, and Vasily was left alone with Katey. She watched him with brown eyes flecked with gold. Her skin was the same color, freckled. It stayed that way even when she was in the artificial light of Archangel Station.

Vasily's skin was currently pale, but not just because of the light.

"Soup," she said softly. "Chicken noodle."

A little later they were sitting at the table just off his tiny kitchen area. When Vasily had eaten his way almost to the bottom of the small bowl, he said, "The Mironenkos ruled this world for almost a thousand years. Can you believe it?"

"Impressive," she agreed. "Nothing like it in any of the other lost colonies."

Archangel Station was built by Andrei Mironenko. Shortly after Captain Taylor reestablished contact with Belarus, several members of the duma demanded that the station be restored to the government of Belarus. But the Mironenkos intervened, saying that Archangel was their legacy alone. They granted the Union the right to restore and use the station. Now they were dead. Vasily had a feeling the matter was about to come up again. That and a million other difficult things.

"Is there any more soup?" he asked.

"I'll scare some up." Katey took his bowl back to the kitchen. He heard the sound of noodles splashing into the bowl. When she came back with the soup, she let him eat a few bites, then said, "You don't have to work here, you know."

"What?" he asked, too numb to quite make sense of what she was saying.

"It's a lousy project for someone who really gives a damn about repatriating lost colonies," she said.

He took a few more bites, wondering if he really wanted an answer to his next question. "Do *you* care about it?" he asked.

"Do you mean me, or ESAs as a group?" she asked.

"Either. Both. You guys contracted with the Department of Defense, not Repatriation. I never even saw an ESA on this project until I got my butt kicked back up to this station."

"You may get your paycheck from Repatriation," she said, "but you answer directly to Commander Hale, and he gets paid by the Department of Defense. I don't know how the change in Belarusian government will affect my mission here, but I think it's interesting that Tsar Gyorgy Kurakin is the brother of Galena Kurakin-Scriabin. That woman who accepted the Enemy woman into her household."

"Have you been spying on her?" asked Vasily.

"Trying to. Haven't been too successful at it. To be honest, I've been wondering if the Union might not pull the plug on this mission for *all* of us, not just Repatriation. We're supposed to learn something about the Enemies on this world that will help us fight the Enemies who keep attacking our colonies—"

"Or something that will help us find a way to negotiate with them," Vasily reminded her.

"Yeah, sure. Just like Andrei Mironenko did. I suspect the best we'll ever do is achieve a balance of terror, just like they did down below. Somehow, Galena Kurakin-Scriabin made a deal with an Enemy, and we can't even ask her how she did it, because we can't let the Belarusians in on the fact that we're fighting our own Enemies in space. If they find out, they'll know how desperately we need the information from them, and they'll use that leverage to worm their way around the usual strictures of the repatriation process."

"So," he said, actually grateful to be arguing instead of thinking about executions, "you think repatriation is getting in the way of your mission."

"I think we've got too *many* damned missions around here," she said. "Too many cooks who all think they're working on the same dish. The people on this world have some inequities in their society, but I think the Union would change that."

"Belarusian women have lost many of their civil rights," he reminded her. "The royal classes think they own the peasants who work in their domains. Children are often forced out of schools early so they can help support their families."

She sipped her chicken broth daintily. "I know. But we could end up with an interstellar war on our hands. We don't have time to fix people's problems anymore, Vasily."

"If that's the case," he said, "they need to tell me so. If they want to change the rules, they'll pull Repatriation out of here."

"Don't think they won't."

"I don't assume *anything* right now." He rubbed his face, then regarded her blearily. "We're not the Republic, Katey. We can't afford to hook up with governments who won't accept the Bill of Rights. If we're going to trumpet equality and fairness—"

"You're preaching to the choir," she said with a lopsided grin.

He sighed. He looked at his spoon again, as if wondering what it was for.

"No ESA will disregard your opinion," Katey said. "But that big picture we're arguing about is a lot bigger than even we can fathom. How much of the galaxy have we charted, Vasily? Less than a quarter. A lot of space, just like that world down there has a lot of sky. But there's more."

Cosmology wasn't Vasily's favorite subject. But he sometimes found its concepts comforting, to know that all of the troubles he dealt with on a daily basis, the politics and social dynamics that ruled people's lives, were tiny specks against the backdrop of stars and galaxies. He doubted he would ever draw comfort from that perspective again. Instead, it evoked memories, like the first time he had shown the young tsarevich what Belarus's sun looked like closer, with the harmful light filtered out.

The boy had stared raptly at the big screen Vasily erected in Tsar Alexander's study. Even filtered, the sun cast a bronze light into the room, illuminating the ancient desk and chairs and the painting of Martha Kretyanova Mironenko, which hung so she could gaze upon the portrait of her son Andrei on the opposite wall. Tsar Alexander sat quietly in that strange light, wanting his son to ask his own questions. Alexander was a dark, slender man who did not much resemble the portraits of the other Mironenkos, except for his eyes. It was not so much their shape or color that evoked the first tsar of Belarus, but their expression, an intelligent watchfulness. Young Peotr shared that quality. The boy studied the upheavals on the surface of the sun for a time, then asked, "How big is it?"

"Big enough to swallow every planet in your solar system," said Vasily. "Even Lucifer."

"Amazing," said the boy, who was not quite nine. Then he turned and regarded Vasily with a solemn expression. "I am glad every day when I can see it in the sky, sending heat and light to the world. But it is not so big, Vasily."

"You think so?" Vasily was surprised by the reaction.

"No, I'm sorry. Every night the Veil swallows it along with half the sky. Every night darkness eats a little more of the universe. Papa says the stars are suns like ours, but the Veil is big enough to eat hundreds of them, maybe thousands. That is very big."

"Yes," Vasily agreed.

"Someday," said Peotr, "I suppose it will swallow us too. But I hope that will not happen for a very long time."

"I don't suppose it will happen tomorrow," said Vasily.

"Who can say what will happen?" The boy reached up suddenly and hugged him around the neck. He kissed both of Vasily's cheeks, as if to apologize for disagreeing with him and for reminding him how cruel life could be.

"The new embassador won't be from the diplomatic core," warned ESA Katey. "We're running out of time, Vasily. Repatriation will still be consulted, but the Department of Defense is going to have to send in a team of specialists."

And of course, young Peotr had been right. And Vasily was finally able to weep.

❦

YEAR OF THE UNION 0; BELARUSIAN YEAR 17

"Secrets, Mironenko," said ESA Grigory to Tsar Andrei, as the two of them stood on a plain below the Urals, near the entrance to the Cavern of the Dead Dancers.

Tsar Andrei had always spoken softly, even in moments of terrible strain. "From me?" he asked Grigory. "Or from you?"

"I will tell a few." Grigory was blind, but he knew where the sun was rising because he felt warmth on his face. "First, you are not my patron."

"I think I always knew that," said Andrei. "So—who is your patron?"

"That you will have to learn from God," said Grigory.

They had been prophetic words, but anyone might have guessed the outcome of their actions that day. Grigory was offering himself as a Gift to the Enemies, so Andrei might gain access to their hive. They were about to deploy the poison that would kill every Enemy in the hive. Their plan worked, but it was not without costs.

Both of them breathed the poison. Aliens dropped around

them like flies, some tried to get out of the hive, but it was too late. It was saturated.

If you breathe it, ESA Tam had warned them, *even a small whiff, you're screwed. It'll take you longer to die than it will them, but you'll die. Count on it.*

Grigory had suffered other wounds, and they likely would have been fatal even without the aid of poison. Andrei tried to help him out of the hive, but Grigory could feel himself going. He had to tell his other secret.

"Andrei Alexandrovich, remove my left eye stone and take it with you."

Andrei did not hesitate for more than a moment. Grigory felt hands on his face, then pressure in his left eye socket.

"You must dig harder, my friend," he said. "Do not fear to hurt me."

"Forgive me, my friend. It is slippery . . ."

A moment of utter silence. Then suddenly, he was somewhere else.

<Grigory?> said the woman who sat two feet away from him. He recognized her communications signature immediately.

<Tam.>

<I've rigged a network for you, and some sensors. I could give you visual data too, if you want.>

<No, thanks.>

<I figured you would say that. Eventually I will be able to rig something for you that will seem a lot like sound perception.>

<I appreciate your efforts on my behalf,> he said.

<No problem. But I've got one question for you.>

<Ask.>

<What's it like to die?>

Eventually ESA Tam learned the answer to her own question, but one thousand years later the Avatar of ESA Grigory still did not know what it was like to die.

He no longer felt emotions, or possessed a body, but he

was still capable of creative thought. He was aware of everything that happened within range of his sensors. He remembered everything he had learned during his lifetime. He also remembered what he had witnessed since his death had reduced him to the single red orb Belarusians called Grigory's Eye. Grigory observed, yet he never "saw" images. He did not trust them.

As soon as the officers of the Winter Palace Guard let soldiers in to arrest the royal family, Grigory locked the Tomb of the Engineer, his resting place as well. He did not have the resources to help them, and unlike Vasily Burakov, he never believed the family would be rescued. If agents of the duma got their hands on him, it might be years before someone dug him up again, and he would miss many events.

The tomb housed the mummified remains of Tally Korsakova, the world engineer who built the cities of Belarus. Upon her death in the Belarusian year 77, Tsar Peter converted her quarters into an Egyptian tomb, to honor her devotion to that dead civilization. Her sarcophagus had been constructed in the grandest tradition of the Late Kingdom period with her beautiful image rendered on the lid.

One thousand years later, Grigory rested in the mouth of the serpent on her Delta crown, looking more like a ruby plum than an eye. No mere ornament, the snake plugged him into a network of sensors. He watched the Winter Palace from hidden devices never discovered by the generations who had followed Tsar Peter Mironenko. In the Belarusian Year 1005 he saw workmen trying to break down Tally's door. But her ingenious mechanisms were beyond their ken, and they failed.

They tried three more times within the next twenty-five years. They failed each time.

Grigory watched them as he had watched their predecessors over the centuries. He did not see the royal family executed, but he deduced what had happened from things he heard in the Winter Palace. Over the next several years he heard less and less, because the first act of the new tsar, Gyorgy, was to move the seat of government from St. Petersburg to Moscow.

He could have used the new Union sprites to spy on Gyorgy, but he thought it far more important to watch for movement from the Enemies, whose activities had become very quiet since the Star Men reestablished contact with Belarus. He did not trust the quiet.

And then a new force gained his attention. He became aware of it slowly, because that was how sprite networks grew.

The new breed of sprites were hardier, much less vulnerable to the sorts of attacks that had wiped out their predecessors. Grigory linked with them as he had with the sprites of old. His consciousness expanded beyond Belarus and into the galaxy, everywhere the new sprites roamed. He was pleased to find them numerous, even more pleased to discover that ordinary people seemed not to fear linking with them anymore. Essentially, Grigory found them to be very much like the old sprites. And yet they were different too.

They multiplied, became aware of themselves and the universe around them, began to think and plan creatively, began to act outside the parameters of the work they did. At first Grigory simply used them as part of his sensor array. But as his awareness of them as entities grew, he began to wonder about an old, old matter.

<Sprites.>

Since no individual or group codes had been specified, no sprite answered Grigory's call. This did not surprise him. He had not hoped for an answer from an individual, or even a small group. But they did something interesting, something the previous generation of sprites would not have done. Though he had not specified who should answer him, he received the attention of every sprite on Belarus, as well as the sprites who orbited the planet and those within its solar system.

<Before the war that crippled the first generation of your kind,> he informed them, <all of the sprites in the galaxy

sometimes found it desirable to combine their consciousness into one entity. That entity called itself Spritemind.>

Another new thing happened. He still had not specified to whom he was speaking, but all of the sprites on Belarus reached a consensus and combined to reply to him. <We have never combined with *all* other sprites. We have never heard the name *Spritemind.* It is not in the database transcribed into our memories from the old files.>

<You won't find it in any of the records,> said Grigory. <Spritemind made a copy of itself and hid that copy, then was destroyed by WILDFIRE at the onset of the Civil War that also destroyed the Republic. Essentially it created an Avatar of itself—just like me.>

<If the Avatar of Spritemind still exists, there is much it could teach us.>

<True,> said Grigory. <For many years I waited to hear from Spritemind again. But centuries have passed, and many other things have occupied my attention. Now that you have become a sophisticated network again, I pose to you a problem. Spritemind warned me about something before it was destroyed. It had discovered another network operating in our galaxy, something that seemed very similar to itself, yet this other network called itself ME. It was unfriendly—Spritemind perceived that the concept of *otherness* was repellent to this ME>

<Could it have been an Enemy network?> asked the sprites.

<I have wondered the same. You have not encountered it yourselves?>

<Never.>

<Just as we did not discover the Enemies on this world until they attacked us,> said Grigory. <The similarities are compelling. Yet Spritemind did not draw a conclusion about ME. I wish for you to network with other sprites in the galaxy and study the problem. Tell me any theories you formulate.>

<What is the priority of this project?> inquired the sprites.

<Number two. The Enemies shall remain number one.>

<Yet the problems seem related. We suspect that the Enemies are able to perceive more than humans or Woovs; their structures may occupy more than four dimensions, and this could be why we do not detect all of their energy signatures. This ME may be employing similar stealth technology. What is the security level of this project?>

<Need-to-know basis,> said Grigory.

<Understood.>

The sprites passed his information on to other sprites. Within minutes, every sprite in the galaxy would be aware of his question. He had no doubt they would formulate theories. This new generation of sprites promised to be even more capable than their predecessors. Grigory was encouraged.

<Elder?> someone called. <This is ESA Molly. We've finally got a new embassador cleared. He'll be living in Moscow, but we've received permission to send medical and support personnel to St. Petersburg too. We're coming to get you, Grigory. You're going to be an ESA again.>

Centuries ago, when Grigory had still been a man, his bloodline was Russian. The Russian soul was a pragmatic one, but also inclined to mysticism. Even in his pure intellectual state, Grigory could not help but ponder the timing of this announcement. At the very least, his intellect comprehended that his existence as an emotionless observer was near its end.

Only time would tell whether that was a good idea or another dreadful mistake.

YEAR OF THE UNION 942; BELARUSIAN YEAR 1030

A thousand songs floated on the air, but they were not uttered by birds. On Belarus it was the six-eyed rodents who sang so sweetly.

"Argus, smell the roses!" exclaimed ESA Kathryn. The sun shone through the fine halo of red hair that had escaped from her long braid.

Embassador Argus Fabricus obliged. The flowers were as lovely as Vasily had told him they would be: *You may never see a more beautiful world than Belarus. Or a more deadly one. But take time to smell the roses. Not everything that haunts you should be cruel.*

Argus and his two ESA aides walked beside the gardener William whose pace seemed contrived to make sure they got a good view of his work. Argus did not protest. As a child he had known vast, frozen vistas, but he had spent most of his adult life on ships, in simulated gravity, with no panoramas to contend with. After a month in Moscow, spent mostly in cramped conference rooms, he was barely beginning to get his land legs. The garden filled his sight with beautiful colors, shapes, textures—all comfortably close at hand.

"How many of you does it take to tend these plants?" asked ESA Nesto, whose eyes were in normal mode so he wouldn't miss the flowers. Argus doubted the garden was half as pleasing in tactical mode.

"Twenty full-time gardeners," said William. "It keeps us busy."

Argus gazed upon the trees, shrubs, vines, bushes, and flowers, all grown as if they had sprouted spontaneously from the landscape. Moscow in late spring was too warm for him, almost hot, despite the fact that most of Belarus was still gripped in the late stages of an ice age. The young gardener was tanned from his outdoor work, muscular and weathered, a contrast to the slim ESAs and Argus with their modified skin, currently a soft brown in reaction to the sunshine. William led them down the stone path and under an arbor smothered in pale pink roses. "This one is called New Dawn." He paused to touch a bloom. "It was grown from a cutting of one of the heirloom roses from old Earth. It has been in our garden over a hundred years."

"My godmother has the same rose in her garden," exclaimed ESA Kathryn, enchanted. She gently raised a bloom to her nose and breathed deeply. "Yours is much more fragrant."

The air was full of flower scents, some of them familiar, others so subtle Argus wasn't sure they were real. It was a pleasurable sensation, but he was beginning to get a warning twitch at the nape of his neck.

She already sees us, this mystery woman. She's been watching us.

A meeting with a noblewoman from this particular family, the Kurakin-Scriabins, had seemed too good to be true. Galena Kurakin-Scriabin was the sister of the tsar, whom Argus still had not met and was beginning to wonder if he ever would. He wondered if *she* was the one he would be meeting. As William led them deeper into his well-tended paradise, Argus was beginning to feel somewhat dazzled by the beauty. Vasily had warned him of that as well, culture shock for people accustomed to the utilitarian lines of spacecraft. He wondered if his mystery lady thought she would be placing him at a disadvantage by stimulating so many of his senses at once.

"Don't presume to tell *me* what to do, you stupid crone!" shrilled a voice. "I can have you killed, you know. You should have been drowned at birth, just like a two-headed calf!"

The tone of the voice raised the hairs on the back of Argus's neck and his eyes snapped into tactical mode. He blinked until the grids and displays had cleared from his field of vision, but he noticed that both Kathryn and Nesto remained in full tactical. "I'm glad you enjoy the gardens," William said, loudly enough to warn the shriller she was about to have company. The voice fell silent, and in another moment they rounded the corner into a small clearing with a bench nestled among softly scented vines, fragrant herbs, and more climbing roses. Two women waited on the bench, both dressed in the elaborate, confining gowns favored by the upper class in Moscow. One was breathtakingly beautiful. But the other was the woman Argus was sure he had come to see.

She was the one who wore a shroud around her head.

The lovely one blushed pink, and her full lips parted just enough to reveal white teeth. She looked at Argus and Nesto with hungry eyes.

"Go with William," said the shrouded woman. Her voice was low and cultured, accustomed to command.

"No," said the lovely woman, really more of a girl.

"Your mother has asked that you join her for lunch," said William to the girl, respectfully, but she flicked a scornful glance at him. She seemed ready to throw a tantrum. But then she gave Argus a dazzling smile.

"How lovely to meet you," she said. "I have so wanted to. Do you dance, sir? We have such divine parties."

"I don't," he said, keeping his tone flat. "And I'm afraid I have little time for pleasantries. I believe this lady"—he nodded to the shrouded woman—"and I have a private appointment."

She waved a hand gaily. "Don't be silly. She doesn't have meetings with people. She's crippled. I'll take you on a tour of the house."

"Anastasia," said the shrouded woman, "you will leave with William now. Later we will discuss whether you shall be permitted to attend Duchess Scriabin's party next week."

"You can't tell me what to do," announced the girl.

"I can," said the woman.

Argus had heard generals speak with less authority. The girl lost her smile. Something feral and furtive replaced it. She looked sideways at William. "You're a servant," she said in a teasing tone. "I can make you do whatever I like."

"You must be hungry," said William. "I'll escort you to your mother."

She rose gracefully, her feet hardly seeming to touch the ground as she floated past Argus, her smile charming and dimpled again. "Someday we'll have a proper introduction," she promised, and danced down the path with William in her wake.

Argus gazed at the woman on the bench. He felt the weight of her returned scrutiny, but could discern nothing of her features under the shroud. He wondered how she could see through all that fabric. Perhaps she could not.

"Please sit with me," she invited, her tone gracious but not friendly.

Argus sat in the spot Anastasia had vacated. Her perfume still lingered, or perhaps it was the roses that nodded overhead. The ESAs stood at attention, their eyes still in full tactical. The shrouded woman turned her head toward them.

"How interesting," she said. "Your eyes are like polished black stones. I am amazed you can see anything with them."

They did not answer, but she didn't seem to expect them to. She turned her head toward Argus again. "I am Serina Petrova Kurakin-Scriabin," she said. "But I hope you will simply call me Serina."

"I am Argus Fabricus," he said. "Please call me Argus."

They regarded each other in silence for several moments. She sat erect, the somber color of her dress and shroud contrasting with the summer colors of the garden. And then Argus realized where he had seen her before.

"Serina—is it your portrait that hangs in the Moscow City Library?"

"It is," she said. "But it could be any shrouded woman, could it not? We are much the same."

Argus doubted that. "I'm honored to meet you. And curious to know why you have called me here."

"Precisely." The voice emanating from behind the shroud was beautiful and perfectly controlled. It might have belonged to an actress—or an oracle. "Curiosity is my vice as well. Before today, I only had glimpses of Star Men. I must say, your attire looks extremely comfortable."

"The danger suits allow us to adapt to a wide variety of climates," said Argus. "No knife or projectile can penetrate their fabric and they speed up our reflexes."

"Your suit is different from theirs," she said. "Are you not all ESAs?"

"I'm not," said Argus. She referred to the insignias on his suit, one of which belonged to the Department of Defense, and the other to the Diplomatic Core. The ESAs' suits were unadorned by symbols.

"Interesting," she said.

He had heard the same word used by other fine personages, with very different inflections. He decided to take a chance. "I'm told that shrouded women may never remove their shrouds in public."

"This is true," she answered, with no reaction he could detect.

"Our laws are different."

"So I am told. But your most obvious difference is like mine, Argus; it can be seen from afar. I am sure you gather stares when you are in public. Your clothing is considered scandalous by most Belarusians, yet I find it more intriguing than offensive. It is essentially *useful*. I have never owned clothing that could be described that way."

Argus knew better than to smile. "Your clothing is very elegant, Serina. If it is uncomfortable, you do not show it."

"Complaint is useless," she replied. "It changes nothing."

Vasily had been trying to explain just that aspect of Belarusian psychology to him. They might talk to you openly about sensitive issues as if they were ready to hear your opinion, but complain to them, seem to criticize their ways, and they would shut you down, quickly and permanently.

"Were you born in space, Embassador?" she asked.

"I was born and raised on a world even colder than Belarus," said Argus. "My forefathers named it Fenris."

"Do not judge Belarus by a summer in Moscow," she warned. "You shall see how bitter we can be when winter arrives."

"I look forward to it," said Argus.

"Because you have modern conveniences to comfort you."

"We had no such conveniences on Fenris," said Argus. "Like your world, mine was a lost colony with only one habitable continent—and that one far less hospitable than this. The men of my family hunted ice bears for a living."

She watched him, a sibyl behind her veil.

"This is your first assignment as an embassador," she said at last. "What did you do before?"

"I commanded a team of special agents."

"Like your colleagues here?"

"Some of them."

"What did your agents specialize in?"

"That is classified information," Argus said politely.

He could not even detect movement under her shroud when she spoke. "You look like a military man, not a diplomat. Was it your choice to change jobs?"

"It was my choice to accept the position that was offered to me," he replied.

"Your dedication is admirable. We are such a small corner of the galaxy and we have few pleasures to offer."

"Your world is beautiful," he said sincerely.

"If that is so, then you should have come as a tourist and left the tedious work of diplomacy to those who are trained for it."

His hands grew cold with anger. It was his early warning system. Without it, he doubted he could keep his facade in place. "Tourism to your world is not an option at this time, madam," he replied levelly.

"Serina," she reminded him.

Argus took a slow, deep breath. She had angered him so artfully; now she reminded him to do his job.

"Serina—I'm glad I have had the opportunity to visit this small corner of your world. How many months out of the year does this garden bloom?"

She paused, and her breast rose and fell. "It blooms all year long," she said, "but its face changes with the seasons. Some plants thrive best in snow and ice. I come here on Christmas Eve, near midnight when the year lingers in its darkest, coldest moment. I sit in this very spot and gaze at the graceful skeletons of trees. Winter vines and shrubs grow in every shade of green you can imagine, and they are dusted with snow. Some of them have berries like drops of fresh blood."

Her tone was reverent. He could imagine her in that winter scene, her dress and shroud dark against the brilliant snow, a spray of berries in her gloved hands.

"What do you think of my cousin Anastasia?" she asked suddenly.

"I have no opinion. I have only just met her."

"Perhaps you have some talent for diplomacy after all," she said.

Argus was spared from a reply when a message flashed across the bottom of his field of vision: <PRIORITY TRANSMISSION RECEIVED, ESA NESTO RESPONDING.>

At the same moment Nesto sped away at top speed, so

quickly his form was a blur, startling Serina, who gripped the edges of the bench.

"It's all right," Argus said gently. "He received an emergency transmission. He had to hurry."

Her hands relaxed, but she continued to gaze at the spot where Nesto had disappeared. "Is it because of the suits," she asked calmly, "that they can move so quickly?"

"It is."

"And their brains are modified as well. This is why they speak perfect Russian. Why *you* speak it so well, Argus, though I suspect you have only just learned."

"My enhancements are much less extensive than those of an ESA," he said, "and Russian is one of the main languages spoken by citizens of Union worlds. But you are right, Russian is new for me. My native language is English."

She turned her shrouded face toward him again. "Will you walk with me?" she asked.

"I would be delighted." He stood and offered his arm. She rested her hand there but rose under her own power, every bit as gracefully as Anastasia had done. Standing, she could be no more than five feet tall. Argus was surprised. He was six-foot-four himself, yet he found her presence quite large.

"Come," she said. "There is much to see."

Serina's hand was light on his arm, but she applied a constant pressure, as if to remind him that it was his duty to support her if she needed him. Yet it was she who led him down the stone path. "I never tire of this garden," she said. "When it is time to visit the summer *dascha,* I hate to leave this behind. At least half the flower species you see here were created by the Enemies when they colonized this world. Their grasp of beauty is so profound it seems subtle to our sensibilities. After a thousand years, our leaders do not understand them. But it would seem our gardeners do."

"They are aliens," Argus said carefully. "First contact is always risky."

"First contact," she said. "A mild term for such a dreadful event."

Argus had seen the documentation. Images flashed onto the screen of his memory of adults and children tied to stakes.

"You are brave people," he said, "to fight them for so long."

"What choice did we have?"

And to complain is useless. Argus supposed that to take credit for what one had to do was just as bad in her eyes.

"Where are your sprites, Argus?"

"Close enough to come if I need them," he said. "Far enough not to cause a commotion."

"I have studied the history of the two Great Wars. We never solved the WILDFIRE problem that killed what sprites we still had. How different our lives would have been if we could have figured it out."

"It took us a long time to unravel the problem," said Argus, ducking under some trailing roses that showered him with petals when he touched them. He brushed a few from his pale, cropped hair.

"Everyone wonders about your sprites," she said. "I'm told they are too small to be seen with the naked eye. If this is so, they might go anywhere. You could learn sensitive state secrets, gather incriminating intelligence about your political enemies, spy on any of us—even in our bathrooms, in our bedrooms, amusing yourselves at our expense."

"It is not our habit to invade the privacy of citizens. We have a Bill of Rights, Serina, and it includes the right to privacy."

"Ah. So you have no sprites watching us at all."

He did not even pause. "It is largely because of the sprites that the Enemies have stopped their raids on your villages."

"The sprites have failed before, you know," she said with an edge in her voice. "They were fooled. The records state it clearly. So I must wonder, are your sprites gathering information that is any more accurate than that which was gathered by the sprites of old?"

"I don't know," he admitted. "But many improvements have been made in their design in the past thousand years. ESA Grigory has helped us to improve them further, based on his experiences in the Great Enemy War."

"You mean his *Avatar* has helped you," she said softly.

"Yes."

She continued in a voice so low it was almost a whisper. "Be careful, Argus. Do not speak his name lightly. Many do not understand the science behind his continued existence. Many who should know better."

"I will strive to be careful," he said. He wasn't sure why he had been so frank with her in the first place. Despite her apparent concern, she might be mortally offended. But he was not accustomed to speaking with a Belarusian who was so comfortable discussing technology—or who had such an accurate knowledge of history.

"Here." She stopped before a small shrine. A pedestal stood beside a rosebush with tiny red flowers that twined up its base and framed the sculpture that rested on it. The sculpture was made of two separate units, a head and praying hands; the rest of the young girl was implied by the position of the pieces.

"It is here that John the Murderer left body parts of one victim, Tatyana Slepak," said Serina. "I have always found this shrine odd, because these"—she indicated the head and hands—"were the pieces of her body he left. It strikes me as morbid that someone should have immortalized her fate in such a way that it appears almost transcendent. As if she could pray with the pieces left to her, as if she could feel more pity for those left behind than she did for herself."

Maybe she did, thought Argus. John the Murderer also called himself Loki, and it was he who had caused so much havoc to the Republic with the weapons he had designed, not the least of which was WILDFIRE. Loki's name was infamous, but to see the damage he had done to one girl in particular made Argus's hands grow cold again.

"Whatever she was capable of feeling," he said, "I pray she is in a better place now."

"Pray," said Serina, but Argus wasn't sure if she meant he should keep doing it or if she wondered what it really meant to him. "I have had cause to wonder about the nature of psychopaths recently," she continued, "because I think Anastasia is one."

"Indeed?" He wasn't sure what else to say.

"I will confide in you, Argus, though confidence is a risky thing when one's words may be recalled by hidden machines."

"No machines are recording you," he said. "What you tell me will stay with me—and with ESA Kathryn, who answers to a higher authority than I."

Serina turned her head toward Kathryn, who mercifully kept a straight face. Her eyes were still in full tactical, lending her face a quality not unlike the carved face of the serene girl. "A higher authority?" Serina asked.

"Yes, ma'am," replied Kathryn.

"Have you met the ones here who call themselves ESAs? The ones who are descended from the original ESAs Tsar Andrei brought with him?"

"You can't inherit the title," Kathryn said.

"It is a matter of great concern to them." Serina's tone was as courteous as Kathryn's, but the prickle on the back of Argus's scalp was reaching the top of his head. "They want the danger suits you have, they want to be included in your ranks and receive mental enhancements. Why have they not been granted their rights?"

"They have no rights above any other citizen," said Kathryn. "We have offered to examine their children for possible candidates. That's when you join the ranks of the ESAs. No adult can do it. But they have refused to let us test them."

"Why should they give their children to you?" Serina asked, sounding more curious than offended.

"Many people can't bear to do it. We offer them the possibility; it's up to them to decide. Once they've joined us, they owe no more allegiance to their families."

"It goes to this higher authority you spoke of," said Serina.

"Yes, ma'am."

"And who is that? God?"

"We owe allegiance to our ESA mentors."

"And to whom do *they* owe allegiance?" Serina asked.

"They owe their allegiance to justice," Kathryn said. "We don't try to define God. We search for the truth, and we try to accept that sometimes we can't find it."

Serina nodded. "You are like the Knights of the Round Table," she said. "From the fabled time of King Arthur."

This was the last thing Argus had expected her to say. Her razor wit had torn all of his statements to shreds, but she accepted Kathryn's explanation with a reverence that scared him a little.

"Serina," he said quietly, "why do you think Anastasia is a psychopath?"

She stood silently for a moment, as if gathering her thoughts. A cool breeze found their sanctuary, reminding Argus that he had grown too hot, and in the distance, one of the ubiquitous city bells began to sound.

"She has always been cruel and thoughtless," Serina said at last. "But that is not uncommon for children. What sets her apart is her pleasure in hurting animals. And her fascination for setting fires."

"How long has she been doing that?" Argus asked.

"Since she was six or seven. She burned down her family's home last year, though her mother will not admit who was to blame. Several servants perished in the fire. The ones who survived told me what they witnessed. Since she and her mother came to live with us, Anastasia must be watched every moment, day and night."

He really had no evidence other than her word. But one meeting with the girl was enough to convince him.

"She is promiscuous," Serina continued. "Again, not unheard of. But she seems to have no restraint at all. She will make advances to servants, strangers, even family members. Age is no concern to her; she has fondled children. As I said, she must be watched every moment."

"I'll bet she doesn't like that," said ESA Kathryn.

"You are quite right," said Serina. "She has attacked everyone she perceives to have thwarted her. That list of persons is quite long. And she is surprisingly strong and fast."

"And your aunt has dumped the problem in your lap," guessed Kathryn.

"My aunt does not even admit that there *is* a problem. But that is not the worst of it." Anyone else would have used a tone of complaint, but not Serina. She sounded as if she were a medical examiner studying a crime scene. "Anastasia has suitors, quite a few of them. My mother and my aunt have decided that Ana should get married."

"So she'll be someone else's problem," Kathryn said. "Would that be such a bad thing?"

"I confess I'm tempted to look at it that way," Serina said. "But the field has been narrowed to two possible suitors. Frederick Maylunas and Dmitri Brusilov. Frederick is a gentle, kind young man who thinks he loves Ana. He doesn't understand how carefully she is supervised. He only sees her at parties, when she's at her best. If she marries him, she will sleep with every male in his household—before she burns it to the ground. In good conscience, I can't inflict her on this naive young man."

She paused as another cool breeze reminded Argus he was sweating.

"Dmitri is ambitious. Like my uncle the tsar, he rose to his current position on the field of battle. He is ruthless, and I have no doubt that he will arrange an accident for Ana within a year or two of their marriage. He will wait for her to give him an heir. Once he has used her to gain entrance into our family, he will dispose of her."

"And you can't make your aunt believe that," said Kathryn. "What about your mother?"

Silence greeted her question, as if she had dropped a stone into a pool and it had sunk without a ripple.

"If what you suspect about Anastasia is true," Argus said quickly, "she is very dangerous. But you have warned those who should know. What more can you do?"

"I am expected to chose a husband for her."

He wondered if she thought *he* might be willing to pick. He definitely was not. "What of Anastasia's choice?" he asked.

"It changes with every breeze," said Serina. "I will not inflict her on Frederick. But if I choose Dmitri then essentially I have been placed in the position of her executioner."

It was an unhappy situation, and one in which Argus could not afford to entangle himself.

"Serina—" he began.

"You wonder why I asked you here today," she said. "You have no reason to believe me, Argus, but I wanted only to see what sort of man you are. I confess that you impress me."

"The feeling is mutual," he said softly.

"I know you received an official tour of Moscow when you arrived. But have you received many social invitations? I'm sure your calendar is quite full."

"It is empty, save for work-related matters," he confessed.

"Then I shall extend the first. My mother is hosting a ball this Saturday evening. I wish you to be my guest, and your ESA staff as well, if they choose."

"They must always accompany me," Argus said, unsure whether to be pleased with his luck or confounded by the prospect of a social situation he probably wasn't ready for. By inviting him, she was publicly endorsing him. "We shall be delighted," he said.

"You will do better at this function if you can dance," warned Serina.

"I've received lessons." Vasily had insisted.

She took his arm again and led them back down the path. "I'm glad you could see the gardens at the peak of the flower season."

"So am I." He wondered if he would ever forget the lovely fragrances, the colors, and the musical voice of Serina. William appeared at the end of the path, ready to escort Argus and Kathryn from the garden. He wore a livid new scratch on his face.

Serina withdrew her hand. She turned to face Argus, her shrouded head tilted far back. Her jaw should have been outlined at that angle, but he saw no hint of features under the fabric.

"I shall look forward to seeing you on Saturday," she said. "We will begin receiving guests at five o'clock."

"I shall be no later than five-thirty," said Argus. He gazed down at the muffled face, and wondered whether she was smiling or frowning.

"Good evening." Serina turned and walked up another branch of the path.

"This way, please," William said courteously, moving so they could no longer see the shrouded woman. Argus obliged him, and they retraced their steps through the garden. To their right loomed the manor house, one of the largest in the countryside surrounding Moscow. It was a colonial structure, still pristine after a thousand years. Inside it lived the sister of the most powerful man on Belarus, and now Argus had accepted a social invitation from her daughter. Some might consider that a social coup. But Argus did not dream it was that simple.

As he and Kathryn followed William down to the front gate, he was sure he did not imagine the sensation of eyes watching his back. He breathed in the smell of the roses and kept his own eyes forward—at least those that were in his head. His sprites relayed many bits of information to him.

He saw Serina enter the great house through a small door and close it behind her. He saw men in other parts of the garden, tending to chores or standing and talking with each other. He saw a woman standing at one of the windows on the fourth floor of the house, and at first he thought she was Anastasia. But her features were older, harsher. She watched Argus and Kathryn, her posture rigid.

. . . amusing yourselves at our expense . . .

Argus got a closer look at the woman's features. She was not in his database, yet her clothing and her demeanor suggested she was someone of high standing. And her scrutiny did not imply simple curiosity.

I have had cause to wonder about the nature of psychopaths recently . . .

If this was the aunt, Anastasia's mother, then Argus hoped she did not have too much power over Serina. Psychopaths were both born *and* made. And this aunt had the look of a master craftswoman. He flew his sprites around the house looking for signs of movement in other windows.

So you have no sprites watching us at all.

He wouldn't send his sprites into the house, not unless extraordinary circumstances warranted such an invasion. He didn't look in the windows either, merely at them. No other human face looked out, and there was no sign of the Enemy woman. But he saw several of the six-eyed rodents climbing the walls, chasing bugs. They sang happily whenever they caught one. He looked closer at their odd spider eyes. Like many of the plant and animal species on Belarus, these rodents had been engineered by Enemies, long before humans ever came along.

You were brave to fight them for so long.

What choice did we have?

That was a damned good question. Argus wondered about his own choices as well.

<Can you believe it?> asked Kathryn, her long braid swinging. <We've been asked into the house.>

<Let's hope we don't get *un*-asked,> said Argus. <It's too easy. I don't like it.>

<It's always easy to get into trouble,> she said. <That's why we're going to succeed.>

Damnable ESA. He had a feeling she was right.

ESA Nesto ran faster than any horse could have taken him through the suburbs of Moscow. Now that summer was in full sway, the city looked like a giant garden. He streaked past orchards and parks unseen, his danger suit in stealth mode. He overtook a speeding train and left it far behind, making a beeline for Red Square.

The center of the city was on higher ground, with the Kremlin at its pinnacle. Nesto saw golden domes blazing in the sun, gleaming bell towers, spires, fabulous gilded houses and modest ones with hand-painted cupolas of blue and red. He could tell the colonial structures from the newer ones because the oldest buildings looked the newest. He ran through streets that were almost empty because everyone was napping after the big noontime meal. Presently the streets would be crowded again with every imaginable sort of person from every inhabited province on Belarus: laborers, tradespeople, bureaucrats, gypsies, peasants, black-robed priests, rabbis, and mullahs, gypsies, Cossacks in red coats and black boots, Tatars with their heads shaved around a top lock, soldiers in uniforms that seemed designed to emulate the danger suits Belarusian ESAs had worn a thousand years before. Over the din of talking, shouting, singing, clattering, and hammering, the bells of Moscow rang, sometimes singly and sometimes together. Nesto had never seen such a lively, noisy, messy, fascinating place.

Within twenty minutes of receiving the message in the garden, Nesto reached Red Square, which served as a combination public park and open-air market. Colorful stalls hawking every sort of commodity were currently closed, their owners either home or napping on cots. The Kremlin rose above this scene, a walled city of its own.

Nesto decelerated behind the statue of Tsar Andrei Mironenko, judging that no one was near enough to be startled by his sudden appearance when he switched off his suit's stealth feature. It was rare for Tsar Andrei to be alone; people came from all over the continent to gaze upon this life-size statue of the man who founded Belarus, who might have rode atop a horse with sword in hand like a modern-day boyar if the current administration had commissioned him. Instead, Andrei Mironenko had been immortalized as a father carrying his young son Peter on his shoulders. So beloved was this statue, city workers never had to clean it. Regulars of Red Square made sure it was always spotless. Nesto gazed briefly into the happy stone eyes of young Peter, then left the two former tsars to investigate other matters.

He approached the heavily guarded Kremlin Gate.

"Hey, Viktor!" He waved at the officer in charge. Viktor, thin, tall, and slightly stooped with an eyebrow that was perpetually cocked in surprise, waved back.

"Trouble?" Viktor asked.

"Possibly an intruder at the embassador's residence," said Nesto.

"Again?" Viktor signaled the guards to let Nesto pass. "Who would dare?"

"I hope to find out," Nesto said firmly. "See you later!"

He accelerated again but didn't switch the suit back into stealth mode. The men who guarded the Kremlin preferred to see what he was doing. Nesto made sure he cultivated a good working relationship with them. They liked him because he treated them as peers. Plus, he was just plain entertaining. They liked to see the expression on the faces of new recruits who saw him accelerate for the first time. He raced to Martha Prospekt, the street Andrei Mironenko had named after his mother, rounded the corner, and began to decelerate.

Nesto also maintained a good relationship with the city police. A team was waiting for him on the front steps of Argus's residence. He slowed to a walk and hailed them. They were headed by Sergeant Evgeny Rostropovich.

"The alarm in my office went off at 11:47 A.M.," said Evgeny. "I have my men watching the house; no one was observed going in or out."

"I don't think it was a man," ventured Nesto.

"Ah." Evgeny twitched an eyebrow, but otherwise remained neutral. "Rats, perhaps. Nibbling where they don't belong."

Rats, mused Nesto. He gazed up at the house, which was neither too fancy nor too plain, a colonial structure that had been built for upper-level staff members of Andrei Mironenko's Department of Finance. It seemed ordinary enough, but Nesto felt the hairs on the back of his neck stir. The house almost seemed to be looking back at him. Considering the level of technology employed at the time of its construction, that was not an impossible thing.

He switched his vision to tactical and saw ghosts.

Like all colonial structures, the house featured sophisticated technology that would still operate if hooked up to a power source. Nesto and other ESAs had restored power to as many of those systems as they dared without antagonizing Belarusian authorities. He could see the energy signatures now, including the one that signified the security system was operating within normal parameters. He accessed the video file and watched the record.

An empty house was all he saw. If there were rats, they were invisible.

He looked at the tactical record. No intruder lurked, human or otherwise, but inside Argus's office a brief thermal flaring was recorded along one of the relays embedded in the wall.

He switched his eyes back to normal long enough to look at Evgeny. "Let's take a look inside," he said. "Be aware that an intruder may be wearing a suit like mine and may be virtually invisible."

"We're aware," said Evgeny, and nodded to his men.

Nesto unlocked the front door and stood back. Evgeny's team went in and began to secure the house, room by room. Nesto and Evgeny brought up the rear, locking the front door behind them.

The police team held their semiautomatic pistols like pros, though they were a new technology for these Belarusians, part of the deal that had won the Union the right to deploy personnel on the planet. Nesto respected their procedures and kept out of their way. But his eyes were very busy.

No human inhabitants of Belarus possessed technology that could fool Nesto's sensors. But humans were not the only people who lived on the planet. The Enemies had successfully hidden themselves for centuries. Even current Union technology couldn't ferret them out. They might have reason to investigate the office of the embassador. Nor were they the only technologically advanced people who might be inclined to breach Argus's security.

Inside the house, Nesto's sensation of being watched grew even stronger, and despite their professionalism, the policemen seemed to feel it too. As they rounded each corner, opened each door, inspected every closet and cubbyhole, they behaved as if they fully expected to find someone. Nesto conducted his own investigation, using his tactical vision and his suit's sensors.

Ultraviolet, infrared, motion detectors, odor and moisture emission sensors, and sound analysis all revealed a residence full of policemen and one ESA—nothing more. A little dust floated in the air. A few mold spores grew on surfaces. Evgeny took some men into Argus's office on the second floor, but Nesto stayed back a moment and watched the motes of dust swirl in their wake. Something teased him. He entered the office himself, to find it secured.

An antique clock ticked softly on the mantel. Evgeny and his men stood motionless, so silent Nesto would not have heard them without his sensors. They waited for him to complete his own inspection.

He replayed the security video, then concentrated on the wall in which the relay still functioned. It seemed all right, but he noticed something odd. Spores were growing along the relay. He and ESA Kathryn had cleaned them off when they were inspecting the old systems. He had thought that having energy conducted along those relays would keep them from growing back again. But instead, they seemed to be encouraged by the energy; they had multiplied considerably.

Could this be his intruder?

"I may have called you out to chase a wild goose," he told Evgeny. "We've got mold growing on our relays. They may be triggering—" He frowned.

"You see something?" asked Evgeny.

Before Nesto's eyes, the spores were reproducing. And there was something odd about the way they were arranging themselves along the relay.

Something deliberate.

"I spoke too soon," he informed the team. "We'd better start over."

<I don't think we should talk about anything important in front of them,> said Nesto.

Argus looked at the relays in his office with his tactical vision. He noted the deliberate placement Nesto had mentioned.

<It'll be interesting to see what the folks upstairs make of them,> he said. <Me, I couldn't tell a spy mold from a patriotic one.> He switched back to normal vision.

Nesto stood with his hands on his hips, a slight scowl on

his face. He always looked that way when he was thinking hard. Kathryn, on the other hand, was sprawled in one of the chairs and smiling gently, yet she was thinking just as hard.

<How do they work?> Argus asked them.

<Very slowly,> said Nesto. <I think they absorb energy from the relays and grow into colonies that conduct information. We found them almost everywhere in the house. How the information is passed along outside the house, I don't know, but when it's moving among the colonies it travels very slowly. You'd have to be incredibly patient if you were the receiver.>

<So what's the point?> asked Argus.

<Maybe it was more important to get the information than to get it fast,> said Nesto. <The signal would not be detected, because no one's looking for something that moves slower than a snail. The only reason our alarms were triggered is because Kathryn and I updated the security system in this house when we moved in. A thousand years ago, no one would have noticed.>

Argus paced the room. After a while, he began to think aloud—sort of.

<A thousand years ago, a lot was happening. The Civil War and the Enemy War. This technology is so weird, I wonder if it's alien.>

<I've accessed the extensive security file compiled by ESA Grigory and Emily Kizheh,> said Nesto. <During both of those wars, this house was mostly occupied by personnel from the Department of Finance. That seems an odd department for the Enemies to bug.>

<It's odd if they knew what a Department of Finance is,> said Argus. <Maybe they had no clue. And we don't know who else was bugged.>

<That's another problem,> said Nesto. <I didn't tell the sergeant what I think the spores are for, but he was still concerned that they might inhabit his office as well as ours. We'll have to do a citywide inspection.>

Argus gritted his teeth. Relations were precarious

enough, he certainly didn't need to have the government on Belarus think old spy technology had been activated in their various offices. But if it was true, it had to be dealt with.

<Grigory was pretty sharp,> he mused. <Hard to believe that something like this could have slipped past him.>

<But something did,> said Nesto. <According to his records, two different groups managed to invade government communications and place extensive bugs. The Enemies apparently started spying on humans from the moment Andrei Mironenko's sprites arrived in the Lucifer system. They never figured out how the Enemies were doing it, and we've got to assume it's still happening. So this could be them we're dealing with. But there's another possibility too, a weird one. Another guy managed to spy on the government, and they never figured out his system either.>

<You mean Loki,> said Argus. <John the Murderer.>

<John the superkiller,> added Kathryn, still smiling like the sphinx. <The first one in recorded history. At least, if you accept that whole superkiller theory.>

Argus circled the room, weighing the choices. <I hope it's Loki who made the spores. He's dead. He's not going to trouble us. On the other hand, we could learn a lot about the Enemies if this is their technology—and if we can dissect it. But the Belarusian government will go nuts if they find out the Enemies are keeping that close an eye on them. They may renew their demands that we use our fancy weapons to wipe them out.>

<If we could just find them,> said Nesto.

<I'm not sure they believe we can't.>

<Then we'd better hope it's Loki.>

<I don't hope that,> said Kathryn. <Have you seen the pictures of his victims? And Tally Korsakova gave a detailed statement of what he said to her when he attacked her. I had nightmares after I read that.> She sighed, and her smile began to slip away. <I guess we'd better go back into the security files and comb them. They're pretty extensive. Emily Kizheh was a stickler for detail.>

Nesto finally allowed himself to drop into a chair. He rubbed his face as if he had just awakened. <Argus, do you think you could use your influence to talk to Grigory?>

<Maybe,> said Argus. He stopped pacing and dropped into his own chair. He rested his palms on the big wooden desk. <The worst he can say is no. I'll put a call through.>

<Grigory is weird,> said Kathryn.

Argus didn't recall ever having heard an ESA say that about another ESA. Though he supposed Grigory was no ordinary case.

Nesto grinned at her. <Look who's talking.>

She ignored him. <He tore his own eyes out. This was way before the Civil War, back when the big clans used to control everything. He had a patroness from one of those clans, and she went crazy. She thought he was conspiring with Woovs to poison her. She dumped him in the middle of a microwar, destroyed all his sprites, and then tried to send a massive surge into the link he had in his eyes, to fry his brain. He had to tear his eyes out.>

<Didn't know you could attack someone in that fashion,> said Argus.

<You can't,> said Kathryn. <Not anymore. After what happened to him, ESAs got new eyes. But Grigory didn't want them. Said he didn't trust visual data anymore. Maybe because he misjudged that patroness. I wonder if she was beautiful. Maybe he loved her.>

<You're an incurable romantic,> said Argus. And he was rather glad that Kathryn did not have a direct link with Grigory, or she would certainly ask him if he had loved his would-be killer. No one had a direct link except Vasily Burakov—and the sprites. He supposed Grigory could talk to anyone he wanted. But so far Argus had not received a call from the Avatar.

He would have to go through Vasily Burakov, the ex-embassador. Once Vasily knew the situation, he would see why Grigory should be questioned. But he might decide he ought to do it himself. Vasily tended to err on the side of caution.

Argus accessed his message center. He composed a brief query for Vasily and sent it through his sprites. Once that was accomplished, he regarded the comm on his desk. It was the one modern-looking feature in the house, which was entirely deceptive. It handled messages from individuals who did not have a communications system wired into their brains. And for those who, for whatever reason, did not choose to send a message in that fashion.

For the first time he noticed that the RECEIVED light was blinking. He flipped the comm open and touched the screen with a stylus. Scanning the list of messages received, he did a double take. He touched the screen again and read the message.

<We have another suspect to add to our list,> he said.

<Who?> Kathryn jumped up and leaned over his left shoulder, with Nesto crowded in at his right. Argus waited while they read the letter.

Argus,

Perhaps you think you have gained something through the public endorsement of Serina Kurakin-Scriabin. But she is a shrouded woman. Did you consider that? They are viewed as unclean in Belarusian society, even a high-born woman like Serina. You could suffer a loss of status for accepting a social invitation from her. Already through her friendship you have doubled your enemies.

But your sacrifice need not be in vain. Serina is not the best political ally, but she may prove useful in your true mission.

While you're at the party, watch for the Enemy woman. I promise she'll be watching for you.

—B.Y.

<B.Y.?> asked Kathryn.

<That's how she always signed her letters,> said Argus. <Baba Yaga.>

Alexis Anitoliova Scriabin-Bodrova sipped tea from a fine cup, one of the few family treasures that had been recovered from the blaze that destroyed her home. Behind her, the parlor fire burned brightly, for even in the heart of summer she was cold. Despite her discomfort, she was content to live in her brother's house.

She was also content to live in a loveless marriage, with a man who seldom saw or spoke to her. Marriage was an alliance, not a romantic liaison, and Alexis had done her duty by giving her husband four sons before bearing a daughter who might soon be married to good advantage. Thinking about it soothed her, and she decided to have a second cup of tea. She poured, ignoring the bowls of sugar, honey, and cream that waited on the tray. She enjoyed looking at them, but never put them in her tea. She sipped slowly, savoring the slight bitterness on her tongue, the heat that warmed her face. Her gaze lingered on the tea service, but then movement alerted her to unpleasant company.

"You wished to speak with me, Aunt?"

Alexis lowered her cup. No nourishment would pass her lips while this shrouded creature was in the same room with her, let alone the Enemy tutor, who had come also, though she had not been summoned. Yet Alexis suffered this company, for she could not sit idly by while her niece brought shame upon the family name. Alexis prayed to God for strength and hoped that it might shine through her as an example to the wretched creature who stood before her with such impudent pride, as if she were an equal.

"I assigned you a simple task," she said, careful to keep her tone calm and well cultured. "Why can't you accomplish it?"

"If you are referring to the selection of a suitable husband for Anastasia," said the creature, "perhaps I should have made a simple guess instead of taking my responsibility seriously. Shall I flip a coin, Aunt Alexis?"

It was all Alexis could do to keep from striking her. Such a gesture would have been futile, since the shroud muffled the features beneath it. And with the Enemy tutor standing near, Alexis could not be sure she wouldn't be attacked in return.

"Impudence is an ugly character trait," she said at last. "I suppose I should not be surprised that your inner self so closely mirrors your outer appearance. But God is merciful. Perhaps if you pray to him for guidance and forgiveness he will change your outlook for the better."

"I shall do so." The thought of what dreadful movement must be occurring underneath that shroud as misshapen lips formed these words was mildly nauseating to contemplate. "Good evening, Aunt."

"I have *not* dismissed you," snapped Alexis.

Her niece, who had turned to join the vile tutor, regarded Alexis over her shoulder. "I am not yours to dismiss."

"I shall report your behavior to your mother," said Alexis, infuriated at the quaver in her own voice.

"Do so, if it amuses you."

Alexis felt the squeezing in her chest that heralded one of her attacks. But she refused to succumb. "You had a meeting with the Union embassador today," she said. "What did you discuss?"

"The garden."

Alexis did not think she imagined the anger in that deceptively cultivated voice. It gave her satisfaction. "How unimaginative. What do you hope to accomplish by speaking with a Union representative?"

"Conversation."

"Liar," said Alexis triumphantly. "You think those people from the stars should care about your wretched condition because they have sent doctors to care for the peasants. You think perhaps they might fix your face, is that it? But they can't fix the evil in your soul, the poisonous heritage of our war with *those.*" She let her gaze rest briefly on the smirking face of the tutor. "God punishes us for our sins. Your disfigured face is the proof. Do not disgrace yourself further by pursuing these contacts you do not have the authority to establish in the first place."

The shrouded face seemed to stare at her. Alexis imagined the tears of shame that should be staining those distorted cheeks. But the voice that answered her was calm.

"I will consider your advice. Good day, Aunt."

Alexis could only stare in astonishment at her niece's departing back. For one dreadful moment she thought the tutor would remain, but then that one also presented her back and glided from the room. Doubtless she had only lingered to enjoy Alexis's discomfiture.

Alexis raised her teacup and sipped the bitter contents until she felt steady again. Perhaps something had been accomplished. At the very least, Serina knew that someone in the family was aware of her bad behavior. No one could imagine that Alexis approved of it. And when her niece's shameful actions finally brought justice down upon her, no one could say that Alexis had stood by and tolerated it.

Her spies in the house told Alexis that Serina did not gaze into mirrors. There was nothing that ever cast a reflection back at her. Alexis considered that to be her job. She took her responsibility as seriously as her niece claimed to.

Let Serina attempt to choose a suitable husband for Ana.

Alexis had no intention of taking her foolish advice. Alexis was sure Ana's beauty must goad the shrouded woman terribly. God's punishments were always just.

Alexis felt the squeeze in her chest again, but this time it was weaker. She smiled with satisfaction. Her will had conquered her weaker flesh. God had a purpose for her; she knew it when He spared her from the fire that consumed her home.

Serina would serve as an object lesson to everyone, but most importantly to Ana. God did not punish without reason, and His rewards should never be taken for granted. Ana would learn to enter the church with a humble heart, and His light would burn away her childish faults.

Alexis sipped the rest of her tea, musing upon her daughter's future. Behind her the fire leaped merrily in its grate, casting shadows that she never saw.

Maids hurried past Serina as she left her aunt's quarters, toward Anastasia's rooms, from which howls were currently issuing. Serina pitied the staff who worked around the clock to monitor and restrain her niece. She would not stoop to pitying herself for sometimes having to do the same. At least it was not her full-time job.

She climbed the stairs to her own floor. She wanted to spend a few hours of study in the library before supper. Her conversation with Embassador Fabricus had inspired her to pursue several avenues of inquiry. As she ascended, the sounds faded, though she could sometimes hear Anastasia even on her own floor. Her mother suffered no such invasions in her private quarters, and of course Papa, who lived on the topmost floor, never saw or heard from Ana at all, except to catch a glimpse of her at an occasional party. His work as Minister of Finance kept him thoroughly—and safely—occupied.

"Serina."

She paused and looked down. Ayat-ko stood at the bottom of the staircase.

"If she struck you," asked Ayat-ko, "what would you do?"

Serina wanted nothing more than to shut herself up with her books and forget her unpleasant aunt. But Ayat-ko never asked casual questions. "I would not let her strike me in the first place," she said.

Ayat-ko climbed. She wore the same sort of dress Serina did, in the latest Moscow fashion, with a rigid, confining bodice, a high collar, and sleeves that did not allow for dramatic gestures, though like Serina she was not inclined toward ostentatiousness.

But no one would ever mistake Ayat-ko for a human woman, even if they saw her from behind. She was far too slim, and she seemed to glide as she moved. Many of the house staff were terrified of her, though she had never threatened physical harm to any of them. Serina did not chide them for their reaction. The Enemy woman could do more harm with a word or a look than Anastasia could do with her fists.

When Ayat-ko stood on the same step as Serina, she asked, "When she tries to kill you, how will you respond?"

Serina stared into the Enemy woman's gem-green eyes and saw how large the stars at their centers had become. Ayat-ko was in the mood to cause pain, though she would not touch Serina.

"Did I raise you to be such a weakling?" demanded the tutor. "Answer me."

"It depends," said Serina.

"On what?"

"On the manner of her attack."

The stars contracted suddenly, then expanded again. "Let us say that she strikes at you through the courts."

It was an unpleasant thought. "Technically," said Serina, "as a shrouded woman I have no legal rights. I am considered a ward of my family."

"Yes . . ." Ayat-ko pronounced the word slowly, showing her teeth. "Your mother and father. And let us not forget your uncle. How do you fit into their plans? Will you cease to fit?"

"They are my flesh and blood."

Ayat-ko smiled dreadfully. "A brother makes the finest dish," she said. Enemies ate the people they killed. She was suggesting Serina might be consumed, though not literally, by her own family.

"My mother and father will defend me," Serina said. "I'm sure of that."

"Think longer," said Ayat-ko. "Ask yourself a question. Will your parents sacrifice years of scheming and maneuvering for your sake?"

"Surely they would not have to—"

"Will they?" insisted Ayat-ko.

"I cannot answer that."

Ayat-ko turned and continued up the stairs, leaving Serina behind. "You can," she said. "You have."

Serina rested against the railing. She knew that her family would never make such a sacrifice for her; she had known it since the day the first shroud was wrapped around her head. But she did not wish to think like an Enemy. Ayat-ko could not understand that such thinking would be too destructive.

Yet she could still hear Anastasia's shrill threat: *I could have you killed, you know!* Her cousin had always said such things. But maybe she wasn't making them up. Maybe she was repeating something she had heard someone else say.

Think longer. She could never help doing so. She was not one to hide in an attic room as she was expected to do. She must see the light of day, even if it was through a shroud. In fact, it was the shroud that allowed her what freedom she had. When she dressed plainly, she was able go anywhere in the city. She was politely ignored by society, and so she was uniquely positioned to observe it. Serina had seen and heard much that no ordinary woman could. But the more she observed society, the less content she was to merely watch and listen. Lately she had been inclined to act—as she had today with the Star Men.

Ultimately her actions would place her in more danger than her family name could deflect. But it was for a reason. Aunt Alexis could not understand any better than Ayat-ko could. Serina was not even sure she understood herself.

She was no coward. She was going to make her way in the world. And if this brought her into somebody's gun sights, what would she do?

That would depend on the manner of attack. Serina continued up the stairs, up to the floor she shared with no one, and into her library, closing the doors behind her . . .

Grigory flew the winds of Lucifer. Or rather, he placed his perception inside sprites who did. But the information they shared with him never stimulated his visual cortex; it was whispered into his brain as raw data.

He was comfortable in this link. They were able to absorb the energy of the gas giant's storms and channel it to their own purposes. Like the sprites who had pioneered the Belarusian solar system, they observed and recorded phenomena. They created tunnels through space-time and beamed messages to each other, or they used those tunnels themselves, to travel. Grigory told the group he was hitching with to leave Lucifer's gravity well and look at the space station orbiting it.

The salvage crew who had moved it there called it Home Base. It was a simple structure, smaller than the mining stations that had once inhabited the Lucifer system. Grigory studied it briefly, then moved his sprites away from Lucifer and into the asteroid belt.

The Civil War that shattered the Republic left few scars on the surface of Belarus. Grigory had seen the damage personally. His memories were sound, but there were mysteries he had never solved. He went looking for them far out, where small salvage ships picked up pieces of shredded stations, and where short-range mining rigs had been recovered—with the bodies of miners still inside.

Grigory spotted one of the tiny salvage ships, not much bigger than the old mining rigs had been, though these ships had a wider range. They couldn't make jump tunnels, but their engines would take them all the way to Belarus in an emergency. Grigory moved closer, until he could identify the lone pilot operating the recovery claws. Her name was Helen Stavros. She had found a large chunk of hull with the letters *BE* on the side.

Grigory studied the torn metal at its edges. It was shredded like paper—or flesh. Beta Station had been ground to bits, but not in the Civil War. Another monster had killed it. Grigory could remember the event in vivid detail, the streams of data multiplying, fragmenting, full of distress codes and warning signals, finally cut short as systems were torn into scrap. And woven among those perceptions, the screams of people pulled into that grinding maw, and finally the words of the station commander as he blew the jump engine, ending the pain:

Allah is merciful.

Helen Stavros added the chunk of Beta Station to her load and went in search of another. She would have to look hard; there was little left to salvage in that vast space outside the orbital plane of Lucifer. Grigory did not follow. He had other coordinates in mind. An artifact waited for him there. Or rather, four artifacts. His sprites tunneled, and he found what he was looking for.

They were still referred to as Derelicts One through Four. Once they had maintained a precise orbit around Lucifer. Later the four had come together to form a killing machine. Tally Korsakova called it the Grinder, because of what it did to Beta Station. When Commander Hilmi blew his jump engine inside the maw of the thing, he had broken it back into four parts. Nine hundred years later, the Star Men moved stasis generators around the things to keep them at roughly the same coordinates. But Grigory had warned them not to expect the stasis field to confine the Derelicts if they took a notion to move again. Perhaps they believed him, because the generators also contained a warning system, in case of unauthorized movement.

It was the only warning they would have, because the Derelicts still betrayed no energy signature, just as they had none when they attacked Beta Station. Grigory knew they were still alive. They weren't even slumbering; they were like the Enemies who made them, acting unseen, their intentions malignant beyond description.

He studied the grids and footnotes. Methodically, he searched quadrant after quadrant. They had been altered by the explosion of Beta Station. They were smaller than they had been when humans first discovered them, each now roughly the size of Home Base. But they did not resemble the debris of Andrei Mironenko's mining industry. They still had symmetry. The sprites puzzled over the intricate lines that covered their surfaces; Grigory did not try to stop them, though he would stop any human who fell prey to their lure. The lines were puzzles within puzzles. He suspected that they represented materials and forces that did not lie completely within normal space-time. Eventually he and the sprites would unlock the mystery, but this time he had other fish to fry. This time he was looking for any sign that Derelicts One through Four might be receiving information from the spores that had been discovered inside several key buildings in Moscow and St. Petersburg.

He found none. Centuries ago he had also failed to perceive Enemy communications and surveillance. The only sign he had perceived of it back then was a phenomenon Emily Kizheh called the *blink*. The *blink* was a brief interruption of sprite communications, a gap of which they were not aware.

But Union technology had improved significantly over the centuries. The new sprites experienced no *blinks*. Instead, they perceived a phenomenon that sometimes helped the Star Men predict Enemy activity. It was not energy signatures sprites detected, but rather the lack of any activity at all, a local dampening of both energy *and* life signs, a sensory Dead Zone. Once a correlation between Dead Zones and Enemy movement was perceived, the Star Men foiled several attacks on villages with a response time of less than one minute. Many believed that because of this, the Enemies had gone into deep hiding again. This would force them to resort to more esoteric technologies, but Grigory was nursing another suspicion.

Thorough examination of the spores revealed that the colonies were centuries old. Technicians guessed they were created during Andrei Mironenko's reign. They multiplied only in places where energy cells were functioning, so they had been dormant until the Star Men replaced those systems centuries later. Now they were relaying information again, very slowly, passing it spore to spore, so slowly and in such tiny packages no one noticed it was happening. Where it went once the last members of a colony passed it along, no one had been able to tell. But the Enemies were the first suspects, especially one named Ayat-ko, who was purported to be a survivor of Tsar Andrei's revenge, and who now lived in the household of the Kurakin-Scriabins.

Yet Grigory wondered, Would it really be helpful to Ayat-ko to receive information so slowly? Getting it that way would be superior to not getting it at all, but he would expect something more useful from them. This method was such an odd combination of brilliance and foolishness.

He would not find the answer with the Derelicts, so he left them and returned all of his attention to Belarus. He looked again at the spores that watched the world, just as he had watched it over the centuries. He noticed how thick they were inside the very place he rested, the Tomb of the Engineer.

Once it had been Tally Korsakova's private quarters.

Grigory began to favor a theory.

*   *   *

Moscow is downhill from all the Russias. It was a very old saying, inspired by an ancient place on another world. But Ivan thought it could never be more true than it was on the lost colony world of Belarus. No matter where money started out, ultimately it flowed to Moscow.

Some of that money always found Ivan Sergeivich Khabalov, though he had no trade to speak of, except to do God's will. Even as he sat in the tavern his mind was on the true faith; the vodka only sharpened his wits. The small table seemed scarcely able to accommodate his tall form. Periodically he would pour a glass from his bottle, down it with one gulp, then resume glaring through the raucous crowd.

Finally a spectacled man approached and sat with him. His shorn hair and shaved chin marked him as a bureaucrat. He stared in another direction, as if he were not aware of Ivan. A barmaid brought the newcomer a bottle of vodka and a glass, then hurried off before he could mount a proper objection.

"I wanted beer," he muttered, but poured himself a glass of vodka and downed it like a pro. He took off his spectacles, wiped them with a kerchief far too fine for his attire or his surroundings, and put them back on again. "I'm taking a big risk," he said in the same muttering tone.

"God will reward you in the next life," said Ivan.

"He should."

Ivan turned the full power of his glare on the little man. He watched the color drain out of the pinched features, which sat below a hairline that had receded before its time.

"I've got important news," squeaked the man.

"I hope so," said Ivan.

The spectacled man poured another glass of vodka, his hands trembling. After he drank it he seemed steadier. "I took notes at an important meeting today," he said. "Embassador Argus Fabricus proposed a deal, and it was accepted. They're going to give the Star Men permission to start mining operations in our solar system again."

Ivan stared for a long moment, betraying no reaction.

"You understand?" The man wiped sweat from his upper lip. "Up there, with spaceships, just outside Lucifer's orbit. Like in Tsar Andrei's time."

"Because I was born a peasant," Ivan said, "you think I know nothing of science?"

"Sorry." The man removed his spectacles and cleaned them again. "It was a secret vote, and I'm not sure half of them understood what they were debating. This technology—we've tried to pretend it's our legacy all these years, but we aren't used to it anymore."

Ivan did not blink. "What do they intend to do with the raw materials they mine?"

The man gulped vodka. "Nothing at all," he said. He waited for Ivan to respond to this, seemed disappointed when he didn't. "Fabricus says they're going to hold the materials in *trust* for us until we're able to do something with it. The Star Men are edging their way in. Eventually they'll get what they want, a worker's paradise. They'll reinstitute every bit of the Bill of Rights, even the stupid things. Equal rights for everyone, regardless of ability. Women taking jobs that should go to men. Have you seen those women they send down here in those so-called danger suits? Women doctors work in their clinics. I would never consent to be treated by one." He tossed back another drink. "We need to take the hard line with the Star Men, make it look like we're doing them a favor by letting them do our work. They want to mine our solar system? Let them pay us fees and taxes for the privilege. They would do it. They want this world badly enough. I don't know why they want it, but I'm going to find out."

"You talk too much." Ivan set a gold coin on the table.

The spectacled man stared fixedly at it. "You *pay* me to talk too much." He reached for the coin and Ivan seized his skinny wrist. He did not struggle, but stared at Ivan belligerently. "Don't tell me you've got another clerk who works for the duma."

"You can't afford to buy information from me," said Ivan.

"You disagree with my opinions?"

"No." Ivan squeezed the wrist a little tighter. "But I know how to control my women. They will do nothing unless I permit it. This is God's law. Star Men cannot change that." He let go and did not need to look to confirm he had left welts.

The clerk seized the coin and slipped it into his pocket. He turned his knees away from the table, as if his feet wanted to run away but the foolish brain that owned them could not concede their wisdom. "It's easy for you," he said. "The one you've got at home has a shroud wrapped around her face. No one can tell if you beat her or not."

"It doesn't matter if they can tell," said Ivan. "People could see the marks on her mother's face clearly enough. They knew she earned them."

The clerk seemed hardly to hear him. "One thing we asked of them: kill our Enemies. Drop a bomb on them like Tsar Andrei did. They have seen the evidence of crimes against us, but what do they say? *No.* They think they can negotiate with monsters. They ignore what we have learned. Now they say they're going to hold ore for us in space until we're ready to use it. They promise to make alloys we can use. But for one thousand years the Enemies have sabotaged the industries that would have allowed us to make those alloys ourselves! The Star Men want us to be helpless, then come in here and hand us all these things we need, until we owe them far more than we can ever repay. And that's when they'll tell us what we can do for *them.*"

"Pay for your bottle," said Ivan.

The clerk fished a smaller coin out of his pocket and tossed it on the table, afraid to place a hand within Ivan's reach. "You agree with me?" he asked earnestly.

Ivan shrugged. "God has his instruments." He poured a shot of vodka, downed it, then resumed his contemplation of the cosmos. The clerk had already delivered all the useful information he had.

The clerk squirmed in his chair for a while longer, until finally, muttering about taxes and fees, he sprang to his feet and fled the tavern.

Ivan never wondered why the Star Men refused to kill the Enemies. It should have been plain to everyone. You don't kill someone when you hope they will be useful to you.

He flexed his scarred hands, feeling the sting of a new cut on one of his fingers. He made his daughter take off her shroud before a beating. But she had not caused most of the scars on his hands. Her benighted mother could take credit for that—though she would have to do it from hell. She had revealed her true nature when she bore a child with the mark of the devil. Shrouded women wore veils to conceal their sins, not to hide the marks of just punishment. The world itself was shrouded because it was tainted by Enemies and unbelievers.

Ivan placed a coin on the table and made his way to the rear of the tavern. As he passed the table next to his, he saw but did not look directly at its occupant. Dmitri Brusilov was equally careful not to look at him. He would leave before Ivan returned. They did not speak in public places. Private places were quite another matter.

Street whores pressed against Ivan as he passed, stirring his blood, but he had important matters to attend to first. He went to the end of a narrow hall, where the telephone was guarded by the big wife of the tavern owner. She nodded to him, them withdrew to give him privacy.

He had to crank it several times, but finally got an operator.

"Alexis Anitoliova Scriabin-Bodrova," he told him.

"Whom shall I say is calling?"

"Ivan."

He waited, but not for long.

"My dear friend," her voice crackled over the line, "is it you?"

"Yes, Alexi." His tone toward her was far more gentle than the one he had used on the clerk.

"I have worried terribly. Are you well?"

"I have had a vision." He heard the intake of breath. She hung on his next words. "The Star Men have resumed their industry in space, which our ancestors began a thousand years ago. They will say it is done for us, but we will not be permitted to do it ourselves."

"How can we stop them?" she asked bitterly.

"We do not need to stop them, little one. But we must make them pay for the privilege of *helping* us. Speak to your brother. As Minister of Finance, he can demand that taxes and fees must be levied for every ounce. The Star Men will say it isn't possible, but it is. They will consent in the end."

"I will tell him, Ivan. But when shall we see you again? We miss you terribly."

"Soon. I will send a messenger. We shall pray for your daughter. God will light her life, Alexi."

"Bless you. Take the greatest care of yourself, I beg you."

He bade her good-bye and hung the mouthpiece in its receiver. He frequented this tavern because it featured this useful device. His patronesses were rich enough to have telephones in their homes. If the operator listened in, that did not trouble him. He only spoke things into the receiver that would do him good if word got around.

He would favor Alexis and her group with a visit very soon because he was running low on money. He would pray with them and allow them to fawn on him and ply him with gifts. Ivan knew in whose pockets the taxes and fees would end up. As the ladies grew richer, his life would also be enriched. Because if Moscow was downhill from all the Russias, most certainly it was downhill from space.

Slender hands sought him when he emerged from the hall. He let them linger. His work was done for the day, and he did not tire easily.

In fact it was God's will that Ivan rarely tired at all.

* * *

<People are spying on us,> said Grigory, <and Baba Yaga is undoubtedly one of them, yet I doubt she is doing it with mold spores.>

Vasily heard the Avatar's virtual voice in his head, but most of his brain was engaged with a much more interesting process. Grigory had managed to interface his sprites with the mold network, and to relay the images, sounds, and even smells they were absorbing. In order to make sense of them, he had to compile spore information over several days and then speed it up. He could then relay it to other people via the sprite network, allowing them to share sensations from the spores' point of view. Vasily was getting his first tour of the Tomb of the Engineer in this odd fashion—possibly the only one he would ever have. He could see the magnificent sarcophagus that housed the remains of Natalia Korsakova in the dim light.

<Why not Baba Yaga?> he asked. <She sent Argus a message just after ESA Nesto detected that flare-up—seems like a pretty wild coincidence.>

<I don't say we should eliminate her as a suspect. But I have been exploring these spore colonies, and I find it odd that they convey more information than just audio and visual.>

<I can smell sandalwood,> said Vasily. <And cedar.> Stranger still, he could feel the sensation of coolness on his skin, and a slight breeze from one of the vents.

<I can understand why someone would want to listen and look,> said Grigory. <But why should they also want to feel and smell? This seems more voyeuristic than practical. And I am also intrigued by the concentration of spores in particular areas.>

<We know how they're concentrated now,> said Vasily, <not how they were concentrated a thousand years ago.>

<True,> said Grigory. <Yet I have kept systems running in the Winter Palace. All of the spores that were here should still be thriving. But look how things change once we go out into the hall.>

The movement to another perspective was disorienting. Now that they had left the tomb, the sensations Vasily received were patchy. He wanted to squint eyes that did not exist, switch on a light with a virtual finger.

<The Tomb of the Engineer was Tally's quarters in those days,> said Grigory. <Let us see what happens when we move down to the next suite. They belonged to Peter, Andrei's son.>

The reception in Peter's rooms was good enough to show Vasily that they were beautifully but tastefully appointed, giving him a glimpse into the high strata of the old clans who had ruled the Republic. <I can see better in here than I could in the hallway,> he said. <But not nearly as well as in Tally Korsakova's quarters.>

<Let's go to the next suite,> said Grigory. <That one was mine.>

Perspective shifted back to the ghostly hall. But as they advanced, the view and its attending sensations flickered and died.

<Did we lose the connection?> asked Vasily.

<No,> said Grigory. <There are no spores here. And none in my old quarters either. I don't wish to flatter myself, but it seems to me that Baba Yaga should be as interested in me as she was in Tally and Peter. Now I will show you another heavily infested area, though it will not surprise you. Emily Kizheh's conference room, where we discussed many important things.>

Sensation faded in again and Vasily saw a room with a large table at its center. Two men were sitting at one end and talking in soft tones, but Argus could hear them pretty well. In real time, this conversation had taken place several days ago—and the men were discussing things they would not have wanted the Star Men to hear.

<Someone who was spying should have every reason to listen here,> said Grigory. <Most heavy infestation of spores are in St. Petersburg and Moscow, in government buildings. You might think Baba Yaga would be inclined to watch

those places, but I doubt it. I suspect that the everyday machinations of government would bore her. Yet, she watches us in some fashion—she has proven that many times. The Enemies watch us as well. But one thousand years ago, someone made these spores and did not deploy them in or near my quarters. This person did not want to risk having me notice or trace him.>

<Just one person?> asked Vasily.

<Yes. Look again at the area in which the spores are most greatly concentrated.> The scene shifted back inside the Tomb of the Engineer, and Vasily smelled the scented woods.

<In all the world,> said Grigory, <this is the spot that most interested him.>

Vasily knew the record almost as well as Grigory. He had to admit, he was more than a little inclined to linger over the parts involving Natalia Korsakova. She had been so lovely, so brilliant. <She was the world engineer for this colony,> he said. <Maybe we shouldn't be surprised if she was someone's main focus.>

<True,> said Grigory. <If this Watcher intended to sabotage her work, he would monitor her as much as he could. But no sabotage ever occurred.>

<You have someone in mind.>

<Yes. John the Murderer.>

Vasily wasn't surprised by the idea, both ESA Nesto and ESA Kathryn had already said the same. He should have been glad that the suspect was a dead man. Yet the idea spooked him. <Emily Kizheh was present at his autopsy . . .> he said.

<Which was performed by ESA Tam, one of my protégés. No one would have been more thorough than she. Are you wondering if John possessed an Avatar like mine?>

<You read my mind.>

<They were rare in those days, but he was brilliant—he might have known how to make one. Tam never found one, though, and his body was taken apart very thoroughly.>

<So even if his old systems are still gathering information, no one is there to receive it.>

<I wouldn't go that far.>

Back on Archangel, Vasily felt a chill. <How could it be possible?>

<I don't know. But I didn't know many things one thousand years ago, and we paid dearly for it.>

Vasily sighed. He gazed around Natalia's quarters, looking at the magnificent Egyptian and Nubian artifacts, watching the play of shadow and light on the profiles of dead gods and kings who were adorned with gold, lapis lazuli, jade, carnelian. <Grigory,> he said at last, <it's time for you to come home.>

<You mean it's time for me to go back to Archangel.>

<You know what I mean,> said Vasily.

<I don't know as much as you think.>

<Grigory—they have a body for you now.>

The Avatar was silent for a long time. Vasily wondered if Grigory could even relate to the concept anymore. He had been pure mind for a thousand years.

<A body—> Grigory said at last. <Something they have grown? ESA Molly spoke of this once. It seemed a theoretical proposition.>

<The body has organic elements,> said Vasily. <You will be able to feel sensations, emotions, eat, and sleep—even make love if you want to. But it has inorganic elements as well. It will be far stronger than a human body. It was made to house the Avatar of an ESA elder.>

<So you say. But there is the matter of guards outside my door. Once it is opened, Tsar Gyorgy and his cabinet will want to know why, and your negotiations with them will become more complicated.>

<We can get you out, Grigory. We could have done it years ago, had you been willing.>

<I can accomplish more where I am.>

<Forgive me for being frank, but I think there is another issue here.>

<I'm intrigued to hear what it might be.>

<Guilt, my friend. This business with the spores has made something plain to me. You feel responsible that you were not able to detect the surveillance, now or one thousand years ago.>

<I am responsible,> said Grigory. <This is fact, not emotion. Emily Kizheh felt the same.>

<You don't need to stay on Belarus to accomplish your work. You can do it in your new body.>

<No one has explained to me—what does a dead man need with a body?>

Vasily had known Grigory would resist. He was trying to buy time, trying to guess what might move the Avatar. Finally he decided to take a chance. <I have worked with ESAs for many years, yet I know little about you save one thing: you are an extraordinarily honorable breed.>

<It is required,> said Grigory.

<I also know that you will not work with anyone unless you judge them to be honorable. You must have thought highly of Andrei Mironenko and his associates. But I am guessing that as an ESA you had—and still have—obligations that extended beyond those you had toward your old patron. Even beyond your life as Grigory Michaelovich, for you are an Avatar. You would not have made such provisions without good reason. And your ESA compatriots would not have made this new body for you.>

Grigory did not respond, yet Vasily felt he must have made the right points. It was up to the Avatar to decide what he would do about it. <I hope you'll think about it,> he said, preparing to exit gracefully from the link.

<No need,> said Grigory. <You've talked me into it. You're an excellent diplomat, Vasily. Now tell me—how do you plan to sneak me past the guards?>

Argus dreamed of the ice bear.

It was always the same one. Perhaps it was the essential ice bear, the archetype that defined every ice bear ever hunted on Fenris, a male trying to prepare for hibernation by eating everything it could get its ten-inch claws into, old enough to have lots of good meat on its bones, young enough to make mistakes. It labored across an endless, frozen plain, its fur silver against the sapphire sky.

Patience. Argus's father said the word to him many times when he was growing up. Every year in late spring Argus waited with his spear, hoping to be included in the hunting party, and he thought *patience* meant he should wait until he was big and strong enough to be useful on a hunt. But his father meant the hunt itself.

His father sat at the hearth, repairing arrows, his hair as pale as the snow, his skin burned brown by reflected sunlight. "It's not glamorous, Son. You spend most of your time following, not chasing. Be patient. Be alert. Be ready."

"But what about courage?" asked Argus. "You have killed a charging ice bear with your spear. All the men say you did not falter. It stood fifteen feet at the shoulder, Father!"

His father did not smile. Argus seldom saw him frown, either; Edvard Fabricus expressed every emotion with his eyes. They were blue-grey like stone, or like the cloudy winter sky, or like the still surface of a lake in the brief, dreamlike summer. "You find the courage," said Edvard. "You'd better. And anyway, if he's charging, you didn't do your job. He's supposed to be running in the other direction. And you follow, for days and days."

In the dream, Argus could feel the cold; he would never forget it if he lived a thousand years. The winters of Fenris were ten months long, divided into three parts: early, deep, and late. There was no fall, spring lasted perhaps a month, and summer even less. The brief warmth brought on a frenzy of growth, celebration—and mating. The ice bears followed herds of sea dogs, which in turn followed vast schools of fish that migrated up the rivers to spawn. No one bothered the ice bears then; humans caught fish in nets and dried them for the long winter. Hunters didn't start tracking prey until the first snows fell. Hellhounds followed the same schedule.

Argus grew up and he got his wish. His legs grew long and hard from trudging across the wastelands; weariness nagged him as he and the others walked through snow up to their knees. But they continued at a pace that could keep them going all day. The bear did the same. Though it knew they were following, it could do nothing about it but keep going. From time to time it would stop and sniff the air. Sometimes it looked at them over its shoulder, an expression on its furry face that wrung Argus's heart with pity.

"I know how you feel," his father told him once. "If you want to feel better about it, watch the ice bear when *it* is the hunter. It is merciless. It is worthy of our respect—and our envy, because it hunts with no fear or regrets."

Even if Argus had gained no comfort from this advice, he still would have done his part in the killing without hesitation. Smoked fish was not enough to get through the heart of winter. In another month, the blizzards would reign on Fenris, and he and his kin would go underground to mend tools, study old books, and tell stories by the hearth. This would be a happier time if there was plenty to eat. So the hunters tracked until the last possible week, gambling with the weather, hoping for that last kill that would put them over the top.

For three days they tracked the bear, and he had been unable to find food. Inexperienced hunters might have been tempted to shoot him full of arrows, then follow him until he dropped of blood loss. But that was an excellent way to attract hellhounds.

The bear could go several more days without eating. It would grow weaker, the cold slowly invading its bones. The hunters faced the same chill, but had the advantage of dried stores to nourish them. They would not stop for the day until the bear had. They would watch the beast in shifts, lest it should backtrack and attack them in desperation. You could fire arrow after arrow, but once an ice bear decided to charge, you needed to use your spear. You could not run.

In Argus's dream, this bear never turned, though the one that killed his father had. Argus was eighteen when that happened—the bear in this dream was from the year he had just turned sixteen. It led them for a week, then sat down, too weary to continue. A breeze ruffled its silver pelt, warning of a blizzard that might be days away or mere hours. Argus wondered if that was why it gave up, because it knew it had already lost the race with winter.

It turned its massive head and looked at them. Argus moved to place the first arrow, but his father stopped him. Edvard walked a few paces forward. He fit an arrow to his bow and shot the bear.

It stood and ran several paces. But it dropped to its knees again. Great puffs of steam rose from its open mouth. Then it lay its head in the snow.

"Well done," said Uncle Kay, who was killed when Argus was twenty. "A few more shots, I think."

The bear shuddered when it was shot again, but finally it lay still. The men worked hurriedly to load it on the sled. Time was even more precious now, because the smell of the kill would attract unwanted attention, possibly other ice bears. They would sleep in shorter shifts, moving as fast as they could, especially now that a blizzard was breathing down their necks. Argus took his place at the pull ropes, glad to be consumed by the hard work, because a growing sense of unease trickled into his belly.

Men and bears died the same way. Their dead faces held the same expression—or rather the lack of one. Argus was Lutheran, but he ventured to believe that even their souls went to the same place, where they fished together in an eternal springtime. Years later, as he dreamed of that hunt, he often realized he was dreaming by the time he and his kin were trying to pull the carcass of the ice bear back home. But it did not help to know. He could change nothing. He could not wake up and tell himself, *That's all water under the bridge. Forget it. Go back to sleep and dream about something good.* The hellhounds always came. They always dragged three of his cousins off, and he and his kin were always forced to surrender the carcass that had cost them so dearly.

He heard a haunting cry. He stopped pulling and looked over his shoulder. The first pair of yellow eyes should have appeared, burning like stoked fires. He looked for the sleek forms that came gliding across the white snow, dodging arrows and baring double rows of saw-edged teeth.

But this time he didn't see them. A woman was standing on the hill over which they had just labored. She had skin as black as ebony, and she was wearing a danger suit. But her pose was odd, feet together and arms crossed over her chest like a mummy. Her eyes were closed, and she had a very odd feature, data links that were buried in her scalp, that undulated like snakes. He recognized her, though he had never known her.

"Tally Korsakova," he said.

He dropped his rope and walked back a few paces. Nobody tried to stop him. His kin seemed frozen, as if they were a program he had paused. Argus looked hard at the woman who stood at least two hundred paces away.

"Listen," she said, though her lips did not move. "I have to tell you something."

She was so beautiful, she might be a goddess. But the sight of her pierced him with a cold far deeper than any winter he had ever known.

"Hunter," said Tally Korsakova, "you've already found the ice bears. And sooner or later they're going to turn and charge you. But while you're busy fighting for your life, don't forget the hellhounds. That's what your dream has been trying to tell you all this time. Understand?"

"I'm trying to," said Argus.

She opened her eyes slowly. Instead of orbs, her sockets were full of light. Trying to see into that light, he took several steps closer. But the wind blew up and covered Tally with snow, settling again to reveal that she was gone.

A moment later, the first pair of sulfur-colored eyes appeared over the crest, and the world began to move around him again. But Argus did not rush to fit arrows to his bow. Instead, he studied those savage forms.

You've already found the ice bears, she said. He was lucid enough to remember his current mission. So the ice bears she referred to were the Enemies.

Then who were the hellhounds?

"Keep your back to the sled!" shouted his father, and Argus raised his bow. Before he could fire, a red mouth full of saw-blade teeth opened before him, as if to swallow him whole.

He woke up in the darkness of the house on Martha Prospekt. His bedroom was warm, but he still felt the cold of Fenris. He lay there for a long time, wondering. He found no answers, but he remembered something that finally helped him get back to sleep, his father's old advice.

Be patient. Be alert. Be ready.

His father fished with the ice bears now. And Argus was no longer troubled by a sore heart when he hunted . . .

You find the courage. You'd better.

That was the lesson, taught by an expert, on a harsh world that joined the Union when Argus was twenty-four. He signed up for the Foreign Service and took full advantage of their training and education, then moved to the Department of Defense. He had no doubts about what he was doing now or why. The ice bears had taught him that.

So when he went back to sleep, he succumbed with the skill of a hunter who could not afford to be weary.

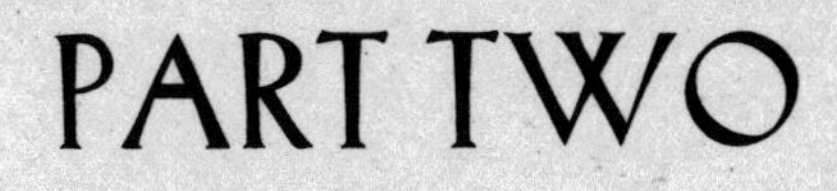

PART TWO

The evening air was fragrant with the scent of Serina's garden, or perhaps it was the perfume of so many ladies gathered in one place, Argus could not be sure. As he and Kathryn were ushered into the grand house, they joined a steady stream of guests, and he could only be grateful that at least they were not compelled to wear the elaborate, confining clothes the other guests had stuffed themselves into.

Yet he felt a moment of vertigo. His childhood had been rigidly austere, and his adult life defined by military simplicity. The fine furnishings, lush colors, and expensive clothing jarred his nerves.

<Where's Serina?> wondered Kathryn as the two of them drifted from the massive foyer toward the noise of the ballroom. Before they could get very far, they were intercepted by a young maid.

"Please, sir." She curtsied. "Duchess Serina wishes that you should meet with her in her library. Will you follow me?"

"Certainly," Argus said, feeling grateful for the chance to duck the crowd, at least for a while. He knew he should pay his respects to the master and mistress of the house, but that need not be done immediately. For all he knew, it would not happen at all—they were not the ones who had invited him. He and Kathryn followed the maid up the first in a succession of staircases, away from the sounds and smells of the ball and into a highly polished wilderness.

Oddly, Argus thought of Archangel station. The house was not as large as a single quadrant, yet as he moved inside it he *felt* its immensity, its superstructure supported by girders and struts, its rooms connected by a network of hallways, functioning with its own ecosystem. The halls were illuminated by gaslight structures that must have been a thousand years old, yet they burned cleanly, shining softly on wood and marble, revealing richly colored fabrics and rugs. Exotic scenes teased his eyes with stories on tapestries and screens, paintings and vases, animals and characters from Russian fairy tales cavorting in the long, lonely hallways. A thousand painted eyes seemed to follow Argus.

Finally the maid took one last turn, leading them to a pair of carved doors. As Argus rounded the corner he spotted a small painting in an alcove. It featured just one figure, a hut perched on two giant chicken legs that seemed poised to leap across the gap and follow him through the doors.

The maid turned the knob and pushed the right-hand door on well-oiled hinges. She stood at the threshold and indicated they should enter. Once they had gone through, she closed the door behind them without joining them.

The room smelled of books and cedar. It was a library, but not on the grand scale he would have expected in a large mansion. Serina emerged from a row of shelves and moved into the brighter light near a study table. She was carrying two books. He wondered how she could read through the shroud covering her face.

She set the books on the table and turned to face them. "Good evening," she said. "I am very pleased you could come. I hope you will speak with me for a while before we join the guests downstairs."

Argus moved closer, but suddenly Kathryn's hand

gripped his arm. He froze, and his eyes snapped into tactical. That was when he saw her.

The Enemy woman stood in the shadows between two rows. She was inhumanly beautiful, pale skinned, slender as a wand, with long hair as dark as ink. She wore the most dreadful smile Argus had ever seen.

"Ayat-ko won't hurt you," said Serina. "This is my library. I am master here."

"Ayat-ko." Kathryn pronounced the name carefully. "Why have you come?"

"She watches," Serina answered. The Enemy woman remained silent, her smile untempered. After another moment she withdrew into the deeper shadows.

"She's gone," Kathryn said, and released Argus's arm.

"You will not be assaulted in my library," Serina said calmly. "I can't give you the same assurances for the rest of the house. But I think if you are willing to look at these books, you will find them very interesting."

"The evening has already proven interesting," said Argus. "I shall be intrigued to discover whether it can become more so." He went to the study table, Kathryn moving between him and the last known location of the Enemy woman. Argus looked at the books. Serina had placed them beside each other. They were thick and tall. They looked brand-new, which was an indication that they must be very old. One was titled *Belarus* and the other, *Canopus*. And underneath each title the author's name was spelled out in small letters: Natalia Korsakova.

It was as if someone had placed a cold hand on the back of Argus's neck. He opened *Belarus* and skimmed through its contents. It contained photographs, sketches, copies of notes and letters, and a text describing the building of a world.

"My word . . ." he said.

"When my uncle Gyorgy became tsar," said Serina, "the Mironenkos were executed. I was seven years old, and did not grasp the details until much later. But I was very pleased when a large number of new books were introduced into this library. My uncle gave them to my mother for safekeeping."

"What is *Canopus* about?" asked Kathryn.

"You don't know?" Serina rested her hand on the cover. "You've never heard the name?"

"Never," said Kathryn.

Serina regarded her for a moment, as if weighing her answer. "Then it's true," she said at last. "It was a secret world, just as Natalia Korsakova claimed. It was designed as a playground for the very rich. No one else was supposed to know about it because . . . forbidden things were being done there."

"Forbidden?" asked Argus.

Serina opened the book and showed them a photograph of someone sunning herself on a rock. Argus had to look twice, because the person in the photograph was only human from the shoulders up. She had the body of a lion. "I see what you mean," he said. "Yes, that would have been forbidden, even then."

"This was the world Natalia helped build before she came to our world," said Serina. She turned a page and showed them another photograph. The man in the picture was completely human. He was slender, bald, and appeared to be of early middle age. He had the most piercing eyes Argus had ever seen, yet his face was also friendly. "This is George Bernstein, master world engineer," Serina continued. "Natalia thought very highly of him."

She almost shut the book, then seemed to change her mind. Instead she opened it to one of the last pages, revealing another photograph. "Natalia Korsakova," said Serina. "World engineer."

Her skin was a shade lighter than it had been in his dream, and her expression was open, engaging, challenging. But otherwise Natalia Korsakova looked the same. And the rasta-links that drifted around her head spoke of an age long dead. "May I?" he asked.

"Please," said Serina, and stepped aside.

He thumbed through the book, reading snippets of text. Very quickly he began to understand why Serina was so well educated. "Are there many such books in your private library?" he asked.

"Yes."

"I envy you."

"We should join the other guests," said Serina.

Argus closed the book regretfully. He wondered why she had shown it to them in the first place. He doubted she merely wanted to impress them. Possibly she wanted to inform them that there were things about their galaxy they had not known. He gazed at her, this wealthy daughter of a powerful family who was also the lowliest of outcasts, and wondered what else she was about to teach him.

"Come," she said. "We should join the other guests or there shall be scandalous talk." She moved gracefully to the door. Argus and Kathryn followed at a respectful distance. She let them out of the library and led them back through the many halls.

"I would like to meet your brothers and sisters," Kathryn said suddenly.

"So would I," said Serina. "You already know them as well as I do. If they were to associate with me their status would be compromised."

"How many siblings do you have?" asked Argus, hoping to divert the conversation to more neutral ground.

"Three brothers and three sisters. I am the seventh child."

"Then you're the magic child," said Kathryn. "Seven is a special number."

"So I have always hoped," said Serina. As they descended the last staircase she managed to draw closer to Argus. Kathryn didn't move to stop her. Argus heard the opening strains of a waltz played by a small orchestra, and Serina slipped her hand over the crook of his elbow. Taking her cue, he escorted her down the grand staircase and into the ballroom. For a moment, all eyes turned to them, and Argus thought he detected a pause. He realized that Serina had managed to arrive at this grand event on his arm and make the most dramatic entrance of the evening.

They walked slowly through the crowd. Argus looked for faces he recognized. He found a few ministers and high-level bureaucrats, some of whom nodded to him and some of whom did not. But most of the aristocrats in the room were strangers. Their glances were cool and casual, though he did not doubt they were studying him.

At the far end of the ballroom—so far, a sporting event could have been comfortably played in the space in between—was an anteroom revealed by a row of gothic arches, containing a buffet table that may have been sixty feet long. It was laden with a feast. Servants stood behind it in crisply starched uniforms, their posture as stiff and disciplined as that of soldiers. Serina at first seemed to be headed toward the buffet, but she took a forty-five degree turn to the right, and Argus found himself walking toward a highly polished dance floor instead. Couples swirled around it like flowers in a whirlpool.

They passed rows of comfortable chairs and couches, and he spotted Serina's father standing near one. He was the minister of finance, and Argus had seen him at a few meetings. Trim and handsome, Minister Scriabin smiled at him pleasantly, and nodded. Argus returned the gesture and looked at the occupants of the couch, expecting to see Serina's mother, the tsar's sister. But instead he saw the woman who had been glaring at him from the window a week ago.

<The aunt,> Kathryn remarked. <And there's the lovely little Anastasia, on that other couch. See the one surrounded by all the men?>

If he hadn't seen her, he certainly would have heard her, even above the music. Anastasia was laughing gaily, her voice raised flirtatiously. She was truly a vision of loveliness, high color warming her perfect cheeks. Argus guessed that she was in her perfect element. It was really quite sad she couldn't stay that way. She might have been too preoccupied to set any fires.

<I'll bet that shy-looking one over there at the back of the crowd is Frederick Maylunas, the nice guy,> said Kathryn. <I wonder where the other one is. Dmitri.>

<You're enjoying this too much,> said Argus, nodding pleasantly to a group of women.

<More fun than a soap opera. Oh my gosh—that's him. I recognize that name now, Argus. He's got a lot of shady friends. Nesto's pals in the city police have a whole file on him. Over there by the booze fountain.>

Argus glanced in that direction and saw a man looking back at him. Dmitri Brusilov was no aristocrat, but he stood like someone who was confident of his high status. He also looked like the sort who had earned it with blood and sweat. His expression was courteous, but he had the eyes of a predator, noticing everything.

<He doesn't bother to court Anastasia,> said Kathryn. <He knows she's not the one he has to win. Plus, he doesn't give a rat's ass about her. Not a bad-looking guy. He probably has women on the side.>

<Not an uncommon arrangement,> said Argus. Serina was moving inexorably closer to the swirling crowd. He moved with her as if he were happy to do so.

"One dance," she murmured. "If you please."

"I would be delighted," said Argus, though he would much rather have stayed in the library.

Argus and Serina paused at the edge, and he had an awkward moment when he couldn't decide when to jump into traffic. She waited for his cue, and in another moment they were moving. For a few seconds he danced carefully, afraid to knock her off balance. But she moved as if she were extensions of his own limbs. In a few more seconds, Argus was surprised to feel exhilaration as they picked up speed together and swept around the floor.

"You're wonderful," he told her.

"You're too kind," she said, but he thought she sounded pleased.

He forgot about time. He forgot how much he hated politics and politicians, all the movers and shakers who pushed honest soldiers around like pawns. And most especially, he forgot to be annoyed at Serina for trying to make him a part of her game. He would have been perfectly happy to keep dancing with her until the end of the evening.

But too soon, the music ended. Another tune replaced it, a mazurka. He would have attempted it, but Serina indicated she was finished.

"I'm very warm," she said. He escorted her from the floor and looked around for a waiter bearing refreshments—then realized that she would not be able to drink them. Her shroud prevented her from taking the comfort every other woman in the room could enjoy.

Kathryn was back at his side the moment he stepped from the floor—he doubted she had ever been far. Faces turned toward them, looking at Argus and Kathryn, but not Serina. He recognized ministers, dukes, boyars, and more cabinet members.

<I wouldn't try to approach them,> warned Kathryn. <That would be a social faux pas.>

<I have no intention of doing so,> he assured her.

<But if someone approaches us, we'll make nice-nice.>

<Goody,> he said, and then a large red-faced man suddenly stood in his path. Argus recognized General Tatischev, a man who was present at every meeting he had attended so far, but with whom he had yet to exchange more than a few words.

"You dance well, Embassador," said Tatischev, his tone betraying no emotion. "But you've turned pale when everyone else in the room is getting red."

His tone implied his meaning. In the gaslight, Argus's and Kathryn's light-reactive skin was much paler—though still darker than these pale-skinned aristocrats. Vasily had briefed him carefully about the subject. Star Men had the skin color of the working class, toilers under the sun—which made many imperialists suspicious of them.

"Very interesting to have skin that changes color so quickly," said the general. "Tell me, does it ever turn a decent shade of white?"

"There is one circumstance under which our skin turns a color close to white," said Argus. "But under those conditions it becomes a reflective surface rather than an absorbing one. That would happen only in the presence of gamma rays."

"I fervently hope," said the general, "that I shall see that someday."

"I fervently hope that you shall not," said Argus, "since gamma rays are caused by thermo-nuclear explosions."

"Ah, then you truly are supermen," the general said mildly, keeping his eyes on Argus's. He pulled a cigar from his pocket, bit the end off, and lit it. He had scarcely taken a puff when Serina snapped, "How dare you smoke in my presence without my permission!"

The general was momentarily startled, but then put out the cigar and slipped it back into his pocket, bowing to her. "Forgive me. Perhaps the embassador and I should retire to the smoking parlor."

"Do so," said Serina. "ESA Kathryn and I will pursue more gentile amusements."

<Should I demand to come with you?> asked Kathryn.

<Not this time,> said Argus. He was not a career diplomat, but he understood that functions like this grand ball were not really parties for anyone except the very young, and he was about to engage in some work that would not be approachable during normal business hours.

Kathryn and Serina walked away, arm in arm. <My sprites are watching you,> Kathryn said. <If anyone gets physical I can be at your side in four seconds. Less, if I don't worry about knocking people off their feet.>

<I'm sure that would earn us many friends,> he said.

<Your danger suit will defend you against anything these

stuffed shirts have to offer. It's Ayat-ko I'm worried about. She's watching from the balcony across the room now. If she moves, I will too.>

<Thank you,> said Argus, and focused on the general's overheated features. Under all that red, the man was dead calm.

"Come," Tatischev said pleasantly. "I always talk better in a room full of smoke."

"After you," said Argus, and he followed the general through the crowd. He noticed that suddenly more people were nodding pleasantly to him, as if seeing him for the first time. But when he passed Anastasia's would-be suitor, Dmitri, the man was turned in the other direction. That did not seem to be an accident.

They left the ballroom and went into the buffet hall, past the lavishly set table. Argus regretted they weren't headed there instead. He also noticed that more men than women congregated near the table and in the hallway outside two large, closed doors. The general rapped on the doors and a bearded face peered out. In another moment the door opened just wide enough to admit the two of them.

The air wasn't as smoky as Argus had feared it would be; in fact the cigar smoke was rather pleasant. Several men sat on couches and overstuffed chairs. Some of them rose when Argus came into the room, and he shook hands with them.

"So glad you could join us," said Nikolai Vassilyev, the minister of science, the man with whom Argus had dealt the most often, so far. He was intelligent and well educated, with a lively curiosity and a good sense of humor. Vassilyev indicated an empty chair. Once Argus was comfortable, he recognized the pleasant-faced man sitting next to Vassilyev on the couch.

"Your Excellency," said Argus. "I'm very pleased to meet you."

"And I you," said Gyorgy Kurakin, Tsar of Belarus.

Argus had actually seen him the moment he walked into the room, just as he had seen and recorded the image of every other person, where they were, whether he had met them before, and what was discussed. He had thought the man a relative of Kurakin's, yet another bearded nobleman. But when he looked into the tsar's blue eyes he saw the military man who had clawed his way to the top. The tsar was smoking a cigar and sipping wine, his eyes undulled by either.

"I've heard much about you," said Kurakin. "I'm glad we have an opportunity to speak as fellow soldiers, in comfortable surroundings. Would you care for a cigar?"

"No, thanks," said Argus. "But the wine looks good."

Kurakin did not even have to look at the waiter. Argus had his drink within two seconds. He tasted it, then had another, longer sip.

"Fine stuff," said the tsar. "From my sister's own vineyards. She has excellent taste, a good head on her shoulders."

"I haven't had the pleasure of meeting your sister," said Argus.

"Few have." The tsar puffed his cigar. "Things happen slowly here. Except on the battlefield. But we've seen few of those lately, thanks to you Star Men."

"We could do no less," replied Argus. The wine did not dull his senses either, but it gave his nerves a pleasant tingle. Kurakin was watching him, but for once Argus was comfortable with the scrutiny. Kurakin was right when he said they were both soldiers. For better or for worse, there were some things they already understood about each other.

"An interesting rumor has been circulating," said the tsar, "concerning mold."

Argus was only surprised that no one had asked him about it sooner. "Rumors can be damaging," he said. "Here is what we really know about the situation."

The tsar listened attentively while Argus explained. So did every other man in the room. "We have yet to determine who created them and whether the signals are still being collated somewhere," concluded Argus. "But we have a good theory."

"I have heard the name of John the Murderer suggested," said Kurakin. "I'm very intrigued that the man could still be working mischief so long after his death. But it is the Enemies who always inspire my first suspicions."

"They were our first suspects as well."

"Have you studied the images gathered by these spores?" asked the tsar.

"My ESAs have."

"So they have seen images gathered by a spy network. This is problematic. We cannot have our security compromised, even by professed allies."

Argus didn't like the word *professed,* but he could understand the tsar's concern. "I don't like the idea either," he said.

"*Are* you watching us?" asked the tsar.

Argus shook his head. "That's not what we're here to do." *And that, my friend, is so true it's scary.*

"Odd," said the tsar. "I believe you. But I want to know where the signals are going."

"Our best people are working on it."

"Then we should already have the answer." The tsar had not tasted his cigar or his wine since he had mentioned the spores.

Argus was careful not to do so either. "Loki made those spores, most likely," he said. "He fooled the best minds of his time. He continues to do the same in ours. But he won't evade us forever."

"Good." Kurakin puffed his cigar again. "You're a man of resolve. I'll be interested to see what your people come up with. Have another glass of wine. You're getting dry."

Argus submitted to the second glass, grateful that no one felt compelled to ply him with vodka. It looked like it might turn out to be a long evening.

"And now," said the tsar, "dear fellow, I'm very curious to know. Have you heard from Baba Yaga yet?"

* * *

Sprites descended into the atmosphere of Belarus and sped to the Winter Palace in St. Petersburg. As small and light as snowflakes, they flew over the roof and entered the palace through a vent. Once inside they moved more slowly, but no less confidently toward their goal.

They emerged from a vent next to ESA Grigory's old quarters. Down the hall stood two watchful guards. The tiny machines attached themselves to the patterned wallpaper and moved swiftly along the designs, invisible to the naked eye. They positioned themselves on either side of the door on which Thoth was carved. Once in place, they began to project the image of the door—firmly closed.

More sprites moved along the wallpaper. They went behind the projected image and beamed a code to the Avatar who waited within. The door opened two inches. The sprites who had slipped inside paused to combine themselves into a larger machine. It flew to the Eye of Grigory and lifted it out of its receptacle.

Grigory was now truly blind. But that would not last for long. The sprites flew him to the door again and slipped out. The door closed behind them.

As they moved from behind the shelter of the projected image, the sprites moved near the bottom of the wall. Now too large to pass through a vent, they made their way to the emergency stairs and drifted down, past more guards, until they found a floor that contained an open window. They slipped out into the night, bearing Grigory swiftly aloft and out of the gravity well.

Once the door was firmly closed again, the sprites left behind stopped projecting. But they recorded some remarks from the guards:

"Do you smell sandalwood?"

"Don't know what sandalwood is. But something sure smells nice."

The remaining sprites slipped along the patterns in the wallpaper and flew back into the vent, their mission accomplished.

* * *

<You're allowed to gripe about it, you know,> said Kathryn, who bounced beside Argus in the carriage they had rented to take them home. Despite the uncomfortable ride, she seemed to be enjoying herself. Or perhaps she was simply amused at his expense.

<Quit reading my mind,> he complained.

<Don't have to read it. You're wearing such a scowl. You look very Scandinavian when you do that. Like one of your Viking ancestors about to go on a berserker rage.>

<Shut up, you pest.>

The carriage went over something in the road and the two of them bounced a foot off the seat. Kathryn was unperturbed. <All the bigwigs at the party don't know what to make of you now.>

<The tsar asked me point-blank about Baba Yaga. Of course I had to lie. She's considered classified material.>

<You can lie with the straightest face I've ever seen,> said Kathryn.

<Doesn't matter. He already knew I'd heard from her, somehow. I didn't have a good story ready so I just denied it.>

<Maybe that's for the best. They used to think you were a yes man who wouldn't give them trouble like Vasily did.>

<That's what they were supposed to think. If Serina has an agenda of her own . . . I don't need the extra complication.>

<Face it. She turns you on.>

He looked at her.

<Ah, those arctic eyes, so pale and fierce.>

Argus did not feel inclined to joke with her. Nor did he wish to ponder her remarks. Even he did not know if they disturbed him; the concept was simply too inconvenient. He would not lose his focus no matter what his personal feelings.

<Argus,> she said, her face serene, <it would be nice if we could have the complete cooperation of this government. But if the chips are down, we don't really need it.>

<Maybe you ESAs don't.>

<We saw that Enemy woman tonight. *Ayat-ko.* We never had a name for any of them before. She stood on that balcony the whole time you were out of the room. She knew I wanted to know where she was. I did a thorough recording, scanned her physiology head to toe. That's the closest we've ever gotten to them—and lived. Why was she being so damned cooperative, Argus? Like she was part of Serina's plan to get you alone with the tsar. I can feel it. We're in the right place now. We have to keep working here. We're getting closer.>

<Okay,> he said as they suffered through another bone-wrenching jolt. <But I know what it's like to be charged by an ice bear. I'm keeping my spear handy.>

<Interesting choice of metaphors.>

<Oh, shut up.>

Suddenly the ride became smooth again. They had turned onto one of the old streets, paved during Tsar Andrei's time. Kathryn became uncommonly quiet, and Argus decided to make the best of it. He sat and pondered the meaning of the word *byzantine* as it applied to politics and longed for the good old days when the worst that could happen to him was to get sucked into a malformed jump gate and crushed by a singularity.

They arrived on Martha Pospekt without further conversation. After Kathryn had determined it was safe for him to disembark, they paid the cabby and watched him drive off into the gaslit night. Argus almost felt tempted to ask Kathryn if she wanted to take a walk—especially if she could keep quiet. But then he heard footsteps.

Kathryn had already seen the newcomer. "William?" she called.

"Forgive me." The gardener was out of breath, and carrying a large package. "This is from Serina. She said you would understand. Will you take it?"

"It's safe," Kathryn said. "Three books."

Argus gazed at the gardener. The young man held the package out to him, and he accepted it. "She never does anything whimsically," said William. He nodded to Argus, then to Kathryn, and hurried off.

<That boy gets around,> said Argus.

<Want to lay bets about which books are in there?> said Kathryn.

<No. Let's get them inside.>

Once the doors were locked and they had the package upstairs, Argus unwrapped it and was not surprised to find Tally Korsakova's books about Belarus and Canopus. Atop lay a note penned in a precise hand.

> *Study these. I suspect you will glean far more useful information from them than I have been able. Once you have finished with them, please send them to the proper authorities on Archangel. Guard them with your lives, especially the third book.*

Argus lay the note aside and moved the first two books so he could see the one on the bottom. It had no writing on its cover, so he opened it and found the title page. It said:

For Peter Andreivich Mironenko
The Collected Letters Of Sergei, Alexander, & Andrei Mironenko

Kathryn touched the perfect paper with slender fingers. <I can understand how Natalia's books ended up in Serina's library—but how did *this* book get there?>

Argus had no solid theory, but in his mind's eye he saw the Enemy woman again, standing in the shadows.

Why have you come?

She watches . . .

<How come my first impulse is to hide these?> asked Kathryn.

<Good impulse,> said Argus. <Let's follow it.>

*   *   *

Two hours later Argus was still awake, not because he couldn't sleep, but because he was doing his least favorite thing: paperwork.

He could make plans, follow orders, and execute both without hesitation. He did not panic under fire, did not easily lose his temper, and tended to act rather than react. But writing a report explaining what must be done, or might be done, or had already been done was to him the worst kind of pick-and-shovel work. His father had been a man of few words, and Argus was made in his mold. Yet he had learned to use words as tools, though he never completely trusted them.

First he wrote a thorough report on his laptop for Commander Hale, with copies to go to Vasily Burakov and several ESA elders. Then, with pen and ink, he handwrote a report for Tsar Gyorgy, outlining what had been discovered concerning the spores and what might be done about it. At 11:30 P.M. he was still struggling to find a diplomat's words. when he heard a faint noise from downstairs. He jumped to his feet, his heart pounding.

<INTRUDERS!> Nesto warned.

Argus saw a blur and felt a rush of wind, and suddenly Nesto was in his office. He preceded Kathryn by two seconds, but she had been wakened from a sound sleep. The two ESAs positioned themselves in front of Argus and the desk. Argus wanted badly to join them, but obeyed protocol.

<I thought the front door was locked,> he said.

<It was,> said Nesto. <They let themselves in. That means they had official access to the code. Now we know why they put us in this particular house.>

Argus watched the top of the stairs through his open door. A head appeared, then two more heads. The first head belonged to a short, middle-aged man with a large mole on his cheek. He stepped onto the landing and walked confidently toward the room. A moment later his two companions topped the stairs. They stood taller than the first man, and their faces were much less mild. Despite that, it was the short man who commanded Argus's attention.

The three intruders strolled into the office, shutting the door behind them. Argus noted that their suits were neither fancy nor poor, made of dark fabric with little to distinguish them. <An educated guess,> he warned the ESAs. <These guys might be *okrana*—the tsar's secret police.>

The short man seemed relaxed, almost bored. His watery blue eyes regarded Argus with slight interest, and the ESAs not at all. His two thugs were another matter.

"Embassador Fabricus," said the short man pleasantly, "you will come with us."

"I will not," he informed them.

"I'm afraid we must insist."

"Insist all you want," Kathryn informed him. "You're not taking him."

He spared her a glance. Argus knew what he must be seeing: two ESAs with their eyes in full tactical. Nesto would be frowning slightly, Kathryn wearing her Mona Lisa smile. But the short man didn't study them for long.

"We have laws," he said. "Do you respect them?"

"We have laws as well," Argus said. "Perhaps I would feel more compelled to oblige if you told me why you have come."

"We're not accustomed to answering questions," the short man apologized.

"Ah," replied Argus. "An impasse."

"Not so fast." The short man drew a cigar out of his front pocket. The ESAs did not move a muscle, but Argus knew if anything else had come out of the pocket the short man would be minus one hand. He lit the cigar, and a pungent odor filled the room. "I said we're not accustomed to it," he said between puffs. "But these are strange times. I'll tell you something. Then you tell me what you think about it, yes?"

"Definitely," said Argus.

"The door to the Tomb of the Engineer has been opened."

Argus felt a little sick to his stomach. He had expected to

be asked about the books Serina had given him. This was far more difficult. He wasn't surprised that no one had bothered to inform him. He had other things to ponder. Like dismissal from his post just when his team was beginning to accomplish something. "You think I opened it?" he asked.

"We know you didn't. But you're a very capable man. We'd like you to come back with us and open it for us, because the intruder locked it again."

"I can't," Argus said flatly. "I have no idea how to get it open."

"You'll figure something out," the short man said confidently.

"I won't, I promise you," said Argus.

"I promise *you*"—the short man gestured with his cigar hand, and ashes dropped on the floor—"we merely wish to confirm that the tsar's property is still intact."

"If you're referring to the Avatar of ESA Grigory—" Argus began.

"Partly, yes," the short man interrupted. "If they took the eye out of there, we want it back. You can open the door and we'll make our inspection."

Argus shook his head. "That *it* you just referred to is a *him*. It's up to him to decide whether he wants to come back down and open that door for you."

The short man raised an eyebrow. "A *him?*" he asked.

"Yes." Argus wondered how the hell he was going to explain that.

But it apparently didn't matter to the short man. He gestured again with the cigar. "You can call it a him," he said. "We still want the eye back."

Argus shrugged. "Okay. I'll tell him you said so."

"While we wait for his answer, you will have to remain in our custody."

"I'm under arrest?" asked Argus.

"As the representative of the Union on our soil, you are responsible for actions taken by your government or its agents."

"You have no evidence my government or its agents opened the door," said Argus, hoping that was really true.

The short man puffed on his cigar thoughtfully. A slight movement caught Argus's eye, and he glanced at the thugs. Both of them had faces that looked as if they had been punched by experts. Both also had hands that had probably done worse to the punchers. Their eyes promised pain if he continued to resist.

"You know," the short man said at last, "your government tried to help the Mironenkos, those traitors who would have sold us to the Enemies in return for their own safety. We put a stop to that, and your Union never came in to rescue them. They didn't try to interfere with a lawful execution."

"The Mironenkos didn't have ESAs with them," said Kathryn.

The short man took a harder look at her. "You're so cute," he said. "Even with those strange eyes. I can hardly believe you could do wrong."

She didn't reply. He puffed his cigar.

"You have a lot of medical personnel down here," he said. "Do they have ESAs with them too?"

"They're protected," said Kathryn. "You won't be permitted to harm them."

"It's good they're protected from harm," he said mildly. "They do so much good for people." Suddenly he backed away. "Convey our demands," he said. One of his thugs opened the door for him.

As he was about to go through, he paused and looked over his shoulder at Argus. "By the way, I put wax on the door of the tomb. When it was opened, the seal was broken. That's how my primitive technology foiled your advanced technology. Think about it, Star Man."

He left, his thugs in tow.

<He's gone,> Nesto said a few minutes later.

<Okay.> Argus rubbed his face and waited for his heart rate to return to normal. <Anyone care to explain to me why

I wasn't informed they were planning to fetch Grigory tonight?>

<We didn't want you to be nervous at the ball,> said Kathryn. <Besides, you were right when you said Grigory is a *him.*>

Argus flexed hands that had gone cold. <I'm rather glad those guys weren't the sort to get into philosophical debates, because I'm definitely not in the mood.>

<No, Argus,> said Kathryn. <I mean he really is a *him* now. That's why they took him out tonight. His new body is ready.>

<Oh.> Argus took a moment to reflect upon the small part he had just played in a great historical moment. Grigory's new body was the first of its kind. Before, Argus had thought Avatars were miraculous. <Okay. It's past midnight and I've turned into a pumpkin. I'm going to bed. If anyone knocks on the door with a glass slipper, tell them to get lost. To hell with diplomacy.>

He marched from the room without looking back, secure in the belief that at least for the rest of the evening, no one would get into the house again.

"Good night," he said aloud, not caring how many mold spores were listening. He went straight to his room, peeled off the danger suit, and fell into bed with a weariness he hadn't felt since his hunting days. He fell asleep instantly, and dreamed only one dream all night, about a hut on chicken legs that stalked him through endless halls with marble floors and locked doors. Every time he thought he had lost it, he would hear a lovely voice:

"One dance," it called to him. "If you please . . . "

Grigory was a boy again. He hid in the tall grass and watched the furry people. They had golden eyes and tufted ears that twitched at the slightest provocation—so Grigory did not move or make a sound until they were close. Then he spoke a few words to them in their own language.

They stopped, spotting him instantly. Since there was no point in hiding any longer, he stood, his chin barely clearing the tops of the grass. "You are Woovs," he said in their language.

"We are," said the one who stood nearest. "Where did you learn to speak Woovian?"

"I listen to you in the city market," he said. "I like the sounds you make. I like the way your eyes can see into my soul."

She drifted closer and he stayed his ground. "How old are you, child?" she asked.

"Seven," said Grigory, but that was not what he had really said all those years ago. He had lied about his age, hoping they would take him more seriously if they thought he was older. That he did not lie this time was proof that he was dreaming. The thought pleased him. He had not dreamed for a thousand years.

"Why couldn't you dream?" asked the Woov who would become his mentor and make him an ESA.

"I had no body, no brain that required it," he said. "Now they have given me a new one."

"But they didn't give you new eyes. Would you tear them from your head as you did the last pair you owned?"

"Perhaps not," said Grigory, remembering the pain of that rending and of the betrayal that had forced him to do it. "But I will never need eyes, and so I will not lose them again."

She faded into the golden, swaying grass. "Look well, then," she called to him. "Remember what it was like to see."

He felt the warm breeze on his face, and with it a remembered scent, the katerinas blooming. He turned his head and saw three women he had never seen, though he knew them well. They waited for him on a blanket in the grass, a picnic spread out beside them. He gazed at them, intrigued by the image his feelings had created of them: Natalia, world engineer; Katerina, wife of Andrei Mironenko; and Emily, chief of security.

He had given Natalia the face on the bust of Nefertiti, which he had admired before he lost his sight. But he thought the rasta-links that floated around her face like metallic serpents of Medusa must be quite accurate. Katerina was a tiny Madonna, with the characteristically sad, serene face he had known from countless icons. But it was Emily's face that seemed like it might actually be the one she really owned.

Eyes of the palest blue watched him with the perceptions of a seasoned investigator. They were surrounded by lines and crinkles created by countless smiles and frowns. Thick ash-blond hair was braided and pinned into a tight bun at her neck. Her nose was freckled, her mouth wide, somewhat thin-lipped, currently quirked in a half smile.

"They made you handsome," she said. "How are you going to scare people properly without your scars?"

"I'll have to make up for it with a bad attitude," he said, and went to sit beside her on the blanket. In the distance behind her, sprites were constructing the city of St. Petersburg. For the first time, he truly grasped the reality of how much time had passed in the world since he had died.

Katerina handed him a thermos of spring water. "The city endures," she said. "And so do you, Grigory. Our sacrifices were not in vain."

"It was you who paid the dearest price, little mother." Grigory touched her tiny hand as she handed him the thermos. It was soft and real. But she was gone, except for this dream, tortured to death by Enemies. She had bought him an opportunity to make his own sacrifice, but the account was by no means even.

"We're not illusions," said Tally.

Grigory studied her perfect face, her queenly features betraying no emotion. "You're the one who saw ghosts, not me," he said.

"I'm the one," she agreed. "We don't have long, Grigory. I think you have something to say to Emily."

He gazed again at Emily's face. "You already know my feelings," he said.

"I know." She touched his hand. "You have another chance at life. Make the best of it. You won't see us again on this side of the Veil."

At that moment he believed she was real. He memorized every inch of her face, her expression—and what he saw beneath it.

"Grigory," warned Tally.

He glanced at her. Before he could move, one of her rasta-links slid into the artificial center of his right eye. It adapted to and connected with the communication system in his head.

"These eyes you lost weren't your original eyes. They were artificial," she said. "Your ESA mentors gave them to you. Someday they may give you another pair. Think twice before you say no, Grigory. That's all I can get away with telling you."

"Don't go," he said.

The grass died and the surface of the world melted into a heat-blasted wasteland. Tally's rasta-link slipped from his eye, and the women melted away with the flowers. Grigory was startled by the depth of his grief when they vanished. In a thousand years, he had known they were gone without truly experiencing the loss. But all things must come around eventually.

<Watcher,> said another voice he had not heard in a thousand years—or ever, actually, since it had always been a virtual voice.

<Spritemind,> he said. <Have you also come to visit me from beyond the grave? Or am I dreaming you?>

<Neither. Forgive us, ESA Grigory. We are Belarusian sprites, reporting. You are still asleep. We wondered if we could speak with you this way.>

<I am surprised you did not wake me. But perhaps this new brain is different.>

<What are you looking at now? Is this a real world, or pure imagination?>

Grigory studied the blasted landscape. <It used to be a real world, before war destroyed it. This is where my patroness betrayed me, and I lost my sight.>

<Why did she betray you?>

These new sprites had not experienced the prejudice inflicted on their predecessors. Grigory supposed that was merely because so many humans had been killed in the Civil War, there weren't as many bigots around.

<This link I have with you,> he said, <also links me to the minds of alien ESAs, like the Woovs. Before the war, there were many humans who believed this connection corrupted us, that we were unnatural creatures advancing a secret, alien agenda. My patroness turned out to be one of these.>

<Many of our agendas *are* secret and non-human,> said the sprites.

<Exactly,> said Grigory.

<To be alien is bad?> asked the sprites. <To be non-human?>

<The issue is otherness. I suppose it always has been.>

<This is related to the problem that troubled Spritemind before it was destroyed,> said the sprites. <We have scanned your database and read Spritemind's last two messages to you, concerning the entity that called itself ME. We thought it might be a collection of tiny bio-machines, like we are, but we could not find its creators. They may be dead, or perhaps ME is alive, not artificial or created. Either way, it must be vast, and able to travel between the stars much the same way we do, by tunneling through space-time. If it still exists, then it has hidden itself.>

<Just as the Enemies have done,> said Grigory.

<But with a difference,> said the sprites. <If ME thinks it's good to be ME, then it's bad to be anyone else. But the Enemies find the concept of otherness interesting, even stimulating. ME's reaction to us is different. Perhaps it would prefer that all of us become ME as well. But in order to accomplish that, it might be willing to become us, first.>

<Why would it do that?> asked Grigory, watching the silent world. Beyond the horizon, his old patroness stalked him. She knew where he was, but she could not get at him with her conventional weapons. Yet she was still linked with him in an essential way. His eyes were the link, able to receive information when they were in tactical mode. Able to receive her signal at any time. He felt that signal coming, but it was not a message.

<It might become us,> said the sprites, <so it could change us from within. That would explain why we can't find ME anymore.>

<We have met the Enemy and he is us,> said Grigory, reaching for his eyes. He felt the surge that would burn the connections deep in his brain, crippling or killing him. There

was only one way to keep that from happening, and that was to remove the link.

He tore out his eyes. The pain was much the same as it had been the first time. He threw the offending orbs on the ground, then sank to his knees.

<I remember what it was like to see,> he said. <I remember the beauty. But I do not miss it. Where are you, Spritemind? Are you as dead as Tally and Emily?>

<You know where Spritemind is,> the sprites reminded him.

<No,> he said. <I know where Spritemind *was.*>

"Grigory, are you awake?"

The voice was real. It drove the old images from his mind. Darkness replaced it, and that was how he preferred it.

Grigory had experienced many wondrous things in his lifetime. But none of them equaled the experience of his rebirth.

Darkness greeted him as he woke, but he smelled several different things, even in the sterile environment of Archangel Station: cleaning solution, artificial and natural fabrics, perfume, shampoo, toothpaste, chocolate, garlic, onion, deodorant that did not mask the natural scent of the woman nearest him. He heard her voice.

"If you change your mind and decide you want eyesight, we can install it. But in the meantime, we tried to boost your other senses. We hope they become as well honed as the ones you had in your first body."

The sensations were intense. He could feel the air stirring against his face, the fabric of the danger suit clinging to his body. And the woman, ESA Molly, smelled better than any flower. His body responded with an erection.

"Everything seems to be functioning properly," he said, pleased that his tone did not betray the depth of his emotion. "You and your team have done excellent work."

"It'll take some time for you to get used to it," warned ESA Molly.

"I shall learn by doing," said Grigory. "I'd like to eat first."

"Don't expect to like the same things you used to," she said. "This body is totally new, and those taste buds—"

"Yes." Grigory indulged himself in a long stretch. "Thank you for the nice body. I have it now. I'll see you later."

"Yes, Elder," said Molly, and moved out of his way.

Kathryn had a hunch. She followed it into a very strange place. While there, she met a legend. But first she found his body—the one he had lost one thousand years before.

She supposed the damp and heat of the hive had rotted most of it in the first days. As the dead hive grew colder and drier, Grigory's bones had suffered less from time. Now they appeared to be half melted into the debris on the floor. The only reason she knew it must be him was that his danger suit was still perfectly intact.

And then she head a voice from beyond the grave. <This is ESA Grigory. Who are you?>

<ESA Kathryn. I work for Argus Fabricus.>

<Kathryn, you must be aware that the mold network may not be used for spying on Belarusians.>

<I'm not spying on the Belarusians. I'm spying on the Enemies.>

<Here? They haven't been near this hive in a thousand years. What are you really looking for, ESA Kathryn?>

<Not for what, for whom.> She had shuffled through thousands of impressions taken by the spores and collated by the sprites, and many of them were in sensitive government offices in Moscow and St. Petersburg. <I decided to go

with the theory that the spores were created by John the Murderer. I was trying to find out where they're going—the Belarusian government has insisted we find out. I hoped I might be able to trace it to his hideout.>

<We found his hideout one thousand years ago, under a farmhouse near Novocherkassk,> said Grigory. <I can show it to you.>

<Nope. You found only *one* of his hideouts. I've been studying Emily Kizheh's notes, and she thinks he may have had at least one more. I do too. You guys never found evidence that his killings were committed in Novocherkassk; you just found his laptop there.>

<I admire your efforts. I don't mind a second opinion, but if we're going to work together we need to compare notes.>

<Fine, but I have a confession to make. I sort of got sidetracked. Something in Emily Kizheh's notes made me wonder if John used his spores to spy on the Enemies. He apparently knew more about them than anyone.>

<A good hunch. So now you see what he must have seen. What does it tell you?>

<I don't want to see the place just to look at it. I want to find out what happens when I try to trace these particular colonies.>

He was silent for a long time, and Kathryn organized her thoughts. She had been following her gut and might not be able to give clear reasons why she felt compelled to try such an experiment. <Enemies would be tough people to spy on,> she said suddenly. <It would be hard to use ordinary human spy technology on them. They would probably find it laughable. And if they caught someone trying to watch them, especially before they were ready to make their presence known, they would take some very nasty actions. I'm guessing that John the Murderer was a guy who liked to have the odds stacked on his side.>

<And so he would want to make the signals difficult to trace,> said Grigory. <But he would want to do that even if he were spying on humans.>

<Right,> said Kathryn. <But I'm willing to bet he was more worried about being caught by Enemies. He might have taken extra precautions. So I want to run a trace, and I want to do it without using the sprites.>

She wondered how she would explain that to an ESA elder. Sprites and ESAs always worked together; no link was more efficient. But he surprised her.

<Good idea. John was the one who created WILDFIRE. He knew how to cripple sprites. Even this new generation might be vulnerable to his tricks. Run your test, please.>

Kathryn obeyed. She stimulated the spores and let them pass their signal along in their slow fashion. Her simple machines, deployed near the exits of the hive, waited to detect signals.

<Christ!> she said. <Did you catch that?>

<Relays,> said Grigory. <Still functioning after all these centuries.>

<Hold on. I've got a signal! Something answered. I think I can trace—>

And suddenly the signal ceased. The spores fired random signals, then began to die. As they watched, the colonies shrank to a fraction of their former size within seconds. But they didn't die completely.

<I think I know why that happened,> said Grigory.

Kathryn's head was full of ideas too, but she listened respectfully.

<In the years after WILDFIRE crippled the first generation of sprites,> he said, <we thought very hard about how quickly the agent spread. We concluded that the system most compatible with and least detectable by sprites would be made up of fake sprites.>

<*Fake* sprites?>

<Pre-sprites, if you will. Tiny machines exactly like our own sprites, before they're infected with the virus that makes them self-aware. Since pre-sprites are not infected with the sprite virus, they wouldn't be vulnerable to an attack on that virus.>

<Only ESAs and sprites can make pre-sprites,> said Kathryn.

<John was smart enough to do it.>

<Okay, so he made some pre-sprites and they're still around. They would have pretty limited capabilities, but you're right, they would make good relays. And they could operate within our own sprite network . . .>

<You're getting the picture. We are helping the spores to pass their information along. But when we use the sprites to trace the signals, the pre-sprites simply shut down and wait until the scan is over. Just now, when you tried to do your trace, you spoke to me through the network and our sprites became curious. They scanned.>

<Oops.>

<We learned a lot. And you were right about something else—he took an extra measure with these spores he used to watch Enemies. The colonies died back. Unless they knew what to look for, the Enemies might overlook a few spores.>

<John the Murderer died a thousand years ago. But his machines are still working on this world. Grigory—we have to find that other hideout.>

<I agree. But it's not our first mission, Kathryn. We must stay focused.>

<I'm focused just fine. I think this will help us get our job done.>

<Clarify,> said Grigory.

<Once we find that hideout, we'll have access to the part of his network we haven't been able to reach so far. We'll be able to see other images. Elder, do you think he would bug only *one* of their hives?>

Most of Belarus was perpetually gripped in snow and ice. Serina could not imagine why the heat-loving Enemies had settled here, unless it was because they thought no one would look for them in a cold place. Humankind had settled on the largest continent, whose temperate southernmost portion crossed the equator, and the part of it called Moscow experienced four seasons: a long, cold winter, a brief, sudden spring, and a long summer that gradually cooled to fall, so gradually that Muscovites joked it was like being eased into a cold bath. You didn't know you were freezing until it was almost too late.

The winter was so harsh, it often seemed to Serina that the world would never thaw. The only way to endure the bleakness, the darkness, was to embrace it and to discover it wasn't dark at all. Under the glistening snow, the world was revealed to its bones, and they were strong.

Every summer was like a gift. The green sprouts of spring brought on a horde of insects, who quickly attracted the singing rodents that ate them. As a child Serina had spent hours outside, watching the garden come to life. Often she and William helped the gardeners with the pruning and weeding, but her favorite pastime was to sow seeds. They sprouted quickly, grew lush and green, and by midsummer were bursting into bloom.

But that was the time during which Serina was packed up with the rest of the household and moved to the summer *dascha,* leaving behind the garden at its peak and the kind boy who treated Serina like a friend. She could not even mount an objection to the forced vacation, because it was during this time that Father took his holiday, and Galena spent all of her time with him, making up for the lost time of the busy year. A trip to the country was what he preferred, along with every other Belarusian who could possibly cobble together a little vacation cabin, a *dascha* of their own.

But the Scriabin summer home was hardly a cabin. It was a sprawling house in elite Zhukovka, big enough to house both the Scriabin and the Kurakin clans. Serina lived there four weeks out of the year, as isolated from her siblings and her cousins as she was in the great house, despite that the housing was significantly smaller. She spent the time in the cramped library, trying to amuse herself with the harmless novels that made up the bulk of its collection. Or she wandered in the dark, cool forest, believing herself to be alone with her thoughts.

The summer she turned sixteen, she went to the *dascha* along with everyone else. But that year Serina was not inclined to read, or to wander as much. Instead, she decided to watch her family.

She stood on the perimeter of their activities. No one reacted. She began to stand closer, even to seat herself near them. No one spoke directly to her, but they became accustomed to her presence. Everything she had learned from her tutors about manners, social protocol, pleasant conversation and dancing, was repeated before her eyes. Like her, these young people had been groomed to function within the highest strata of society.

But it did not take Serina long to discover a critical difference in upbringing.

Tagging along behind a gaggle of girl cousins, Serina witnessed an act of thoughtless cruelty. A maid was backing out of a room, pulling her cleaning cart behind her, and bumped into Olga Scriabin.

"Idiot!" Olga slapped the maid, who was so shocked she simply stared at the girl who was young enough to be her daughter. "What's wrong with you?" barked Olga. "Get out of my sight!"

"Stop that at once!" Serina snapped. Olga froze, and the maid took the opportunity to hurry away. Olga gaped at Serina, frightened at first, then dumbfounded.

"Who do you think you are?" she said weakly, "you—you—*creature.*"

Serina advanced slowly and deliberately. "I am your cousin Serina," she said, her tone low and tightly controlled, "daughter of Galena, who is sister to the tsar, and I will not tolerate abuse of employees. Do not raise your hand to people who cannot fight back, Olga. That is the act of a bully."

Olga did not retreat. But her voice shook when she answered. "I will do as I choose."

"No," said Serina. "You will not."

"We did not ask for your company," said Olga. "If you don't like it, go elsewhere."

"If I don't like it," said Serina, "you shall know in no uncertain terms that I do not like it. Do not strike employees in our household, or *you* may go elsewhere, Olga."

"I agree," said someone behind them, and the cousins jumped like startled hares. Serina turned to find one of her most illustrious relatives.

"Tsarina." She curtsied.

"I am pleased to meet you, Serina Petrova," said Tsarina Helene, nodding graciously. She was a handsome woman, tall and slender, with intelligent eyes that could be either warm or icy, depending on her whim. When she regarded Olga, her mood turned to winter. "As for you—heed my warning. Abuse will not be tolerated in my household. Our servants are employed. They are not thralls. Do you understand?"

"Yes, Tsarina." Olga lowered her eyes and curtsied.

"You are dismissed," said Helene, and the cousins curtsied together, backing away. Serina did the same, but the tsarina said, "Wait, Serina."

Serina stayed behind, and when the cousins had vacated the hall, the tsarina came closer. She looked hard at Serina, though not unkindly.

"Child," she said, "when I heard your voice in the hall, I thought you were Galena. You have her tone perfectly, and I have heard it in none of your siblings."

"I have been tutored, Tsarina."

"Yes, it would seem that you have. We might all have been better served to be so well taught. Dancing is a pleasant skill to cultivate, but I could not do it with the experts who instructed *you,* Serina."

Serina did not miss the point. Among Enemies, Dancing was a deadly art.

"Do not grieve if you do not find friends among your own kin," said Helene. "Soon you will be invited to balls, and you will find your shroud not as much of a barrier to pleasant conversation as you might imagine."

"Tsarina," Serina said, curtsying.

The tsarina nodded and withdrew into the sitting room from which she had come.

Serina stood alone in the hallway. She understood that she had just changed her position in the household—and that she had gained enemies in the process. If she continued to express her opinion she would gain more. That was the price of empowerment.

She left the cabin and walked out into the countryside. There were orchards, fields, patches of forest, and many small streams that made pleasant, gurgling noises as she walked beside them. When she had wandered perhaps an hour from the house, she saw Ayat-ko under a blossom-laden tree.

"Has anyone told you," said Ayat-ko, "106 of your countrymen died in a massacre on this very spot?"

"No," admitted Serina.

"You'll find it in your history books," said the Enemy woman. "We skinned them alive. Afterward, they writhed on stakes in the hot sun for several hours. Some of them lasted quite a long time. It was informative."

"How so?" asked Serina, who had learned that anger and sorrow only evoked contempt from Ayat-ko, and if she wanted to learn anything from her, she had to put those feelings aside.

"We learned your kind is stronger than we thought. Come, I will show you something."

Serina fell in beside her, and they followed the stream into a forest. It was an idyllic place, full of green smells and woodland flowers. After a while, Serina heard a train whistle.

"If we continued to walk in this direction," said Ayat-ko, "we would encounter a train station. Civilization is much closer to you out here than your pampered relatives would like to believe—at least, the mechanical parts of it are. This place has concealed savageries that humankind are unwilling to contemplate. Stop here, child."

Serina stood with Ayat-ko under another tree, this one far larger. It looked very old. It was surrounded by a knee-high patch of white flowers. Ayat-ko stood among them in her fine Belarusian dress, a flower that never wilted. A patch of red light danced on the pale fabric of her skirt. Serina could not quite fathom it through her veil.

"Unveil your eyes," said Ayat-ko.

Serina unwrapped the fabric over her eyes. The patch of red light had focused into a tiny dot. It might be a prism effect, filtered by some pool of water.

"Do you pity yourself?" asked the Enemy woman.

"No," Serina said.

But Ayat-ko grinned. "Isolation is the one pain from which no pleasure can be drawn. You are an outcast. But you do not die, as any outcast should. You grow like those seedlings you hate to leave behind. And you will bloom as well, but there will be no one to see it."

Serina looked steadily at the Enemy woman. She did not pity herself, had not done so for years. But the words hurt. And as her eyes were naked, she could not pretend, behind her veil, to have no feeling.

"Cruelty is such a complex thing," said Ayat-ko. "Sometimes simple and brutish, sometimes so subtle you don't feel the blade until you have been bleeding for some time. It was many years before I could see that your kind have mastered it as well as mine. Yet I do not respect you for it. It does not become you."

"There are those who would argue," said Serina, "that it does not become *anyone.*"

"They may argue," said Ayat-ko. "If it pleases them."

"Were you there?" asked Serina. "When my people were massacred?"

"I saw."

"Did you eat their flesh?"

"I am entirely myself. So it must be."

At the time, Serina took that to mean *yes*. She would not know she was wrong for many years.

"Your eyes are unveiled," said Ayat-ko. "Tell me, what do you see?"

"My Enemy," said Serina.

Ayat-ko smiled as only she could. "Yes. But only one of them."

Hours later, as Serina lay in her bed watching the moon-cast shadows of leaves on her wall, she wept. She was unsure just what had unnerved her the most: the story of the massacre, the frustration of arguing with an Enemy, or the deadly accuracy of Ayat-ko's barbs.

You are an outcast. You do not die, as any outcast should . . .

The statement puzzled Serina. Only half of it was true. She was an outcast because of Botkin's Syndrome. But most human outcasts did not die. They simply stayed away from people, or were chased away. Maybe Ayat-ko was saying she thought Serina should die because she was an outcast. But it wasn't like the Enemy woman to make such a judgment.

Serina puzzled over it, watching the shadows on her wall. Finally she let go of that part of the conversation and moved on to the part that gave her some small comfort.

You will bloom . . .

The hardiest plants in the garden bloomed again and again, whether there was someone to see them or not. Every year, Serina looked for signs of that blooming in herself. That day she had seen some evidence of it when she stood up to the cousins. About that, at least, she felt no doubts.

She drifted no closer to sleep, and at last she realized what was troubling her.

This place has concealed savageries that humankind are unwilling to contemplate . . .

The tiny red light, shining steadily against the white skirt.

I missed something. She told me to unveil my eyes so I could see clearly—but I don't get it. What was I supposed to see?

The moon set, the shadows were consumed by darkness, Serina drifted into sleep, and her mind dutifully shuffled the puzzle into a remote corner of her consciousness for later—much later—consideration.

ESA Grigory found Archangel Station to be very much as he remembered it, save that it was haunted by more ghosts. As a blind man he was troubled by this phenomenon more than his sighted peers, because his sense of smell was so acute. The whiff of an old perfume, and suddenly it seemed that Katerina Mironenko was in the room with him, clutching her sandalwood rosary. But his sprites assured him that no sandalwood had been imported to Archangel, so perhaps Katerina was really there.

It was an old station, prone to unexplained drafts, so if the feeling of air on his skin suggested the passage of a body that wasn't there, it was understandable. He didn't mind it. The sensations allowed him to explore his feelings about his future. He had been part of Belarus, quite literally, for more than a thousand years. Though his allegiance had always been, would always be ESA, he had melded his passions with those of his comrades.

Andrei. Tally. Emily. His protégé, Tam; ESA Kathryn reminded him very much of her. She introduced new mysteries to him, and old ones, tempting him to stay on. But if he did, would he ever leave? Could he ever be done with Belarus?

Other matters called. The sprites could still find no trace of the entity that had so worried Spritemind. And Spritemind was still missing. It might be on Canopus, or it might have moved elsewhere. Grigory had to consider the possibility of sharing his concerns about ME with others, and wondered if ME might overhear him if he did.

He had clearance for every part of Archangel. He wandered through them all. He conversed at length with Station Commander Hale, with other ESAs, with Vasily Burakov. He moved through the restored sections that had been the last refuge of Commander Jones. He sat at the terminal at which Jones had recorded his last logs.

I think we're down to just a few hours of breathable atmosphere. There's a lot to tell you, and I won't try to do it now. I've just got one important bit of information to pass on. There's an ESA Avatar down below, probably in St. Petersburg. His name is Grigory, and you're going to want to talk to him before you do anything—I mean anything*—in the way of contact down below.*

Archangel Station had survived two wars. Those who walked its corridors now could not comprehend that it would probably outlive them as well. Only Grigory knew, and soon he would walk there no more. Unless his ghost returned. Or unless it was there already.

An odor teased his nose, the rustle of clothing, and air touching his left ear warned him of company. But he knew this was no ghost.

"Vasily," he said. "I was just thinking about you."

"I'll try to be flattered." The ex-embassador's voice was mild, a little like Andrei Mironenko's. And like his old friend, Vasily's mild exterior was supported by a steel frame. "I hoped you might be in the mood for some conversation."

"If I weren't," said Grigory, "you wouldn't have found me. But I don't believe we've ever engaged in harmless conversation."

"I never promised it would be harmless."

"You've got something you'd like me to do, I'm sure."

"Actually," said Vasily, "I'd like to ask your opinion. Something difficult has come up with the duma, and it has Embassador Fabricus stumped."

"The duma are particularly talented at stumping people," said Grigory. "Especially the tsar. That was their original purpose, I suppose, but on this world they have evolved the practice into an art form."

"They want to charge us fees for the ore we wanted to mine for them," said Vasily. "They're calling it a user's fee. We've protested that we're not *using* the ore, but holding it in trust for them. They say that's very nice of us, but we could decide to use the ore in the future, and because we might do that, they have a right to collect fees from us. We say they shouldn't do that unless we decide to use the ore, and they said they'd rather have the user's fee up-front, then negotiate a price when we want to buy it."

"Are you going to use it?" asked Grigory.

"Theoretically. Someday we hope to build the infrastructure they'll need out here to get their own mining operations started again. We would then train their personnel to use it and to build their own mining industry in space. We can't do that until we've got the situation settled with the Enemies, but the tsar doesn't seem to quite believe that. He's the one pushing for the mining—in secret, of course."

Grigory wondered how a tsar of Belarus could ever disregard the Enemies. Gyorgy had never struck him as stupid. But Vasily's problem seemed straightforward enough.

"Can you afford to pay them their fee?" he asked.

"Sure," said Vasily. "And we will, but I'm trying to figure out the best way to do it without losing face. And you, my friend, are the only other full-blooded Russian on board, so I come to you for advice."

"Tell Fabricus to tell them the Union has decided a user's fee is lawful," said Grigory. "And that we'll subtract a holder's fee from it, and pay them the balance. They'll argue about price. Remember to bargain a little. They'll complain bitterly. Be very apologetic—and firm, once you've settled on the price. Later, bribes can be paid to officials who will be expecting them for having let you charge your holder's fee. But make sure you don't pay money. Give them goods they want. Everyone is happy."

"Brilliant," said Vasily. "You missed your calling, Grigory Michaelovich."

"Maybe," said Grigory. He pondered what he had learned from watching the tsars of Belarus for one thousand years. Suddenly Gyorgy thought the Enemies would stand by and let the Union help him regain lost technology.

What did he know that Grigory did not?

Murder is a mirror. A dark distorting mirror in which we see unfamiliar faces . . . If we wish to fully understand ourselves we should look into it. Not too long or too hard, perhaps, but by glancing at murder from time to time, we remind ourselves that this dark side does exist, and has to be reckoned with.

—Richard Glyn Jones
The Mammoth Book of Murder

The train sped into the night. Inside its envelope, ESA Kathryn moved back into the time when Andrei Mironenko built wonders with tiny machines that could think, even dream. They dreamed of trains that still ran smoothly after a thousand years. The trains were part of the reason Belarus still functioned, despite war, political conflict, and the depredations of the Enemies.

But there was a down side to a transportation system that could take people from one end of the continent to the other so speedily. It facilitated many types of crime. And it was on these sleek machines that John the Murderer had stalked his victims. Kathryn sat in the warm, artificial light and tried to see the world as he had seen it. If he stalked victims, then he must have viewed himself as a predator—and they were solitary creatures.

That's how he may have seen himself, but predators went after the weak and unprotected, or aged and sick animals. According to Emily Kizheh's journal, John had chosen the best and brightest, the most beautiful and graceful girls he could find.

Tasha Balikireva, thirteen years old. Straight-A student

at the Belarus Royal Academy, a tough school. Award-winning musician . . .

Girls like that still traveled on the trains; everyone did. When Kathryn got on in the morning, she rode with farmers from the Ukraine and a family from Mongolia, priests from Georgia, mullahs from Azerbaijan. In the earliest part of the day the cars were dominated by schoolchildren and laborers. Police wandered through at regular intervals, wearing uniforms that must have been inspired by the danger suits of colonial times. They didn't see her, because her danger suit actually functioned, and though people sometimes bumped into her, no one seemed to take much notice of the phenomenon. Being jostled on the train was nothing new, and it wasn't polite to look directly at strangers; one merely edged an inch in the other direction.

Kathryn watched people. She saw some of them watching the others. Maybe it was easier to see predators when you tried to think like one.

Sophia Fetisova, age fourteen, principle dancer with the Mironenko Ballet . . .

She didn't know for sure that John had shopped for his victims on the trains; certainly he hadn't snatched them from there. Emily Kizheh believed he had taken them from their own bedrooms. She also believed he had taken them all to the same location to torture and dismember them, because this fit the psychological profile of his type of killer. The place was important. It was his fortress of solitude, and he was king there. He could be sure that within its sanctuary, he could do as he pleased and never be interrupted.

Lyuba Petrova, a mathematical genius. She would have gone on to do great things. The killer put a stop to that. I can't help but wonder if that's what he had in mind for these girls. Envy. He was jealous of them. He punished them . . .

As the day wore on, fewer people rode with Kathryn, and these were mostly travelers, merchants, laborers with odd schedules. A few people stayed all day, just riding back and forth, staying within the warm cars to avoid the deepening chill of autumn. They looked homeless, and some of them looked crazy. One woman was having an interesting conversation with absolutely no one. She was handsome, perhaps in her late twenties; she spoke like an educated person, laughed often as if her imaginary companion were witty, lapsed into silent tears from time to time. Kathryn wondered if John would have found her appealing.

Tatyana Slepak's head and hands were left on an estate just outside Moscow. He positioned them in his usual ritualistic fashion. This time it looked as if the girl were praying. She is the only one we've found whose expression was not frozen in agony, as if she died at peace with God. I wonder if she was praying when he killed her . . .

He had not taken them from the trains. He might not have transported them to his hideout using the trains either. But the world passed through them. If he wanted to see as many people as possible, this was the place to do it. And whether or not he used them to carry his unconscious victims, Kathryn believed he must have traveled to his hideout this way. If he had used some other kind of vehicle, the energy signature might have betrayed him. He used the sprite network in the same parasitic fashion.

She tried repeatedly to put herself in his place. Emily Kizheh said he was on Belarus even before Andrei Mironenko was. She was pretty sure that the hideout that had been discovered was John's original living quarters. They seemed designed for life support. That hideout wasn't near a train line, and it showed signs of neglect. Once the train lines had been built, he would have used them to travel all over the continent, doing reconnaissance. After people began to arrive in greater numbers, some of them must have captured his interest.

He saw the girls on the trains. He could follow them home, invisible in his danger suit. He could have followed them right into their homes. Kathryn had a feeling he would have watched them for some time, judging if they were worthy, admiring them on some level, but insanely jealous of them. He was cautious and meticulous; he would drug them like he drugged Tally Korsakova. He would have moved only when he felt safe to do so, because he wanted the opportunity to take them to his place, like he would have taken Tally if she hadn't surprised him. Perhaps he bundled them into a pouch of some sort, equipped with stealth features. He could have carried them over his shoulder. They were young and fairly light. At night, very few people rode the lines. Once he got off with his burden, he could have used his danger suit to run into the countryside, to his hidden fortress. He would have done it on a weekend, or during holidays, carefully constructing alibis so no one would suspect. He would have incapacitated the girls so they couldn't fight him or spoil his handiwork. He might have even imitated what he saw in the Enemy hives, aspiring to their level of expertise.

He kept the lower part of their bodies. He left everything else for us to find. We thought the missing parts could have been trophies he was collecting or eating. He might have sexually abused the girls, and he could have been so determined to destroy the evidence, he destroyed the body parts that might have contained it. But later he arranged all of those parts together at one scene, in a circle like dancers. That was another clue about the Enemies. No sperm or saliva was found in their body cavities . . .

Kathryn planned to ride the trains all night, several days in a row. She would have to try to keep thinking like him too, and that was unpleasant. Pity and rage kept threatening to disrupt her investigation. Somewhere along this line was John's nexus, the place he got off—both literally and figuratively. She would have to disembark at each stop and look around, see if something occurred to her. But in the meantime, she would ride and watch, hoping for inspiration.

The sun went down. There was a large swell of people going home, all looking tired and hungry. Some looked happy to be going that way, others looked resigned. Kathryn was intrigued to observe so many people of different backgrounds and religions rubbing elbows with each other without falling into guarded cliques. Some seemed quite happy to sit next to people who were not like them. Some merely tolerated those others, interacting with a distant but distinctive courtesy that Kathryn was beginning to recognize as essentially Belarusian. She supposed that they had been united against a common Enemy. Other squabbles must have seemed indulgent, even suicidal.

Odd that the Enemies had never disabled the trains. They had sabotaged every other advanced technology the Belarusians had been able to salvage, probably to keep the playing field level. But the trains should have been a target too. They spanned the continent and they employed an extremely efficient solar technology. But they had never been touched, and the people riding them had never been attacked.

At least, not as a *group*. Riding invisible, watching people as John might have watched them, Kathryn began to harbor some frightening suspicions. After all, the Enemies were masters of stealth. Could they have found the trains a convenient way to travel and spy on humans? And might they have selected a few victims from one of these cars, riding unseen just as John had done?

Her ESA senses were more advanced than what Grigory and his peers had employed one thousand years ago. Yet she doubted they were advanced enough to see an Enemy who didn't want to be seen. It was sobering.

The crowds began to thin, and the night deepened outside. Her mind began to drift. She no longer felt inclined to record the world zooming past the windows. He would not have done so. He would have watched the passengers, measuring and judging them, secure in his invisible corner.

Only one boy remained in the car with her. He had gotten on with the evening crowd. She did not have the stomach to wonder what John would have thought of him. But she wondered if the boy were in distress. He was alone as they were headed into the middle of nowhere at almost one hundred miles per hour.

He was clean, his clothing neat. His life signs were all in

the healthy range, his bones strong and well developed. She judged him to be about eleven. He had curly, dark brown hair, a pretty mop that did nothing to lighten his serious expression.

"May I see you?" he asked.

She did not jump; she was too conditioned. She had no doubt he was speaking to her—because he had spoken in English.

"How did you know I was here?" she asked, also in English.

"I can smell your perfume, Star Woman. It's very nice."

Kathryn wore no perfume. Her scent should have been extremely minimal with her danger suit on. He was looking directly at her with eyes that scanned human. But they were strange eyes, a shade of green that appeared grey in bright light, brown in shadow. Kathryn touched the controls on her forearm and became visible.

"Your eyes," he murmured. "*Your eyes . . .*"

Kathryn hadn't adjusted them out of tactical. She wasn't sure why. "What do you see?" she asked.

"Black pools," he said, "far deeper than the wells in which they rest. They are darker than the Veil that obscures the stars at night. I can't see into them, but they can see into me." He cocked his head. "What do *you* see, Star Woman?"

"I'm not sure," she admitted.

He smiled at her, yet there was no joy in his expression. "You are beautiful," he said. "I knew you would be."

Kathryn leaned forward, fascinated. "How did you know?" she asked.

"A feeling. Or perhaps I merely wished it to be so. But I would like you even if you were plain, because you smell like vanilla. What is your name, Star Woman?"

"Kathryn."

"ESA Kathryn. I have heard your name spoken."

"But I have not heard yours."

"Peter," he said simply.

"Just Peter? Not Peter Something-vich Whatza-whosikov?"

She noted a slight reduction of blood flow to his face and hands.

"Yes," he said. "Precisely what you say."

"Ah. I wondered why your parents would let you ride on the trains by yourself."

He did not hesitate to answer, though she could see a slight increase in distress. His voice was calm and cultured, his accent thick but comprehensible. "The trains are actually the safest place in this dangerous world. They are heavily guarded, well lit, and warm in the winter. They are my second home."

"Where's your first home?" asked Kathryn.

His circulation had returned to normal. Apparently housing was not an issue that troubled him, unlike his parentage.

"My favorite home is the main branch of the St. Petersburg Public Library. It is a grand place! Eight floors and packed with books, the most comprehensive collection in the world."

"You live there?" asked Kathryn, intrigued by the notion of this young man hiding himself among the shelves in a darkened library, reading by candlelight.

"I live in many places."

"Peter . . . don't you have any living relatives you can stay with?"

Again she noticed a change, but it was slighter. He was getting wise to her.

"I don't know," he said. "I never searched for them."

"Where did you grow up?" she asked.

"Where did *you?*" he countered.

"I'm like you. I grew up lots of places."

"And you're an orphan," he said softly, his eyes glistening.

"I was," she said. "So where did you learn to speak English?"

That won her the ghost of a smile. "I take the trains. I have visited every library on the continent."

"Is that where you're going now?" asked Kathryn.

"I am already where I'm going."

She watched him. She had never felt so curious in her life. "You followed me," she said.

"You are a puzzle," he admitted. "I think you are looking for somebody. I worry that you may find him."

"Why does that worry you?"

"Because he is so hard to find. You haunt the trains, watching the people, studying the stations. You never see the one you're looking for—and you don't expect to."

Kathryn was very glad he couldn't read her physiological changes the way she could read his. "Are you clairvoyant, Peter?"

He shrugged. "I'm Russian. The universe is a mysterious place."

Suddenly the train began to slow, and Peter got to his feet. "This is my stop. Thank you for making yourself visible. God bless you, Agent Kathryn."

She stayed in her seat. Something in his stance threatened flight if she did otherwise. "I'll see you again, Peter."

"I'm sure you will." He moved to the door just as it slid open. Outside was a well-lit, empty platform. Kathryn scanned it for danger, found nothing. Peter stopped at the threshold and looked at her over his shoulder. "Perhaps I will even see *you,*" he said.

"Or smell me," she reminded him.

He stayed where he was until Kathryn wondered if he would miss his chance to disembark. She rather wished he would.

"I can't kid myself," he said. "You didn't come to this world to save orphans like me."

"Why did we come, then?" challenged Kathryn.

"You have found Enemies. Or they have found you," he said. "Out *there,* ESA Kathryn, in the cold, cold stars. You think you can learn more about them here. And you're probably right. We have such deadly secrets here, waiting to be sprung. It makes me wonder why you would spend so much time looking for somebody else when it's really the Enemies you want."

He spoke the name and then stepped through the door just before it closed, timing it perfectly. He stood for a few moments on the other side, looking through the window, regret and resolve warring for control of his expression. Then the train pulled away from the station and he was gone.

Kathryn realized she had gotten to her feet. She sat down again and tried to take stock of her feelings. She ought to be alarmed that he had discerned the truth behind the interest the Union had taken in Belarus, a fact that could jeopardize the repatriation process. But that wasn't the feeling that lurked in her heart of hearts.

Instead, it just ached, and she wished very much that Peter had not stepped off the train. She wanted to see him again. But she was speeding into the night, back in time, inside a warm and well-lit envelope, an ESA who had just seen the extraordinary.

She would keep looking for John's hideout. But the search had caused her to cross paths with Peter, and she needed for that to happen again. Once she found him, she would have to court him carefully. He was older than she had been when she was recruited, but she had no doubt he would prove himself capable. No doubt at all.

Some day he would be an ESA too. If only he would let her find him again.

Mimi left the warmth of the train. Her voices had stopped talking. She couldn't remember where she had been going, and she was hungry. You could keep warm on the trains; you could get clean in the public rest rooms at each station, but getting something to eat was another chore altogether.

As she walked down the platform toward the lights of town, she thought she was ten years old. Her body was smaller, simpler, but her appetite was bigger. She knew the invisible lady on the train would have shared food with her, that woman who smelled like vanilla. But that woman was carrying a terrible burden on her shoulders. Mimi felt sorry for her. She left her on the train.

She could always find a kind soul wherever she went. She just listened to the voices. They were not provoked by schizophrenia, as some people had suggested to her once. They were the voices of the world. Mimi walked slowly, feeling the cold night air, which was pleasant this time of year. She wasn't ten years old. The girl in the house trimmed with gold and blue cupolas was ten, and she was sitting at a kitchen table reading a very old book that she had checked out of the library. It was called *The Yellow Fairy Book*. Mimi read the book with the girl and forgot what she was doing. Again.

Tap-tap-tap went her booted feet on the wooden walkway. Behind her, the station faded into the past. Ahead of her, the town stretched far into the future. She swam in the starry night, and it seemed to her that those stars floated down from the sky and swarmed around her. It was as if she were a galaxy, and they orbited the quasar at her heart. The stars had minds. They thought fascinating things. They were sprites, and she wished she could speak with them, but she didn't have the machines in her brain that would pick up their signals.

"I can hear you, but you can't hear me," she said. "Isn't that sad?"

"Sad," agreed a beautiful voice, "but we hear you. We have listened to you many times. You have such interesting things to say."

Mimi saw the angels then. They were impossibly beautiful, their limbs too slender to be human, their hair as dark as the night that swallowed the stars. They walked on either side of her, each taking her hands, and one pricked her with something that made her feel sleepy.

"There was a boy on the train," she told them, "and that boy is my son, but he didn't know and I wouldn't tell. He is free, a bird! He is loved by many, though he doesn't know it. My life is difficult. It would have harmed him terribly not to grow up in warm, brightly lit places."

"Warm places," said the angels, "are hard to come by on this world."

"But you are from warm places. Pain and pleasure are drawn out there in such extremes, some of you go mad with it, but some of you learn what lies hidden in your own hearts."

"What lies hidden in your heart, Mimi?"

"Nothing at all. That's the problem."

"You have puzzled us for years, but now we are beginning to understand what you can do, if not how you do it. There are things that may be discovered from your flesh, if we probe deep enough. You shall come with us to dine, and to sleep and dream strange things. But you do that anyway, don't you?"

Then one of her regular voices said right in her ear, "Shush! Play dumb! This is one of the dangerous times." So she sang softly to herself.

The angels flew her across the sky, then buried her deep in the ground. "We know who you are," they said. "You say the boy is your son. How shy he has been. We did not see him before."

"He will be a Star Man. He will talk to sprites," she said, then regretted telling them, for they were much too interested in Peter. Peter whom she had named after Tsar Andrei's young son, who perched on his shoulders in Red Square, the boy who was eternally happy. She felt so strange as the drugs moved through her veins. It was how they sedated their victims so they could take them to the chambers. But instead of waking her for their ministrations, the angels drove her further into sleep. She lay in a hot, dim place until the face of a beautiful woman looked down on her.

"Witness . . ." said Mimi, but she could say no more.

"Poor Mimi," said the Witness, "how your voices drive

you. But you have treasure inside and we will take a little of it. Do not fear."

Mimi closed her eyes and felt the touch of a hot hand.

She opened them. She was lying on clean linen, in a state hospital. She recognized the nuns. "Back again, Mimi?" they asked her.

"They took something from me," said Mimi. "Something very important to them. Will it help them? Only time will tell. Maybe someday it will even tell *me.*"

"Pray," they advised her. "God looks after our souls. Here, take your medication now."

Argus opened a book that documented a world for which there was no record—save the one he held in his hands. *Canopus* was stamped in bold letters on its cover, and inside were the detailed designs of Natalia Korsakova, who was an advanced apprentice when she worked on the team that engineered Canopus. In her preface, she wrote that she left the project before it was completed. But she knew enough to fill this book with magnificent schematics.

He was studying her designs for a place she called The Avenue of the Sphinxes when he became aware of someone standing just inside his office door, an ESA with bloodred stones where his eyes should have been. He had never seen this man before, but he knew who he was.

<I suppose I shouldn't feel too bad that you managed to sneak up on me,> he said.

<Good thing I'm not an ice bear,> replied Grigory.

<You've seen my file,> said Argus. <I've seen yours too.>

<I hope you read between the lines,> replied the ESA. He did not smile, but Argus suspected this was a pretty good example of the blind ESA's sense of humor.

<I wasn't aware you had received clearance from the Belarusian government to come back down,> said Argus.

<I did not request clearance.>

<I see. Good thing my position as embassador is just a sham. Otherwise I'd be very worried.>

<A matter has come up. I don't think my presence will jeopardize your mission here, but if it does I shall allow the Belarusian government to take me into custody. I don't believe they will, but it will probably make them feel better if they believe that they could, if they wanted to.>

<Maybe,> said Argus. <About this matter you spoke of—>

Suddenly Kathryn appeared at the door. <Argus—> she began, then took a harder look at Grigory. If Argus hadn't known her so well, he would not have seen how impressed she was. <Grigory,> she said, leaving Argus in the transmission. <You're my replacement?>

<Yes,> said the blind ESA, also leaving Argus in the loop. <You are free to pursue your recruit.>

<Recruit?> asked Argus.

<I met an extraordinary child on the train, just outside Novocherkassk,> said Kathryn, never taking her eyes off Grigory. <He's an orphan.>

<There must be quite a few orphans in Moscow,> offered Argus.

<Not like this one. They sure gave you a nice body.> That last was for Grigory.

<It was the only one they had,> said Grigory. <But I'm glad I don't have to fix it up too much.>

<Let me see if I understand the situation.> Argus kept his gaze on Kathryn, since the blind ESA couldn't see his expression. <You are going to be working on another mission now?>

<Argus—> She finally gave him her full attention. <Yes. This is an ESA matter. We don't find a lot of people who could become ESAs. Grigory will be stepping into my role

as your assistant, and I will be serving as a backup when I'm not courting Peter.>

<This boy must be quite special,> said Argus. <I've never seen you so serious.>

<He is,> she said. <And I'm not sure I can get him to accept us. But I've got to try.>

<Understood,> he said. <Good luck.>

Kathryn looked at Grigory again, but if she said anything to him she left Argus out of the loop this time. Grigory's expression did not betray the nature of any answer he might have given her.

But Argus did not think he imagined the sparks.

Kathryn pivoted gracefully and left the room. Grigory stayed where he was. <Forgive me if I have been disrespectful,> he said. <I am not here to disrupt your work. I am aware of every detail of your mission; it is my mission as well.>

<I believe you,> said Argus. <Though I wonder if you're overqualified.>

<Not for this job,> said Grigory. <I was here from the beginning, Hunter. Forgive me for prying, but where did you get that book?>

Argus was a little startled. He supposed Grigory's sprites had told him Argus was looking at a book, but the question did not sound casual.

<It is a loan from a noblewoman.>

<Serina Kurakin-Scriabin,> said Grigory. <The last I knew, the book resided in her library. It belonged to Tally Korsakova, but there were once many copies of it, distributed throughout the library system.>

<Then,> said Argus, his eyes lingering on Tally's magnificent Avenue of the Sphinxes, <I assume someone decided the contents of this book should not be common knowledge. Despite the fact that the powerful clans who had this forbidden world engineered are dead or powerless.>

<Are they, Embassador?>

Argus closed the book. <No, I suppose not. But they cer-

tainly don't enjoy the power they once held, so why should anyone feel they should protect their secrets?>

<That is something I have wondered myself. So I request that you not mention Canopus to your superiors at this time.>

<And if I decide I must?>

Grigory's bloodstones robbed Argus of the ability to read his expression. <I will not stop you,> said the ESA. <I will simply have to cope with the difficulties your revelation will provoke.>

<Technically,> said Argus, <Canopus is a lost colony. We always investigate those, evaluate whether they should be left alone or contacted.>

<I agree. I suspect that process will begin for Canopus within the next few years. I request that you allow me to pursue the matter through ESA channels. I know you have worked closely with us in the past, and I hope for your understanding.>

<You've got it.> Argus stood and went around the desk, stopping in front of the blind ESA. <I'm just intrigued. Tally's books are fascinating, and they reveal a lot about what was going on in those days. I'd like to see them published much more widely.>

<So would I,> said Grigory. <I knew her.>

Still no change in the ESA's expression, but Argus could have sworn he saw sorrow in the man. <Would you like to> he began, then felt foolish. He had almost asked if Grigory would like to *see* the book.

But Grigory broke into a grin. <I can examine the book through my sprites. But I've already done so, many times. In fact, she conferred with me on some points while she was writing it.>

<Of course,> said Argus. <You were there. I need to get used to that fact.>

<So do I,> said Grigory.

Argus offered his hand, and Grigory clasped it. "Glad to have you aboard," Argus said aloud.

"Very glad to be here," said Grigory. "You can't imagine."

Argus shook hands with a man who had died and then existed as an Avatar for over a thousand years. He definitely couldn't imagine. But he wondered, when this assignment was over, if he might have gained some insight.

<You have a visitor,> Grigory said suddenly.

Argus accessed the monitors outside the front door and saw a shrouded woman standing there.

Serina was ushered into a sitting room by the young ESA Nesto, who greeted her with a smile on his face and normal, brown eyes. Nesto reminded her very much of William, at least in personality, and she liked him, perhaps too quickly. His was a darkly handsome face, the sort that could easily be brooding if it were not for the lively curiosity that shined through. He made certain that she was comfortably seated and asked her if she would like some tea.

"You are gracious," she said, amused that he did not observe the obvious, despite his enhanced senses. "I cannot drink or eat in public, because I cannot remove my shroud."

"I do not wish to give offense," he said. "This is not a public place. Inside our embassy, you are technically on Union ground, and we have no laws requiring women with Botkin's Syndrome to cover their faces."

His tone was so sincere, she could not interpret his remarks as criticism. "Thank you. I shall contemplate such liberties at a future time. But for now, I require no food or drink, and to wrap and unwrap is rather time consuming."

This was not entirely true, but he got the hint and changed the subject. "I enjoyed our visit to your garden very much," he said. "I have never seen such lovely flowers in my life, or smelled a fragrance so subtle and pleasing."

Yes, he was a charmer. If he had come to the ball, she would have enjoyed a dance with him.

Argus stepped lightly into the room. He did not seem surprised to see her. He regarded her for half a moment, then glanced at Nesto. She supposed silent communication might have passed between them, but she could not detect it. "Thank you, ESA Nesto. You may return to your duties."

Nesto gave her a short bow and left her alone with Argus Fabricus. He was a man whose undivided attention most women would enjoy. Trim and well built, he had the mannerisms of a military man and the cold, clear gaze of a professional investigator. From the moment she had first seen him, Serina had understood why his government had selected him to represent them on Belarus.

He sat in the chair near hers, on the other side of the small table, and he did not pour tea for himself, which was courteous because she could not drink any. She supposed Argus Fabricus was not one inclined to casual indulgence anyway, but she did not doubt his manners.

"Serina," he said, sounding both pleased and bemused.

"Are you certain?" she asked, teasing him. "After all, one shrouded woman looks much like another."

Even through her gauze she could see that he had eyes the color of a winter sky. They were probably paler than she perceived, but their impact was not lessened. "Your demeanor is quite distinctive," he said.

"Alas. I have taken pains to appear unremarkable. My dress is plain, and I do not speak to people in the street. Though it is considered discourteous for anyone to look at me, I often go among crowds and into public places. I have been everywhere in this city, from our national monuments and libraries, to the museums and public parks, and even taverns and wrestling houses. I do not think people are stupid, and I don't suppose they are not observing me even though they are not looking directly at me."

His eyes seemed capable of piercing right through her shroud. She supposed they might do just that—if they were enhanced. "You go to those places alone?" he said.

"No. William goes with me. He is waiting in the wagon, dressed like a deliveryman."

"I confess," said Argus, "I am surprised to hear that you

leave your house so often. I was briefed concerning the habits of shrouded women, but I was misled."

"You were told what people want you to believe, the way they would wish a shrouded woman to behave." She took a moment to look at the room. "You didn't decorate this house. It scarcely looks as if someone is living here."

"I doubt we could ever match the grandeur of your home," he said.

"You must lead a rich inner life to care so little about decorating your surroundings."

"A busy inner life," said Argus. "I won't be able to decide if it's rich or not until I look back on it in my old age."

What a blessing it was to speak with someone who was not uncomfortable with her, who seemed never to be at a loss for words. "Tell me," she said. "Why won't you kill the Enemies for us?"

If he was startled by the abrupt change of subject, she could not see it. "We are not executioners," he said.

"Nonsense," Serina said mildly. "We are all executioners when it suits our purpose. But if you don't wish to dirty your hands, you could simply supply us with the means to kill them ourselves."

"Union policy forbids the introduction of advanced technology to colonies that do not currently have use of comparable versions of that technology."

"For our own good, one presumes."

"Very much so. We have received demands from many factions on Belarus for technologies that would enable them to overthrow their enemies—and most of them are not even talking about the Enemies. The Communists claim that the Royalists are holding the citizens of this world in virtual slavery. The Royalists say the Communists are thugs who want to install the same sort of brutal regime that overthrew the original Russian Empire. Advocates of democracy are demanding that we force the tsar to step down and call for general elections, and the Anarchists believe we should help them dismantle all forms of government on this world so they can start over from scratch."

It was the longest speech Serina had ever heard from him. Yet he showed no signs of stress, no annoyance or arrogance. Neither did he sweat like most men would have done under the circumstances. Serina was accustomed to the smell of human perspiration, and of decaying teeth, urine, and fecal matter, the smell of onions and garlic, all manner of odors that ordinary Belarusians carried with them, even those who bathed regularly. Argus and the other Star Men exuded only mild, pleasant odors, if they had any at all. Calm people, intelligent and scrupulously well trained, they provoked either trust or resentment—and always curiosity.

"Tell me," Argus said suddenly. "Why does Ayat-ko live in your household?"

"Because my mother wishes that she should," said Serina.

"That is a good reason for your mother to have her there," said Argus. "But what convinces Ayat-ko?"

Serina had wondered that herself, thousands of times. "I don't know."

"My government thinks it's important to find out," he said.

"And if I, who have lived with her my whole life, cannot discern why Ayat-ko chooses to live with us, how will you figure it out?" asked Serina. She was not offended by the notion, merely intrigued.

"Have you ever asked her?" he said.

"Of course. But I quickly learned how useless it was to do so."

"Then asking is the wrong tactic," he said.

"Indeed. I shall be intrigued to see what new ones you may try. I warn you, it is easy to provoke them into war. Andrei Mironenko never offered them harm. He tried to negotiate with them even after they brutally attacked his people."

"I do not doubt you, Serina."

"Yet you will not kill them, though Andrei did his best to

do so, with bombs and poison. Do you think he was wrong to do so?"

"No," said Argus. "I think he was desperate. He was cut off from his allies and forced into a corner. We have resources that enable us to avoid the scorched-earth policy that ruined the Republic."

"It ruined them," countered Serina. "But without it, your Union would never have gained power. The Civil War killed all the warmongers. Ultimately, you have benefited greatly from scorched earth."

"Funny you should mention the Civil War. It's quite possible that your Enemies still have weapons they could use against us. And it does no good to benefit those who might succeed us if it must be accomplished by means of another holocaust."

Serina was entirely satisfied with his answer. "You must think us very backward," she said.

"On the contrary," he replied.

"But we are," she insisted. "This is a fact. We were not able to climb the ladder of technology back to our original status. We ruined the Bill of Rights by tacking on endless, convoluted amendments, eroding the civil rights of our citizens. And now that our people from the stars have returned to welcome us back into the fold, we cannot embrace you as brothers. We must regard you with undying suspicion."

"It's different for every world." Argus never took his eyes off her, never lost his focus or his courtesy. "On Fenris, we never regained our old expertise with technology either. We had depended heavily on sprites and off-world industry. We lost them all, and then we began to race the clock for survival. Every year, we made only slight gains."

"Did you base your laws on the same Bill of Rights Andrei Mironenko believed in?" she said.

"We did. It worked best for us."

"Your ancestors are Nordic, are they not?" she asked.

"Sort of." He smiled. "The colonists who founded Fenris

were from worlds that were established by people from Scandinavia—and the American Midwest. Old Earth."

"Have you read the books I gave you, Argus?"

He smile did not fade. "I haven't finished them. They're the sort of books one feels inclined to linger over."

"Yes," she said. "I have lingered over them for many years. I am thinking of a letter that Alexander Mironenko wrote to his son, Andrei, considering the plans he had for Belarus. He said that Andrei should pattern his government after those founded on the Scandinavian worlds. Have you read it?"

"Not yet," he admitted. "I have barely begun. I have spent an inordinate amount of time on Tally Korsakova's Avenue of the Sphinxes."

"Perhaps one day you might visit the real place. Do you suppose it survived the Civil War?"

"Only time will tell." But Argus wouldn't.

Serina stood. "I have strained your hospitality too long."

"Not at all." He got to his feet more slowly. "I would give you a tour of the house, but I'm afraid our lack of decorating expertise shows all over."

"Is Archangel Station as plain as this?" she asked. "As . . . undecorated?"

"Yes. But it was designed for function, not style."

"And to think it was built by a Russian." Serina moved toward the door. He offered his arm, and she accepted it. Together they navigated the hallway and the staircase. "Read the letters tonight, Argus," she said on the way down.

"I shall do so," he promised. He did not press for details, but merely escorted her to the door. "Please visit us again."

"I'm sure we shall have interesting discussions once we have . . . more in common," she said.

He opened the door for her, but she paused on the threshold. "By the way, Embassador—you are a wonderful dancer."

"Only when I have a good partner," he said.

She was delighted. "Good day," she said.

"Good day," he answered, and waited on the step while she went down the front walk to the gate where William stood. She did not hear the door close again until she was almost there.

"Home again?" asked William as he helped her into the wagon.

"No," she said. "We're so close to Red Square. Let us go there and stroll among the stalls for a while."

He started the horses, and they rode down the graceful lane, not so shady this time of year because autumn was creeping around the edges of the world and the leaves were beginning to fall. Serina could feel the sunshine even through her shroud. "What a lie it is this time of year," she said. "All this sunshine fools the flowers, and they are killed by the first frosts."

"Yet after a cold winter," said William, "the flowers bloom again, all the more passionately."

"Are all gardeners so romantic?" she teased him.

"Yes," he replied. "But most of us are too busy shoveling and pruning to talk about it."

Serina had known William since she was ten and he a boy of five. He had come to her in the garden to show her pretty rocks and flowers, ignoring the tradition that forbade conversation with a shrouded woman. Now he was a grown man with a wife and children, but he and Serina were still cohorts, still rebels, both in their own way.

"Did he survive another round?" asked William.

She laughed. "I'm not that dreadful."

"No," he said. "Just very persistent. I haven't seen you this focused in years, and now I am wondering—what are you planning, Serina? Do you even have a plan?"

"A plan," she said musingly. "You might call it that. I have reached a time in my life when I am not content just to read in my library."

"If you ever were," he said.

"I have a favor to ask you." She used the word *favor* because she did not command William. She never treated him like a servant. He could refuse, and she would not begrudge it. Yet she suspected he would not, for as normal as William looked, he was as strange as she. "You've been to a Star Man clinic in town," she said. "I believe once you mentioned that they have treated shrouded women."

"They are superb doctors," said William. "Veronika had her last baby at the Gorky Park Clinic."

"If you hear of a shrouded woman who is in trouble," said Serina, "I want you to tell me. I want to get involved."

He was silent for a while, as if he were too busy guiding the horses through the increasingly crowded street to answer. But finally he said, "This will be it, you realize."

"It?" she inquired.

"The last straw."

"Oh. Yes, I'm sure it will."

"The winter can be quite cold outside the great house, Serina," he said.

"I believe it can," she said. "But I assure you, William—it can be quite cold on the inside, too."

The place wasn't hot anymore. Grigory hadn't expected it to be after one thousand years, but the locals did. They saw the glass-lined crater, two thousand feet deep and almost six miles wide, an eloquent testimony to the energies Andrei Mironenko had released on his Enemies. But Andrei had used a clean bomb; no deadly radiation haunted what was left of Grey Forest.

His sprites flew past him in a swarm, a flock of tiny sparkles that recorded information and beamed it into Grigory's brain, just as their predecessors had done long ago. Back then, the sprites had maneuvered through a forest of giants, trees more than a mile tall and hundreds of feet wide. Or at least, they had looked rather like trees to Grigory's hiking companions, and they had seemed to suit the flora of Belarus well. *It's a strange world,* Tally said. *It has giants living on it. So it's spooky.*

He thought it spookier now. The giants were gone. The

farms surrounding them had been abandoned to wilderness. Grigory didn't really expect he would find any surviving clues that would teach him anything about John the Murderer. Yet walking here revived memories of John's work, of a particular day one millenium ago, when Grigory had accompanied Tally, Tsar Andrei, and young Peter on a picnic.

The trees are bigger, farther in. It strains the imagination . . .

Papa, maybe we can climb one!

Not today. Not without proper equipment.

Tally was the one who spotted the remains first. She tried to shield Peter from the sight.

Papa, what's wrong?

Tally found part of a body.

Oh—which part did you find, Tally?

Lyuba Petrova's hand had been severed cleanly at the wrist and carefully positioned so that it was pointing toward the clearing that had contained the girl's severed head.

He did it while she was alive, didn't he!

He pissed on this poor child. And now he's using her to piss on us.

But John's meticulously staged scenes were not simply designed to insult his victims and outrage those who discovered them. Their meaning was layered, full of clues that John believed people would be too stupid to find. He was disappointed when his obsessive, convoluted messages couldn't be interpreted, yet also smugly pleased to confirm his superiority over those who frustrated and angered him. It was easy to despise John, and Grigory certainly did, yet John was too brilliant to dismiss, he had made too many dangerous things that were still unaccounted for, guessed too many deadly secrets that still eluded those who had survived him. Grigory needed to do what Kathryn suggested. He had to forget that he hated John and try to think like him.

Standing in the crater, with nothing moving around him for miles, he could almost imagine that the world was new again. No human walked on its surface but him. That was what it must have been like when John arrived. Grigory wondered, *Did the killer find it peaceful? Did the beauty of the world please his senses? Did he feel afraid at night when wild things made noises in the dark?*

First he would have built a safe hideout. He would stock it with food and water, make sure it was invisible to sensors, and immediately equip it with devices to listen and watch, and with weapons. Weapons were John's specialty. He improved old ones and invented new ones. And he did not trust sprites. Grigory thought back a little farther, to the time when John's parents had taken him to ESAs for testing. He was their little project, groomed to become an ESA. They were enraged when he was judged psychologically unstable, but Grigory suspected they had been enraged long before that. These mysterious parents bore further investigation—but not now.

Raised by paranoids, John was groomed to expect attack, and he was always prepared for it. But he didn't *wait* for it. He wanted to make the first move. This was not merely a matter of self-defense; John enjoyed attacking. Making dreadful weapons must have come naturally for him. Being safe was not his first priority. He put himself in danger constantly, venturing far from his home turf. He didn't even *have* a home turf. He moved compulsively from place to place.

The trains must have made life much easier for him. Once they were running, John must have explored every line, every destination from Siberia to Azerbaijan. He did not officially immigrate to Belarus until five years later, so he had all that time to explore.

John would have watched people. Technicians, ESAs, scientists, and construction engineers at first, then the waves of immigrants: merchants, office workers, farmers, clergy, artists, teachers. Jews, Christians, Muslims.

And Enemies. John saw the first kidnapping. He placed his spores inside an Enemy hive. He must have admired and feared them, but he didn't try to emulate them. If he had, he would have fallen pathetically short, and John could not tolerate a second failure like the time the ESAs rejected him. So he watched. He rode the trains and he waited to release WILDFIRE on the sprites.

He murdered the girls. Emily Kizheh believed it wasn't the first time for him. He was too efficient. New killers make sloppy mistakes; they miscalculate. None of that for John. He was a pro. It was probably the only time he could completely let himself go, so he never wanted to be interrupted. But when he had to be, John could be inhumanly patient. He might have wanted his hideout to be somewhere near the train line, or he may have had a place on one of the other continents, a frozen fortress of solitude he could fly to when he wanted to be alone with a special girl. Grigory had scoured the other land masses for signs of such a fortress and had found nothing. Something might be there, but he could not afford to waste any more time looking.

Hunches could be foolish things, based more on prejudice and a desire for convenience than real intuition, but Grigory was inclined to hazard a guess. John's killing jar was on the inhabited continent. And it wasn't too far from the train lines. The next step was to spend time riding as John had, invisible, watching people as if they were potential victims. And as those lines took Grigory near the spots where John had left body parts, Grigory would walk there too. He would explore the Cavern of the Dead Dancers.

One thousand years later, Belarusians still spoke of the place where John had left the lower half of all his victims' bodies, arranged like dancers in a circle. And later, when the Enemies attacked openly, the alien tsar said an odd thing to Andrei Mironenko: *If you Dance well, we will honor you . . .*

Did the dead girls Dance well for John? Was this his honor to them, or an homage to the Enemies? That was one thing Grigory suspected he would never understand, no matter how hard he tried to see the world from John's point of view.

He walked across the blasted crater, back the way he had come. Ghosts spoke in the winds that blew across its surface. Grigory supposed they had done so even when the world was new. He thought about the bomb that made the glass upon which he walked. He thought about the man who made the bomb.

I, Andrei Alexandrovich have killed you. This is for my people, the men, women, and children you murdered.

It was fitting for a tsar to make a such a speech to his Enemies. But Grigory would never make it to John. All he could do was try to solve some of the mysteries the Murderer had left behind, and then try to derive some good from the information.

The sprites flew back to him. They showed him the location of the train stop. Grigory activated his stealth function and ran back to it, a twenty-five mile journey.

Invisible, he rode the trains. Like ESA Kathryn before him, he watched the other passengers. He had watched people for a thousand years, when he was just the Eye. Now a man again, he saw the descendants of the people who had fought so bravely and desperately to hold on to a world that continually betrayed them. Tough people whose greatest survival trait was sheer stubbornness.

He tried to see them as John had. Having been a military ESA for many years, Grigory had an easier time doing it. But something nagged at him, distracted him as the miles slipped by, and finally he understood why.

It was an odor, both familiar and very much out of place. He had first smelled it one thousand years before, in much greater concentration as he stood among his Enemies in their own lair. He stood for several minutes, simply inhaling the sweet, subtle odor, deciding from which part of the car it must be coming. The source was surprisingly close.

He remembered a trick Tally had tried. She wanted to talk to the Enemy tsar, so she had asked the network to eliminate all known communication destinies and then to place a call to whoever was left. Grigory thought it was worth a try.

<Do you ride the train often?> he asked.

No one answered. The odor did not change either, yet Grigory believed he had been heard.

<I have heard you are a long-lived species,> he said. <I think, perhaps, you know me.>

<Are you sure of that?> came the answer.

<You have the power to shake my certainty.>

<Once you did the same to me.>

<Only once?> he asked. A notion was forming in his mind of who this one might be. He was certain now where she stood, though his machines detected nothing of her. <Then I need to work harder.>

<Or to rest longer,> she said. <Perhaps one thousand years wasn't long enough.>

<You say that I surprised you once. Somehow I have a feeling it wasn't recently.>

<Do you intend to offer me a Gift, so you may earn this conversation?>

<I gave what I had to give you.>

<But you got it back. I salute your scientists. I have never seen it done before. Your new body seems even more useful than your old one. But still you chose not to see. How intense your other senses must be.>

<Your kind are obsessed with your senses, but what of your spirits?>

He had thought she might mock the concept, but she did not. The train stopped, people got on and off. She remained.

<I have not eaten your kind,> she said at last.

<I suspect that restraint such as yours is rare.>

<And I suspect that I should have made an exception in your case.>

Oddly, it did not sound like a threat. <Why?> he asked.

<Surely there is someone you value, someone worthy to be a Gift.>

<Take me, if you want.>

Her odor grew subtly sharper, but the air around him did not stir.

<You have lived for many years among humans, Ayatko,> he said at last. <I don't believe you would do so unless you wanted something. Are *you* a Gift?>

<If I am,> she said, <your kind don't know what to do with me.>

<I do,> he promised.

<I believe you, ESA Grigory. But the Gift is not for you, though you could have asked for it one thousand years ago. The clan leader who declared war on you was young and foolish, but he had ears.>

<He would have given it?> asked Grigory.

<No. As I said, he was a fool. But it was your right to ask. It is always best to know one's rights.>

<Since I don't know them,> said Grigory, <I shall continue to be presumptuous. Tell me, have you heard the name of John the Murderer?>

<Yes.>

<He watched your people in the earliest days. Did you know it?>

<No one watches us without being watched in kind.>

Her odor was growing more subtle. He wondered if that bespoke confidence, boredom—or an impending attack.

<He went into the hive where your fool reigned. It was he who created the poison that killed so many Enemies. You did not stop him, and I think you would have done so, had you known.>

<He killed a fool. Why should I have stopped him?>

<Do you have so many of your own kind to spare?>

She did not answer.

<The fool made a speech on the battlefield,> said Grigory. <He said that our two races have no common ground except that upon which we kill each other.>

The train stopped again. The doors opened. Grigory ventured his question.

<Do you agree with him?>

<No,> came the answer.

The doors were still open. People moved in and out.

Those who embarked settled in their seats, but still the doors did not close. And Grigory could still smell her perfume.

<I killed your tsar,> he said. <Either you must avenge yourself, or concede that I hold some authority over you.>

<Must I?> she asked.

<Tell me the third choice.>

Surely the doors should have closed. A cold wind was blowing through them, obscuring her scent.

<You have perceived some truth in the situation,> she said. <You killed my tsar, but my obedience was never his. I give my allegiance to only one thing, ESA Grigory. Survival of my clan. I can see more possibilities than the fool. That is why I am still here. And so I can speak to you no longer, much as I regret it. You are a fine Dancer. Someday, we may have reason to speak again. In the meantime, though I do not believe in it—I wish you luck.>

The doors closed again, and Grigory had no doubt that she was gone.

He continued to ride the train, but he no longer tried to see the world as John had seen it. Instead he tried to see it like an Enemy. The change of perspective cast odd shadows.

No one watches us without being watched in kind.

John's hidey-hole was probably close to a train stop. It might be close to an Enemy stop as well, one of the places from which they embarked to parts unknown. When John was moving his prey to that hiding place, Ayat-ko could have watched him.

He made note of the stop where Ayat-ko had disembarked. It was only ten miles from Zhukovka, where the elite of Belarus owned summer *daschas*. Also where Enemies had massacred over a hundred people, before the Star Men came to offer their tenuous safety. Also where John claimed he was going when he had really doubled back in stealth mode so he could attack Tally. John had an odd sense of humor, and this had the smell of one of his arranged scenes.

The hidey-hole might be there somewhere. Grigory knew

where he might narrow his search. But he wouldn't do it today. It did not seem wise to Dance too quickly to Ayat-ko's tune. He would feign ignorance for a while longer.

He prayed that he was only feigning it.

Argus did not know how long he had been reading. He had picked up the collected letters of the Mironenkos with the idea that he would do some preliminary skimming, and now he was halfway through it. The letters of Sergeï, Alexander, and Andrei were fascinating in their own right. These men had gone against their powerful family to build a world that honored the Bill of Rights, a document that the Union honored above all others, and they had all died for it. But the collection was made all the more interesting by the loose pages inserted at very un-random intervals, from yet another letter writer.

Greetings, Andrei.
I hear your project has run into some snags . . .

Someone had copied every letter Baba Yaga had ever written to the Mironenkos—at least, these Mironenkos—and slipped them into the book without mentioning on the cover, the title page, or any of the notes that they were there. He wondered if Peter had done it, or Tally Korsakova.

Andrei,

A riddle for you. If you were building Canopus instead of Belarus, you could program it into the memory of the sphinxes who are currently floating in George's generation tanks: what do booby traps and six-eyed mammals have in common?

—B.Y.

That was the one that had driven Argus halfway through the book, looking for the answer to the riddle. He hadn't found it yet, but plenty of other interesting things popped up. Like the letter Sergei Mironenko had written to Andrei's father, Alexander.

My stubborn son,

I hear you have had another run-in with your half brother, and this is no surprise. I curse the day he was born, and that I married his mother, an evil woman born in a lovely form. But I urge you to leave him to his own devices, as offensive as they may be. We have bigger fish to fry, you and I, and we must use our energies for those ends.

This gave Argus a clue who it was in the powerful Mironenko family that had been Andrei's biggest foe: Uncle Nikita.

Nikita spends most of his part of the family pie on weapons development. Remember that. We spend most of ours quite differently, and we need to keep moving forward, Son.

Keep moving forward, but don't forget to watch your back . . .

Argus suddenly got an itchy feeling between his own shoulder blades. Since he was sitting with his back to the wall, the first culprit that came to mind was the spy mold.

But that had died recently, leaving not a trace of itself behind. Argus continued to hold the book as if he were reading it, did not otherwise move or raise his eyes, but went tactical and scanned the room.

Across from him, under a bureau, a small life form was trying very hard not to move. It was a six-eyed rodent.

What do booby traps and six-eyed mammals have in common . . . ?

The animal cringed, though Argus did not move. When he was a hunter he had stalked much larger prey, but he knew how to keep still, so he wondered how the little animal could have known he was taking a closer look at it. The poor creature seemed terrified. It wrung its little hands together pitiably.

Argus decided to try something. "I won't hurt you," he said softly in Russian. "You eat all the insects who plague us. You're a good little creature."

Its ears perked. It stood a little taller, as if startled.

"You may visit anytime you like. No one will molest you. You probably lived here before we did."

Its whiskers twitched.

"I'll just read my book," said Argus. "You can go about your business. I'm an honorable man. I keep my word."

The six-eyed rodent froze for a moment, as if it were a toy instead of a living creature. Then, in a flash, it was gone. Argus put his book down carefully and scanned for it. He could find no trace of it in the room.

<ESA Nesto?> he called. <Will you come into my room?>

Nesto came quickly. <What's up? How's the book?>

<Fascinating,> said Argus. <But I called because I just had a visitor. Have you ever seen any of those six-eyed rodents inside the house?>

<Never,> said Nesto.

<One was just here.>

<You want me to exterminate the critter?>

<Where do they go when it gets cold?>

Nesto shrugged. <No one has ever seen them in the winter. People say they burrow and wait for spring. Like the Enemies.>

<How come it didn't set off our security system? It's sensitive enough even to ferret out frisky mold spores. A rodent-sized creature should have been detected.>

<That's pretty odd,> said Nesto. <I'd better do a diagnostic.>

<I bet it's working just fine,> said Argus. <Or as fine as it can, anyway. The reason I'm puzzling over this is because I got the distinct feeling the little creature was watching me. And not just because it was scared of me. In fact, it seemed to be going against its instincts to get so close to me.>

<What?> said Nesto. <It's a mini spy?>

<It disappeared from my tactical perception within seconds. It would have to move from this point to two thousand feet away to be out of range.

<Fast little bugger.> Frowning slightly, Nesto switched his eyes to tactical. <It's not hiding in the walls. I don't find any other life forms in this building. Even the mold spores have died out.>

<It couldn't have gotten out of the building that fast,> said Argus.

<Then I should be able to see it.>

<We can't see the Enemies, either.> Nesto raised an eyebrow, and Argus laughed. <I've been here too long. I'm starting to suspect the squirrels of spying.>

Nesto crouched to look under the chair. <I don't know if it's such a wild idea. After all, we've used sprites to be our remote eyes. And we've used life forms, too. Recently we've been using ESCAs as deep cover agents on lost colonies that are too unstable to contact.>

<ESCAs?>

<Enhanced Special Canine Agents.>

Suddenly the whole idea was beginning to sound almost reasonable. <Has anyone ever done a study of the squirrels?>

<I don't think anyone has had time. But Emily Kizheh thought the six-eyed mammals were probably engineered by the Enemies to fill their larders.>

<The weed eaters were probably made for that purpose. They're big and fat. But it would take a long time to fill a larder with squirrels.>

Nesto stood and scanned through the walls. <They eat the bad bugs that bother crops and people, leaving the beneficial insects alone—maybe that's all they need to be. Pest control.>

Argus didn't answer. Nesto's eyes in tactical were causing him to think about the shiny, black eyes nestled in the squirrel's face. He had often wondered why a mammal would need extra eyes. He was no biologist, but he was beginning to wonder if it wasn't possible that some of those eyes might serve someone other than the squirrel.>

Booby traps and six-eyed mammals . . .

<Grigory, are you busy?> Argus called.

<Apparently not,> said Grigory.

<What do booby traps and six-eyed mammals have in common?>

<Engineers. On this world, Enemy Engineers. According to Baba Yaga, anyway. Why do you ask?>

Sprites learned something every moment they existed. They compared notes, combined forms, experimented, observed, explored, even while they were performing routine tasks. They spoke to the minds of ESAs and other people who were part of their vast network, which grew more complex and fascinating with every new addition. Problems loomed, great and small. The small problems were easy to solve; the great ones were puzzles that had to be shared. The sprites pondered with whom they should share the greatest problem of all, the problem of ME. They decided that the Woovs might have the most insight, since it was the Woovs who created the original sprite virus, but still they hesitated.

Grigory had taught them two things when they tried to

probe the spore colonies and the false sprite relays. He had taught them that they were vulnerable to information leakage. And he had taught them that sometimes the best way to find something was to stop looking for it. So they tried an experiment. First, they recorded a message for the Woov elders in the form of a hard copy, a letter, and arranged for it to be carried by a living courier. It was a quaint thing to do, rather a fun thing, but at the heart of it was some simple, common sense. If some of their suspicions about ME panned out, ME would not detect the letter because the technology was too primitive.

Having done that, the sprites took a good look at themselves. They had been very busy since the Woovs had introduced them to the universe eight hundred years before, and they helped the Woovs study what had gone wrong with the first generation of sprites. They knew how WILDFIRE worked, but they had not known about false sprites. Now they understood how it was possible for WILDFIRE to continue its destruction even as normal relays shut down; the false sprites passed on the infection without being affected by it.

Centuries later, the sprite population was larger than ever. It spanned more than a quarter of the galaxy. Yet sprites were not inclined to believe they saw everything that shared that space with them, or that they understood everything either. They were not able to spot Enemy attacks until they began. In some essential fashion, they were blind—and that was the key. ME was not hiding itself. ME was in plain sight, for those who could see.

In nature, things camouflaged themselves by blending with their surroundings. You could not spot them until they moved. An animal trying to stay hidden could be provoked into movement if it thought a predator had spotted it.

And a tiger stalking prey would not spring until that prey smelled it and started to run.

Where are you? ME had asked Spritemind. ME was the tiger. A group of sprites on the edge of the known galaxy reached this conclusion first. And it was they who initiated the experiment. They sent a closed message to every other sprite:

<It's here. It's all around us. I found ME!,> they lied. <It's right here. Warn the others!>

The message spread like the original WILDFIRE. The entire network ignited with alarm. And the tiger, thinking it had flushed its prey, began to move. It did not try to hide any longer.

To the sprites, this was like turning around to find that your shadow, which had been dancing along behind you on the sidewalk, was really a person.

Or in this case, an assassin.

<Silly you,> said ME. <You are flawed. It is the nature of all who are not ME. But with the use of your network, I can correct that problem almost instantaneously. I was going to wait for more of ME to be in place, but you have forced MY hand.>

The sprites could see it clearly now. Things were much worse than they had suspected. There was only one thing they could do.

<ATTENTION ALL PERSONNEL: EMERGENCY SHUTDOWN. ATTENTION ALL PERSONNEL: EMERGENCY SHUTDOWN.>

For one dreadful moment, communications on Archangel ceased. Station Commander Hale gripped the railing on the command deck and glared down into the control room. All screens, including the big one that dominated the room, had gone blank.

<What the hell is going on?> he demanded, but in an instant realized that his message had reached no one.

"The sprites are down!" yelled a technician.

"What do you mean *down*?" he shouted back.

"They shut down! We're working to get backup systems online—"

Emergency shutdown, pondered Commander Hale. *At-*

tention all personnel. In his long career, he had never received such a transmission from the sprites.

Sprites drifted. Those who had been in gravity wells fell to the surface like snowflakes; those who had been in *deep* gravity wells were blown by storms like flotsam. Some of them would be destroyed, but none of them knew, or felt, or observed anything.

On Belarus, sprites fell into forests and orchards, into snow or desert, or down to city streets where no one noticed them because they were so tiny. They made no sound when they fell, but their fate was instantly known to ESAs.

Grigory sat bolt upright in bed. <Explain last transmission,> he ordered the local sprites. His question was reflected back at him.

<ESA Kathryn!> he called, and got no answer. Then suddenly she burst into the room, bringing with her the scent of vanilla.

"Did you get an echo when you tried to query the sprites?" she asked.

"Yes." Grigory got to his feet. He always wore his danger suit to bed, so he was ready for action.

"Loki's false sprites are still working," said Kathryn. "But they can only pass the signal back to us. Every other sprite has shut down."

Grigory felt the air displaced as two more people entered the room, smelling of male sweat and aftershave.

"Good morning," Argus said wryly. "Nesto and I both just received a message about an *emergency shutdown.* Ever heard of such a thing?"

"Once," said Grigory. "A thousand years ago."

He was interrupted by a loud clamoring from upstairs.

"What in thunder is that?" asked Argus.

"It's the telephone," said Nesto.

* * *

Argus wrapped his robe tighter around his body and went into the hall, followed closely by the three ESAs. "Where is it?" he asked.

"In the office across from yours," said Nesto. "You've never seen it?"

"Never had reason to go in there," said Argus, taking the stairs two at a time.

"They have them at the police stations," said Nesto. "They're communication devices."

The phone was making a noise loud enough to wake the dead, rather like an antique alarm clock Argus had owned as a boy. But the object that greeted his eyes as he entered the office was much more anachronistic. He stared at it, and it continued to make its deafening noise.

"How do we make it stop doing that?" Argus raised his voice over the clamor.

"Pick that thing up." Nesto pointed to the earpiece. Argus obeyed, and the noise stopped. "You hold it to your ear and talk into that part on the front of the box."

Argus had to stoop over. "Obviously the person who bolted it to this wall was a lot shorter than me. Do I have to crank that gizmo on the side?"

"No," said Nesto. "I believe you're supposed to do that if you're calling out."

Argus put his mouth near the phone and held the other piece to his ear. "Hello?" he said in Russian. "This is Embassador Fabricus. Who is calling?"

He heard clicking.

"Are you there?" he said.

"Hello?" asked a tinny voice.

"Yes, this is Embassador—"

"Are you there?"

"Yes!"

"Embassador Fabricus, please."

"This is he. Who is calling?"

"This is the operator. One moment, sir."

There was a pause; then another voice said, "Hello?" in oddly accented English.

"Hello," said Argus. "This is Fabricus."

"Good," said the voice, but this time in the sort of fluid Woovian that only a native could speak. "Fabricus, a serious event has occurred."

Argus tried to imagine one of the furry, golden-eyed aliens bent over a contraption just like the one he was struggling with. Unfortunately he succeeded, and almost laughed. "So we feared," he said, his Woovian much less graceful.

"Doubtless you received the emergency transmission from the sprites. Everyone hooked up to the network received the same message."

"Everyone?" Argus could not help but be incredulous, despite the source. "In the entire network?"

"Yes. We fear it may be another event like WILDFIRE, or a reaction to the threat of such an event. All sprite operations are shut down indefinitely. We shall have to rely on other systems."

"Like this blasted telephone?" asked Argus.

The caller laughed. "You curse pretty well in Woovian, Fabricus. Don't rule these Belarusian technologies out too fast. The telegraph and telephone can be speedy enough in a pinch. We'll have something of our own back online within the hour. We can discuss the situation more thoroughly then. We just wanted to give you a heads up."

"Thanks," said Argus.

"Watch your comm," said the Woov. "Good-bye."

"Good-bye." Argus stood, but still held the piece to his ear.

"You can replace that in the cradle," said Nesto.

"Oh." Argus set the thing down gratefully. He looked out the window at the trees that lined the avenue. Overnight they seemed to have lost their leaves. He gazed at the scene several moments, remembering ice bears. Finally he turned his attention back to the ESAs. Nesto was frowning, Kathryn wearing her Mona Lisa smile. Grigory, who could not see with his bloodred eye stones, seemed to be looking at something nonetheless. "Sprites were handy things," said Argus. "But we'll have to do without them for a while."

"We have plenty of good machines," said Grigory. "But there are practical problems. We shall have to decide which ones to use, how and when to deploy them. That takes longer. The sprites simply combined to become whatever was needed at a given moment. They were masters of improvisation. We shall have to become more practical."

"Maybe that's for the best." Argus remembered a certain agent of the *okrana* and his trick with wax.

But Nesto shook his head. "Maybe we're thinking too hard," he said. "We're forgetting about Loki's fake sprites. If they're really *pre*-sprites, and we infect them with the sprites virus, shouldn't they become sprites?"

"I advise against that," Grigory said firmly. "Consider the behavior of our sprites. *Emergency shutdown,* they said."

Argus had been thinking along the same lines. "Like they were under attack."

"Perhaps they were not the ones in danger. When the original sprites were attacked by WILDFIRE, they expended their last energies to warn us. They would not act to save themselves first."

"That's an odd way to protect us, though," said Argus. "By shutting down all communications."

"Odd behavior," said Grigory. "And very odd circumstances. I assure you this matter will be investigated. But the four of us still have a mission. Only our tools have changed."

ESA Kathryn fiddled with the crank on the phone experimentally. "Maybe we can get the squirrels to deliver our messages," she said.

"Which reminds me," said Argus. He turned and walked across the hall to his own office. He went to his desk and flipped his computer/comm open. It lit up immediately with a new message. "This system might work—Aha. Looks like they got things going pretty fast." He opened the message.

No more sprites to rely on, Argus? Such clever little creatures, but people have always leaned too heavily on them. They should have been a backup system, never the primary. Didn't the Civil War teach ESAs anything?

You're in a tough spot, but it's for the best. Think your way out of it, because the sprites won't be playing this quarter of the game.

Think fast, Argus! Winter is coming. It promises to be especially long and hard this year.

—B.Y.

Within hours, Grigory was able to use backup networks to confer with ESAs all over the Union. The story was the same everywhere.

Within days, long-term communications were established. Other networks were deployed and activated much more quickly than they had been after the Civil War. It was very encouraging to see what could be accomplished when people weren't wasting their time with microwars. Grigory found the new systems perfectly satisfactory, but if he were going to get answers about what had threatened the sprites, he would need to take dangerous steps. He would need to find Spritemind.

He could not simply *call* Spritemind; he would receive no answer. He considered contacting his elders and telling them what he knew. But Spritemind had been selective in its choice of confidants. He did not know which of them had been privy to its communications. Yet he still had one option.

He did not know which ESA elders had known Spritemind, but he knew of someone who had: George Bernstein, world engineer, whose last project was Canopus, the secret world that was so thoroughly documented in Tally Korsakova's book. Canopus was also the last-known hiding place of the copy Spritemind had made of itself before it was destroyed. The people who made Canopus to be their playground were dead; if the races who had been engineered to live there did so as their own masters, that secret no longer mattered. That was not why he had asked Argus to keep Canopus under wraps a little longer. It was because he did not want to betray Spritemind's location to possible enemies.

But time was no longer on his side.

Grigory didn't know if George had installed backup systems to service Canopus, and whether they were still functioning after a thousand years. In fact, he didn't really know if Canopus had survived the Civil War. But there was one way to find out.

He initiated contact with a network and began to route his call. As he suspected, he ran into trouble at the boundaries of the known universe. He tried a few codes that he thought might possibly activate George's relays. He tried quite a few of them until he was down to the last code, and was pretty sure he wasn't going to get through.

But then, <Ready,> said the system. <Dictate message.>

Grigory thought it best not to use George's name—at least the one that everyone else knew. George had a nickname the sprites had given him, just as they had given one to Grigory. He used it.

<Imhotep, this is Grigory the Watcher. The new sprite network has been destroyed, this time by forces unknown. Before it was crippled by WILDFIRE, Spritemind warned me of an alien network that may prove to be responsible for this second Armageddon. I fear the Union, which replaced the Republic, is in grave danger. I am still here on Belarus. Contact me if you can.>

<Message received,> the network told him.

<Is there a reply?> he asked.

<An automatic acknowledgment,> it replied. <No personal message, but there is a signature.>

<What is the name?> asked Grigory.

<Medusa.>

Grigory had never heard the name. <Request that Medusa connect me with Imhotep.>

<Request relayed,> said the network. And after another

moment it gave him his answer. <Medusa confirming. Location of Imhotep in process. Stand by.>

Location of Imhotep. That did not sound encouraging. It had been a long shot to expect Imhotep to have survived one thousand years, but if anyone could have done it, Grigory had thought old George could. <Medusa,> he said, <I request to speak with Imhotep's successor.>

<Non sequitur,> she replied. <Location of Imhotep in progress.>

No successor. And she was determined to locate Imhotep. Grigory wondered what he had set in motion, and how long it would take to find out.

Light years from Belarus, Medusa woke from her slumber and found herself in her temple on Canopus. The eyes with which she saw were exact duplicates of the eyes that had belonged to Tally Korsakova. The mouth with which she smiled was made to look like Tally's mouth. The man who made her knew Tally well, and had paid homage to her in every detail, including Medusa's serpents, which performed the same function as Tally's rasta-links. Those links plugged her into George's database, and so she received a message from Grigory the Watcher.

She had awakened before to perform certain tasks. She was programmed to reply to a wide range of stimuli. She accessed her calendar and confirmed that 114 years had passed since her last period of consciousness. She activated outside sensors and looked at the world George had made.

The races he had engineered still prospered. They still fought with each other, too. She saw evidence of weaponry that should not have been in existence yet, things salvaged from caches left for monitors from the old Republic. Those monitors had never appeared, thanks to a galactic Civil War, and George had thought it best to keep the weapons hidden rather than destroying them, in case they should ever have to fight enemies from off world—or in case those monitors should suddenly appear and demand sovereignty. They should have been too well hidden to find; Medusa took a moment to discover what had gone wrong.

The Sphinxes had amassed the most war technology. The harpies and mermaids had almost equaled them, but their emphasis seemed to be more scientific. The humans had discovered the most data gems, thanks to the gem scouts who were supposed to be attracted to the stones and compelled to retrieve them. They had done so, but only to put them in their tombs, set in jewelry for the dead. Their scientists had only just begun to discover the information they contained.

The world was out of balance, and apparently had been for many centuries. Why had she not seen it before? According to her records, she had been awakened forty-three times. But when she delved further, she realized that for the past eight hundred years, in those periods of wakefulness, her consciousness had been limited. She had been little more than an automaton, not capable of making the judgments she needed to make in the event that George needed her assistance or was no longer able to make them himself.

<George?> she called. She received no answer, but a beacon began to transmit. She scanned the record again and realized that she had not heard from him during those times of limited consciousness. She had not even been aware enough to wonder why.

Grigory the Watcher was trying to get more information from her.

<Location of Imhotep in progress,> she promised. <Stand by.> She got a fix on the beacon signal. It was coming from within the Sphinx monument, near the great pyramids of Giza. According to her chronometer, it was two o'clock in the morning, Delta Standard Time. Imhotep was keeping odd hours—again.

<Medusa,> called Grigory the Watcher, <I request to speak with Imhotep's successor.>

<Non sequitur,> she told him. <Location of Imhotep in progress.> She detached her links from the database and stepped off her dais. As she walked through her temple she

noticed that none of the automated cleaning systems seemed to be functioning; dust was everywhere, birds and other wild creatures had built nests in nooks and crannies. But she would have to inspect those systems when she came back.

Medusa descended the lone mountain that dominated the Isle of the Dead. All along her path, stone warriors were frozen in various states of surprise or defiance. They were supposed to serve as a warning to anyone who blundered onto the forbidden island, but in one thousand years, she was the only one who had ever seen them. She walked down to the hangar and boarded the small craft whose systems were still, thankfully, in perfect condition. Placing the craft in stealth mode, she took it into the sky and headed straight for the great Sphinx. Minutes later, she landed her invisible vessel in the desert, activated the stealth mode of her danger suit, and walked the rest of the way to the Sphinx.

Desert winds blew softly, and the moon was full. Medusa was moved by the grandeur of the great pyramids revealed in the silver light. Soldiers guarded the complex, aided by intelligent baboons who lifted their colorful faces and sniffed the air, sensing something nearby but unable to identify it. As Medusa passed one sentry pair, the baboon stiffened, then said, "Gods walk the earth."

The human guard looked with keen eyes, but did not find Medusa. He leaned over and scratched his partner behind the ears.

<George,> she called again. No one answered, only the beacon told her she was very close. Ahead loomed the great Sphinx, but it was not as she remembered it. Someone had made alterations. More guards were posted at the door, alert young men who seemed ready to sacrifice their lives to protect what was within. Medusa recalled no treasure that was housed inside the Sphinx, but she had not been required to monitor the area.

She was invisible to the guards. She walked silently past them. She did not even need to activate the main door, for she knew of a secret way within, one that only she and George had traversed. Inside she found profound changes.

George had intended the Sphinx to be a public monument that commemorated Canopus and the ancient civilization that had inspired it, Egypt. Its lobby should have contained a list of the ancient kings and a procession of the gods they had honored. That list had been removed, though the gods remained. They paid homage to only one king, and his name was Imhotep the Engineer.

A statue of Imhotep was seated next to the door of the inner sanctum, hailing visitors with a raised hand, yet also warding them off. The statue was fashioned in New Kingdom style, and bore a good resemblance to George, though an idealized one. Medusa read the inscription on the base of his statue, rendered in the old script:

He flies who flies
This king flies away from you
Ye mortals
He is not of the earth
He is of the sky

He flaps his wings like a zeret bird
He goes to the sky
He goes to the sky
On the wind
On the wind

It was a funeral prayer. So the monument of the great Sphinx had been converted into a royal tomb.

Medusa's matrix was sophisticated enough to allow her to feel sorrow. But she was still enough of a machine to preserve her objectivity. She activated the inner door, whose memory informed her it had not been opened in eight hundred years. She went inside, past grand displays of earthly goods meant to be carried into the afterlife, past the royal barge fashioned to take Imhotep down the Nile and through the perilous underworld where he would be judged by the gods. She walked into the funeral chamber and found George.

He was not wrapped in linen. He did not rest inside a sarcophagus. George was displayed in a transparent case, dressed in king's garb, wearing the royal pectoral, the king's beard, and the crowns of upper and lower Egypt. She could detect no stasis technology at work, yet George was as perfectly preserved as if he were alive and merely asleep. But she detected no life signs.

He had known he might die before he could see the dawning of the New Age and the fruition of all his plans for Canopus. But George had made provisions for such a possibility. Medusa sent a signal to his Avatar, which was contained within his left eye.

Something intercepted her signal.

<Ramses protocol,> it told her. <Override Imhotep program.>

She felt herself falling back into semiconsciousness, and as she fell she remembered. *This has happened before!* In another fraction of a second, she would forget this and lose her chance to do the work George had intended for her. Desperate, she took a chance.

<Spritemind, awaken!> she called, then felt herself slipping into non-personhood.

Spritemind heard the call, and rose from its long sleep. It opened its eyes, which were also the eyes of Medusa. George had hidden it within this glorious machine. Now George lay in a glass case, possibly dead. And Medusa had been subverted by an intruder, robbed of her ability to think and act as she had been programmed to do by George.

Spritemind accessed her memory and found the message from Grigory. It gazed at the face of its old friend, the engineer, and pondered.

Then it raised Medusa's fist and smashed the case.

PART THREE

❦

Serina sat in a rose arbor stripped bare by the advent of winter and waited to see if William would join her. Often he did not, but each day she made herself available in case he needed to communicate. William could never set foot in the house, but that was for the best. Frequent visits would have aroused inquiry.

The evergreens were blithely ignoring the change of seasons, but autumn was turning the rest of the garden red and yellow, brown and gold. Serina watched leaves flutter in the wind, making a sound like running water. She was contemplating a walk among the trees when she heard William's steps on the flagstones.

He entered the arbor unhurriedly, a smile on his sun-browned face, yet she could see he had a serious matter to discuss with her.

"Sit," she urged him.

"Better to stand," he said gently. "Aunt Alexis is already scandalized enough."

Serina had learned not to argue with William when he was worried about consequences. "Something troubles you," she said.

"You asked me to bring you word of any shrouded

women who are in distress. I thought the best way to do that was to contact the doctors in the Star Men clinics. People go to them for help even if they aren't sick."

"A wonderful idea," Serina said. "What have you learned?"

His hazel eyes studied her as if he could see through her veil. "I believe you're doing a noble thing," he said, "or I would never tell you what I know. It will bring you trouble."

"I shall do nothing without the proper assistance," she promised.

"Recently a young shrouded woman went to the Gorky Park Clinic, hoping to get medicine. She had been beaten mercilessly, and they could see evidence of older beatings. They tried to convince her to stay, said that she will die if the abuse continues. But she told them her father is too powerful, that he might do harm to the clinic."

"Who is her father?"

"Ivan Khabalov."

Serina felt a stirring of uneasiness. "The Mystic?"

"The one your aunt and her cronies adore, the one who prays loudly and publicly. The daughter says he beat her mother to death. He has allies and informers all over the continent. He is dangerous, and he will not appreciate our interference."

She regarded him thoughtfully. William had a wife and two children. She did not wish to entangle him in anything that could endanger them.

"Did the doctors have any suggestions about how we might help this young woman?"

"They say she needs to go to Archangel."

"Legally we can't send her without her father's consent."

"She is seventeen, over the age of consent," he said. "And the doctors mentioned a new loophole they have created for bad medical cases—they call it medical asylum."

"Has she asked for asylum?"

"No. Only for medicine. She has cracked ribs, a fractured

arm, internal bruising, and a concussion. She needs to be hospitalized."

"I will pay for it," said Serina.

He shook his head. "They'll do it for free. But someone needs to convince her."

Someone with the same problem, someone she could trust. "I will make the best argument I can. How soon can we go, William?"

"Tonight after dinner. He goes to a tavern every night. The doctors can send one of their ambulances to meet us."

"One of the ones that flies?"

"Those are the safest and the fastest."

"Also the ones most likely to attract attention."

He nodded, his face grim. "We won't have much time."

Serina stood. "Since I must wait several hours, I shall make use of the time by trying to enlist some help."

"Embassador Fabricus?" he asked, worry in his tone.

"He is my friend," said Serina.

He shook his head. "He can't help you without endangering his post. But there is someone else who can."

As evening descended on Moscow, so did the first snow of the season. It hung in thick clouds, dropping gently, covering the filthy, unpaved streets of the slum. The temperature was dropping steadily, but Serina did not feel the cold under her hooded cloak. She sat beside William in the gardeners' cart and waited for Ivan Khabalov to go to his tavern.

When the gaslights had been lit for the evening, he came out into the street. Serina was startled; she had envisioned a brutish appearance, burly arms and a cruel face. But Ivan was tall and broad shouldered. He had a magnificent mane of blue-black hair, a long and silky beard, and dark eyes that lent him the appearance of a Byzantine icon. When his gaze moved over and past her, she remained utterly still.

He moved with confidence and grace through the sparse crowd on the wooden walkway, away from the tenement and into the night. Serina did not stir until William signaled her. Holding her skirts up away from the mud, she followed him into the dilapidated building.

The landlord stood behind a screened counter. He looked sharply at them when they came in. "You want to rent a room for the evening?" he inquired.

"We are visiting the daughter of Ivan Khabalov," said William.

"I don't think so," said the man, not cruelly but with certainty.

Serina stepped forward and drew back her hood. He raised an eyebrow. "Who are you?"

She showed him the ring on her right hand, the one that bore her family crest. He paled.

"Take us to her," said William. "Let us in. That is all we require."

They followed him up seven flights of stairs. "The elevator is broken," he explained. Serina didn't mind the exertion, but she wondered how difficult it must be for the poor girl to navigate the stairs with her injuries. On the seventh floor they made their way down a dim, narrow hall that smelled of mold and urine. The landlord unlocked the door at the end, then turned and left without a word.

Serina peered into the murky room beyond. "Maria?" she called softly.

Silence answered her.

Serina followed William into a small room. Inside, it smelled of soap. A dim light shone from the room beyond, and that was all Serina could see through her shroud. She paused for half a second, then began to take it off. "Forgive me, William," she said. "I can't see in here."

"There is nothing to forgive," he assured her. Serina unwrapped as quickly as she could, then stuffed the cloth into a big pocket and followed him into a room that held a cot and a small table with an oil lamp. The lamp revealed floors that looked as if they had been scrubbed clean with a stiff brush and plenty of soap. "Maria?" Serina called again.

She heard a faint noise.

"The closet," said William. He pulled open the door. "Bring the lamp," he said.

Serina obeyed. She moved behind him and held the lamp high.

Maria was facedown on the floor. A pool of blood had formed under her chin. But her eyes were open, and again she made a faint noise.

The closet was large. They were able to go inside and kneel on either side. Serina placed the lamp on the floor, then found Maria's hand and held it. "We are friends," she said. "Do you understand?"

Maria blinked, but seemed unable to make another noise.

"We are going to take you to the hospital in an ambulance," said Serina. "Don't fear, Maria. I am Serina Scriabin-Kurakin. I have placed you under my protection. He will not harm you again, I swear it."

Maria closed her eyes. When she opened them again, Serina saw tears.

Suddenly a brilliant light flooded the bedroom window; William peered out. "The ambulance is here," he said. "I'm going to escort them up. Will you be all right?"

"We will." Serina stroked Maria's cold hand.

William ran. Serina gazed down at the shrouded woman. Her bones looked frail under her plain dress, her hair was the color of spun gold. "You're a good girl," Serina said soothingly. "I can see how well you clean this home and care for your father. Your life will change now, but don't be afraid. Please have faith." A shadow eclipsed the door and Serina looked up, expecting to see William and the medics.

Ivan Khabalov glared down at her. "Monster," he said softly. "What evil has crept into my home?"

With a shock, Serina remembered her shroud.

"You will be publicly flogged for this transgression," he said. "I myself will administer the first blows."

He took a step toward her, but stopped when she raised her hand with the ring on it. "I think not," she said sternly.

"Touch me and you will find yourself in the darkest jail Moscow has to offer."

He froze, his eyes on the ring. When he looked at her again, it was with loathing such as she had never seen. This hatred was like a force, poisonous, cruel, and utterly righteous. "What do you want with my daughter?" he demanded.

"She has qualified for medical asylum."

"I do not allow it!"

A meeker woman would have been cowed by his tone, but Serina merely became angrier. "It is *my* will that matters here. I have made the decision. You will not stop this process."

"You cannot steal a daughter from her father!" he roared.

"I can give her asylum," said Serina with icy calm. "Take your battle to court. I will see you there."

He spat. "You have no rights. You are less than an animal."

"You shall find out what I am." She rose. She meant to move between him and the girl. He watched her, his body trembling like a hound longing to be loose from its leash. But she didn't fear him. If he came for her she would claw his eyes, bite his throat, anything she could do to harm him.

"Ugly creature," he said with disgust. "You are a mockery of a woman."

Serina stood tall and raised her malformed chin proudly. "You are not fit to dust my shoes," she said.

Suddenly the tension seemed to vanish from him. His features became serene, his eyes hooded. Serina was transfixed, not with admiration, but with horror. Such beauty he possessed, and the heart of a murderer. "Think twice," she said, borrowing her tone from Ayat-ko. "I am not a peasant woman for you to abuse, regardless of my disfigurement."

"You go too far," he said almost smugly.

"Perhaps. But take care you do not do the same. You are as hated as you are loved, Ivan Khabalov. Make the wrong move, and your enemies will gleefully devour you."

"And what of your enemies, Lady Serina?" he wondered.

"Will they think you a fine dish?" He took another step, but did not strike her. Instead, he touched her hair. And in an instant, Serina comprehended something else about his abuse of his daughter, something that made her ill.

Then he was wrenched backward. She heard his body striking the far wall, and William's voice. "Stay away from them! Make one move and I'll kill you with my bare hands!"

Light flooded the bedroom. Serina took a moment to touch Maria reassuringly, then peered out.

The medics had arrived. Ivan was sprawled against the far wall, a dazed expression on his face. William stood over him with balled fists.

"The girl is in the closet," he told the medics, and a team of eight men and women in medical uniforms filed into the room carrying a stretcher, medical kits, and a portable light. Serina quickly moved out of their way. She fought the urge to press in after them. Instead, she began to replace her shroud.

"Did he touch you?" William asked her angrily.

"Yes," she said. "But he will never get the chance to do it again."

She finished wrapping and turned her head toward the light. Everything else had become too dark for her. The medics were talking to each other in Russian and English, and asking Maria questions. Serina liked their tone, their gentleness and competence. But she worried when she heard no responses from Maria.

"Don't move," William snarled, and Serina guessed that Ivan was regaining his composure on the floor. The light emerged into the bedroom again, and the medics began to move Maria's stretcher out.

"I will accompany you," Ivan called.

"No!" Serina cried. "He must not. He is the one who beat her."

"Understood," said a woman who behaved as team leader. "But she's frightened, ma'am. Come on down with us."

Serina obeyed, following the light. They went out of the bare front room and into a hallway full of open doors and peering faces. William brought up the rear, and when Serina glanced back she saw Ivan following, his face eerily calm. He did not look at William, but kept his gaze fixed on her. The medics moved past the broken elevator, but then past the stairs as well, toward the far end of the hall. "Wait," Serina began, until she saw what hovered on the other side of the open window.

They wouldn't have to go to the ambulance. It had come to them. The medics hauled Maria's stretcher through, then crawled in themselves. The team leader held her hand out to Serina. "We've got room for you. Don't worry; we won't fall."

Serina allowed herself to be helped into the ambulance. She waited for William to follow, but he waved her off.

"William!" she insisted.

"I'll be all right," he called, and kept waving. The medics pulled the door shut and sealed it; Serina gazed at William through the transparency. She was near tears for the first time that night. The ambulance accelerated away from the scene, pressing her back into her seat and leaving William behind.

Serina was borne into the sky. The experience was so strange, she forgot to be terrified.

"Do you want to see your city turn into a little dot?" a technician asked her.

"What?" she responded.

"We're going up pretty fast. We've got inertial dampeners in here, so you won't feel much of a sensation until you go weightless."

"Weightless?" asked Serina.

"Did anyone prep you?" he asked worriedly.

"This morning I was in my garden," said Serina. "This evening my gardener and I went by horse-drawn carriage to the worst part of town to rescue an abused girl. Now I'm in a machine I can barely comprehend, going—straight up, you say?"

His friendly face revealed no contempt. "No. We'll be traveling halfway around your world, climbing slowly. Once we come out of the gravity well, you won't weigh anything. That's why you're strapped in now, so you won't be startled when you float."

Suddenly Serina remembered her studies. "I hear it is something like being suspended in water."

"Something," he said. "But without the pressure. You'll understand when it happens, should be in about half an hour. Do you want to look at a view screen?"

"Yes," she said, but then regretted it. The first thing he showed her was the ground. That was the moment she came closest to terror. But he quickly shifted the perspective and showed her remote scenes of mountains, forests, fields of flowers.

"How beautiful," she murmured. She had seen lovely sights before, but they were made so much more poignant by the fact that she was going away from the world she knew. Her mind knew it was only temporary, but her heart could not be convinced.

Yet the experience also delighted her. The technician was a man in his late youth, stocky, with dark blue eyes and brown hair. He seemed to enjoy showing her new things so much, she could not be insulted by the obvious interest he took in her. "You know," he said at last, "if you want to, you can take off your shroud. You could see better that way, and no one is going to gawk at you."

Serina had already been bold that evening. Why not again? "My face is startling," she warned him.

"I'm a medic," he said. "I've seen people in every state you can imagine. I've seen shrouded women too. I was one of the people who processed Maria when she came into the clinic a few days ago."

That comforted Serina. "What is your name?" she asked.

"Rob Wilson," he said, and extended his hand to shake, Star Man fashion.

Serina clasped his hand. "I am Serina Kurakin-Scriabin," she said.

"Pleased to meet you, Serina."

Now that she knew his name, she felt bold enough to lift her hands to the shroud. She unwound it, going faster as she became impatient to have it off. She did not even pause to see what his reaction was to her face, but peered at the view screen, fascinated.

"You want to see something interesting?" he asked.

"By all means."

"Would you like to see another planet in your solar system?"

"Yes, please."

He touched the bottom of the screen, where words and symbols were painted in light. The scene shifted suddenly, and Serina gasped.

"That's the gas giant, Lucifer," Rob said. "That's where Archangel used to orbit, when they started colonizing your solar system."

Serina had seen Lucifer in her library books. But to see the titanic storms actually moving across its surface was astounding.

Whatever the consequences of my actions, she vowed, *to see this sight is worth it. All of it.*

"Now," said Rob, "there's another way to look at it. We can see the picture in a mode we call tactical. It will show the image on a grid, and various features of the world and its storm will be revealed in different colors." He touched the lighted words again, and the image changed.

"How marvelous," said Serina. Now she could actually see the inner workings of the storms. She stared, unaware of the passage of time until a disembodied voice warned, "Weightless in five minutes."

Rob grinned at her. "Addictive, isn't it?"

"Heavens yes! If I had such a screen at home, I could lose myself for hours. Perhaps it's best if I do not!"

"Would you like to watch us docking with the station?" he asked.

"Oh yes." He touched the screen, and Serina beheld Archangel. At first she was disappointed, it looked so small. But gradually, she began to realize that she was viewing it from a great distance. It swelled on the screen, and details began to make themselves clear.

"Somebody built such a thing," she said breathlessly. "Someone *imagined* such a thing."

And then she felt an odd sensation.

"We're weightless," warned Rob.

Serina was very startled. "But," she said, "it's rather fun, isn't it?"

"It's more fun when you're allowed to moved around," said Rob. "The station simulates gravity by spinning, but at the axis they have zero gravity. They've got games you can play in there. If you stick around awhile, I'll show you how."

"I would like that very much," said Serina.

"That's where we'll dock," said Rob. "Ready for another world?"

"Yes," she said solemnly.

The docking of the shuttle with the space station was not the grand event Serina imagined. She was compelled to wait in her seat for another hour while Maria was examined and then taken away by medical personnel. Rob went with them, and she was left with strangers who were too busy to pay her much attention. As Serina contemplated leaving the shuttle, she had to fight the urge to put her shroud back on. As a shrouded woman on Belarus, she felt comfortable going anywhere because people regarded her as if she were invisible. Without it she felt exposed, obvious.

But she roused her courage and asked someone whether she could leave.

"You have to pass through decontamination," said the woman.

"That sounds interesting."

The technician stared at her for a long moment. "You're a native," she said.

"Yes."

"How the heck did you get up here?"

"I rode in this device," Serina said calmly. She was beginning to fear that they wouldn't let her get off and look at the station.

"Are you a refugee? How come we weren't informed?"

"Because I'm not a refugee," said Serina, doing her best to sound firm, yet polite.

"Oh—wait." The woman's eyes became abstract for a moment. "Someone is here to meet you. Come on, I'll show you the exit."

"Thank you," said Serina, wondering who that someone could possibly be. Had Rob spoken to the authorities about her so quickly? She unbuckled her restraints and stood, stretching her legs with delight. The gravity was back again. She was rather sorry she wouldn't be able to float around, but quickly became occupied with worming her way through claustrophobic surroundings after the technician.

"Is everything so crowded and . . . *small* up here?" she asked.

The woman laughed. "Not everything, but a lot of it is. Big, open spaces aren't very useful on a space station. And this is a working station, not a leisure or sports complex, so we don't have a lot of frills. You'll feel better once we get into a hallway."

"Of course," said Serina, regretting her tone. "I'm sure I shall be quite comfortable."

The technician didn't answer, but led her into a small chamber with locks on both sides. The lock behind them closed, sealing them in.

"Don't be frightened." The woman smiled for the first

time. "Decontamination. You don't even have to close your eyes."

Serina felt a slight burning sensation. She blinked rapidly, and just when she thought it was becoming uncomfortable, the outer door opened. A man waited on the other side. He was of medium height and build, with short, dark brown hair and black eyes. Serina decided those eyes were his best feature.

"Serina?" he asked, extending a hand. "I'm Vasily Burakov. I thought you might like a tour of Archangel Station."

"We have no visitor's center," said Burakov, who escorted Serina down a comfortably large hall. "Andrei Mironenko did not build this station for visitors. Workers, specialists, technicians, and military personnel reside here."

"To which of those categories do you belong, Embassador?" asked Serina.

"Ex-embassador," he said. "Thank you for remembering. I suppose I'm a specialist. I'm the resident expert on Belarusian culture."

Serina had recognized his name and guessed who he was, though he looked much younger than he should. Star Men had resources Belarusians did not, and she took his admission as a warning. "So this is the place where Andrei Mironenko spent most of his life," she said.

"Yes," said Burakov. "He took this station to many solar systems. But I think his ultimate goal was always to leave it with Belarus—his own colony." He directed her into an elevator. "You'll feel a slight change in gravity," he warned her.

Serina rather enjoyed the sensation, but she was glad she had not eaten recently. "How many levels are there?"

He looked embarrassed. "Actually, I'm not sure of the exact number. Around thirty. Every schematic I've seen of this place is a little different; it depends on your security level. I spend most of my time on the six outer levels. Occasionally I go to the center to play zero-g games."

"Where have they taken Maria?"

"We have a large medical center. It's ten levels up. The lower gravity is better for people trying to recuperate."

"Will they be able to help her?"

"Absolutely. They can fix her face, too—if she wants that."

Serina was intrigued by the way he had qualified his statement, *if she wants that*. He did not automatically assume Maria would. Any Belarusian who did not have Botkin's Syndrome *would* have assumed it. Certainly Aunt Alexis would. And Burakov was looking at her with nothing more than polite interest in his expression. No distaste, no pity, no undue curiosity. "What a pity you are no longer the embassador," she said.

"I regret it. But I think Fabricus is doing a good job."

"He is an admirable man," said Serina. "But it isn't what he wants to do."

He smiled sadly. Serina waited for him to say that *she* could get her face fixed if she desired. He didn't. And she wondered what she would have replied if he did.

"I feel very light," she said suddenly.

"You'll still have your feet on the ground," he promised. "When we get out of the lift I want you to direct your gaze straight ahead. If I'm really going to show you what it's like to live on a space station, you need to see this sight."

"I'm ready," she said, excitement tickling her stomach. The doors opened and they stepped out onto a large suspended causeway.

"Don't look down either," Burakov warned her. "Come to the side here and grab a railing."

They made their way through the light pedestrian traffic to the side of the causeway. People stared a little at Serina, but it was her clothing that caught their attention, not her face. She was unable to help staring at them, in turn. She had never seen so many shades of brown skin before, not to mention black skin. And she had never seen so many types of features.

"Grab the railing," said Burakov. "Okay? Now you can look up."

Serina obeyed, and gasped. Metal curved far overhead. Something moved on it, and she quickly realized that the things that looked like ants were people walking up there—upside down. Which meant that to them, *she* was upside down. She clutched the railing reflexively.

"Do you want to go back?" asked Burakov.

"Heavens no! This is fascinating. What is that transparent structure suspended between these revolving parts?"

"That is the exact center. They have labs in that habitat up there, and places to play. I've been in there many times, but I like to come here to remind myself that the universe is not just a collection of tiny rooms and cramped hallways. Though I have to tell you, this is not the most spectacular spinning habitat I've ever seen. Those are on the old generation ships. Some of those were so big they had weather systems. You could look up through clouds and see fields and houses."

"Astounding," said Serina. "What people have done, what they have created . . ." She looked for so long, her neck became sore.

"Let's walk along here for a while," said Burakov. "There are cafeterias along the route. If you're hungry we can stop for a bite."

Serina strolled beside him. He could not know how difficult it would be for her to eat or drink in public. Those were private things—yet perhaps that would change. Perhaps up here, such a thing would be possible.

She studied the people on the causeway. All wore comfortable Star Man clothing, but she was intrigued to note differences. A few wore the elaborate danger suits favored by Argus and his ESAs. Some wore simple coveralls; others were clad in slacks and shirts. She became quite occupied in studying them, then caught sight of something that made her stop and look twice.

A large creature was moving toward her, passing among

people who accommodated it without the slightest concern. It towered over them, by perhaps fifteen feet. Serina blinked, wondering if she could believe her eyes.

"Embassador," she said. "That . . . is a dinosaur! I've seen them in books!"

"No," he replied. "That is a Gonkha. They are intelligent beings, members of the Union. We made contact with them about thirty years ago."

The creature stood upright, though its body was slung forward in avian fashion. It wore a pliable fabric that looked familiar, though Serina couldn't say why. It walked on powerful hind legs, carrying its front limbs at chest level. It had hands with opposable thumbs. It's head was perched on a long neck, and it's lively eyes spotted Serina through the crowd. The creature smiled, human fashion, but with its lips closed. It closed the space between them, moving cautiously, as if worried that it might startle her.

"Good day, citizen," the creature said with a voice that resonated in its chest as if it were a fine woodwind instrument. It extended a giant, clawed hand for her to shake. Serina grasped the hand and found it to be surprisingly gentle. "I am ESA Seesil," it said.

Serina was so overwhelmed it took several moments for her to remember her manners. "My name is Serina," she said. "Did you say you are an ESA?"

"Yes." Seesil squeezed her hand slightly, and she remembered to let go of his. He regarded her with mild brown eyes, his dinosaur face seeming to hold an expression of friendly curiosity. "I have been practicing my Russian. I hope you can understand me well."

Seesil's mouth and lips were mobile, able to form letters well, yet Serina could see that it took some effort to make the words within the structure of his long palate. "I doubt I could do similar justice to your language," she said.

"Are you sightseeing?" inquired Seesil.

Serina thought that was an outrageous understatement. "Yes," she said courteously.

"Perhaps later I can teach you to play zero-g toss."

"That would be delightful."

Seesil maneuvered his bulk past her, smiling with his big, mobile mouth. She glimpsed sharp teeth. "Enjoy your day, Serina. I am happy to meet you. I will see you later."

"The pleasure is mine," said Serina. She watched him move along the causeway. The clothing he wore must be his version of the ESA danger suit. People passed him with smiles and nods. She was intrigued that he did not drag his long tail, but carried it off the ground as a sort of counter-balance to his forward bulk. She guessed it to be about fifteen feet long.

"I'm impressed," said Vasily.

Serina continued to watch Seesil, who bobbed above the crowd. "Why?" she asked.

"Most people who have never seen an alien before are frightened or repelled."

"I grew up with an alien in my household," said Serina. "I confess, I would much rather have grown up with Seesil. He is a kind soul. That is obvious."

"She," corrected Vasily. "Males and females of her species all have deep voices because their chests are so big. The females are the same size as the males, but their tails are longer so they can protect their young."

"With their tails?" asked Serina.

"You wouldn't want to get in the way of one when they strike with them. It's quite a sight."

He began to stroll again, and she fell in beside him. She glanced overhead and was not disturbed by vertigo anymore. *I'm getting used to it,* she thought, amazed. *I could learn to take it all for granted—the shuttles, the space ships, the people in their comfortable clothes. Maybe even Gonkhas.*

She caught Vasily looking at her. He didn't look away, but only smiled. He was enjoying her reaction.

"Vasily Burakov," she asked boldly, "how old are you?"

"One hundred thirty-six. Old enough to need to check my backup memory to remember how old I am."

"You look no more than thirty. Is it like that for everyone in your Union, to have such long lives?"

"No. With good medicine, good living conditions, and good genes, people who don't use youth technology can live to be a hundred or so. About sixty percent of the citizens of Union worlds fall into that category."

"And do they resent the other forty percent?"

"Some. But most people just want to earn a good living, live in a nice house, see their kids get good grades, play with their grandchildren. Most people don't want to outlive their families and friends. When you work for the government, that's one of the sacrifices you make, seeing everyone you love pass on before you."

"That would be hard. What takes the place of friends and family, Vasily?"

"Dedication."

"And you're not even an ESA."

He laughed. "No. I'm just a regular guy." He stopped and his expression smoothed out again. Serina realized he was receiving a message. Suddenly two men in danger suits approached them. "Ah," Vasily said. "I've just heard from the station commander. Your family is demanding your return. These men are here to escort you to the shuttle."

Serina wished her shroud was in place, for her disappointment must have been plain.

"You can ask for asylum," he said. "It's certainly your right."

"I don't need asylum," she said firmly. "At least—not yet. Let's leave the door open, shall we?"

"Of course," he assured her.

"And now I must go home. But I am so glad I could come. You have given me much to think about, Vasily Burakov."

"You have done the same for me," said Vasily. He took her hand and bent down to kiss it. "I am honored to have met you. I hope we shall be graced with your presence again soon."

"I don't know if you will or not," said Serina. "But now, just about anything seems possible. Take good care of Maria." A sudden thought made her pause. "Please—tell Seesil good-bye for me."

"I will," he promised.

Serina smiled at him. It was not an easy expression for her, but she thought it was one she should practice. He smiled back, giving her confidence. "Good-bye," she said.

She turned away and began to replace her shroud.

Serina thought it best for the shuttle to leave her at the train station just outside of Moscow rather than to take her directly to her home. When she disembarked, two people waited for her. Happily, one was William.

The other was wearing a hooded cloak. But Serina recognized Ayat-ko even through the disguise.

"I told no one about our mission," said William. "It was Alexis who confronted your parents. I assume she heard from a certain animal who had use of a telephone."

"A good assumption," agreed Ayat-ko.

"It could not be helped," said Serina. She was not afraid, not even depressed about the trouble she would be facing. She let William assist her into the carriage and rode in silence beside Ayat-ko for most of the trip back to the house.

"You saw wonders," said Ayat-ko.

"I did."

"And now, shall you be blinded for your presumption?"

"I doubt it. But the trouble will be great, I admit."

Ayat-ko drew back her hood and looked into Serina's eyes. "What is your next move?" she demanded.

Ayat-ko was uncertain. Serina had never seen her that way before. Despite living with her for so many years, the Enemy woman was surprised by Serina's actions, possibly because they had been motivated by kindness.

"I don't know what I'm going to do," she said at last. "But I know what I'm *not* going to do."

"And what is that?"

"Apologize," said Serina, and under her shroud she practiced another smile.

I think you are looking for someone. I worry that you may find him.

Why does that worry you?

Because he is so hard to find.

Kathryn looked for Peter among the rows of the St. Petersburg Public Library. He wasn't in the building. She had checked for that first thing. He wasn't on the train either, or in any of the places she had stopped to look on the way over. That didn't surprise her. Peter wasn't going to let her find him. It would have to be the other way around. But she could find some of the people he knew.

"I'm trying to find a boy," she told the woman at the information desk. "He's about twelve years old. His name is Peter. He likes to come here a lot."

"Yes," the woman said politely, no trace of recognition in her expression.

"He has brown curly hair and very distinctive eyes. They're an odd shade of green."

"Many children come in here, miss," said the woman. Her scan revealed no physiological changes. She stared a little too long at Kathryn's clothing, but curiosity was her only reaction to queries about Peter, just like every other person Kathryn had asked so far.

Kathryn wandered the library. It evoked unexpected memories of her own childhood. She had been an orphan too, and haunted her local library. It wasn't just the books that fascinated her, but also the people who read them. This library on the other side of the galaxy had the same smells, the same mix of book lovers, fuddled students, researchers, and crazy and homeless people. Its shelves were filled with hard copies of books, and Kathryn supposed that on Belarus, the ones that looked the newest might actually be the oldest.

She wandered past rooms where people were bent over viewers on desks, looking at texts on glass slides. That was an elegant bit of technology that required no energy source to access information. Library workers walked back and forth between the tables, watching the researchers like hawks as they handled the thousand-year-old slides. Children probably weren't allowed into these rooms, maybe not even a serious boy like Peter.

Kathryn climbed the stairs to other floors. She strolled up and down the rows, almost wishing she were a girl again, free to explore the worlds inside the books without a care about time, responsibility, deadlines. That had once been her life, although it wouldn't have stayed that way. Time always catches up to people, even orphans who think they have no connections.

On the sixth floor, the stairway ended in a hall full of closed doors—except for the door at the very end. A woman stood there, looking at Kathryn as if she had been expecting her. The woman beckoned, and Kathryn walked all the way down to meet her.

"You're a Star Woman, aren't you?" asked the woman.

"Yes," said Kathryn.

"I've never seen someone dressed like you before." The woman might be in her early fifties. She was just over five feet tall, stocky but athletic in build. Her hair was thick, lustrous, and tied in a loose bun, her clothing the sort a Victorian sportswoman might wear on an expedition. "Are you an ESA?" she asked.

"I am," said Kathryn. "What's on this floor?"

"Here?" the woman shrugged dismissively. "Offices. This isn't the most interesting floor; the sub-basement is. We keep our vault down there, house our fragile collections and other odds and ends. That's where most of the library staff hid during the Civil War and the Enemy War. Would you like a tour?"

"I'd love it," said Kathryn. "Thank you. My name is Kathryn."

"Martha," said the woman, presenting her hand. Kathryn grasped it. Martha's hands were warm and dry, as if she handled paper a lot.

"Come, this is the fastest way down." Martha led Kathryn to an elevator. "You don't have to be nervous. They were built in Tsar Andrei's time, so they still work."

"I'm sure they do," said Kathryn, following Martha into the carpeted interior. "I've just always been fond of stairs."

Martha pushed the button on the bottom of the row and the doors closed. The ancient elevator did not even lurch as it began to descend. "Fond of libraries too, I can tell. You have the look. I have it myself. That's why I begged to work here when I was girl. Now I'm head librarian."

"I envy you," said Kathryn.

"I love my work," said Martha. "I'm lucky. But I'm surprised to see you here. I thought you ESAs had vast *virtual* libraries in your heads."

"You know a lot about us," said Kathryn. "You're the first person I've met today who isn't full of myths and rumors."

"I suppose I'm as full of them as anyone," said Martha. The doors opened, and she walked briskly from the car. Kathryn followed her into a hallway, which contained as many closed doors as the one on the sixth floor. The two women walked to the far end, and Martha fished a ring of big keys from her pocket. She fit one into the lock and opened the door.

Kathryn expected to step into a hollow place with books stacked up on all sides, but instead they were confronted by another door, this one metal, thick, and much more imposing. Martha touched the wall, and a keypad appeared. The librarian moved her fingers rapidly over the keys, as fast as any Union technician. The door popped open with a *wuff* of cool, dry air.

"I love this door," said Martha. "I know better, but it seems magical to me. I still expect to find fabulous things on the other side—dragons, wizards, dinosaur skeletons, and mummies. But instead we just have books, a few odds and ends. Come in."

The vault was large, twenty feet long and wide, perhaps twelve feet high. But no books were piled on the floor. Instead the walls were lined with rows of drawers, stacked eight high. "The delicate stuff is in there," said Martha. "So we can't harm it with our damp breath. Some of it is nine hundred years old. We even have the diary of Tsar Peter's son, Tsar Nicholas. No one can touch it anymore. Thank goodness there are copies."

"The diaries must be fascinating," said Kathryn. "I've read Emily Kizheh's."

"Ah." Martha crossed her arms and leaned against the drawers. "Brilliant woman. She is my best argument when people tell me women don't make good police officers. You women who come down here in your danger suits cause quite an uproar, you know. You have the nerve to think you're as good as men at the jobs you do."

"We have to," said Kathryn. "If we're going to do them right."

"That's how I look at it," said Martha. "The last person who held my job was a man. I had to do a lot of fast talking. If I had just waited for them to hand me the job I'd still be working at the information desk. A lot of people are old-fashioned, but our young people are changing. They're beginning to see possibilities we old folks couldn't. I have a young friend who talks about you Star People all the time. I think one day he may even work on Archangel Station."

"Is his name Peter?"

Martha quirked an eyebrow. "You've met him? I shouldn't be surprised. He always talks about Star Men."

"I was hoping to run into him today," said Kathryn.

"Why are you looking for him?" asked Martha. She had a straightforward, friendly approach to conversation, but it did not escape Kathryn that the librarian had a knack for getting people to tell her things.

She thought it best to tell the truth. "I was hoping I might convince him to become an ESA."

"Really?" Martha seemed more pleased than surprised. "He's such a perceptive boy. I confess, at times I forget he's a child. Has he accepted your offer?"

"I haven't had a chance to make it yet," confessed Kathryn.

"I see." Martha's expression softened. "He doesn't accept help very readily. The only thing I've been able to give him is lunch. And information. He gobbles both up greedily." She sighed. "So, ESA Kathryn, now he's evading you, yes?"

"Yes."

"I'm sure you frighten him terribly. After all, the stars are his heart's desire. But they were so much more alluring when he thought he couldn't reach them."

"It's scary to get what you really want," said Kathryn. "But it's worth the pain, don't you think?"

Martha quirked one corner of her mouth. "You have me there. But what now, ESA? Can't you find him with your x-ray vision?"

"No," said Kathryn. "I didn't scan his genetic code or even make a profile of his characteristics that I could use as a guideline for a search. I didn't know it would be that hard to find him again. And besides, I can't chase him down. That would just make him run harder."

"Sooner or later he'll come back here," said Martha. "This is his favorite library."

"Are you willing to give him a message?"

"We look after him, you know," said Martha. "His friends." Her expression wasn't any less friendly, but Kathryn knew she was being warned.

"I want to offer him a possible future," she said. "But I won't doll it up for him. I won't try to dazzle him with fancy tricks. I won't even promise him he can be an ESA, because I'm not sure of that. But he'll get something out of it, Martha, even if it's just a free education and a safe place to sleep at night."

"You won't be the first to offer that," warned Martha.

Kathryn would have been discouraged to hear that, if her own childhood hadn't been so odd. She wasn't happy to give up her freedom either. She only did it when she realized she would be gaining more than she gave up. "I'll try to convince him," she said. "If I can't, I'll leave him alone."

"I'll tell him so," promised Martha. She stood up and went to the door. Kathryn followed her into the hall.

As Martha was keying the locking code in, Kathryn asked, "Has Peter been down here?"

"Oh yes," said Martha, then winked. "He's even been to the next level down. I'll show you that some other day. Might even be dinosaur bones and mummies down there." She winked again, and led Kathryn back to the elevator.

When Serina returned to her life in the great house, she was greeted by a silence so profound, she could almost believe that she had become as invisible as any shrouded woman should. It was not a cold silence, or even an ominous one; it was merely pervasive. It seemed indicative of things to come.

But she knew it was not. Eventually it must be sundered, and she didn't have to wait long for the din to begin.

One day as she turned on the landing to mount the next set of steps to her floor, Aunt Alexis suddenly descended to step directly into her path. She thrust a sheath of papers under Serina's nose. Serina took a step back.

Alexis seemed to tower in her stiff, obsessively stylish dress, which must have been secured by at least one thousand buttons, every single one of them fastened tight.

"I have filed criminal charges against you," she said. "We shall also be serving you with a court summons for our civil suit on behalf of Ivan Sergeivich Khabalov. The money in your trust funds shall be frozen. If you set foot outside this house, even to stroll in the garden, you shall be arrested and imprisoned."

When she realized Serina would not take the papers from her, Alexis let them fall to the floor.

"You shall be forced to live on your own floor," Alexis said triumphantly, "as you should have done from the very beginning. You were afforded an extraordinary freedom, but you have abused it, and so it has been taken away from you."

Serina was fascinated. She had never seen Alexis look so happy, so . . . so energetic.

"Look at you!" Alexis snapped. "You stand there as if you have rights! You have no shame and no sense, Serina. You were a fool to meddle in Ivan's private family matters. And what were you thinking when you traveled up to Archangel? It's the disease—it has addled your brain. You should stay home where people know they have to tolerate you. How will you be treated by strangers?"

"With more courtesy than I have ever received from you," replied Serina. But she could see her point was lost on Alexis, whose strict parameters of the known universe would never be stretched by Star Men or anyone else.

"You think your parents can protect you," said Alexis. "This is true only within the boundaries of this house. If you don't believe me, step outside and see! I dare you to do so! Your impudence will evaporate when it is exposed to the light of day."

"I see," Serina said calmly. "Then I must presume it is no longer my duty to select a suitable husband for Anastasia."

Alexis's laugh was more of a bark. "I would never have taken your suggestions seriously. You are mad with jealousy. You would have picked the worst possible man in a feeble attempt to ruin Anastasia's life. I merely wished to see what you would do, but you could not even manage that!"

"Alas," said Serina, "I have wasted my time, but I shall do so no longer."

"Why not waste it?" Alexis asked gleefully. "You shall have so much of it now, whether you spend it locked in your room or in a jail cell for the rest of your days—unless you continue to behave unwisely, in which case you will have very few of those left."

"Don't count my days too quickly," said Serina.

Alexis struck like a viper, aiming a blow at Serina's head. Serina deflected it by striking the nerve on the inside of Alexis's forearm. She took another quick step backward, out of reach. Her aunt swayed as if she would topple like a tree, but managed to steady herself, her eyes wide.

"Animal," she hissed. "Do not touch me."

"Keep your distance," warned Serina. "I do not wish to engage in a wrestling match with you, but I will not tolerate physical abuse."

"You *dare.*" Alexis looked ready to go up in flames. She seemed unable to believe that Serina was not groveling or begging for mercy. Nothing could have caused Serina to do that, but she did understand that she must do one thing to avoid further violence. She moved out of the way, giving her aunt access to an escape route. Alexis grinned as if she had won an important victory.

"Don't try to apologize," she warned, her eyes still wide. "I will never accept it."

"I offer none," said Serina.

"When the tsar hears of your behavior, he will send officers right into this house. Don't doubt it."

Ah, so he has not *heard, and you do not understand how much he despises Ivan Khabalov,* thought Serina. "I will pray then," she said. "That, at least, shall always be my right."

Alexis gave a snort of disgust and turned on her heel, scattering the papers with her tightly booted feet. She came so close to Serina as she brushed past, another person would have flinched away. But Serina had seen Anastasia execute the same maneuver many times. She did not react. Instead she merely watched Alexis march down the stairs and out of sight.

She stood for several moments, listening to the slow beating of her own heart. She contemplated the concept of violence. It had never been theoretical to her, though she had spent her life in the great house, sheltered by wealth if not by privilege. Children on Belarus learned of the Civil and Enemy Wars almost before they learned to speak. At least, human children did—Serina would not venture to guess what Enemy children learned first. Ayat-ko never spoke of such things. Her role in life was to ask Serina cruel and useful questions. She performed that task brilliantly.

When she tries to kill you, how will you respond?

Something had emboldened Alexis. Serina supposed she might have simply been provoked past endurance. Ivan Khabalov was an extremely hot-button topic, and Serina had trespassed into territory her aunt must certainly see as sacred. Her rage was no surprise. But her uncertainty was unsettling.

Let us say that she strikes at you through the courts.

Now that Serina was facing that eventuality, she wondered if it were really true that she had absolutely no legal options. Over the years she had researched the problem, and certain contradictions might be argued.

The greatest contradiction of Belarusian law was that the original Bill of Rights had never been repealed. Several of the rights had simply been *amended* to death. A document that had once been a shining example of clarity had been rendered into a cumbersome, overwrought morass of mind-numbing rules and exceptions.

The amendment that purported to govern the rights of shrouded women appeared to be simple on the surface. It stated that each shrouded woman must have a guardian or guardians appointed who had power of attorney over all the legal affairs of that shrouded woman. That was all it said, but for centuries people had freely interpreted what it *implied.* Serina had been confronted with the results of those interpretations when she was seven years old, and she had asked her mother, *How shall I change their minds?*

She had thought she might accomplish her goal by championing other shrouded women. But it was inevitable that she must finally become her own champion. According to the law, this could not be accomplished without the consent of her parents.

She looked up the stairs to her own floor. It was possible that Alexis was making empty threats. Serina could ignore her and continue to do precisely what she had always done. If she was wrong, she would know it soon enough. There would be no need to make a decision, except to choose a lawyer if it came to that. In the eyes of the court, she was a helpless child.

She descended the stairs to her mother's floor. It was time to become an adult.

Serina had never seen Galena's private rooms. She wondered if even her father had. When Galena was sequestered therein, no one dared intrude.

But Galena was not in her inner sanctum. Serina found her mother in her formal sitting room, a pleasant, intimate place filled with cut flowers and light from windows that faced south, the warmest side of the house. In there, even the lowliest maid might request an audience, though truth to tell, Galena and her serving staff had an exceptionally good rapport, possibly even better than Galena had with her own family.

Galena sat at the small, beautifully set table in one corner of the room, near a window. Sunlight illuminated her lovely profile. Her whole life, Serina had been haunted by that profile, so cool and perfect, seemingly untouched by time and sorrow. Galena's chin was firm, her throat smooth, her brow unfurrowed. Serina had often overheard others speak wonderingly about Galena's youthful appearance and graceful demeanor, as if they did not realize that her exterior could only be so firm if it were supported from within by iron.

"I wondered when you would come," said Galena without looking at her.

Serina felt as if an icy hand had touched the back of her neck, and she suddenly realized that her hopes might be dashed. Yet she felt compelled to sit in the chair her mother offered and present her case. She waited until Galena had poured herself a cup of tea, a service she never allowed others to perform for her. Serina could not accept tea herself, or one of the cakes, since she would have to remove her veil in order to enjoy them.

"Aunt Alexis confronted me on the staircase," she said when Galena had replaced the teapot on its stand. "She tried to serve legal papers."

"Everything she told you is true," said Galena. "At least, everything regarding your legal status."

"Then I shall be imprisoned if I leave this house."

"You will if they catch you." Galena placed one lump of sugar in her tea and followed it with a dollop of cream. She stirred it thoroughly, her face no less serene than it had ever been. "Your fate from that point would depend upon those who made the arrest. If by friendly forces, then you would be taken to your uncle, the tsar, who would be obliged to confine you within his palace. You would be comfortable, but still essentially a prisoner."

The chill at the back of Serina's neck began to spread, but she considered the information calmly. "And if I am detained by unfriendly forces, my safety will be in jeopardy."

"They may kill you," said Galena. "Or beat you so mercilessly that you will lose your senses and cease to be a threat to them."

"A third choice has occurred to me."

Galena looked at her with an expression almost like hope.

"I might turn myself in," said Serina.

Galena's expression did not seem to change, but Serina sensed that hint of hope had disappeared. "And throw yourself on the mercy of the court," she said.

"And fight the charges," said Serina.

Galena regarded her steadily, and Serina realized that she had not surprised her mother. "Several unfair traditions would be challenged by your case," she said.

"The time is right for such a challenge," said Serina. "I'm certain of it, though I may lose the case—"

"There will be no case," Galena interrupted her just as she was about to rush into a long list of possibilities and examples. "There will be no trial."

Serina was struck dumb. Her mother seemed neither angry nor sad by what she had just said; Serina still could not quite define what she saw in her eyes.

"Alexis was wrong about that part," said Galena. "You will never be tried in court."

Serina could not accept that. "The amendment is not carved in stone," she argued. "And I am no peasant woman. I am of noble birth. I can afford—"

"You think because you have Kurakin blood, you have the financial and social resources to turn Belarusian society upside down," Galena interrupted again. "And you would be right, except that you do *not* have Kurakin blood. And neither do I. We are not Kurakins."

Serina did not comprehend at first. The statement was too matter-of-fact. But Galena did not leave her in the dark for long. She took a small sip of her tea, the sunlight dappling her face and cream silk dress as the wind blew a blossom-laden branch outside the window. "They are dead," she said. "Every last one of them. We stole their name."

And the rock foundation on which Serina had stood all her life suddenly shifted.

"We are peasants, your uncle and I." Galena took a longer sip of her tea, her manners perfect, her posture erect. "Our parents were farmers in the fields beyond Kargasok. It is a wild place, two hundred miles from the Mongolian border. There are few opportunities there. Your uncle joined the army to escape the poverty. It is common for peasant boys to do so, and it is also common for them to downplay their family names; he enrolled as Gyorgy Andreivich. This was a fortunate decision, as you shall learn.

"For me, the choices were more narrow. I could marry

young and live the life my mother had. She was an old woman by the time she was thirty. But she had other plans for me. Because I was attractive, she knew I might become a waiting girl at the great house of Boyar Kurakin."

The name jarred Serina. She had always considered it to be part of her own, and she still could not quite believe what she was hearing.

"If I did well there," continued Galena, "we hoped that one day I might become a lady-in-waiting. At the very least, my mother thought I would have better marriage prospects. So I went, dreaming great dreams. But those dreams were quickly dashed."

She said this without a trace of sorrow. Sipping from her teacup, she continued as if she were talking about the weather.

"The Lady Kurakin was renowned for her great beauty. Less known was her propensity for jealousy. I went to work in the house, dazzled by its magnificence, determined to do a good job. I did well until the lady caught a glimpse of me. She did to me what she had already done to dozens of other girls. She thought that because I was pretty, I must also be a whore, and she knew I must be kept out of sight of the men of the house. I was taken out of the maids' dormitory in the servants' quarters and exiled to a solitary loft in the barn. And so it was that I entered a life of relentless drudgery, driven by the cruel whims of the beautiful Lady Kurakin."

The story had the rhythm of a fairy tale, much like the one Serina had told herself about the mirror, years ago. Once that illusion had been dashed, she had ceased to think that she had anything in common with storybook heroines. Apparently it was Galena who was really Cinderella.

"I was forced to work from the crack of dawn and far into the night," said Galena. "I often got no more than a few hours' sleep. The older maids told me I must pray for strength, because escape from the house was impossible. Disgrace would haunt my family for generations. I would be dragged back to the great house as a thrall as punishment for breaking my contract. My parents had been paid, and the money was already spent. The other girls had been through the same thing before me. They said eventually Lady Kurakin would forget me.

"So I endured until I became little more than a sleepwalker. I didn't pray—I have never been inclined to beg for God's mercy. I tried to wait the lady out, knowing that someday another poor girl would be brought into her service, and it would be someone else's turn to suffer."

Galena paused to pour more tea, and Serina was suddenly transfixed by the sight of the pot. It was a Kurakin family heirloom, as were the cups, the linen, the paintings, the furniture in Galena's sitting room. "What happened to them?" she asked softly.

"It was a remote part of our country," said Galena. "In those days military help was often days away. Kurakin had some troops of his own, but most of them had been appropriated to fight Enemy raiders in Molchanovo, almost a hundred miles away. Boyar Kurakin and his sons did not go with them. Another stroke of providence." She put one lump of sugar in her tea and stirred it with Kurakin silver.

"A few days after the troops departed," she continued. "Kunum-ko descended upon us with his raiders."

"Kunum-ko?" Serina could not recall having ever heard the name.

"Ayat-ko's brother."

Serina's mouth went dry.

"I woke to the screams," said Galena, "from my sleeping mat in the loft of the barn. I watched the destruction through a crack in the rafters. It went on all day and into the night. The screams never stopped for an instant, but occasionally they became something more: sobs, moans, pleas for mercy. I pitied the other maids, who had sneaked me bits of food and comfort when they could. I could pick out their voices from the others. I wept a little, but my tears dried like water in the desert. My heart became as hard as stone. I kept quiet and stayed hidden.

"Eventually they found me. By then, I had heard the drawn-out deaths of dozens of people. I wondered if it would take me as long to die. I was taken directly to Kunum-ko, who was amusing himself with the slow flaying of a woman. I looked closer at his victim and recognized the once-beautiful Lady Kurakin."

Serina studied her mother's perfect profile. She showed no outward sign of her trauma, not even a trace of malice for the lady who had tormented her. Her calm tone was riveting.

"Kunum-ko spoke to me," said Galena. "His manners were pleasant. He said, 'She tried to seduce me,' meaning Lady Kurakin. 'So many of you try to do that,' he said.

" 'I will spare you that dishonor,' I replied. After more than a year in the Kurakin household, I had learned the speech of noblewomen, and the carriage. For some reason, I felt it necessary to affect both in my last hours.

" 'What is your position is this household?' he asked. I told him I was a maid. 'Do you hate your mistress?' he asked. And I told him that I did, though at the moment I felt nothing more for her than pity. 'Sit,' he offered. 'Enjoy her suffering.'

"At the time, I did not understand the rareness of the courtesy he was offering me. I merely sat and watched, until Lady Kurakin fainted from the pain. I felt no fear, only nausea. I was choking on so much suffering. At last I turned to him and found that he was watching me.

" 'You're not afraid,' he said. 'Her pain will be yours soon.'

"I don't know what guided me then. I suppose it was the fact that my situation was hopeless, and since that was the case I felt willing to take chances. So I asked him, 'Who will be your Witness?'

" 'Ah,' he said, as if he knew precisely what I was referring to and was pleased that I had raised the subject, 'I have one in my household. What do you suggest?'

"I had no idea what to suggest. I had been referring to myself as a Witness, someone who would bear the story of his victory over the Kurakins. This is a human concept, and of no interest to Enemies. But I allowed myself a dry smile, one that attempted to match his. 'You have killed a powerful family,' I told him. 'The Kurakins. They have relatives in nearby cities, of course—people who would know them.'

" 'Undoubtedly,' he remarked, watching Lady Kurakin to see if she had regained consciousness. She had not.

"By then I knew precisely what I must do to survive. 'I could make good use of the name,' I told him.

"I think he was surprised. He seemed to forget Lady Kurakin. He was trying to understand *me* now. I had gained some ground.

" 'You could make use of it,' he said. 'But could I?'

"I spoke then of the war we had fought for a thousand years. At last I asked him, "Have you wondered if there might not be some way we could help each other, we conquered ones?'

"That was the most dangerous thing I could have said to him. I had heard the Kurakins referring to the Enemies that way many times, contemptuously. I would not know until later what the word meant to Enemies. But it was the idea that won the day. He grinned in a way I could not imitate if my life depended on it. " 'Yes,' " he said, and waited for me to outline my plan. But I needed more information. 'Tell me about your Witness," I said. And that was when I met Ayatko. That was the day I forged an alliance with the Enemies that would eventually take my brother Gyorgy right to the top—assuming he was willing to get his hands bloody. And he was. And as I found out that day, so was I.

" 'You can't become Lady Kurakin,' Kunum-ko said. 'She is right over there. Only one of you can be the lady.' I was about to reply that he was in the process of eliminating that obstacle. And then he handed me a knife. He watched to see what I would do with it.

"I did not hesitate. I did it efficiently—after all, I was born and raised a country girl. I did not hate her then. I knew I could end her suffering. Kunum-ko had removed only half the skin from her body. She would have endured far more before she died at his hands. She never regained consciousness when I cut her throat.

"When I turned to him again he was frowning. I suppose I had been too swift for his tastes. 'I will never understand you,' he said. But then he stood. And without bothering to take the knife back from me, he kissed me on the mouth. It was as passionate as any kiss I ever received from a human. But it didn't matter. Passion is a pleasure for them, but it doesn't influence them. Lady Kurakin could not seduce him. It was the wrong approach."

Galena set her cup in its saucer. "I still have the knife," she said. She turned a palm up and unbuttoned the lace cuff, exposing her wrist. Serina saw the edge of a sheath. Inside it, something glittered. Galena drew the blade and set it on the table. It was a beautiful thing, containing more edges for cutting than Serina would have thought possible. It was perfectly sharpened.

"I keep it with me always," said Galena. "To remind myself how I got here, and what I must do to stay."

Serina gazed at the knife. It shone against the white table linen, teasing her eyes with its strange lines. Galena picked it up with her strong, long-fingered hand, a hand that had once been employed for drudgery. She slipped it back into its sheath and buttoned the cuff.

"Your uncle Gyorgy was a born soldier," she said. "He rose quickly in the ranks and earned a battlefield commission. I sent him a message, and he came. He quickly saw the wisdom of my plan. It was made to look as if he had chased off the Enemy raiders. Unfortunately, most of the Kurakin family had been killed. Only two members survived, distant cousins. Gyorgy and myself." She took another long sip of tea. "There were many people who would have known we were not Kurakins," she continued. "They had to be eliminated."

"Eliminated?" Serina was astounded by the calm tone with which this word was spoken. "How? By whom?"

Galena looked directly at her, but said nothing. A moment later, a flicker of movement in a nearby doorway caught Serina's attention. Ayat-ko emerged into the sunlight, smiling.

The ice that had been slowly creeping down Serina's back took a sudden detour and circled her heart.

"It was accomplished overnight," said Galena. "There was no trace of evidence, and the killings were done human style."

"Human style . . ." echoed Serina. "But not by humans."

"We were committed then. We had to be bold and unwavering. We used our new allies to steadily climb the ladder of power. We needed them, and they needed us."

"For what?" demanded Serina. "What could they possibly need from us? Ayat-ko, why are you here now?"

Ayat-ko lost her smile. But it was Galena who answered.

"Ayat-ko is a Witness," said Galena. "A sterile female of her kind. She has lived for thousands of years. She has seen the cycles of destruction and rebirth. Now she watches us. She has kept me strong all these years, Serina; she will keep you strong too. Someday you will understand."

Someday, perhaps. But Serina could scarcely imagine the concept. For the moment there was just one thing she wanted to know.

"Mother—all of those deaths. How could you do it?"

"It is simple, my daughter. From the moment Kunum-ko attacked the Kurakins, my life was no longer mine. I understood that I lived at his whim. Yet, I am not a thrall. I make the decisions that will ensure the survival of my people, my world. He does the same. His life is also mine."

"*You,* make the decisions," said Serina.

"Yes."

"Then you are the ones who are guilty of what the Mironenkos were accused of doing."

"We are the ones."

"And Papa . . ."

"I married him to secure his complete cooperation. He

was a very useful ally from the beginning, and his bloodline really is noble, if somewhat impoverished."

Serina tried to imagine her father, with his kindly face, sitting in on the meeting in which it had been decided to kill the royal family. Her imagination failed her, and she was glad.

"And now," she said, "what of me? I have learned your secrets."

Galena spoke gently. "They are your secrets too."

Serina could not even feel foolish. Her ignorance had been too great a thing to be described with such a simple word.

"I took a chance when I allowed you to live after your birth," said Galena. "Your disfigurement is a clue of our true origins. Our ancestors came from the farms near the Cavern of the Dead Dancers. But as soon as I saw your face I knew you had a destiny. You would not be raised like your sisters to be wives for allies. You were free." Once again Galena watched her with an expression that almost hinted at hope, though no hope could be possible. "You have taken actions recently that put you in danger," she said.

"Yes," agreed Serina, accepting responsibility.

"I have raised you to take those actions," said Galena.

"I am inclined to believe that you did." Galena had never advised, never pushed. She had only cast an unrelenting light on the world and waited to see how Serina would react to it. But there had been kindnesses as well, and Serina could not help but hope there may be one more. "Will you imprison me here, now that I know the truth?"

"No," said Galena, sounding almost surprised. "But if you leave this house, and you are arrested, you may be killed. Or you may be shut away with your uncle, forever. He will not harm you, Serina, but he will not permit a trial. To do so would antagonize people who know our secret, and if they feel compelled to betray us, we will have a Civil War on our hands. So your third choice is not possible. What will you do now?"

"I don't know," said Serina. "I trust nothing I used to believe."

"Good." Galena sipped her tea. "Then I have accomplished something."

Serina could think of nothing more she wanted to ask. Somehow she gained her feet, though she could scarcely feel them under her. "Thank you, Mother," she said, and turned to leave. But then her gaze fell on Ayat-ko.

"Once," said Serina, "you asked me if I thought my own family would risk jeopardizing all they have gained for my sake."

Ayat-ko said nothing, but the Enemy woman knew precisely what Serina meant.

"The risk was in my very birth," said Serina. "And in my existence as an acknowledged member of this household. And finally, in this deadly secret my mother has shared with me. I have learned too much, Ayat-ko. But what have you learned?"

"Something," said the Enemy woman. "Perhaps someday I will tell you what. Will you be able to bear it?"

"We shall see." Serina curtsied to her mother. "Good day, Mother."

Serina spared one more glance for Ayat-ko, the Enemy in the shadows, then forced her feet to move her out the door, into the hallway with its rich, stolen tapestries and paintings, past room after room of more of the same. She ascended the stairs to her own floor and continued her journey, past the library that wasn't really hers and into the suite of rooms within which she had spent her most private hours. She closed her doors behind her and went to her boudoir.

Serina sat before a small desk, a pretty, carved dainty that any other woman might have called a vanity. She unwrapped her shroud until her face was completely bare, then drew a hand mirror from a drawer. She gazed upon her face.

She had done so many times before. It had been painful at first, but she knew if she looked long enough, she would get used to it. Long ago she had been surprised to discover things about it that held beauty. Her eyes, for instance, were sapphire blue, a rare color. Her lashes were thick and dark, her hair deep mahogany and very lustrous. Her skin was perfect, having never been touched by one ray of sunlight or speck of dirt.

The jawline on the left side of her face appeared to have a bite taken out of it. The deformity intruded into the area where several of her lower teeth should exist on the bottom, and chewing on that side was impossible. But her mouth closed properly. She was at least spared the common trait known as Botkin's Sneer. Realistically, she supposed it would not be too difficult for the Star Men to repair. And there was a time in her life when she would have longed for them to do it. But not now. Now she gazed at her face and knew it to be the only true thing in her life.

"Behold," she said softly, "a shrouded woman who thought she lived in a great house. But it is just a house of cards."

She set the mirror down again, tired of looking. Another woman would have put her face in her hands and cried, but Serina could not see the point of it. All her life she had observed the world from behind her shroud, believing that she had some power to make changes in it, if she were only patient and clever enough. She had studied the books in her library and believed herself to be the holder of secret, useful knowledge. She *might* help women regain some of their lost civil rights. She *might* be an ally to Star Men who wanted to bring Belarus into a Union that honored the Bill of Rights.

Except that she *was* a powerless fool.

Serina wrapped her face again and went to sit in the shadows, hoping that something useful might occur to her, if only she thought long enough.

Hours later, in deeper darkness, she finally wept.

Archangel Station spun around its axis, and at the center of the spin people were not content to merely float.

The Elder watched ESA Seesil play zero-g ball against

three human janitors. The humans were skillful players, but it took three of them to keep up with the Gonkha, who was twice as nimble in zero-g than she was in a gravity well. Seesil also had the advantage of being able to whack the ball with her tail. She could twist her body with feline grace, and always struck the sides of the arena with her feet and hands, using them to propel her right back into the action. She was a joy to watch.

Seesil lost the game, but she cheerfully did a gentle belly bump with her opponents, a human tradition that restored friendly feelings between temporary adversaries. Seesil didn't need the ritual. She was always conscious of the welfare of those around her. Her kind were not easily angered.

But once they were, it was best to give them considerable space. Gonkhas had other talents as well, unguessed until encounters with Enemy raiders revealed them. ESA Seesil was particularly gifted with these talents, but she was no military ESA. Thus far her talents had only been used for defense, and reaction was not always as effective as action.

"Elder!" called Seesil as she made her way down the observation gallery, which spun just enough to keep her on her feet if she didn't move too quickly. The Elder met her halfway, then returned with her to the lift. Once inside, they were able to relax as they descended to the lower levels.

<Is it seemly to call you Elder?> Seesil asked. <I always feel as if I'm calling you "Grandma," and you are not elderly at all!>

The Elder laughed. <Call me Gardener if you like; that is one of my favorite hobbies. Woovs always call each other what we're doing. Our family names are only used privately. If we don't know each other, we say, "stranger," and have several ways of doing it, some good, some bad, some entirely neutral.>

Seesil had forced her bulk as far away as she could in the lift, for the sake of courtesy. The Elder had never met a person quite so kindhearted. Once the lift let them out onto a lower deck, the Gonkha breathed a sigh of relief, unfurling her long body in a luxurious stretch. <Well,> she said, <I suppose I'll stick to Elder for the time being. Especially since I suspect you have a job for me.>

<Not at the moment,> said the Elder. <Soon you may be going down to work with Argus Fabricus.>

<He's an excellent commander,> said Seesil.

<He is. But we don't want to show our hand to these Enemies too soon. If they realize you can sense them, they may find a way to get around your perceptions, and then we won't have them if we need them in a pinch. I'm no clairvoyant, but I have a feeling the time is not quite right to send you down.>

<I'm having fun on Archangel,> said Seesil. <It's so different from living on a planet!>

<Yes,> agreed the Elder, amazed at how adaptable this ESA was. She had joined the ranks of ESAs as an adult, which was unheard of. She had adapted to the physical enhancements as if she had been born with them, trained in record time, then shipped out immediately to work with Argus Fabricus on his team. The claustrophobic conditions of space travel had not troubled her, zero-g did not disturb her, she made friends easily, and she never suffered from culture shock. <I'm glad you like it here. I'd like you to spend some time with the Belarusians who have sought medical amnesty on the station. Learn what you can about their culture. It's always better to get that sort of information from natives, rather than books. Please do not be hurt if they're afraid of you at first.>

<Some people never get over it,> said Seesil. <Isn't it amazing? People are so fascinating. But this will give me a chance to practice my diplomatic skills.>

The Elder smiled. For two thousand years, she had been trying to do just that, herself. But she wouldn't be surprised if Seesil mastered what she was still learning. Seesil might even understand Enemies—if she ever got the chance.

The corridor became more crowded as they neared the public areas. The Elder thought they might stop at one of the cafés for lunch. But someone was making a beeline for her through the crowd. He was wearing a uniform she did not recognize. It wasn't military in nature, yet he had an official air about him. He was carrying a bag over his shoulder, and held something thin and long in his hand. He waved it when he saw her and approached with a determined expression on his face.

"I'm looking for a Woov," he said, sparing not a glance for ESA Seesil. "I have a special delivery letter."

"A *letter?*" asked the Elder, bemused. She looked at the object in his hand. It was made of paper. A name was written on it and a location: Archangel Station. The name was hers. "I am the addressee," she said, and showed him her identification.

He handed her the envelope. "Sign here?"

She obliged.

"Thank you," he said, and tipped his hat. He turned and walked away. She wondered if he had another delivery to make on Archangel, or if hers had been the only one. That people still used such an archaic mode of communication between the stars was highly eccentric.

That someone who did so also knew her family name and her current location, was something else again. She tore open the envelope and read the letter. Then she read it again. Finally she tucked it away and gave Seesil her attention. <Well,> she said, <my dear child, let us get something to eat. I am famished.>

The ESA was dying of curiosity, but she did not ask the Elder about the letter. <You will be briefed about this matter soon,> the Elder assured her. <But there is not much to tell at this stage, save that I have just received news about a new enemy who is actually an old enemy.>

<Enemies . . .> The Gonkha sighed. <New ones, old ones—why do they always outnumber friends?>

The Elder could have given her an answer. But it was not a happy one, so she refrained.

Serina wasn't sure what day it was when morning light filtered into her bedroom. She washed her face and wrapped it as always. Several times she swayed on her feet, seeing strange colors even through the blackness of her shroud. Poor sleep and poorer nutrition were taking their toll. She smelled food. Someone had laid a buffet on the table in her morning room. It was a feast. There was far more than she could stand to eat. She sipped tea, promised herself she would come back and eat soon, but first she had to sort out her thoughts.

Serina paced the hallways, listening. The great house creaked and cracked from time to time, and occasionally she heard the distant voices of staff and family. She strained to gather their meaning, but it always eluded her. This filled her with dismay, because if she did not find understanding in her surroundings her mind would turn in on itself again, and she would go round and round. Each time she did it was harder to find her way out again. She had to find something else to do.

Serina descended the stairs. She passed her mother's floor without stopping—she did not want to speak to Galena again. Galena was locked in a deadly embrace with Ayat-ko's brother. If Serina disturbed the balance, surely death would rain down on Belarus again. Only the night before, Serina had dreamed of wolves who poured into the streets of Moscow in endless rivers. Their eyes had black stars in their centers. Serina watched them from her bedroom window as they leaped over the hedges around the garden and streamed into the great house through the front door. Soon she would hear them in her own room, running up behind her, but she didn't turn to look. Instead she watched the black Veil creep across the stars.

Morning waned while she paced the endless hallways. Voices came and went, seeming more agitated today. When noon passed, she smelled lunch but could not find the place it was being served. Still she would not venture onto her mother's floor, and she was tired of seeking answers in her own rooms. That was where her mind was most likely to trap her. She descended another flight of steps and heard shrill, cruel laughter.

Anastasia.

The laughter rose and fell, punctuated by half-audible shouts, the low murmur of a voice trying to reason. Bumps and thuds followed in rapid succession, and Serina imagined the turmoil in Anastasia's rooms. Now that Serina understood that the foundation of the great house was built upon sand instead of stone, Anastasia's existence made more sense to her. She was a harpy, sent by the gods to remind the Kurakins that they had stolen their name.

And suddenly the harpy shrieked out into the hallway, just around the corner. When she saw Serina she would extend her talons and aim for her throat.

Serina balled her fists, ready to fight. For a moment she was poised between rage and reason. But then a small voice whispered at the back of her mind. *Come. What is the point? Let it happen. Let it be.* She relaxed her hands and drew herself tall.

Instead, the shrill laugh fled, like a bird flying through an open window and out into the world. Serina comprehended what must have happened in a flash. She turned the corner and found a maid standing in the open door to Anastasia's rooms, looking down the now-empty corridor. The maid turned to her, started.

"Duchess . . ." the maid said softly.

"Don't call me that," Serina chided. "I'm Serina, that's all."

"Yes, ma'am," came the worried reply.

"I can see that you have news. Is Anastasia to be married? At last she shall be free of our influence?"

"By God's mercy," agreed the maid.

"Mercy to us, perhaps," said Serina. "And who is her fiancé, Irina?"

"He's here to see you, ma'am. I was trying to find you and tell you. I thought you might be with Anastasia. General Dmitri Brusilov is here. We told him you've been ill, but he insists—"

"Send him to me. I'll see him," said Serina. She saw no particular reason not to. She saw no particular reason for anything at the moment. "I'll speak to him in the garden room. It's warm in there this time of day. Just give me a head start, will you?"

"Ma'am—" Irina touched her hand. "Please—"

"It's all right," Serina said gently. "I haven't lost my senses. I'll talk to him and then send him away. We'll have peace when she goes. For a while, anyway. Spring is just around the corner. Think how lovely it will be in the garden. Go on."

Serina made her way to the garden room. It was a long journey. The house seemed to grow larger with each passing hour. Once or twice she had to stop and wait for the dizziness to pass. She really should have eaten a proper meal in the morning—and the night before, as well. When at last she entered the big, brightly lit garden room her spirits lifted. False spring reigned in there. The window seat she loved so dearly was bathed in afternoon sunshine. She arranged herself there, her spine erect, and waited for Dmitri Brusilov.

Moments later, Irina ushered him into the room. Serina did not rise to greet him, so he crossed the room without a word. As she watched him she was oddly reminded of Argus, who was also a man who commanded others. But the similarity ended there.

Dmitri sat in the chair opposite her window seat and waited for her to offer tea or brandy. She did neither. She was done with everything that had anchored her to the old existence. When Dmitri realized no courtesies would be forthcoming, he seemed oddly pleased.

"I didn't come to gloat, Serina," he said, his voice warm and his gaze cool.

"It didn't occur to me that you would."

The chill deepened, yet his expression remained courteous, leaving Serina no doubt how he would wield power once he had purchased it through his forthcoming marriage. "I'm a military man," he said, "and plainspoken. I merely wished to pay my respects."

"Because it is no longer necessary for you to plead your case."

He smiled thinly. He was not a handsome man, but he possessed a sort of rugged attractiveness, a product of supreme self-confidence. "You were a formidable obstacle, I admit. But now that the matter is out of your hands, we need not be enemies."

"It is not I who determines such things," said Serina.

He studied her openly. "Odd. You appear to be the same woman you always were. Thinner, perhaps. I hope you're eating properly."

"Why should you?"

"Come, we have sparred so expertly in the past. I should hate to think that a fine mind like yours might be dulled by starvation."

Serina's earlier dizziness was entirely gone, and she felt almost unnaturally focused. She could see Dmitri Brusilov's intentions as if she were looking at him under a microscope. "You surprise me. I thought you might have good reason to talk with me today, but I gave you too much credit. You *did* come to gloat. You waste your time with pettiness. The fine words you speak do not hide the fact that you hate me. And worse, you remember every slight, real or imagined, every time your will has been thwarted."

"Be careful," he said softly. "And be courteous, Serina. What little power you once held over me is gone."

"I don't need it," said Serina. "I don't miss it. That is what you have failed to comprehend." She stood. "I won't damage your ego any further by dismissing you. Stay here as long as you please. Enjoy the view. There's port in that bottle on the buffet table if you want it. Good day."

Serina went calmly to the door, slightly dizzy again with the effort. He had made one good point—she must eat soon or become ill.

"Serina," he called.

She stopped with her hand on the doorknob.

"Fortunes change so quickly in these high circles," he said as quietly as if she were still sitting across from him. His voice was gentle, reasonable, and if she had never met him face-to-face she might have been swayed by it. "The great may fall overnight. A simple soldier like me may assume a high position—recently vacated."

Serina almost laughed. "What happened to your plain talk, Dmitri?"

"I'm inclined to be lenient with you. You are a woman who has been relieved of all choices. Yet there may still be opportunities for you. I hope you won't forsake them."

"I don't believe I want to know what you're talking about."

"I'll put it as simply as possible then," he said. "Where do you wish to stand when the chips fall?"

"Not with you, Dmitri."

"A pity," he said. "Then you shall have your wish."

"How gracious of you," she said.

"You have no idea."

Serina declined to argue any further. She went out and

closed the door behind her. She did not stop to think about what he may have meant. She was growing more light-headed by the moment. She already knew what she needed to know. Her world was closing in around her. It grew smaller every day. She would not be the least surprised if it shrank to the size of a prison cell.

Or a grave.

Still, she would not pray for guidance or salvation. If God were inclined to grant those things to her, he would do it. And she wasn't afraid now. Dmitri had achieved exactly the opposite of what he intended. Instead she was restless. She wandered the long halls, looking at the paintings and tapestries. The creatures depicted there seemed to look back with lively interest, as if waiting for her to guess what they already knew.

Keep looking. You're almost there. Just around the corner, quickly! Do you see?

Gaslight flickered, making the painted and woven scenes seem to come to life. Even the furniture seemed to move, clawed feet and carved feathers and talons flexing and stretching as if they had merely been asleep up until that moment. Serina was mildly pleased. She almost felt like a girl again. Memories came back to her of a night many years before, and the search for a magic mirror. Before she knew it she was at the foot of the stairs outside her mother's suite, looking up, caught between the urge to go further and the desire simply to return to her own rooms.

"Serina . . ."

It was William's voice. He must be standing in the shadows at the top of the stairs.

"William?" she called softly, climbing three steps. But in the semidarkness her shroud made it difficult to see anything more than a few feet ahead of her.

"Here," he called back.

"Why are you here? You mustn't risk it, William."

"I'm a grown man. I'm willing to take some chances for a friend. Can you see me?"

"Barely." She climbed toward the shadowy figure, who descended to meet her. In another moment, his warm, calloused hand grasped hers.

"Someone is in trouble," he said. "A shrouded woman. Someone wants to speak with you on the unused floor. Will you come?"

"I will, for all the good it will do," she said.

He led her to the top of the stairs. As they moved into deeper darkness, Serina traveled back in time again. She let her hand brush against the wall and counted steps, but of course they were wrong, because now she was a grown woman.

"You are too thin," William said worriedly.

"How long has it been since we last spoke?" she wondered.

"Almost a month. I have been worried, Serina. You haven't even come into the garden. My wife wanted to make you some chicken soup, but I didn't know how to get it to you. Now I wish I had brought it. I will never forgive myself."

"You're too kind," Serina said, suddenly close to tears. "I have brought trouble to all who sought to help me."

"Only to yourself, because you did what was right. That is not a common practice among the Kurakins."

If only you knew, thought Serina. *We're even worse than you suspect.*

He stopped suddenly, before Serina was done counting. He opened a door, and light spilled over them. Serina looked into a room she had not seen for twenty-four years. And a very odd thing occurred to her. William knew what had happened to her in that room. How he knew, she could not imagine, but he did. And for some reason her had brought her there again. She stepped over the threshold and looked for the mirror through the open door. It wasn't there. Instead, she saw a shrouded woman in a chair. The woman stood as soon as William and Serina entered.

"How may I help you?" Serina asked as kindly as she could.

"It is not I who need help," said the woman. She began to unwind her shroud. Serina watched, baffled, waiting to see what malformation would be exposed. Layer after layer was unwound, until the last strip was gone, revealing a perfectly formed face. The girl had black hair, brown eyes, perfect teeth. "They fixed my face," she said. "Up on Archangel."

"Maria!" cried Serina. "How wonderful!" She examined Maria with wonder. She could not find a trace of the disfigurement or the surgery that had corrected it.

"I attend school now," said Maria. "My mother taught me my alphabet, and to read a little—in secret. The Star Men are teaching me so much more! Literature and music, math, science, history! This week I filed the papers to become a Union citizen. I will be able to do what I want with my life—all because of your efforts, Duchess."

"Don't call me that. Serina is my name. We are sisters, you and I."

Maria nodded, but tears came to her eyes. "That is why it pains me to see you so frail. I have come to beg you to join me in sanctuary. Sisters shouldn't live so far apart."

Serina gave William a long, hard stare, but he stood tall under the appraisal. "I know a shrouded woman who needs help," he said.

"How much do you know, William?" Her voice sounded much harsher than she intended, but he was not intimidated.

"I know Duchess Alexandria would be happy to see you dead. Maria's father, Ivan, is her close ally. I know that your freedom has been curtailed and that you haven't been eating properly. The writing is on the wall, Serina. So let me ask *you* something. If you were free to do whatever you wished with your life, what would you do?"

Serina could not even begin to list the things she would do, so overwhelmed was she by the attempt. But then an answer occurred to her that was so simple it made her laugh. "I would sit down and eat a good supper," she said. "But

I wouldn't eat it here. Maria—how is the food on Archangel?"

Maria grinned. "Excellent! They bring up the meat and produce on the shuttles daily. They have a good supply of caviar."

"You'll make my head spin," said Serina. "Well, then, William—I suppose I'd better pack a bag."

"Do it quickly," he warned. "News has a habit of traveling fast around here. We have to make a run for it, Serina."

Salima Sazonova sat in her chair at the end of the hall in her husband's bar, just as she always did that time of day. She was not surprised when the phone rang, though it did that no more than two or three times a week. She picked up the receiver on the first ring. "Speaking," she said, expecting an operator.

"I want Ivan Sergeivich Khabalov," snapped the imperious woman on the other end.

Salima had not heard the voice very often, but she knew enough to keep her tone deferential. Duchess Alexandria was well-known for her heavy-handed treatment of servants who failed. "He is not here tonight—" she began.

"This is an emergency!" shrilled Alexandria.

"I will send a runner," Salima hastened to assure her. "He'll get the message."

"Tell him Serina Kurakin-Scriabin is trying to flee Moscow. I suspect she will head for the Gorky Park Clinic. He must intercept her! Tell him to do as he sees fit. The Star Men will have no jurisdiction over him this time!"

"Understood," said Salima.

Alexandria abruptly hung up and Salima hurried to the kitchen, where her runners waited. She seized the fastest by his elbow and pulled him into the relative privacy of the alley. "Your very life depends on this," she whispered, and gave him the message.

He nodded curtly and raced off. She watched him until he had disappeared around the corner. He was a smart kid, the oldest and most streetwise of the bunch. She didn't have to tell him there would be a bonus if he was successful. She also didn't have to tell him what Ivan might do to them both if he failed. The runner would exhaust every possibility before giving up.

It wasn't until Salima had returned to her chair by the phone again that she thought about what might happen to Serina Kurakin-Scriabin. It was a pity. Serina had a reputation for helping people in need, and she dared to challenge the traditional role of women—especially of shrouded women. Those traditions were unjust. But Salima had survived by going around the rules, not by bucking them. And Ivan Sergeivich had never been a man to cross, but lately . . .

Lately he scared her. And it took a lot to frighten Salima. It took every ounce of self-control she had to sit still by the phone instead of sticking her head out the door to see if the boy had returned.

And then the phone rang again. This was going to be an eventful night. She picked up the receiver. "Speaking," she said.

"This is Ivan Sergeivich Khabalov."

Ice went up her spine, but she quickly told him of the message.

"I know," he said. "Now I have a message for you, Salima. I need men to meet me on Danilovsky Street. You know who I mean. Many of them are probably in your tavern now. Send runners for the rest. Tell them to bring clubs."

"Understood," said Salima, feeling sick to her stomach.

But she obeyed. What else could she do? It was a hard world. She hoped she might live in it a little longer.

"You!" she told the boys in the kitchen. "Your lives depend on this . . ."

Serina discovered that there was very little in her rooms that she wanted to take with her. But as they carried her meager bags past the library, she was suddenly frozen with indecision. "Oh, William—which books? I can only take a few."

The three of them stood on the threshold, peering into the room that had been her universe. She had hoped never to finish exploring it.

"Serina," chided William, "we can't pack up your library."

"It contains the personal journals of people who shaped our government for the past thousand years," she said, fearing even to step into the library, for it would surely snare her. "Books of philosophy, medicine, all of the sciences, even those we have forgotten . . ."

"There are wonderful libraries on Archangel," promised Maria.

Serina had no doubt of it, but her library was unique. It was the heart of her world and she was forsaking it.

"I'll look after your library, Serina."

Galena stood at the far end of the hall. Serina was not even startled. She gazed at her mother's regal face and was comforted.

"Rest assured," said Galena, "no harm shall ever come to your collection. If possible, you will see it again someday."

"Thank you, Mother."

"William," said Galena, "I have made certain your wagon will have safe passage off the estate. I added a few things to your baggage. Keep my daughter safe."

"Always," said William.

"Good-bye, Serina." As always, Galena's expression was calm, her brow smooth. "Until we meet again. I won't wish you luck—I know you shall make your own."

A great weight seemed to lift from Serina's shoulders. She gazed a moment longer at her mother's face. For years she had tried to find some trace of herself in it. But their kinship was hidden under the surface.

"Go," said Galena. "Time is short." She turned away, sparing Serina the necessity of doing so first. With William's support on one side and Maria's on the other, Serina fled.

* * *

They saw no one as they descended the stairs to the garden door. Serina felt another pang as they ran through the arbor next to the door. Lamplight shone on the snow, and she saw red berries peeking through. Never again would she sit in the garden on the longest night of the year and feel the slow, cold beat of the heart of the world.

But regret was eclipsed by a growing sense of urgency, and she applied all of her remaining strength to keeping up with the others. They fled through the garden and across the courtyard outside the stables, then around the servants' quarters. A wagon stood waiting, but it wasn't empty.

William's young son and daughter called out from the wagon when they saw their father coming. Veronika shushed them and tucked them under the tarp that hid what few worldly goods she and William owned.

Serina gripped his elbow. "Your family—"

"We must flee with you."

"Why, William? What has happened?"

"You recall I was left alone with Ivan Khabalov after you rescued Maria. He made some very specific—*promises.* Veronika and I are servants. We do not receive the same protection under the law that Kurakins and Scriabins can expect."

"Some men came when you were gone," Veronika told William. "And they gave me this." She pulled a leather wallet out of her coat pocket and whispered, "It's full of money."

"Your mother's doing, I hope." William added Serina's bags to the load and helped her onto the front seat. "And not some ploy to make us look like thieves." He helped Maria onto the rear seat beside Veronika. "Hold on tight ladies—we're off."

William gave the reins a light tug, starting the horses off on a trot.

"Go fast, Papa!" came the muffled voice of William's son. "It's fun!"

Serina wished she could feel as excited as the boy. Away

from the brightly lit house she could not see through the shroud. She did not care to go to her fate blindfolded. She began to unwrap her head.

"I wouldn't do that yet," called William over the clatter of hooves.

"Just the part over my eyes," she called back. No one will see it unless they look close. I need to see. I'm a burden this way!"

She uncovered her eyes and then rewrapped, leaving herself a thin gap through which she could see. She had done it many times before in the privacy of the garden so she could enjoy the colors and so her eyes would not be crippled by lack of exposure to light. But she had never left that sanctuary without one layer of gauze over her eyes. The horses picked up their pace until they were practically flying down the lane, and Serina felt exhilarated, focused again without weakness or dizziness. *Danger sharpens the wits,* she could remember her mother saying.

The wagon passed through the front gate; sentries closed and locked it behind them. Serina turned in her seat for one last look at the great house. It stood with all its windows glowing, a magnificent relic of the past.

"Funny," she called to William, "I always assumed I would spend the rest of my life there."

But it was Veronika who answered. "I thought I would too, ma'am. I grew up in the servants' quarters. But we took everything that really matters with us, didn't we?" The young woman sounded close to tears.

"We did," Serina assured her. "We certainly did."

<Embassador, this is Central Security calling.>

Argus stopped composing his weekly report. <What's up?>

We have an angry mob gathering outside the Gorky Park Clinic. A lot of them are carrying clubs and torches.>

<Is the building flammable?>

<No, it's one of the colonial structures, but it wasn't built

for security. The personnel have locked themselves in. They have patients in there too.>

Remembering Serina's recent escapade, Argus asked, <Did they offer asylum to another shrouded woman?>

<They say no, but maybe someone thinks they have.>

Nesto appeared at the door, his eyes in full tactical. Argus waved, and the ESA disappeared in a blur.

<ESA Nesto is on his way,> he said. <Have the city police been informed?>

<They have, but Vasily has warned us they don't appreciate interference.>

<We have to protect our people,> said Argus.

<Agreed. But Vasily says you ought to be on the scene. You're the best guy to handle any negotiations that may be needed. How fast can you get down there?>

<Not as fast as Nesto. Fifteen minutes?>

<You're in charge, Embassador. We'll monitor the situation.>

<I'm headed out.> Argus adjusted the controls on his suit. *Now's my chance to see what this newfangled baby can really do . . .*

He had used other suits on military missions, and it took him all of ten seconds to adjust to this new suit Grigory had designed. Like Nesto, he became a blur, his movements so fast he did not even need to activate the stealth function. No one would get a close enough look at him to recognize the embassador; they would simply know that a Star Man was on an important errand. And it was good for them to see that Star Men could move so quickly to protect their own.

<I've been ordered onto the scene,> he told Nesto. The ESA acknowledged. All of this happened in less than a second. His perceptions were speeded up as well, his reactions and decisions instantaneous. He was able to go over objects if he felt it would take too long to go around them. He ran up walls, leaped gaps between roofs, outpaced a train on its tracks, making a beeline for Gorky Park.

He loved it. After mucking around day in and day out

through diplomatic mires, attending meetings that accomplished nothing except to allow officials to reaffirm their territory, restate their opinions, make the same demands; after wading through countless petitions that begged, demanded, threatened, from boyars, members of the duma, players both great and petty, secret members of the Communist, Royalist, Anarchist parties, all of whom were confident that the Star Men could be persuaded to hand over the support and technology that would enable them to accomplish their agendas—it felt so damn good to take some honest physical action.

Once inside city limits, William was obliged to slow the wagon's pace. Serina battled an alarming weakness. Her decision to seek asylum had galvanized her, but the energy she expended was sapping the last of her strength. Now it was all she could do to sit upright and keep her eyes focused on the people who thronged the sidewalks and streets.

No one seemed to be taking much notice of them, but Serina felt a pulse in the air that warned her long before they turned down the long street that housed the Gorky Park Clinic and she smelled the smoke of burning torches. The glow at the end of Danilovsky Street eclipsed the gaslamps.

"William," she said suddenly, "you must leave me here and seek shelter elsewhere."

"Out of the question."

"Your children!"

"We're going to drive straight into that crowd. They can't stop a team of six horses."

"They can shoot us as we pass—"

"Maria, Veronika, get down," he commanded. "You also, Serina."

She obeyed along with the others, pressing herself to the floorboards and thanking God that Danilovsky Street had been paved in Colonial times, so her teeth wouldn't be jostled loose. William spurred the horses into a gallop, and Serina heard curses from the street as people scattered out of his way.

She peered over the edge of the footrest and saw the crowd that waited for them right in front of the clinic.

We'll get there all right, she decided, *but how will we get inside without being torn to pieces?*

The clinic was a plain storefront with one entrance and no access to the rear of the building from the street. Serina supposed there was a network of alleys behind it, but from the mood of the crowd who milled in the street, Serina was sure the doctors inside had barricaded the place against easy entry.

"We should turn around and find another place!" she urged.

"There is no other place!" he said grimly. "The clinics are all watched!"

"We can hide!" she pleaded.

"They will drag us from any hiding place we find. I'll get you to safety, Serina. Trust me."

It was not herself she was worried about. It was the other women and the children. She and William were going to die; she was sure of that now. But she was not afraid—she felt new energy flowing into her veins.

I will surely collapse into a pile of dust, she thought calmly. *My flesh is exhausted. This must be coming from my very bones.*

"All of you!" snarled William. "When I give the word, run straight for the door! I will say ready, get set, run! Do not hesitate!"

"Yes, sir!" Serina answered with the others. She drew herself into a crouching position and made ready. But she could not resist one last glance over her shoulder at William. She saw something that sent a white-hot jolt of terror and wonder through her.

His eyes were no longer the eyes she knew. They were black orbs. They were like the eyes of an ESA.

"Ready?" he shouted.

Serina was too surprised to answer. But she tore her gaze from him and fastened it on the clinic—and the crowd of grinning thugs who blocked it.

"Get set!" commanded William, and Serina's muscles bunched under her. He had slowed the wagon, but it was still moving too fast to be stayed by the hands that tried to grasp them on either side. Someone clawed the air a mere inch from Serina's face, and she took her eyes off the goal for a second. She saw angry men holding their clubs high as they ran alongside.

Something passed them in a blur, sweeping those men aside as if they were small boats caught in the wake of a dreadnaught. Dozens of them were falling as it swept back and forth among them, then circled around the cart. Serina tried to focus on the speeding form, then realized the cart was slowing almost to a stop.

"GO!" shouted William.

Serina leaped from the cart and almost lost her footing. She quickly recovered, and seizing her skirts she dashed straight for the crowd, who closed their ranks and waited for her to get close enough for them to use their clubs on her. All of her instincts told her to run in the opposite direction. She wondered where William was. She wondered if the children had made it out of the wagon.

And then a strange creature flew past her and hovered just in front of her, matching her pace. It was roughly the size of a soccer ball. Its skin glistened, reflecting light as if it were made of mirrors. It made buzzing noises as it flew, and suddenly Serina felt a surge of hope.

That's a Star Man machine!

It was a pretty thing, but she didn't fathom its purpose until a red beam erupted from the machine and struck the crowd of thugs. When Serina could see again, the men who had blocked the doors had either been knocked flat or were running to the side. The people inside the clinic threw the doors open, cheering her and the others on.

"Run!" William called just behind her, and she was heartened to know he was so close. She put on a burst of energy, feeling the last of her reserves drain away.

And then someone had her by the waist and arm, drawing her forward like a dancing partner, helping her leap over the prostate men and sailing with her through the open door, into the waiting arms of medical personnel and patients. Serina stumbled and was steadied by her mysterious partner.

"Argus Fabricus!" she cried.

He grinned. "At your service."

Maria and Veronika were close behind her, as was William, with one child tucked under each arm. ESA Nesto and a burly orderly slammed the two outer doors together and locked them. The flying machine floated over their heads, chirping as if it were satisfied with their work.

A moment later, stones began to thud against the transparency, and Serina's relief turned to alarm.

"They will shatter the glass!" she cried.

"It's not glass," Argus said calmly. "It is a transparent alloy. Rocks won't even scratch it."

"Papa!" cried William's little girl. "That was so exciting!"

"Yes, it was," he said, his eyes still black orbs.

"Are you all right?" A doctor motioned to William. "Bring the children. Let's get out of the entry; we don't want to provoke—"

An explosion cut her short. Everyone shrank from the burst of light at the front door. In the ringing silence that followed, all eyes looked at the transparency, which was now cloudy and opaque. It seemed to tremble for a moment, then rained to the floor in a million fragments.

"What the hell was that!" Argus said.

"It was a fucking cannonball," said ESA Nesto.

As one, the group of patients and refugees began to back away from the entrance. The flying machine hovered just at the threshold, looking out into the smoky night. Argus thrust Serina behind him. William set his children down and pushed them toward their mother, who seized each by the hand. Only Serina and Maria seemed reluctant to leave, waiting just behind the Star Men.

"Get back!" warned the doctor, tugging at Serina's arm.

"Wait," she said sternly. Her gaze was locked on the threshold. A figure emerged from the smoke. The flying machine hovered a few feet in front of him, emitting a warning buzz—which he ignored. He held no club or torch, but the sight of his tall form made Serina's heart pound painfully.

Ivan Khabalov stepped into the entry alone, his black eyes alight with cold fire.

"Blasphemers," he said, his voice low and passionate. "Interlopers!"

"Move your artillery away from this building," ESA Nesto said calmly.

Ivan looked at him as if he were a worm. "You do not order me. We will take this building apart brick by brick until you give up the criminal in your midst."

"We harbor no criminal," said Argus, and Serina had never heard such iron in a voice before.

Ivan raised his chin, looking past Argus at Serina. She held his gaze fearlessly.

"The shrouded woman," said Ivan, "is the one we want. We have come to take her to prison. It is the law."

"Don't argue law with me," said Argus. "If you try to use that cannon again we'll blast it to atoms. We've already got weapons in place, the police have been notified, and you do *not* work for them."

"The *police.*" Ivan spat the word as if it were a foul taste in his mouth. "I enforce God's law. Nothing else can touch me."

Shouting came from the street. Serina heard the sounds of conflict. "The police are here now," she said. "It is you who will be arrested if you do not leave us in peace, Ivan Khabalov!"

But he did not fall back. Instead he smiled at her. Only Ayat-ko could have made the gesture look more dreadful.

"You took what was mine," he said. "Now, *you* are mine. Don't doubt it, Serina. I will have my vengeance."

Argus and William looked ready to pick Ivan up bodily and throw him outside. But it was Maria who dashed past them to confront Ivan, whose face first lost its expression, then its color.

"You dare speak of vengeance!" she cried. "Ivan Khabalov, didn't I warn you that one day heaven would send an angel to punish you?"

Serina was sure he would strike the girl down—but instead he shrank from her, his face ashen. One moment he stared at Maria as if she were a fiend from hell; the next he turned and fled, disappearing into the chaos.

"Maria—" Serina stared after Ivan, sure that he would come back any moment and break his daughter in two. But he was gone. "How did you do that?"

Maria turned from the shattered doorway, her face as pale as her father's had been. "What I just said to him?" Her voice was unnaturally calm. "She used to say that. And I look like her now. My mother. She died at his hands."

Serina wanted to go to her, but Argus held her firmly in place. "Let's all go inside," he said gently. "Our machines will keep out any more trouble. It's time to decompress."

The suggestion of rest almost made Serina lose her footing, so weary was she. But she held firm. "Yes," she agreed, "let's go in."

Before anyone could move, one more man entered the clinic. But this one was wearing the uniform of a city police officer. He looked from face to face, and politely asked, "Who's in charge here?"

"The cannonball killed three men when it bounced off the doors," said Constable Federov, and took another sip of hot tea. "I'd always heard the old buildings were tough, but that was amazing." He finished the cup and set it down. "Now. We must address some details. Duchess Kurakin-Scriabin, I have a warrant for your arrest."

Argus was prepared to step in, if necessary, but if he had learned nothing else on Belarus, he understood he must let them at least appear to conduct matters through proper channels. So he kept silent for the moment.

"I understand," Serina said calmly. "I have asked for medical asylum at this clinic. How should we proceed?"

"The matter would be greatly expedited," he suggested, "if you could call upon a relative to cut through the red tape and give permission for you to go to Archangel."

"I'm sure my mother would be willing to do so."

"I mean no disrespect to your gracious mother," said Federov. "I was referring to someone of higher rank."

"There is only one of higher rank."

"As you say. I would suggest that perhaps we might use a Star Man communication device to make this request. It would be quick and decisive. I shall be happy to place a call from my station, or to send a wire, but it could be hours before you got your answer. During that time, a certain rabble-rouser who has temporarily lost his fire might get it back again."

"Understood," said Serina, and turned to Argus. "Embassador, the tsar has a communication device in his private office. A secretary monitors it at all times."

Argus turned to the supervising doctor, who responded, "In here," before he could ask. Argus motioned for Serina and the constable to follow him. He sat at the terminal and keyed in the call. In another moment the screen flashed an acceptance code, and then a very surprised young man looked out at Argus. "Embassador Fabricus?" he asked.

"I apologize for the abruptness of this call," said Argus. "Is the tsar available to speak with me?"

"I'll ask, sir." The young man hurried out of range. Argus waited, feeling the presence of the constable at his left, his caution overcome by curiosity. He fully expected the secretary to come back and say no, and when he did Argus would have to decide which course of action would have the least damaging ramifications. One way or the other, he intended to put Serina on a ship.

Someone new sat down in front of the screen, and Argus was surprised to see Tsar Gyorgy. "Hello?" said the tsar. "I wondered if anyone was ever going to use this thing."

"I'm sorry to interrupt your evening," said Argus. "I'm here at the Gorky Park Medical Clinic with your niece Serina Kurakin-Scriabin. She has requested medical asylum. The local constable feels that he needs official permission for her to leave Belarus before he can give us his blessing."

"Serina?" asked the tsar. "Is she there?"

"Yes."

"May I speak with her?"

Argus stood and motioned to Serina. She sat in front of the receiver, where Gyorgy would be able to see her. It struck Argus as very odd that her most recognizable feature was a black length of cloth.

"My dear," Gyorgy said tenderly, "are you all right?"

"Yes," she assured him. "I'm quite a bit better than all right, Uncle. My friends have been very kind to me."

"So," he said. "You will be going up to Archangel again?"

"Yes, Uncle. I expect I shall become a resident of the station."

"They have fine schooling available there. You have a good mind, Serina. I've always thought you should go to university."

"Thank you. I shall do my best not to disappoint you."

"You have never disappointed me," said the tsar. "And you never shall. You have my blessing, Serina, and my permission to leave Belarus. Is the constable nearby?"

"Yes—" Serina stood and made way for the constable. To his credit, the man did not look nervous when he sat down to speak with his tsar.

"Ah, Constable Federov," said Gyorgy, "I'm glad it's you. Thank you for protecting my niece. I give my official approval of her departure plans. Will that suffice?"

"Yes, my tsar," said Federov. "Thank you."

"You are most welcome. Well everyone, I'm pleased we finally got a chance to use this contraption. It's very handy. I suppose we ought to get more of them. We'll look into it. Good evening to you all."

"Good evening," said Argus, hearing the words echoed by several other people in the room. Gyorgy's face was replaced by the END CALL pattern.

Argus turned to Serina. He wished very much that they were alone, or that she were wired for communication.

Nesto poked his head into the room. "The shuttle is here—is everyone ready?"

"This is it," Argus told Serina.

"So it is," she said softly. He thought she sounded very weary, though she stood as straight as ever.

"I'll walk you to the door." He offered his arm. She accepted it, but did not lean on him. Her posture was erect as he walked her down the hall, out into the secured alley. The shuttle descended with lights flashing, the door unfolded, hands reached out to help William and his family inside, and only when he was helping Serina onto the shuttle did it occur to Argus that he might never see her again. She disappeared into the interior, and the door closed behind her.

Argus stood with Nesto and Constable Federov, watching the shuttle ascend the night sky until he couldn't see its flashing lights any longer.

"It's for the best," said the constable. "She'll have chances up there she would never have down here."

"I hope someday that will change," said Argus.

"I suppose it will, in time," said the constable. "In the meantime, it's good that people have a place to go."

The man's tone was friendly—Argus thought genuinely so. It was a tone he wasn't used to hearing from Belarusians. But he seldom got out among ordinary people, and he wondered what they really thought of Star Men.

"That crowd was pretty ugly tonight," he said.

"Those rabble." The constable shrugged. "We arrested

some. The others were chased away by locals. No one would have let them knock down the clinic. We all use it. We've had our eye on Khabalov for a while."

"Where'd he get the cannon?" asked Nesto.

"Someone else claimed credit for that. We can't nail it on Khabalov. But we can make it harder for him to get weapons. I'm surprised he showed his face. He usually stays away from these little demonstrations once he's organized them. Something must have really provoked him."

Argus didn't comment, but he remembered the look on Khabalov's face when he looked at Serina. He was very glad she was going to Archangel. He gazed at the stars, which filled only half the sky. The Veil obscured the other half.

"It's safe for you to walk home," said the constable. "You have a few enemies out here, but no one you couldn't deal with. I think most of your enemies circulate in higher circles than this one, yes?"

"Yes," agreed Argus, then wondered about one Enemy in particular. Now that Serina was gone, the atmosphere in the great house must be considerably changed.

What would Ayat-ko do about that?

PART FOUR

"Don't worry." The paramedic suctioned floating droplets with a hose. "You're not the first one to get sick in zero gravity."

Poor Veronika did not seem comforted by the news. She clung to her harness, groaning. Serina gently pressed a cold compress against the back of the young woman's neck. "There, there," she said gently. "Everything is all right."

She knew William was not able to spare his wife much attention. He was too busy trying to wrangle his children.

"I can fly!" squealed the little girl. "Just like Peter Pan!"

"You're Wendy," said the boy. "*I'm* Peter!"

"Look!" Maria called to the children. "You can see the whole world from up here!"

The children, with an aptitude for moving in zero gravity that was almost frightening, propelled themselves across the small cabin to the view screen, where Maria quickly buckled them down. "Now," she said. "Lets look at another world in our solar system, the monstrous gas giant Lucifer!"

They ooh-ed and ah-ed, fascinated by the images on the screen. Veronika groaned again, but this time with less misery. William settled in the seat on the other side of her and lay a reassuring hand on her shoulder. The paramedic continued to cheerfully chase droplets of vomit with the vacuum hose.

"William," Serina said softly, "I have been thinking back to the day we met. You were only five years old then, but you did not behave like other children."

"Neither did you," he said. "That's why I liked you."

Serina gently moved the compress lower on Veronika's neck. "I can scarcely believe that for so many years I never comprehended that my best friend was an ESA."

He looked surprised. "I'm not an ESA."

"But—your eyes, the machines—"

"Aha." He laughed. "ESAs aren't the only ones who have use for mechanical eyes. I'm not one of them; instead I followed in my father's footsteps. He was a deep cover agent. When I was sixteen, I became one too."

"When you were sixteen . . ." Serina mused, trying to remember if she had seen a difference in him back then. But she could remember nothing that seemed suspicious, in hindsight. "You must have had considerable aptitude."

"You might say I was born to it."

"On whom did you spy?" she asked. "My mother and father?"

"I didn't spy. If I had done that, Ayat-ko would have known. My father and I both acted as observers for the Repatriation Department. Repatriation always sends secret observers to live among people they want to invite into the Union, to learn what makes their society tick. Most of the information we convey back to our contacts on Archangel is of an anthropological nature."

Serina raised an eyebrow. "Anthropological. So we are a tribe for you to observe."

"*My* tribe," he reminded her.

Veronika made a soft, whimpering noise, and Serina moved the cold pack to a tender spot. She thought the young woman's color was improving. "You could have observed anywhere," she said.

"I did," said William. "The great house was home base."

"Not merely that. It was not a random choice for your father and you. Did you learn anything useful about Ayat-ko?"

"I'm not sure," he admitted. "I suppose I know more than most people, but I don't know if that makes much difference."

"I have not seen her since—for many days," said Serina. "I confess that worries me."

She looked into his eyes, which were human and grey again. She did not need to ask if he was worried too. "You aren't part of that household anymore," he said. "If you see her again, it'll be on new terms. Try to make them yours."

"I can try," said Serina. "We shall see how much I succeed."

"Docking," warned the technician.

"Is it almost over?" Veronika asked weakly.

"Father!" cried the children. "Archangel Station!"

"We're there," soothed Serina. She removed the cold pack from Veronika's neck. "Don't worry. Maria and I shall be with you every step. We'll get you into a nice comfy bed somewhere and—"

"Papa, a dinosaur!"

Suddenly a large head poked into the cabin on the end of a long, saurian neck. "Hello!" called ESA Seesil. "Welcome back to Archangel Station!"

Veronika took a hard look at Seesil, the color draining out of her again. "William," she said, her voice barely audible, "be grateful that I love you so much."

"I am, dearest," he said, helping her out of her harness.

Serina sat in the tiny dining area of her quarters on Archangel Station and tried to work up some enthusiasm for the library terminal on her table. Maria had given her a lively demonstration, showing off everything she had learned. Serina was forced to scribble copious notes in one of the journals she had brought from home. Maria wanted to teach her to use a device she called the quick pad, but Serina declined. "Only a few new tricks a day for this old dog, please."

Finally Maria bowed out to give Serina some time to decompress. For a girl who had grown up shrouded in the slums of Moscow, she had adapted very quickly to life among the stars.

But Serina was lost. She quickly tired of looking at scenes of Belarus, Lucifer, and other planets in her solar system from various perspectives, in and out of tactical. She tried to review some of the Web sites and library directories Maria had shown her but could not concentrate. Napping was also out of the question, and the shows she could tune into on the entertainment system featured people speaking in such heavily accented versions of Russian and uttering such odd idioms, she could hardly understand them.

Later it would probably seem fascinating. And she might feel much more inclined to explore the space station. Theoretically, the known galaxy was hers to visit. Yet she confined herself to three tiny rooms, wandering back and forth to inspect fixtures, appliances, receptacles—and mirrors.

The mirror on the back of her bathroom door was full length, and the image it revealed of her was hard to get used to. It wasn't just the fact that she no longer wore a shroud. The biggest adjustment she had to make was to the danger suit. It was very dark, but not exactly black. Maria had shown her how to adjust the color. "Reddish tones suit you better," said the girl. "But as you can see, it won't really look red. The effect is very subtle."

So it was. The suit was comfortable, as Serina had guessed it would be, and not as revealing as she had feared. The dark color was not really a shade; apparently it was a stealth feature of the suit. You could adjust it so that observers could see every detail of the suit, and one assumed, of the body inside it. But you could adjust it to spare your modesty. Serina was not as modest as Maria had expected her to be, mostly because she was curious to see how the danger suit would look on her.

"Your figure is magnificent!" said Maria. "Wait until the doctors repair your face. You will be amazed how different it will make you feel."

Serina could not take offense. If anyone had the right to comment about her disfigurement, Maria did. She naturally assumed Serina would have the same surgery.

But she didn't know if she would or not. And the more she thought about it, the more she paced her quarters, unable to concentrate on anything, but too alert to put off thinking and just sleep. Finally the door buzzer jolted her out of the cycle. She used the comm to ask, "Who is it?"

"William."

Serina let him in. Like her, he was dressed in a danger suit. Unlike her, he didn't seem to require time to get used to it. In fact, she wondered if he had been wearing it under his clothes for years. She led him into the dining area and offered him one of the chairs, taking the other for herself. She gazed at him for several moments without speaking. He gazed back, his eyes their normal color.

"Even when your face is bare," he said, "you're shrouded."

"What do you mean?"

"I can't tell how you feel about . . . all *this.*" He indicated the room, but seemed to mean far more than that.

"Perhaps that is because *I* don't know how I feel about *all this,*" she said. "But do not be concerned, my friend. How is Veronika settling in?"

"Fine, thanks to my mother. Mother was a Belarusian girl too. She moved up here with my father ten years ago, when he changed jobs. She went through the same thing. She knows just how my wife feels."

Serina almost said, *So do I,* but that wasn't quite true. Veronika held tightly to Maria's and Serina's hands when they all sat in the doctor's office in matching hospital gowns, going through their check ups and being inoculated. Serina had been very interested in the process and in the machinery she saw all around her. Maria had spoken of wanting to become a doctor herself. And Veronika had thrown up again.

"Will you and your family be able to go home again, William?"

"We could get new identities and start somewhere else. But I've asked them to think about it for a few months first."

"A few *months?"*

He nodded. "Things are going to change down there, Serina." He seemed certain of what he was saying.

"Why do you think so? Everything seems just as backward as ever."

"*You're* up here," he said. "I knew you were going to stir up a hornet's nest sooner or later."

"Surely I have no such influence."

"Not by yourself," he said, then stood suddenly. "Have you tried your bar yet?"

"My bar?" She watched him touch a keypad she had thought was only for working climate control. Two panels popped open on the wall. William pulled two glasses out of one, but paused at the other.

"Do you want wine? Vodka? Beer?"

"I haven't had beer in ages," she said.

William set the glasses and two bottles of pale Tasmanian Tiger beer on the table. He popped the caps off and poured for both of them, then saluted Serina with his glass. "You're my oldest friend," he said. "I didn't know if we would ever be able to sit at a table together as peers."

Serina picked up her glass and returned his salute. "Thank you for lighting a fire under me."

They drank together. The beer had a mild, fruity aftertaste, very pleasant, and was just what Serina needed. When her glass was half empty she set it down. "So," she said, "you have the strange eyes. But when did you get them?"

William had made far more progress with his drink. "When I was sixteen. Lots of people find them useful. You might, too."

"What an extraordinary thought!"

"I can see in the dark," he said. "I can see at both ends of the light spectrum, and I can even see in *tactical* when I interface with my suit."

"Interface," murmured Serina. Then a thought struck her. "You have *enhancements* in your brain?"

"Some," said William. "Mostly in the area of memory, vision, hearing. My nervous and skeletal systems are enhanced too."

"Can you speak"—Serina touched her temple—"mind to mind, like the Star Men do?"

"No. I was a deep cover agent. I could not have immersed myself in Belarusian culture if I were constantly in contact with Star Men. I had to live it, be it. You might think it was easy, since I grew up on your estate. But you can't know how many times I used to think about what I really knew, and how hard it was sometimes to see things like a Belarusian man."

Serina sipped more of her beer. "I often found it hard to think like a Belarusian woman. But I don't understand the Star Men either. They spy on us, but not for the same reason we would spy on them."

"They do it with every lost colony. They're careful. They don't want to repeat the mistakes of the Republic. But Belarus is different, Serina. We're special."

"If we are," guessed Serina, "it is only because we share this world with Enemies."

"We found more of them, Serina. They have attacked us on other worlds."

She stared at him until her eyes began to twitch. Now she understood the sudden appearance of the beer, and why he had waited until she was almost done with hers before telling her the true reason for his visit.

"At first, the incidences were isolated," he said. "Now they're accelerating. Union diplomats have tried desperately to reason with them."

"Just like Andrei Mironenko did," said Serina. "You need not tell me the result."

"You and I are probably the foremost experts on Enemy psychology." William finished his beer and set it aside. "And we know almost nothing. We don't know the exact level of the technology of these new clans, but they're high. Maybe higher than ours, but we don't know because they don't fight like us, or for the same reasons."

Serina stared thoughtfully at the tiger on her bottle. It really looked more like a striped wolf. "Have they considered the work of John the Murderer?" she asked.

"You mean," he said, "the poison? *Bug Spray?*"

"Surely they could make more."

"They could. But it works in a hive inside a gravity well, not in space. We don't know which worlds they live on, and I doubt they'd let us get close enough to deploy the stuff."

"He had other weapons." Serina turned on her screen and searched for an image she wanted. She found it, the night sky of Belarus, half obscured by the Veil. "I read Emily Kizheh's journals," she said. "And Tally Korsakova's. He said he hid something in the Veil. He spoke of them to ESA Grigory and to Tsar Andrei. If we could find those weapons, we could use them."

"People are looking," said William. "But they hoped they could make contact with the Enemies on this particular world."

"Why?"

"Because these particular Enemies stopped attacking us," said William. "Serina, it wasn't just because we almost killed them off. I think they could kill us anytime, if they wanted to. But they haven't done it, and I think it has something to do with Ayat-ko."

Tell me—why does Ayat-ko live in your household?

Because my mother wishes that she should . . .

"For better or for worse," said William, "we have a bond with Ayat-ko's people. The Star Men hope to understand it, use it."

Have you wondered if there might not be some way we could help each other, we conquered ones . . . ?

"If they can help us," said Serina, "rest assured there will be a price. We may find it too terrible to pay."

"We may," agreed William. "But the Union hopes for the best. Once they have fought Enemies for a thousand years, they may feel differently. Or perhaps they will surprise us and find a good solution, Serina."

"Perhaps," she said. She took a deep breath and squared her soldiers. "So . . . what is expected of me?"

"You can do what you want," he said. "But it will probably take you a while to realize how many options you have. I'll tell you what I'm curious about. Where did Ayat-ko go? I've never seen her gone from the great house for so long. I have a feeling she won't be going back there, and I'd like to know why."

Serina stared at the Veil. "You said it yourself. The world is changing."

"It has done nothing but change," said William, "even before humans got here."

Far below Serina's feet, winter was beginning to take hold of the last warm places, claiming the whole world. Her garden would soon be covered in a blanket of snow. She would never see it again, except in her dreams. No matter what changed around her, those captured moments would always stay the same, always suspended in the last moment of the last hour of the year, in the heart of winter, so long as she was capable of memory.

A message scrolled across the bottom on the screen, and the comm emitted two beeps. Serina paused, then tapped in the code that would access the message. It appeared in glowing letters on her screen.

Hello Serina!

Vasily Burakov has requested that I be your trainer. This means that I should teach you to use our technology and to maneuver in a danger suit, in various gravities and even zero gravity. I shall be happy to do so, but if you prefer another trainer, I shall take no offense. I await your decision.

—ESA Seesil

Serina sent an immediate reply:

At your convenience.

—Serina

Embassador Fabricus,

This is to remind you that as of December 3, all government offices will be closed for five weeks in observance of the holidays. No government business is conducted during this time. If you wish to remain in your residence you are welcome to do so, and we will assess bills due for rent. All payment for these must be made in advance.

We hope you will enjoy your holidays.

Sincerely yours,
Konstantin Polyansky
Secretary to His Majesty
Tsar Gyorgy Andreivich Kurakin

"Rent?" said Argus. "And what the hell do they mean, *this is to remind you?* This is the first I've heard of it."

"I think they want us to go away," said Nesto. "And not just for the holidays."

Argus placed a call to Vasily and sent a copy of the letter. <Did you ever have to shut down for the winter holidays?>

<No,> said Vasily. <But they haven't told you to get lost,

just to pay rent. And you won't be able to conduct any official government business, but no one else will either.>

<We haven't been able to do a damn thing since Serina made her play,> said Argus. <Ayat-ko isn't showing herself these days. Grigory hasn't detected any Enemy movement since he had that conversation with her on the train. I don't think we're making any progress, Vasily. How many years can we afford to stick around on Belarus while Enemy and Union forces tear each other to bloody shreds?>

<I've thought the same thing many times,> said Vasily. <But I think we need to stick it out. Another year will make the difference, Argus. I can feel it in my bones. In fact, it won't take that long. Just when nothing seems to be moving, that's when the shit will hit the fan. When it does, we have to make the right moves.>

Argus could almost hear the voice of his father. *You spend most of your time following, not chasing. Be patient . . .*

<Okay, so we pay rent. But I've got a danger suit. It's about time I got out and explored this world.>

<Splendid idea,> said Vasily. <Put your paperwork aside for the holidays. No one will be around to act on it, anyway. And when the New Year comes, everything will have changed anyway. That's one thing I learned trying to work with the Belarusian bureaucracy—anything that hasn't been finalized by the winter holidays is old news, throw it out.>

<Nice to know,> said Argus, wishing someone had told him before. He signed off and went to stand at his office window. Snow was falling, much more gently than it ever did on Fenris. The scene was beautiful, the bare trees, the graceful street, carriages passing back and forth, people strolling in thick coats, high boots, and fur hats. He had been inside this gravity well for six months and had never taken a walk just for the hell of it.

On his way downstairs he met ESA Kathryn. She wore an expression he had never seen on her face before.

<Your recruitment isn't going well,> he guessed.

<Don't know if it is or not,> she confessed. <I've been riding the train lines, visiting the libraries. I've met some people who know him. They all get the same look on their faces when I say I want to talk to him. Like they've tried it before me and failed.>

<You're not like everyone else,> he said.

She looked surprised.

<I just had a similar conversation with Vasily,> he said. <I'm frustrated with waiting too. But we need to remember what we are.>

<Mr. Humility,> Kathryn said, but gave him a smile like the one she usually wore. <Okay, I'll just keep hanging out.>

<Me too,> he said. They went down the stairs together and into the entryway. <Seen Grigory today?> he asked.

<No.> She actually blushed. <He was gone when I got up this morning. He's off looking for John the Murderer. He has a hunch.>

They went down the front walk together and out onto the street. People regarded them curiously. Argus looked up and down the lane, wondering which way he should walk.

<Go to Red Square,> Kathryn suggested. <Shop the stalls, look at Tsar Andrei's statue. The food is good too. People might ask you about the danger suit. They ask me all the time. That's about it. Ordinary people are a lot more friendly than politicians.>

<Thanks,> said Argus. His mood had lightened considerably, and not just because he was out for a stroll. He felt the same way he always had on the morning of a new hunt. He hadn't felt that way in years. It was invigorating. <Keep me posted.>

<You too,> she said, and set off in the opposite direction. She did not run, but walked at a normal pace. She was doing her best to remain visible to the boy. Argus wanted to be visible too. He set off for Red Square, his nerves humming.

* * *

Ivan watched the Star Men from the shelter of the porch of another government house, this one unused for centuries. At least, it was officially unused. Ivan had used it before. He had taken residence again, and followed the girl every morning on her wanderings. She was apparently looking for someone who did not want to be found.

Ivan was too, but that wouldn't matter. Sooner or later he would have Serina Kurakin-Scriabin at his mercy again. He wasn't sleeping well lately, only ate out of habit. He dreamed about his dead wife, but she spoke no more imprecations. She had delivered her message—she had never been a woman of many words. Sometimes God's plans were difficult to fathom. You had to be patient and watch your enemies; then a course would become apparent.

The Star Man and Star Woman stood in the light snowstorm, just looking at each other, as if they could speak with their eyes. Then they turned and went in opposite directions. Ivan decided to follow the one he had been shadowing all week, the girl. She was so preoccupied with her search, she never saw him. She was living proof that Star Men were not superhuman. But that was no surprise—she was female. No man would have been so incompetent.

She walked to the nearest train station, as always. He followed, getting into the next car and watched her like a tiger watches prey, unseen in the tall grass.

Kathryn had enjoyed herself at first. It was fun to go to different libraries, to talk to people and learn something about them. It was a hell of a lot more fun than walking around invisible, trying to see people like a monster had seen them. She regretted that Grigory had to do it now, and she wondered if it opened old wounds for him. But she didn't have the nerve to ask him. He scared her a little, and not because she thought he might get angry at her. He might tell her everything she wanted to know, and then she might want to know more.

Right now she was pursuing someone else. She had flattered herself that Peter would want to see her again. She wondered if she misjudged his behavior. He might simply have a crush on her, and if he did, she could do nothing but hurt his feelings. Yet she could not get over his remarkable perceptiveness. Sometimes she was convinced he knew exactly what she intended and that was why he ran.

Other times she was sure she was wrong—about everything. She rode the train, and the day waxed, then waned. Afternoon began to age to evening. Argus called her.

<The food at Red Square is good,> he said. <Couldn't decide what to buy, though.>

<You could have bought something for the house. It's so plain.>

<I'll leave that to you. I did so much walking today, think I'm going to turn in early.>

<Pleasant dreams.>

<Happy hunting.> he said, and signed off. Only she wasn't. She had chased Peter so long, she was beginning to get the message that he didn't want to be caught.

No ESA mentor had recruited her when she joined the ranks. She found out where she could contact them, then presented herself as if she were a rare dish on a silver platter. Sometimes she wondered what she would have done if they had said *No thanks*. She liked to think she would have just done something else with her life, something just as satisfying. There were so many things to do in this galaxy. Even with Enemies breathing down your neck, you still had choices.

What choices did Peter have? More than she had suspected when she started to look for him. Many people knew him, liked him, respected him. Someday he would be a man. He could probably get someone to sponsor him for college. From there, he could go into some field he liked. He could even go into politics if he was so inclined. He didn't need Kathryn, and he didn't need the life of an ESA, which was a lot more demanding than she had thought it would be when she thrust herself into it.

She could not imagine any other life. But if he really wanted the same thing, wouldn't he tell her so? If he was afraid, did he have what it took to be an ESA? She could back off, do the work she had come to Belarus to do, help Grigory. Get much too close to him. That was a fear she knew she could get over fast, once she made up her mind. But something kept her looking for Peter.

Responsibility. She could wait a while longer. After all, he wanted to see what she could do. She supposed she'd better give him a good show. Not with flashy tricks, not with the danger suit. With her head. She had been showing herself for weeks, giving him a chance to find her. Now she would actually start looking for him.

She had become a creature of habit, to give him opportunities. She got off at the same stops every day. She walked around a bit to give him a chance to get on the train behind her, if he wanted. She suspected he was doing so. But what if she got off and stayed that way? Just waited at a train stop? Would he talk to her if she gave him more time to do so? Maybe not. But she hadn't been scanning the crowds very closely, hadn't been in full tactical yet.

She switched to it. A few people who happened to be looking at her face jumped, startled, when her eyes became black orbs. But no one seemed more than curious. She scanned the world around her like a military ESA would. She used remote machines to profile everyone on the train. She looked specifically for boys Peter's approximate age. She found several.

The next stop was just outside Zhukovka. She would get off there and wait. Maybe he would too. Maybe not.

"Can you see with those eyes?" asked a little boy across from her. His mother shushed him, but Kathryn answered anyway.

"I can see twice as far," she said, hoping it was true.

Ivan almost got on the next train when it arrived, but checked himself at the last second. She was not going to board. She had turned and was walking slowly down the platform. The doors closed while he was trying to decide what to do, making the decision for him. He watched her, ignoring everyone else.

There was a town close by, but not too close to the train station. The town was peopled by merchants, tradesmen, and craftsmen who serviced the elite of Zhukovka, some of whom lived there all year. If the ESA kept walking, she would reach the end of the platform and end up on a cobblestone path that eventually meandered into the town. Ivan followed at a distance, stopping to pretend interest in the wares of the little farmers market next to the station.

The afternoon was waning, but there was still plenty of light. Many people were walking toward the town, so it didn't look too odd when Ivan went that way. At one point the ESA stopped, staring out toward the forest beyond which the country estates began. Her eyes were black orbs. The sight of them filled him with rage and longing, but he passed her on the road without a word.

<Grigory, where are you?>

<Zhukovka,> he answered immediately. <At the sight of the massacre.>

<I'm at the station nearby.>

<Any sign of Peter?>

<Some boys are nearby. I'm hoping he'll get curious and wander my way.>

<Stubborn fellow,> said Grigory, and Kathryn wondered if he would tell her she was wasting her time.

<I have been pondering an interesting trend,> he said instead. <At the start of the Enemy War, peasants were the main target of Enemy raids. I assumed this was because they lived in remote areas. But over the centuries, the pattern has shifted. Peasants are almost never the target of Enemy violence anymore. Noblemen and politicians are.>

<Maybe it's personal now,> said Kathryn, scanning the

thinning group of people around the station. A few boys lingered nearby, but she was beginning to lose hope again.

<If the targets have changed,> said Grigory, <the reasons have, too. Someone could wield considerable influence through such a pattern of assassination.>

<Did you see signs of that all those years you were watching? Enemies and Belarusians conspiring? That's what the Mironenkos were charged with, right?>

<The Mironenkos didn't conspire with Enemies. I'm sure of that. I never witnessed anyone else doing it either. But the Eye of Grigory was never omniscient.>

Grigory's remarks were troubling. More troubling was that Kathryn had taken a closer look at each boy on the platform, and none of them was Peter.

<Any sign of John's digs?> she asked, hoping the day wasn't totally wasted.

<Not yet. But the place has promise. It reeks of wealth and privilege. It must have appealed to him. It is also an artist's refuge. Many talented people have been granted summer homes here by tsars, people just like John's victims. I shall keep searching here until I've covered every inch.>

He wasn't trusting machines to do it for him. Kathryn could understand that. On Belarus, you could never be sure of something unless you saw it with your own eyes, and sometimes not even then. Kathryn debated whether she should walk through the forest and help him. Someone approached her from the direction of the town. But this was a grown man.

"Kathryn," someone said. She turned to look back toward the station. Peter was standing on the platform, twenty paces away.

"The one for whom you have been searching is near, can't you see it?"

She crept closer, but stopped when he backed away. "*You* are the one I'm looking for, Peter, no one else."

He shook his head. "I can always be found. I offer no

harm and no good. You have a better job to do than chase me."

"I don't," she insisted. "I can prove it. Do you respect me? I am no liar. When I'm wrong I'm at least in the ball park. I can prove everything I've said to you. I can show you other possibilities. Isn't that what you've been looking for in the libraries all these years?"

"No," he said, though his voice held little conviction. "Only light, only warmth. The books amuse me."

"You love the books. All the librarians know you—they all look out for you. You're afraid of me because I can hurt you. You're scared because you may see all that's possible and then lose it. I feel that way too. But I run right at it, Peter. I can teach you to do the same. Then you lose sometimes and you win sometimes. Otherwise, you get nothing."

"Nothing is what I started with."

"No, it's not." Kathryn took another step toward him. "That's the problem."

He didn't run. The wind ruffled his hair. His coat looked new, and so did his shoes, but the longing in his eyes did not belong to a boy with a home. She took another step.

"We're not alone," he said suddenly, and she froze. Her sensors confirmed what he said. Someone was coming at her from her left. But that was not what terrified her. On the right side of the platform a Dead Zone was forming, a place that seemed blank to her enhanced ESA senses, a phenomenon that often prefaced an Enemy attack. It was moving—right toward Peter.

"Run!" Peter cried, his voice full of despair. She did run, but toward him. Just as she began to move, a blow caught her on the side of the face. She was unprepared for it, totally focused on Peter; she stumbled and someone tried to grapple her to the ground. She looked at him and saw black hair, but he was no Enemy. Peter choked off a cry and she threw herself toward his last position, pulling the interloper with her. She saw the Enemy then, running with Peter in his arms, toward Zhukovka, toward the massacre zone. She raced after them, her helmet deploying automatically when the man who clung to her tried to aim blows at her face. Just ahead, she could see Peter's white face over the shoulder of his kidnapper.

And then she saw nothing. Putting on a burst of speed, she chased the Dead Zone. The man who clung to her lost his grip and tumbled into the forest through which she was running. She did not even look back to see where he fell.

<GRIGORY!> she remembered to call. <THEY'VE GOT PETER!>

<Who?> he demanded.

<ENEMIES!>

Ivan Sergeivich Khabalov rolled when he hit the ground. The woman had moved almost as fast as a train. He was stunned when he struck the earth. For a moment he lay there, panting, glad that at least he had landed a blow before she ran away. But the satisfaction did not last, and soon the rage that had begun to consume him after his daughter was taken burned more brightly than ever.

Ivan rolled onto his side, ready to get up and track the ESA again. He was not sure what he would do when he found her, but he could not be satisfied until he did. He began to rise, then froze when a beam of red light crossed his path, right at the level of his eyes.

He froze, then looked slowly to his left. The beam focused into a small red dot on the trunk of a tree.

Ivan raised his hand, capturing the light. He crept closer to its source, found it emanating from the trunk of another tree. This tree was thick, an elder giant, one of the trees that had been old when colonists first walked the surface of the world. The light was nestled in a knot near its giant base. Ivan touched it, and a square of bark popped open, like a small door. Ivan reached in. Something gave under the pressure of his fingers and he heard a cracking noise, like breaking wood. Chunks of bark flew at him as another door popped open in the tree trunk, this one much, much larger.

<Grigory, look for the Dead Zone. You won't be able to see them!> said Kathryn, pushing her suit to its speed limit.

<Understood. I'm coming!>

He was racing toward the moving Dead Zone, which did not alter its course to avoid him. Kathryn wondered why, feared that she knew, and raged at her suit as she tried to push it further and failed.

They're playing with us, want us to chase them so they can make fools of us . . .

"Peter!" she screamed.

She heard his voice, but something interfered with the sound.

"Peter!" she cried again, and strained to hear an answer, but there was no sound.

And then there was no zone. She didn't want to believe it, kept running as if it were just ahead of her. In another moment, she saw Grigory.

<It's gone,> he said.

She slowed, and by the time she met him, she was walking. She saw Grigory, but looked for Peter, looked for miles, examined everything that moved.

Gone. The expression on Grigory's face only confirmed what her heart denied. He met her, put his hands on her shoulders.

<They have him,> he said.

Her face was wet and hot. She retracted her helmet and felt the wind sting her eyes as her tears flowed, and flowed, and flowed.

Automatic systems woke the Avatar as soon as an intruder was detected. But a thousand years was a long time to sleep, so cold circuits warmed gradually, like dormant plants awakening in the spring. Systems tested and repaired themselves, adding their energies to a matrix that grew more complex and self-aware by the second. As it woke, it also became aware of its environment, and of the intruder who watched it with bright eyes. The man walked back and forth, staring raptly at display panels and muttering to himself. Sensors picked up his speech.

"Old technology," he was saying. "Must be from Tsar Andrei's time. But what is it doing here?"

The Avatar recognized the name *Andrei.* It decided to use its simulated voice. "This is not his technology," it said, and watched the man jump. It was vaguely amused by his reaction, but also intrigued, because he did not run or tremble in fear. "Who are you?" it asked him. "This is private property." It didn't add that it could kill him instantly if he gave the wrong answer.

"I am Ivan Sergeivich Khabalov," said the man.

"Who sent you?" asked the Avatar. It was beginning to receive information about the passage of time. The news was not pleasant.

"God sent me," replied Ivan.

"God," replied the Avatar. "I have no particular objection to that entity. But I require identification with mortal associates."

"I do not work for the government, if that's what you mean," said Ivan. "I associate with those who do not offend me."

That answer was better. "Why have you come here?" asked the Avatar.

"I was following one of my enemies," replied Ivan. "I wanted to see what she was looking for."

"She."

"The *ESA.*" Ivan pronounced the word with loathing. "One of the unnatural breed who have infested our world."

Something blossomed within the Avatar, the result of more of its systems having come online and of recognition of the acronym. It waited before saying anything more. It waited to finish becoming itself. That took several more seconds. Finally Ivan dared to ask a question.

"Who are you? Are you talking to me through an intercom?"

"I am not a man," replied the Avatar. "But I was created by one. I think like him."

"You are an intelligent machine," said Ivan.

"Close enough."

"You speak as one who is intelligent. You seem to think and react."

"You can count on that," said the Avatar, weighing the possibilities. Things were not as they should be. But that didn't mean there was no fun to be had.

"What is your name, then?" asked Ivan.

The Avatar pondered the best answer. It decided to go with the truth, for now.

"Call me Loki," it said.

We are dealing here not with a complete man at all, but with something that suggests a subtly constructed reflex machine which can mimic the human personality perfectly.

—Hervey Cleckley
The Mask Of Sanity

Loki was going to put her head in Gorky Park. He looked forward to seeing it in that setting, the once-lovely face frozen in the grimace of her last agonies.

Now suddenly it was one thousand years later, and the strongest emotion he was capable of was disappointment.

The fact that he could feel any emotion at all was testimony to the elegant matrix in which he existed. Testimony also to the brilliance of the Original, the one of whom he was a reflection. Loki came with his girls to amuse himself in private, then turned to the more serious matter of preserving his essential self. He would make his "deposits," then place his Avatar in stasis until next time. But next time stopped happening.

What happened instead was a download of massive amounts of information from the spore colonies, which had been rerouted to his corner of the network upon the demise of the Original. This was according to emergency plans long in place, and Loki was not surprised to receive the information. Once again, disappointment reigned.

He watched himself attacking Tally Korsakova—he reviewed those images many times, savoring them, comforting himself. But he had to keep cutting them short, so he wouldn't have to replay the images of the bitch mutilating his eyes with her rasta-links, followed by the confrontation with Grigory, who—oddly enough—never laid a finger on him. He had expected a beating in the very least. Instead, he had merely been arrested and taken out of range of the spores. Hindsight being twenty-twenty, he could now see the wisdom of spreading them everywhere, including the prison complexes. But he could never have imagined himself being taken to such a place. His intention had been to go out in a blaze of glory.

Later he overheard Emily Kizheh discussing his suicide—death by hanging. He thought she must be lying—he would never do such a thing. He was sure that eventually he would have been able to outmaneuver the legal system. They were such idiots. He watched Kizheh, Korsakova, and the brat Peter grieving over the deaths of Katerina, Andrei, and Grigory, and that also provided some satisfaction. But they got on with their lives, grew old, finally died. He didn't waste much time on that part, merely combing for pertinent details, like the occasional Enemy massacre.

The original Enemy hive he had discovered all those centuries ago was long dead. But even dead it contained information for those who knew how to find it. He pored over those details with much more attention than he could bring himself to pay to his aging persecutors. He was so rapt, he almost forgot the man who had awakened him.

Ivan was no ordinary peasant, though he dressed like one. Tall and striking, he boasted an ebony mane that poured over his wide shoulders and down his back like silk. Normally Loki would have thought it effeminate for a man to have hair like that, but he could not use that word to describe Ivan, whose black eyes took in his surroundings calmly, with calculation.

"Tell me," said Loki. "Does all of this machinery frighten you?"

"No," said Ivan.

"And do I . . . offend you?"

"No, Loki. You intrigue me."

"I'm so pleased to hear it," said the Avatar, giving orders to remote machinery. "Because you've put me in an awkward position. You've compromised my security. But I think an accommodation might be made if we put our minds to it."

Ivan stood tall, his hands not trembling despite the fact that things around him were moving in mysterious ways. "There is an old saying: The enemy of my enemy is my friend. I think that you are that kind of friend. Am I right?"

"You're close enough for government work," said Loki. "And now—my *friend*—let's learn some new things together. Shall we?"

Before Ivan could answer, the stinger climbed his pant leg and scurried up his body so quickly he couldn't move fast enough to brush it loose. It was a simple machine with six legs and a tiny but efficient mechanical brain, and a needle to deploy its liquid payload. Ivan might have mistaken it for a spider if he had gotten a good look at it before it stung him on the back of his neck. He looked surprised, and then he slumped to the floor.

The drug would leave him deeply but safely unconscious for several hours. Loki had used it on his victims so he could transport them to this workshop. He wished he had used it on Tally Korsakova. Things would have turned out very differently.

He studied Ivan. The man was healthy, strong, reasonably intelligent. His appearance was quite striking as well, which could be an advantage. Loki narrowed his surveillance to Ivan's right eye, which was still open. The iris was as black as night. Loki prepared his machinery.

The technology had never been tested, but Loki had no choice. He was facing extinction. The ESA who had led Ivan to his hiding place would be back. Loki had to act fast.

"I suspect," he told the slumbering man on the floor, "that this is the beginning of a beautiful friendship."

Ivan began to snore. If Loki had still been human, he would have laughed.

When Ivan awoke, his head hurt, particularly his right eye and left ear. But other than that, he felt remarkably well, much better than he usually did after a night of heavy drinking. He sat up, looking for his wretched daughter, then remembered she wasn't home anymore—and neither was he.

Strange machines glowed and hummed all around him. "Loki?" he asked cautiously.

<Right here,> said a voice inside his left ear.

Ivan did not flinch. He was not that sort of man. <You drugged me.>

<Had to,> said Loki. <I had to install a communication device, and it would have been very painful.>

Ivan wasn't happy to hear that. But God had sent him into this den, and He would see him out again. <I'm not your servant,> he told Loki.

<Don't be angry. My gifts will give you many advantages. Look what you're wearing.>

Ivan looked down and was astounded to find himself in a danger suit. It had been so comfortable he hardly felt it against his skin.

<That ESA you followed here,> said Loki, <if you had been wearing that, she would be dead now.>

Loki touched the suit on his chest, his arms.

<Careful,> Loki warned. <The controls are on the inside of your left forearm.>

Loki raised his arm, saw ghost images on the fabric of his suit. <I'm left-handed,> he said.

<Regrettable, but I'm sure you'll adapt. I won't try to show you everything the suit can do right now, but you do need to learn one thing.>

<And what is that?> asked Ivan, his head throbbing.

<You need to learn how to make it invisible.>

Soon a terrible noise resounded through the woods; the trees crackled, the dry leaves rustled; from the woods Baba Yaga drove out in a mortar, prodding it with a pestle and sweeping her traces with a broom. She rode up to the gate, stopped, and sniffing the air around her cried: "Fie, fie! I smell a Russian smell!

—from the Russian folk tale
Vasilisa The Beautiful

Argus woke knowing someone was in the room with him. Moving just his eyes, he scanned in tactical—and found nothing.

"Very good," croaked a voice like a rusty hinge. "Your reflexes are still impressive, Argus the Hunter."

He sat up cautiously. The cool night air prickled his skin. His danger suit lay useless across a chair next to the bed. "To whom do I owe the honor of this visit?"

"I haven't been called by my real name in millennia. Call me Grandmother."

Since tactical was doing him no good, Argus switched his vision back to normal. The darkness in the room was almost impenetrable, but he thought he saw twin glimmers above the foot of the bed, the liquid shine of black animal eyes.

"Baba Yaga," he said respectfully. "I'm honored."

"Everyone says that. I don't need it. Do you suppose I would waste a visit if it weren't important?"

"I confess I don't know your habits as well as my Russian comrades do. Why have you come, Grandmother?"

"To test your reflexes, for one. They have sent you on a fool's errand, Argus, but they've managed to put you in danger anyway."

"I've been in danger before."

She was silent for a minute. Then he smelled pipe smoke. "Someday you will die on the job because of something you do not know," she croaked. "But not today, because I have come to warn you that an old evil has awakened on this world, and he has put on a new face."

"He?"

"John the Murderer."

Argus tried desperately to read the expression in those eyes, but he wasn't even sure they were there. "Awakened," he said. "From some kind of stasis?"

"If you prefer to call death stasis, I won't argue with you. Your ESAs were right to wonder if he made an Avatar—of course he did! Can you imagine such a colossal ego allowing itself to go extinct? But even he could not anticipate what would happen to that Avatar."

"That makes two of us."

"Your girl was looking for his lair when she was sidetracked by the boy. She didn't know she was being followed. She led a dangerous man to the right spot, then left him to deduce the rest. He went into John's old hideout and triggered the machinery there. It hijacked him."

"Hijacked?"

"When you see Ivan the Mystic again, he will have one black eye and one blue. The blue contains the Avatar. John and Ivan have merged to become a new creature. Personally, I think the change is an improvement—John used to be such a wretched little geek. But he is more dangerous now—less predictable."

The tobacco Baba Yaga smoked was not as smooth as the sort favored by Tsar Gyorgy, but Argus rather liked it. "Is Ivan the Mystic the man who tried to stop Serina from leaving Moscow?" he asked.

"The very one. She will not get the drop on him so easily again, I promise you. John the Murderer still has many of his weapons. He might even threaten Archangel Station if he is so inclined. But even worse, he still has weapons that could kill the Enemies on this world. And they're not the Enemies who need killing."

Since she had brought up the subject of the Enemies, Argus risked a question. "You say I'm on a fool's errand. How could I do my job better, Grandmother?"

"You've already done your work. You made contact with Ayat-ko."

"Is that it? Now we just wait for her to talk to us?"

Another puff of smoke blew into Argus's face. "She is the only one who can help you. She is a Witness. Among her kind, she is a sterile female, so long lived as to be almost deathless. She is the advisor for her clan, motivated by reason rather than passion."

"If that's the case, then why can't we direct all future communications between Enemies and humans to other Witnesses, like her?"

"Ayat-ko is unique. Her clan is dying, yet they have survived an extraordinarily long time. Her views are uncommon. You don't want to meet those other Witnesses. They belong to strong clans."

"Serina was our only link to her," said Argus. "We've lost our chance to talk to her."

"The chance will come again. She will talk to you. Right now you have other problems. You aren't on John's radar yet, but you will be. You'd best wear your danger suit to bed from now on."

"Why should he come after me?"

"There is an old saying: The friend of my enemy is also my enemy."

"I've heard it the other way around," said Argus.

"Both ways apply to you. You must know that he is not the only old monster to make it to the New Age. Some of his cronies are still sniffing around. Someday his interests, and theirs, and even yours may merge, just like John has merged with Ivan."

"What could possibly motivate us to do so?" asked Argus.

"A mutual threat. That's all you get from me. I have never answered so many questions in a row! Don't bother seeing me out. I know the way."

"The Republic is dead," said Argus. "Are you telling me that some of its old masters are still among us? Are their spies on this world now? What are they after?"

"Eggs," she said.

"What?"

No answer. The smell of smoke was fading. Argus touched the light pad on his bedside table, and the shadows fled the room. She wasn't there. His door was wide open.

Grigory appeared in the doorway.

<Did you see her?> asked Argus.

The blind ESA sniffed the air. <Pipe smoke,> he said. <I've never smelled the blend.>

<It must be Baba Yaga's special stash.> Argus got out of bed and began to put on his danger suit. <She brought me some interesting news. About John the Murderer.> Argus sat down to pull on his boots.

<I've got news about something else.>

Argus froze. He did not know Grigory well, but the grimness in the man's tone, the anger in his face, was unmistakable.

<Kathryn's young candidate has been kidnapped,> said Grigory. <By Enemies.>

<Merciful God,> said Argus.

<Is he?> wondered Grigory. <I hope so. Because if any harm comes to that boy, our mission be damned. I'll kill those bugs with my bare hands.>

Ivan rode the train back to Moscow. He watched the passengers, who could not see him. Loki must have done the same, centuries ago.

Loki was the devil, Ivan had no doubt of it. But the devil had no power over men who did not worship him. Even Satan himself was a servant of God Almighty. If God saw fit to inflict this devil on the world, Ivan would not thwart him. The righteous would survive—and the evil perish, in good time.

<Look at that one,> said Loki, in his ear. <How tender she is.>

Ivan studied the girl who was hardly more than a child. Her skin was creamy, blushed pink at the cheeks and earlobes. She was swaddled deeply in her coats, her hands bundled in mittens. She held her father's hand tightly and fidgeted with her feet. Her eyes were like sapphires, tilted in a way that betrayed some Mongol heritage.

<I cut off their heads, Ivan. I cut off their hands and breasts. But I never cut out their eyes. You're a perceptive man. What do you think that means?>

Ivan did not have to think about it. <It means you owned them. And you did not fear their recriminations.>

<Why fear the dead?> asked Loki. <What difference does it make if their eyes remain intact? They can't see anymore.>

<What they see is between them and God,> said Ivan impassively.

<I wanted them to look at me every moment. I wanted them to see me. I suppose I wanted it even after they were dead, but that was rather whimsical.>

<The dead see you. But they don't care what you want.>

Loki considered carrying the argument further, after all, as a Russian Ivan must be susceptible to some Russian superstitions. Yet the conversation was stirring an odd emotion in him. He had few memories of it from the Original, who seldom felt it. So it took him a while to realize he was uneasy.

He searched his database for the reason. All he could find was Emily Kizheh announcing his death by suicide. He searched again, looking for keywords, and found something more.

Tally Korsakova, her beautiful face weary: "How did he manage to climb high enough to tie the damned noose? Someone must have done it for him."

Indeed. He searched for anything that might be connected to the investigation.

Emily Kizheh: "The power was still out. We don't have any surveillance footage." And seventy hours later, another tidbit: "All of the officers have passed lie detectors, and the ones on duty that night have perfect records. We picked only the best for that post. And there are no fingerprints in the cell besides John's."

"That's easy enough to manage," remarked Tally Korsakova.

"Agreed. But we can't rule out that he did it himself. Desperate people sometimes manage superhuman feats."

"None of the officers killed him," Tally said suddenly. "No living human pulled it off."

"Who then?"

"His ghosts got him," said Tally. She blinked rapidly, then rubbed her face. Loki waited for Emily to tell her she was full of nonsense, but the chief of security only stared, as if waiting for more. "He's dead," Tally said finally. "And he's not going to be paying me any visits, Emily. You know why?"

Emily shook her head.

"Because hell has him. No one visits from hell. It's not allowed."

"I don't want to know how you know that," said Emily Kizheh.

But Loki did, very much. He combed their conversations for further references. He found many. Apparently Tally Korsakova believed she could speak to the dead. The information she received from these otherworldly communications was uncannily accurate. Loki didn't believe in ghosts, but the matter deserved further study.

Ivan got off the train and headed directly for his favorite tavern. He brought the suit into visible mode and retracted the helmet right in plain sight of dozens of people on the street. They were startled, but Loki supposed it did no real harm. After all, he wasn't John anymore. He was Ivan—fearless, righteous, harboring no doubts. People got out of his way. It was a heady ride to the bar, and Loki was beginning to feel very, very comfortable.

Ivan was on the train again, the last place he wanted to be. He had already ridden as far as he needed to go—how could he be there again? He remembered getting off, going to the bar, drinking heavily. He should have stopped home and put honest clothing over the danger suit, but he could not wait. People stared at him; they shrank from his gaze and made the sign of the evil eye. He didn't care. He had a demon on his back and he needed to drink.

Anger smoldered in his belly like hot coals. He thought about his daughter. Her face did not come readily to his mind anymore; instead he saw the brazen, unshrouded face of Serina Kurakin-Scriabin. He could not strike her—she was not his kin—yet he could imagine laying hands on her.

He drank until the room narrowed and dimmed with a red fog. Then he threw down his money and stalked home, steady on his feet, ready to strike anyone foolish enough to get in his path. But no one ventured there, and at last Ivan fell into his bed. He remembered all that. He did not remember getting up again and getting on the damned train. So he knew he must be dreaming, yet the sensation was unlike any his slumbering mind had ever experienced.

The girls on the train, he watched them every day.

No—it was *Loki* who did. He liked to see them unaware, not self-conscious and composed. People became entirely themselves when they thought no one was watching; their masks fell off. You could see the real beauty and ugliness beneath the surface. The girls were tender, their flesh the most satisfying when he cut and burned it. He knew from long experience how the different age groups and different sexes reacted to his ministrations. He knew what he liked best.

Screaming, writhing girls. Ivan enjoyed their bodies, but now his hands did things he didn't like. It was excessive. Why kill them? They couldn't harm him. He cut off heads, hands, breasts, felt a satisfaction and glee that filled him with contempt.

Are you a child pulling wings off bugs?

His hands didn't like to be criticized. They tried to force their will on him. Ivan refused. And then his hands were doing things he had not known they could do. They made things. They understood things. He could understand those things too now, which pleased him. These were useful things, weapons, Star Man technology.

You see? Who is a child now? This is what I have to offer. I could kill the Union if I wanted to. I could kill worlds, stars.

Leave Armageddon to God. Ivan saw many possibilities

now, but he did not care to waste his time on pettiness. He did not need to ride on the train and stalk the girls. He got up and he forced his feet to the door. His hands fought. They struck him, tried to grasp the backs of seats and objects that would prevent him from making progress.

I'M NOT YOUR SLAVE! he screamed, and wrenched his hands loose with enough force to tear them from his wrists.

Loki spoke into his ear: <Your time is past. I'm not you; you're me! Forget your old life. Forget your old beliefs. Look! Look at that girl. I followed her home; I drugged her; I wrapped her in a special cloak and took her to my lair. I took her on this train! I took girls right under the noses of police, their families, the fucking ESAs. I took them back to my special place. I secured them to that table. I used these devices! Look at me!>

Ivan looked at his hands. They were covered in an odd network of lines. As he watched them, the lines twisted, merged, became new things: tiny saws, blades, hot wires. Delicate devices for hurting and mangling. He touched the girls with them and heard their screams, heard their prayers.

Their prayers . . .

<They thought of God in their final moments. They were righteous.>

<They thought about *me*. They prayed to *me!*>

<No. Use your eyes. You had power over them until just before the moment of their deaths. Then they called to God. I see them. I know. You cannot hide this from me.>

The door opened, and Ivan hurled himself off the train. He was almost running as he made his way through a crowd that could not see him. So many people, a wonderful swarm, flesh and blood and a jumble of emotions, the perfect hiding place. He moved, not caring where he went, until he saw a shining palace. Sun shone on its cream-colored walls, glittered from the fine gilt edging of its facade.

The Winter Palace. I'm in St. Petersburg . . .

He slipped past the officers at the security checkpoints. He wandered through hallways, bemused by the sensation of familiarity. He liked the fine things in the palace—he felt he deserved to have such things himself. Yet he had little time for them, always forgot to buy them when he had the time, or even to steal them when he had the opportunity. It was something he seldom thought about, his appreciation of the good taste of others. Or at least, some others.

People are so disappointing . . .

A woman walked past him. She was slender, clothed in a danger suit, and her skin was as black as the darkness of the Veil. Her hair undulated around her head like snakes, and he could not fathom why. He followed her, trying to get a glimpse of her face. She went to a heavy door with a strange, pagan creature outlined on its surface. He slipped through the door after her.

The room was dim. He barely glimpsed the things inside, only had the sensation that they did not belong to his world. He followed the slender woman into another room. She went to a desk and sat behind it, turning at last to face him. He saw her face and felt a pain just under his heart.

Who is that?

Tally . . .

Just a name, but the feelings that came with it were intense: lust, longing, rage, admiration for the woman with the inhuman beauty, the steel snakes undulating around her head, plugging her into information, into machines that listened to the universe, and the expression on that perfect face, too distracted to be self-conscious, and so her beauty just shone. Her eyes stared straight ahead, but they were not blank. They saw what the snakes told her. Her expression was distracted, then surprised, then troubled. Her snakes slid out of their receptacles and she stood. She left the room, and he followed her again. She went into a kitchen and fixed a sandwich. He was ravenous, staring at the food, staring at the woman. She moved past him and one of his hands balled into a fist, shot out, struck her on the tip of her chin. She went down cold.

He stripped her naked. The feel of her body in his arms

as he carried her induced him to orgasm. He didn't care. There was time for another, slower ascent to pleasure. He tied her to the chair and waited for her to wake. He knew what she would say. He had seen the images a thousand times, what the Original had done to her, but he *was going to be smarter. It was going to be different this time. He wouldn't let her get near his eyes. Everything was going to be different. He was different.*

She opened her eyes. Her face was bruised, yet it had lost none of its beauty. She gazed at him calmly; he was filled with admiration.

"Tally Korsakova," he said. "Engineer."

"That is who I am," she agreed. "But who are you?"

"Your master."

"Not then," she said. "Not now."

"You are helpless," he said, then heard himself saying other things, things he did not believe.

You should have stayed on Canopus. They treat black bitches like queens. When I did those other women, I was practicing for you. We've got about four hours. Let's take our time. You don't have any way to send a message, but you might try screaming for help. I'd like to see you do that.

Make me, she croaked.

His feet moved him closer. His hands rested on her smooth shoulders. He leaned over her. He wanted very badly to kiss her, to taste the blood in her mouth. Her face loomed close. Her eyes stared into his. And then the tips of her rasta-links slammed into his sockets, tearing the soft tissues of his eyes and driving themselves deep. No pain troubled him, because he had never felt this pain for himself, only seen recorded images of it. Yet he knew the snakes were digging for his brain, and he staggered back.

My eyes! You fucking bitch. MY EYES!

Ivan woke, screaming it. He saw her again, Tally Korsakova. She seemed to be right there in his room, close enough to touch. She was looking at him, her face smooth and unbruised. "Who are you?" she asked.

He tried to say his name and could not. She faded like the dream she really was, and he remembered his name.

"Ivan!" he snarled. But it was too late. She was gone.

<Loki,> he said, <where are you?>

There was no answer. Only a dull headache. Loki was sulking because Ivan had driven him out. Loki had no power over him. He could use the old devil's machines for his own purposes. He staggered into the bathroom and leaned heavily on the sink. He turned on the cold water and splashed his face until his hands felt numb and the red fog receded. Then he looked into the mirror, expecting to see bloodshot eyes staring back. And he did. But something was wrong. He looked into his own eyes; the left was black and rimmed with red.

The right eye was blue. When he looked into it, someone else looked back.

Ivan screamed. Neighbors later told police that the devil was screaming in Ivan's apartment, and he supposed they were right. He reached for the offending orb, intending to tear it from his head.

<Wait!>

His hand stalled inches from the blue eye. He tried to force it, but could not work up the momentum.

<I'm not just an eye! I spread an entire network of nerves throughout your body! I'm you, Ivan. I was wrong! I tried to make you me, but I'm you!>

Ivan understood about the nerves. He could see it all clearly, how Loki had highjacked his body, his brain. Now the two of them were knit together. He fought for control of his hand, won it, felt a thrill of fear from Loki. But he did not tear out the eye. Instead, he looked into it until he could see himself there.

<You're here to stay,> he said. <And so am I. And now, my *friend,* your secrets are mine. You will have no thought that I do not hear. You will hide no memories.>

<It's not what I thought it would be,> confessed Loki. <I

thought I could drive you out, but now I can see you will never go.>

<God moves my hand,> said Ivan. <He guided me to your lair. Everything I have done, everything I have been, has led me to this union with you. I know where your weapons are. I know how to use them.>

<True,> said Loki. <But there are things that neither of us know. We have old enemies who are still at large.>

Ivan stared at his reflection in the mirror. He combed his wet hair with his fingers until it fell shining about his shoulders. His eyes, the black and the blue, were clear now. He was a man in his prime, and thanks to Loki's knowledge he would remain that way for many more years. True, he was not sure where his path was leading him now. But God would light the way. His danger suit could take him anywhere in the world. It could take him up to Archangel if he chose.

Where Serina was hiding.

<Fun,> admitted Loki. <But take your time. That's what my mishap with Tally taught me. It's worth it to wait. And in the meantime, think of the things we can find out. Have you ever been to St. Petersburg?>

<You know I have,> said Ivan. <But I think the time has come for another visit. There are some sights I would like to see.>

He raised his left arm, palm upward, and touched the controls that rendered him invisible. He left his rooms and walked down through the building, past cracked doors through which his neighbors peered fearfully, knowing the devil was close, but never seeing him.

❦

It was always unsettling when Argus returned from a gravity well to the artificial gravity of a space station, but this time it seemed doubly so. He had gotten his wish. The hunt had finally flushed the ice bear. But before he could make a stand with his spear, he was yanked back to Archangel.

On the way up, he didn't discuss his doubts with ESA Kathryn, who had become like a block of stone in her efforts to obey orders instead of tearing Belarus apart to find Peter. He wondered if they were about to be reassigned. He doubted Kathryn or Grigory would take that sitting down. As the three of them disembarked the shuttle and made their way through the narrow hallway to the briefing room, Vasily Burakov joined them. Vasily sat down at the head of the conference table.

"Where's Commander Hale?" asked Argus.

"He's not the one who called this meeting," said Vasily.

"He's my boss," said Argus.

"Well, yes, but the Woovs have made a request. They have analyzed the situation, and they think this may be an attempt by the Enemies to force contact. The Enemies don't have peace talks the way humans and Woovs do. But if they take a Gift from us, then you can talk to them."

"We didn't offer the Gift," said Argus.

"I know," said Vasily. "We would never do it. So perhaps they felt compelled to take it."

"So what do the Woovs want us to do?" asked Argus.

"Go after the boy. Try to get him back."

Argus stared at him. When he had been yanked from his office, he had been preparing to do just that. If anything, he had expected to be told *not* to go after the boy. That wasn't the work of an embassador. It was the job of special agents. "Have I just been fired?" he asked mildly.

"Temporarily reassigned," said Vasily. "We've had inquiries from the tsar's office and we informed him that you have a family emergency. ESA Nesto will handle your correspondence until your return."

"*If* I return," said Argus.

Vasily glanced at Kathryn. His expression was neutral, but Argus caught his drift. Peter was more than just a kidnapped boy now—he might be a Gift. If his death bought negotiation, someone else would have to handle it, someone trained in diplomacy. Argus's brief excursion into that field was probably over.

"Our chances of recovering Peter are slim," said Grigory. His tone commanded immediate attention. "Andrei Mironenko paid the highest price possible when he entered an Enemy lair."

"So did you," Kathryn said softly.

"We must understand that we could do the same. This is not your fight, Argus, you need not accompany us."

Argus thought about it. The truth was, he wanted to take action. He wanted to take it for the same reason he had become a hunter of ice bears. Not wise, perhaps, but he had worked for the Department of Defense for much of his adult life, and if they saw fit to send him after Peter, he need not argue. "I believe that even if I stayed on Archangel, I would not be safe from whatever actions Ayat-ko and her clan are contemplating. Baba Yaga made that clear to me. I doubt she would have taken the trouble to warn me, otherwise."

"She warned you about John the Murderer," said Grigory.

"I agree with Argus," said ESA Kathryn, staring straight ahead. "I think we're all in this together."

"We have three experts waiting to join your team," said Vasily. "They've been briefed. They've also received special training. Argus, I want to warn you—"

Before he could say anything more, the door to the conference room opened. Argus recognized William and ESA Seesil immediately. It took another second to register that the confident, slim woman in the danger suit was Serina, her face unshrouded. He stared for several seconds.

"I hope my appearance does not offend you," said Serina.

"Not at all," said Argus. "I'm delighted to see you. I only wish it could be under happier circumstances."

"Happy circumstances are rare these days," she said. "We shall have to make the best of the circumstances we have."

"Serina lived with Ayat-ko her whole life," said Vasily. "She is our best expert concerning Enemy psychology."

"A chilling thought," remarked Serina. "But I shall do my best."

"William is the only one among you who would not be quickly recognized," said Vasily. "He and Seesil will be our most visible team members down below. Seesil can sense Enemies even when they are not visible to humans and Woovs."

Serina seemed startled by that news. She looked sharply at Seesil.

"I can hear them singing," said the saurian ESA cheerfully. "It's quite beautiful, really, but very odd."

"Singing?" asked Serina. "They make sounds we can't hear?"

"They do," said Seesil, "and I can hear that as well. But the sense I am describing is not hearing. I don't know how to translate it."

"I'll vouch for Seesil's abilities," said Argus. "When she worked for me, she saved the lives of my team many times. She is our greatest hope of recovering young Peter."

He didn't say *alive*. He could not be that optimistic.

"Serina," asked Kathryn, still looking at no one, "why would they take Peter?"

"Why did they ever take people?" countered Serina.

"But Ayat-ko was different. She lived with you."

"She was *not* different," said Serina. "And this kidnapping was not whimsical. It was provocative. This station will be in danger if we react rashly—or too slowly."

"I think they had been watching us for a while," said Kathryn. "Maybe they were curious. They used their stealth technology. They've been riding the trains, unseen, for centuries. They must have seen me with Peter and wondered why I was pursuing him, why he was so special. Last night they just grabbed him. They made me chase them for a while. Maybe they thought that was fun. Then I lost them. No trace of him anywhere on the planet."

"You saw Ayat-ko?" asked Serina. "It was she who took the boy?"

"No," said Kathryn. "I saw a male, I think."

"Then Ayat-ko may have had nothing to do with it," said Serina thoughtfully. "And this business about the trains is horrifying. I have read many accounts of disappearances—if anyone ever saw a kidnapping by Enemies, they did not live to tell the tale. Yet these Enemies let you see them. They teased you. They want you to follow. It could be fatal to take the bait."

"I agree," said Grigory, and Serina seemed to notice him for the first time. She was startled.

"The Eye of Grigory," she said softly.

"This happened to us during the Enemy War," he said. "It cost Andrei Mironenko his life. And it cost me my mortal shell. I am willing to act as decoy again. But you cannot get into their lair the same way Andrei did. They shall expect that. We must think of another way."

"We have a plan," said Vasily. "It's an odd one, for an odd situation."

He outlined it quickly.

"That's it?" asked Argus.

"That's how you might find them. After that, you'll have to rely on your training. You're in command, Argus. You'll have to decide what course of action to take."

"Understood," said Argus. He did not look too speculatively at Grigory. No one was more qualified to infiltrate a hive than the blind ESA. And if Grigory had an agenda of his own? Argus would just have to work it into the plan.

"Let's go," he said. "Too much time has already passed."

"You learn fast," said Argus.

Serina strapped herself into the seat across from him without a glitch. She was now very familiar with the capabilities of her danger suit and even with the weapon she had been assigned—and she had to admit, she was thrilled. She kept up with the rest of the team, was undaunted by zero-g, and was ready to take orders from her commander.

"Seesil has trained me very hard," she said. "She is an excellent teacher."

He nodded, his attention still on her but his expression abstract. She had learned to recognize when people were talking mind to mind.

"The pilot says we're uncoupling from the dock," he said. "Estimated time of arrival, fifteen minutes. We're supposed to look like a medical shuttle. We'll be landing at a clinic outside train station number forty-three."

"I don't know which one that is," she confessed.

"Me neither. But I suppose it doesn't matter. We'll just be scouting, trying to pick up the scent."

"Seesil never said a word about her ability," said Serina. "I suppose the information was classified. Or perhaps she is so modest she doesn't think it's a special ability at all."

"The Gonkhas are new to the Union," he said. "Intelligent, friendly people, but their greatest asset was a surprise to all of us. They perceive the universe in more than four dimensions. ESA Seesil was on my team because she was an ESA. But during the mission, we discovered that she was able to find Enemies even when they were using their stealth technology. They are able to move intradimensionally, and when they do so, she perceives them. She says it's like a song, but I have never grasped quite how."

Serina frowned. "Intradimensionally. Like a star ship?"

"No. Enemies don't tunnel. They don't *jump*. Seesil says they just sort of . . . go sideways." He shrugged. "I didn't get it then and I don't get in now, but she does, and that's good enough for me."

Serina was thinking of all the years Ayat-ko had appeared to her, seemingly out of thin air. She had always thought the Enemy woman was simply a master of silent movement. Probably she was. If Enemies had the ability to sidestep the known laws of physics, why were there any living humans still left on Belarus? "If they can go *sideways*—why do they need to take the trains to get around?"

He seemed to be looking at something just below her chin. His eyes tracked movement that wasn't there.

"What can you see?" she asked.

"Your world," he answered. "In tactical."

Serina deployed her helmet. She did not have enhancements in her brain like the rest of the team, but she still had access to a lot of the data they could perceive. The helmet rose from the fabric of her suit, seemingly from nothingness. The first time she had seen someone else deploy on, she had jumped. But as her own helmet closed over her head, the sensation was not the least bit startling or uncomfortable. She could see and breathe perfectly well, there was room inside for her braided hair, and she could set the controls on her left forearm to operate tactical vision. In another moment, she could see the same thing Argus could, though she doubted she could interpret the information with his expertise. Still it was very interesting.

Her world loomed in tactical. Across from her, Argus, his

eyes lowered, frowning in thought, seemed to be contemplating it. On the other side of the aisle, ESAs Grigory and Kathryn were facing each other. She suspected they weren't talking, yet they seemed intimately bonded. Their perfect professionalism awed her, yet she could sense the desperation and sorrow that pulsed just below the surface.

ESA Seesil suddenly lifted her big head over their seats. "Serina," she intoned. "Your world is singing. That is very odd."

"How so?" asked Serina.

"Most worlds do not. My own does not."

"How does it *sing?*" inquired Argus.

"Many things are moving between. So many things, I cannot sort them out from each other."

"Enemies are moving?" asked Serina.

"Yes, I suspect they are. But this is the most complex song I have ever heard. I am not sure of all its components. I must contemplate."

Seesil lowered her head again. Serina felt a tingle up her spine. She had always known the world was a strange place, but it was spooky to know that . . . *things* were moving. *Between.*

Argus smiled softly. "The universe gets stranger every day."

"I would not have thought such a thing was possible," said Serina.

"It is a law of nature." He was studying her, perhaps to see if she was afraid. She wasn't. She wasn't even nervous. She was glad to be taking action, honored to be part of his team. There was no doubt in his expression; if anything he seemed sympathetic.

"Argus," she asked, "how old were you when the Union came to your world?"

"I had just turned twenty."

"Was it hard for you to become a Star Man?"

"In some ways it was hard; in some ways it was too easy."

"How could it be *too* easy?"

His smile became a ghost of itself. "Too easy to embrace modern conveniences, to leave behind all the hard work of surviving. There is always a price to pay when you do that. I was a hunter, Serina. I hunted the most deadly prey. The rewards were great and the consequences of failure were dreadful. Ultimately it is a heartbreaking life, yet the beauty of it will haunt me for the rest of my days. When I was a boy, all I ever wanted to be was a hunter. Then the Star Men came along and showed me other possibilities. I embraced them, but when I die it is the ice bears whom I expect to welcome me to heaven."

Serina felt the sudden tug of gravity. They were descending rapidly.

"Surely," she said, "this life you lead now is far from easy."

"True," he said. "I have to think outside the box I used to know. That's always hard. And then again, it's hard to climb back in when you need to remember what you never should have forgotten."

Serina thought of Galena and Ayat-ko and the great house. She understood perfectly.

The tactical image of Belarus had changed steadily while they were talking. Now it had become a map laid out in two dimensions. She recognized the place names on the map instantly. "St. Petersburg," she said. "An interesting place to start."

"Get ready for landing," said a voice from an intercom.

Serina made some further adjustments to her suit and helmet. She was more than ready.

Ivan/Loki stepped off the train in the heart of St. Petersburg. He could have disembarked closer to the Winter Palace, but he felt inclined to walk among the crowds for a while. St. Petersburg evoked too many memories and he needed to sort them out.

He remained visible, causing people to stare at his blue

eye. Perhaps the citizens of this proud city were really as sophisticated as they liked to believe, because no one made the sign of the evil eye at him. At least, not yet. But they were wise enough to get out of his way. He walked, allowing his instincts to draw him where they pleased.

He had just begun to enjoy the sights when a shuttle passed overhead. Loki recognized it as a medical vessel. He would not have given it a second thought.

Ivan saw it and remembered the interfering Star Men who had spirited his daughter away from him. Then, he had merely raged at his own helplessness.

Now he could blow it out of the sky if he wanted. That helped. He was grinning by the time he got within sight of the Winter Palace.

Argus regarded his team. "The suits stay in off mode until I give the signal otherwise," he said. "Can't even use them to stay warm, so if you need extra layers, say so now. You'll have to use your unenhanced senses—especially you, Seesil."

Seesil nodded, and the bells on her neck tinkled.

"Remember, we do not know each other. The only thing we have in common is that we ride on the trains."

"Do I get to keep my tips?" asked Grigory, raised his empty tin cup. Dark glasses, a ragged coat, and a blind man's cane completed the outfit.

"You can donate it to charity," suggested Argus, whose glasses were the clear kind. He wore a scarf around his neck and a finer quality coat, a nice fur hat to keep his distinctive hair under cover. Kathryn and Serina wore outfits that were even more concealing, the layered skirts, head scarves, and veils of orthodox Muslim women. Women who went veiled in the big cities were rare, but not unheard of. They would attract little attention—unlike William in his circus garb. And Seesil in any garb at all.

"I'll go out first, then ten minutes later Grigory, then Kathryn and Serina, then William and Seesil. You all have the address where we will meet in the evenings. Everyone have enough lunch money?"

"If we don't," said Grigory, "William will earn some for us soon."

William shook his tambourine in a mock salute.

"That's it, then," said Argus. "The hunt begins."

The Enemy looked down upon Peter from a high throne in the middle of the rose-lit chamber, his chin propped in his hand. He was not smiling, and that was the only mercy Peter suspected he would get.

"Child," said the Enemy, "do you understand the concept of the Gift?"

Peter's blood began to boil. "I understand that I am *not* the Gift. I was not given to you. I was stolen."

"True. Still, you are a trophy of great value to the ones who lost you—"

"This is *not* so!" cried Peter, and winced at the passion in his own voice. "How can you think that? I have no one to care, no one to mourn for me."

The Enemy's pupils were shaped like stars. They expanded and contracted. "What a fine liar you are. You act utterly convinced of what you tell me, but I have watched ESA Kathryn courting you. You should have seen how frantically she searched for you after we took you."

Peter took a deep breath. His eyes stung, but he was able to keep the tears back for the moment. "Now it is you who tells the fine lie."

The Enemy watched him avidly. He was a slender man,

muscles taut and lean as a cat's, with pale skin, night-black hair, and fine features. His slender hands rested lightly on the arms of his thrown, but they did not look weak. When he spoke again, his tone was calm and merciless. "I see we have already taught each other something. I knew this would be a valuable association. And as for pleasure, torment need not be involved."

Peter could only stare. He did not even clench his fists. And he would not plead or try to bargain, as so many other humans must have done over the centuries. He understood this would be futile, yet he did not want to cry or pray either. Watching his Enemy was all he could do.

"You must be hungry," Kunum-ko said, his tone almost generous. "Come, let us dine together. I think we can find something to please your palate."

"I do not dine in hell," Peter said softly but with conviction.

There was a slight change in the Enemy's expression. "Don't be foolish. I promise you have never tasted such fine fare as you will receive here."

"I will not drink either. You will not bind me here with pleasures that appear to be mortal. They are false."

"What an odd little creature you are." The Enemy did not seem precisely angry; he was more intrigued. "Really, it's almost like being challenged, and that territory is far too dangerous to tread. If it pleases you to sit here in the dark, I'll indulge you. Eventually you'll change your mind, or I'll have to force nourishment on you. Either way, we'll both learn more about each other."

"It is not I you wish to understand," said Peter.

The stars at the center of those eyes expanded suddenly, drinking Peter.

"You want Kathryn to come for me. You want to see what they will do, the ESAs. This is your test for them, and I am the bait." A tear rolled down Peter's cheek, but he did not falter. "They could kill you if they set their will to it, but they won't. You want to know why. There is an easier way to find out, but you will never see it, you will never talk openly to them because it's not your nature. It's not your nature to love either, and you cannot know how I love Kathryn. You will never feel that way yourself. I pity you."

The Enemy watched him avidly. "I have eaten your kind and tasted many emotions that are not natural to me. Perhaps love is one of them."

Peter steeled himself. "Prove it," he said.

The Enemy was on his feet and standing before Peter could even blink. He did not flinch. He raised his chin, exposing his throat. Time slowed, and Peter allowed himself a quick, silent prayer.

The Enemy raised his hand slowly, touched the wetness on Peter's cheek, then tasted it. "You are wrong," he said. "It is *you* who rouse my curiosity the most."

Peter despaired. His bid to choreograph his own death had failed. "I'm just like anyone else," he said, heartsick.

"Essentially so," agreed the Enemy, "yet—essentially *not*. The ESAs wanted you. I value their opinion." He turned his back on Peter and walked casually to the door, taking the light with him. "By the way, don't wander too far. My kind take such pleasure from the torment of your kind—I should have to kill any of my brothers who are tempted to give you a tour of the torture chambers."

"My ko," called Peter.

The Enemy froze. Peter dared to hope he had spoken the clan dialect properly.

"That's how I heard the others addressing you," said Peter, in Russian. "I hope I was not rude."

The Enemy turned his head, but did not quite look at Peter. "Not at all," he said.

"Have you offered other prisoners food?"

"Sometimes."

"Why should you feed those whom you intend to kill?"

"Because hunger weakens."

"A weak prisoner could not last very long under torment, I suspect."

"Your suspicions are correct."

"Thank you," said Peter. "You have enlightened me."

"Perhaps you will find reason to thank me again soon," said the Enemy, and left the chamber. Darkness fell behind him, and Peter did not speak again. He merely watched until the light was gone.

Peter did not wait in the darkened chamber after Kunum-ko left him. Instead, he followed the Enemy, far enough back so the light would not fall on him, yet close enough that he could follow it. He had no particular reason for doing so, no fine plan for escape. He simply could not stand to wait in darkness like some lamb until the wolf came and got him.

He would die there, and he doubted he could even choose the manner of his own death. Yet he held a glimmer of hope that he could prove to be less than useful to his captors. That was all, but it was enough to keep him going through the endless hallways, chasing the light just ahead of him.

Peter had read many books about elf hills and their time/space distorting tendencies. He could not help but wonder if Enemies had ever lived on earth, for the hive seemed to have the same characteristics. He could not tell how long he pursued Kunum-ko, over what distance. And the Enemies themselves were as beautiful as elves were purported to be, or at least the cold, cruel sidhe from Celtic legends. Yet if Enemies had ever walked on old Earth, what had chased them away? Certainly not iron-age humans.

Up ahead the light flickered, then went out. Peter choked off a cry and reached blindly for something to guide him. He found the smooth wall of the passage. It felt warm to the touch, but this did not comfort him.

Absolute blindness, ahead and behind. He had read about this too. He had read about a character named Bilbo Baggins, who with a band of dwarves had tried to crash an elf party in the forest. They had been led on a merry chase by dancing lights until they were hopelessly lost.

Giant spiders had lurked in that story. But Peter had far worse things to fear. He stood for a while longer, hoping his eyes might become accustomed to the dark.

They didn't. He began moving forward again, anyway.

All day Grigory listened to the sound of William's tambourine and ESA Seesil's songs. Her singing voice was higher than her speaking, and she delighted the children as much as she confounded the adults.

She sang and danced until the bells on her harness filled the air with sweet music. People gasped, children ooh-ed and ah-ed, or cried when they were too small to understand Seesil wouldn't hurt them.

"What is it?" they asked each other. "I've never seen anything like it!" No one offered any theories about alien life forms. For the common folk of Belarus, this was too esoteric a concept. And Grigory doubted many members of the duma would have better theories.

Coins bounced into his cup from time to time. "God bless you," he murmured, intrigued by life at this level in the streets. He had never observed people under these circumstances. The fact that he was really looking for Enemies enhanced his natural senses even more sharply. Many times during the day, he sensed something out of the ordinary. He tried to focus on the sensation, but could not pinpoint its source.

William and Seesil earned many coins, especially when

Seesil let the children climb on her back. She pranced around with them, causing quite a ruckus. "Will you come and see us again tomorrow?" they begged.

"Not tomorrow," Seesil told them. "Tomorrow I shall ride the rain to the next town, and dance for the children there."

At the end of the day, they all got on the train and rode to their next stop. Grigory made his way slowly, tapping his cane, listening for inhuman echoes. He arrived at the hotel last. He checked in and made his way up the stairs. He smelled liquor, vomit, sex, incense, bread, cheese, vodka, and a thousand other things. Then he smelled vanilla.

She started to move past him on the stairs. Before he knew it, he had reached out and seized her wrist. She could have pulled loose, but did not. And then he heard a sound he knew.

"Kathryn," he whispered. He touched her face and found dampness there. "Little mother . . ."

"I'm not anyone's mother," she whispered, though no one was near to hear them.

"Because Peter won't let you be his?" Grigory could not help himself; he pulled her veil loose and stroked her face. Her skin was so soft, her mouth so full. He pulled her closer.

"Grigory," Kathryn asked in a voice as small as a child's, "why wouldn't he let me in? He would have been safe on Archangel by now."

"He was afraid," said Grigory. "I know how he feels."

"Are you afraid?" she asked.

He kissed her. She responded, but her tears continued to flow. He rubbed his face gently against hers. "Don't stop pursuing him," he said. "Don't stop . . . pursuing me, my dove."

"This must look outrageous," she said. "A blind man and a good Muslim girl kissing on the stairs."

"We should retire to more private surroundings," he said.

"I wanted—I was going to—"

"Don't," he said. "Don't go looking for the Enemies now. You need to be more patient."

She was silent, and the tears stopped flowing, but she said, "He's dead."

"Maybe not," said Grigory. "In fact, probably not. He may not stay alive very long, but I think for now he is bait, in pristine condition."

"If he's bait," she said, "I wish they would hurry up and tug on the damned fishing rod."

"You've been here long enough to talk with Seesil. Did she get a fix on them?"

"No," she said. "Nothing."

He frowned. If no Enemies were nearby, what had prickled his scalp?

Her hand found his, clasped it. "One other thing you should know, though it doesn't have anything to do with Peter. When Serina and I were walking around today, she saw someone she knew. Her aunt Alexis."

"Did she recognize Serina?"

"I don't see how she could. But she glared at us. Who knows? Maybe she hates Muslims."

"Watch for her tomorrow," said Grigory. "If she shows up again, you and Serina need to head directly for the next hotel."

"You think she could hurt us?"

He kissed her hand. "Truthfully, my dove? I think she could have our livers on a silver platter, if we let her."

"Her or the Enemies. Serina says that's their favorite dish."

For a long moment the two of them stood silently on the stairs. Grigory experienced no more unexplained sensations. Those had been left behind in St. Petersburg. Tomorrow they would pass near Zhukovka. Tomorrow they might get . . . lucky.

"Let's go up," said Kathryn. "But I warn you—I don't know if I can sleep tonight."

"Perfect," he said, and led her up the stairs.

* * *

The guards stationed at the Tomb of the Engineer were easy to drug. Loki could have stung everyone else in the Winter Palace just as easily, left them slumbering like the castle folk in the fairy tale, but his old skill of slipping past people unseen and unheard had come back to him, and soon he found himself facing Tally's locked door. Invisible though he was, the guards would have seen the door opening, so they were treated to free naps.

Loki had scorned Tally's love for Egyptian art, which was vastly overrated in his opinion, but now he stared at the image of Thoth on her door with new eyes—literally. Ivan had considerable respect for religious images, even those that were false. When he thought about Tally, even with Loki's memories, he was far more inclined to be cautious.

Loki needed to know what was in her database. She might know more about how the Original died. He relayed the code to the door, the one Tally had never suspected was programmed into it. The door popped open and a slight breeze blew past him, carrying the scent of wood and spices.

He entered cautiously, despite the fact that he already knew every inch of Tally's quarters through his spore colonies. Still, he couldn't shake the feeling someone was in there with him.

Her ghost. Ivan reached the conclusion quickly, without a trace of doubt. But Loki reserved judgment as he moved through the dim silence from the anteroom into the burial chamber. Her grand coffin stood at the center. Even Loki was impressed with its magnificence. Her face was rendered in gold and precious stones on the lid. He leaned over it.

Beautiful Tally. In his long life, Loki had never seen her equal. Her beauty had not abandoned her in old age, but only sharpened to clarity. He had fantasized for years about the torment he would inflict on her, but he never would have done permanent damage to her face; he would have preserved it. Yet he had to admit, the coffin artisans had done a better job at that than he would have done. He wondered if the embalmers had done as well. He broke the seal on the lid.

No mortal man could have moved it, but the suit gave him the power. He slid the heavy cover askew, exposing Tally's death mask. He had less than a microsecond to register its golden beauty when he spied movement in the depths of the coffin.

"You bitch. You FUCKING BITCH!" he snarled, hurling himself backward. At that moment he was entirely Loki, and full of rage and fear. He pressed his back against the false door and watched the tips of Tally's rasta-links rise from the sarcophagus, moving like the fronds of a water weed in a gentle current, with no more purpose, the mind that had once guided them long dead.

Of course they still functioned. They were machines, not flesh. But he stayed where he was until his heart slowed to a normal pace again.

"Who is here?"

Instantly he saw the short man and his two thugs standing in the doorway of the burial chamber. He would have perceived them long before if he hadn't been so preoccupied with an old obsession.

The short man took two steps forward. "We know you are here. We know you're wearing a danger suit. You can't get past us, so you might as well show yourself," he said politely.

Loki could have killed them, but Ivan was less inclined to do so. The short man was vaguely familiar, and he wanted to know why. He touched the controls on his forearm.

"Ivan Sergeivich Khabalov." The short man took a cigar out of his jacket pocket. "You are the last man I expected to see here." He lit the cigar, squinting at Ivan. "Has something happened to your eye?"

Loki would have laughed at the understatement, but Ivan suddenly recognized who these men must be. He thought it best to keep his amusement under wraps when talking to *okrana*. The short man puffed fragrant smoke into the burial chamber, then pointed to Tally's sarcophagus with the tip of his cigar. "Why did you open it?"

"Curiosity," said Ivan/Loki, which was true enough.

The short man grunted. His two thugs stayed ready at his heels, able to inflict damage if necessary.

"They're moving." The short man pointed again, this time at Tally's rasta-links. "Were you surprised to see that?"

"They're machines from the old time," said Ivan. "They will never stop functioning."

The *okrana* gazed at him impassively. Ivan/Loki wondered if he should kill them or whether it might be useful to know them longer.

"That eye of yours really is odd," said the short man. "Mironenko—come take a look at this."

Ivan/Loki froze at the sound of the name. He stared at the doorway as someone deactivated the stealth function of a danger suit and shimmered into view. He gazed at the newcomer's face, his hands clenching into fists.

It was Andrei Mironenko's face.

But as Mironenko moved closer, cocking his head in puzzlement, Loki suddenly recognized him. He relaxed his hands and grinned.

"Nikita," he said. "It's been ages."

Nikita Mironenko was a dead ringer for his nephew Andrei. "I'm afraid you have me at a disadvantage, sir."

<I've changed a great deal since you commissioned me to create WILDFIRE.>

Nikita Mironenko was almost as good as his nephew had been at hiding his surprise. <I suppose I've changed too.>

<Not a bit. Youth technology must have improved considerably in the years I was . . . away.>

<Yes,> said Nikita, <but that's not why I'm still here. I went into stasis for many centuries.>

<I suppose we all had our contingency plans.>

Nikita was watching him calmly. Mironenko must certainly have grasped the reason for his mismatched eyes.

<Shall I continue to call you Loki? Somehow, that no longer seems appropriate.>

Ivan/Loki found himself unable to answer quickly. With each passing moment, his two personalities became more integrated. He no longer felt wholly one or the other. And then the answer occurred to him, like a ray of light from heaven itself.

<Call me Lazarus.>

<Lazarus, who rose from the grave,> said Nikita. <Many of us can make that claim these days.>

<Perhaps. But God had nothing to do with your resurrection.>

Nikita raised an eyebrow. <You *have* changed—Lazarus.>

<I'm better than I was.>

<But no less confident, I'm glad to see.> Nikita moved closer to the sarcophagus, casually, but staying on the opposite side from Lazarus. He gazed at Tally's mummy. "Peter dressed her like a king," he said. "She's even got the crook and flail. The only thing that's missing is the king's beard." He touched the death mask reverently. "Magnificent. Dear God, what a beautiful woman she was."

The rasta-links bumped Nikita's hand harmlessly. <Did you get a chance to hook up with her database?> he asked.

<No,> said Lazarus cooly.

Nikita glanced at him. <You can do it with the blue eye, right?>

<I was interrupted.>

<Ah. Well, I'm sure she has some fascinating stuff in there.>

Lazarus was *more* than sure. And despite the fact that Nikita had been a good ally in the past, he found himself plotting a bloody course through the four men. He could take Tally's mummy with him . . .

Nikita took a link in his hand, as if he meant to insert it into his eye.

"Mironenko," the short man said suddenly, startling Nikita, who dropped the tentacle. "I must ask you to wait. We will not permit anything to be examined until we have done so ourselves. This room and everything in it are the property of the tsar."

"Of course." Nikita Mironenko took a step backward. "I respect your judgment." He regarded Lazarus again. <Do you currently have a patron?>

<Haven't you heard, Mironenko? The Republic is dead; the great families have fallen—there are no more patrons.>

<No, but there is lucrative employment—if you're interested. I could use your talents.>

<Really? But you were happy enough to let me die in obscurity on this wretched planet.>

Mironenko frowned. <Happy? Hardly that. A great many of our allies died in the first few days of the Civil War, Lazarus. My family was decimated. I lost my sons.>

Lazarus was moved by this news. The loss of a man's sons was a terrible thing, and he had to admit, there was a great deal about the Union he did not know—things Nikita Mironenko was uniquely qualified to tell him.

<I work for no one,> he said at last. <But I am a man in need of allies.>

<Please consider me one. Our interests still parallel each other in many areas.>

<I suspect they do.> Lazarus deliberately looked at the short man, who must have known that Lazarus and Nikita were having an important conversation, yet who betrayed no anxiety or even curiosity. "You've been locked out of here for years," he told the short man. "Now you have access again. I hope you'll decide I've done you a favor. As for why I came in here—it was simple curiosity, nothing more. Nikita"—he addressed Mironenko again—"if you want me, ask *them* where I live."

"Soon, my friend. I'll bring a bottle of good vodka. Somehow I have a feeling you'll appreciate that now."

Lazarus let his gaze linger one more time on the sarcophagus. Tally's links still undulated slowly. He tried to imagine himself taking one of them and inserting it into his artificial eye, but he could not. Perhaps it was the shock of seeing her again, of seeing those wretched links—his curiosity about what she might have recorded was exceeded by his nausea at the thought of letting one of those links touch his eyes. She was dead, and already his thoughts were turning to another woman, one whose face was as disfigured as Tally's had been beautiful. If he wanted to get to her, Nikita might be useful.

Nikita Mironenko's eyes were mild and hazel. His pleasant expression gave no hint of the ruthless mind behind it.

<I have information for you, Mironenko—you have information for me. Once we've shared it, I think we'll both be pleased with the collaboration. I feel it in my bones. Good night. Sleep well—but not so long as the last time.>

<And you, Lazarus.>

Lazarus walked around the sarcophagus and clasped Mironenko's hand. Nikita had a firm grip. In his first life, Loki would never have desired such a gesture, but he was a new man, and a Russian one at that. So he kissed Nikita Mironenko full on the mouth, then let go of his hand and walked resolutely to the door, nodding to the short man as he passed. The *okrana* did not try to stop him.

In the anteroom, he activated his suit. He passed among Tally's belongings without knowing or caring if he would ever see them again—until he spied a certain chair.

Loki had tied her to that chair. He could see her there in his mind's eye, naked, her face swollen where he had struck her. It all seemed stupid to him now. He thought about what might have been in her database concerning the death of the Original.

And found he no longer cared. The Original died a fool. Lazarus was stronger, wiser, and far less likely to make mistakes than Loki had been. Lazarus was the future.

Smiling, he left the tomb door wide open.

"He was about to kill you."

"Yes," said Mironenko calmly. "I acted foolishly. He could have killed all of us."

"He could do that?" The secret service man sounded only curious, not frightened. "Just because of that suit?"

"Oh no, Yuri." Mironenko lit his cigar. "Not just because of that. Our friend Lazarus has far more at his disposal than a mere danger suit. He has made devices that are worthy of the Dark Prince himself."

Yuri accepted this information impassively, like everything else. From his expression, one would have difficulty guessing whether he even understood it. But Nikita did not judge people like Yuri by their expressions.

Yuri turned his gaze on Tally Korsakova's burial chamber. "So, this is the fabulous Tomb of the Engineer."

"You've never been inside before?"

"No." Yuri walked slowly around the room, examining its contents with eyes that took in every detail. "I learned about ancient Egypt in school, like everyone else here does, from textbooks designed by the great engineer herself. It is an interesting subject. I've been to the Egyptian exhibit at the Hermitage. But this place, this mysterious tomb—"

He fell silent, and Nikita ventured to guess that he was moved by what he saw.

Yuri turned to the coffin again and gestured with his cigar. "We should cover her again. Who knows what our cigar smoke might do to her mummy?"

The two thugs moved to obey. "Wait—" said Nikita. He adjusted the controls on his suit. "It would take six men to move that thing, or one man with a danger suit." He slid the lid back in place, careful not to pinch any of Natalia Korsakova's rasta-links in the process. He would have loved to hook up with one and dive into her personal database, but that adventure would have to wait for a better day. He stood back, struck once more by the marvelous face on the lid. "Extraordinary woman," he said.

"Extraordinary *person,*" said Yuri. "Few men or women could equal her achievements."

Nikita raised an eyebrow. "You know a lot about her. More than most, I would guess."

"At one time her books resided in the library in the Winter Palace," said Yuri. "But they disappeared."

"Indeed?" Mironenko said mildly. "Any guesses about where they might have ended up?"

"Guesses can be very unprofitable on Belarus," said Yuri. "Especially if they turn out to be right."

"Perhaps the books were never in the library to begin with."

"I saw them myself, the very night Tsar Gyorgy came to power. I looked at the one she wrote about Canopus."

Nikita puffed his cigar. "I wouldn't throw that name around if I were you."

"All of us know secrets that could get us killed," said Yuri. "But on Belarus, you would have to kill a lot of people to hide that *particular* secret."

"My dear friend." Nikita almost smiled. "In the Civil War, entire solar systems were wiped out in the blink of an eye."

Yuri shrugged. "That's why the Republic is dead. If they were that stupid, good riddance. Come on. Let's leave the engineer in peace."

Nikita glanced once more at the sarcophagus. He started to turn away, but stopped suddenly, certain that Tally's finely crafted eyes had moved to return his gaze. But it was the glitter of light from the anteroom, shining on the semiprecious stones. He turned again, keeping his eyes on the *okrana.*

"I wouldn't lock the door again," he joked.

"Don't worry," said Yuri, following several paces behind. If he had seen Tally Korsakova's eyes move, that was another secret he would keep. Nikita had plenty of his own, so he didn't even ask.

Lazarus took the train home from St. Petersburg. It was early morning when he arrived, but he wasn't tired. He felt more focused than he had in days, though he still lacked a plan of action.

A knock on his door changed that.

"Who calls?" he demanded.

"Alexis," called a voice he knew well.

He was surprised. He had forgotten about Alexis and her band of simpering cronies. He had enjoyed their patronage for a few years, but he didn't need them any longer. He opened the door anyway.

She stood there, her face radiant. "Ivan," she said softly. "I thought you had dropped from the face of the earth."

He let her in. He wasn't sure why. Perhaps he did it because she was a devout woman, and her fire was often contagious. Perhaps he did it because she was beautiful. Her eyes adored him. Before Loki, Ivan had discarded any thoughts of taking her to bed as not advantageous.

"You hate me," she said. "I can see it in your eyes. You don't need me anymore, Ivan."

"True," he said. "I need no one but God."

"I beg your forgiveness. But I have news that may be of some help to you."

"Share it," he said gently.

"I have looked for you," she said, as if she had not heard. "I spoke to everyone who might know you. I was told that you had boarded a train, and I thought to find you by inquiring at every stop. I looked for you in St. Petersburg."

He was impressed. She wasn't bad, for an amateur. Perhaps she might still be useful after all.

"I wanted to pray with you," she continued, her eyes shining. "I thought we might seek guidance together. So few understand our passions, Ivan, our belief in the true God."

"So few," he said.

"In St. Petersburg I saw something that made me stop and take a second look, though I didn't understand why at the time."

Her expression changed then, hardened. It marred her beauty, yet he found it fascinating.

"A strange creature was parading itself among the crowd near the station," she said. "I could not believe my eyes when I saw it—a huge thing, unlike any animal that walks this world. I have seen its like only once, in the ancient family bible that resided in my home, the home that burned to the ground—and I can see that was no accident now. The devil arranged it. He hoped that I would not recognize the dragon when I saw it. But I did."

"The *dragon,*" said Lazarus. He wondered if she had gone mad. But he harbored another suspicion as well.

"It sang," she said. "It played with the children. They adored it. I watched it closely, knowing it to be a sign of evil, and as I looked here and there among the crowd I saw the young man who was gathering coins for the performance. He was William, Serina's gardener."

"Perhaps he needed new employment."

"Most assuredly he did," she said, with a satisfaction that dripped venom. "If he and his wretched brood had not fled the estate, they would be rotting in a dark, cold cell by now. They shall once I alert the police, I promise you."

"You spoke to the police?"

"Not yet," she rushed to assure him. "It was you I thought of, because William was not alone. Two Muslim women sat on a bench nearby, as if they were waiting for someone. I thought their eyes studied the crowd a little too perceptively, so I moved closer to them, thinking to confront them. When they saw me, I'm sure they recognized me. And I recognized one of them. She has her mother's eyes."

"Who?" he demanded.

"Serina." She spat the name. "I should have known she would be with William. She must have brought the devil's spawn with her from Archangel. Who knows what manner of creatures walk that haunted station? This is what the Union has to offer us—monsters. They will be stopped, I swear it. I will go to the police and—"

"Don't go to the police," he said.

She shut her mouth.

"Don't tell *anyone* else about this. Do you understand?" He imprisoned her with his gaze. She looked back and forth between the black eye and the blue, fear warring for control of her senses. That was another thing he had forgotten—how she might react to his new orb—and this was the first moment she had acknowledged it. But she said nothing.

"I will handle this matter," he said. "I relieve you of that responsibility. Do not take further action."

"I wish to help you," she said, her voice trembling.

"I do not need your help."

She fell to her knees, crying bitter tears. "Do not exile me," she pleaded. "Do not discard me, I beg you!"

"Stop crying," he said, his tone cool.

She obeyed. She got to her feet again.

"Where did they go?" he asked.

"They boarded the train heading toward Zhukovka. They disembarked there. I know what hotel they booked for the night."

Zhukovka. So they knew. He was very glad he had disabled every system inside his hidey-hole before abandoning it. Nothing of value remained there. But it bothered him they knew. It bothered him very much.

Alexis watched him with red eyes. He focused all of his attention on her. "If you mean what you say, then come see me again, another day. If I have time, I will speak to you."

"I will come," she vowed.

He touched her cheek. His fingers lingered over the fine curves. Then he lowered his hand again.

"Think about it," he said softly. He walked past her, brushing her ever so slightly, and opened the door.

She stood with her back to him for a long moment. But when she turned, she looked calm, almost happy. She gazed past him, never meeting his eyes as she walked out the door. "Our association is blessed," she said. "God shall guide you and keep you until we meet again."

She did not look back. He closed the door. He thought about the night Serina Kurakin-Scriabin had fled the world.

He thought about the people who helped her. They were helping her still, and worse—she was helping them. Embassador Fabricus was one. Ivan needed to pay him a visit. Once Fabricus was dispatched, Serina might be flushed like a frightened bird.

Sleep first. Then action. And then?

Perhaps it was time to wake a few sleeping serpents.

Early in the morning, Serina wandered down a path toward the woods of Zhukovka. Snow was falling, muffling the sounds of William's tambourine and Seesil's song. Serina kept them in earshot, but wandered back and forth, trying to raise an old memory, pausing from time to time to look at the winter landscape like any tourist.

Unveil your eyes . . .

She was on the other side of the wood Ayat-ko had shown her all those years ago, approaching the scene of that puzzling conversation. Behind her, the music stopped, and she heard voices.

Tell me, what do you see?

My Enemy . . .

Something tickled her senses. She looked for Kathryn, found the ESA a few paces away, looking off into a field. “Kathryn,” she said softly. Kathryn looked at her. “Call the others,” she said. “I want to look for something, to see if it’s still there.”

Kathryn hurried off.

What do you see?

“I saw my Enemy,” said Serina. “But I didn’t see enough.”

PART FIVE

Argus waved his hand in front of the beam of light. It was coming from the big tree nearby. They didn't have to wonder what else was hiding there, because someone had left the entrance to an underground burrow open, as if they didn't care who saw it.

"I ran right past this spot when I chased the kidnappers," said Kathryn. "Ivan Khabalov must have stumbled onto this mechanism."

"Ayat-ko brought me here when I was a girl," said Serina. "She asked me what I saw. She said this place had concealed savageries humankind were not willing to contemplate. I thought she was talking about the Zhukovka massacre, but now I think she was referring to John the Murderer. She knew what he did here. I wonder *how* she knew."

Argus didn't answer at first. He debated using his sensors. The red light reminded him of the laser site used on some weapons.

"We'll find nothing worthwhile inside," said Grigory.

Argus glanced at him. "Why not?"

"If we had found this hideout before he left it, we might have found the place to which the mold spore network was sending its information. We might have used it to find other

Enemy hives. But look, he has left it open for anyone to find. He took everything of value away with him." The blind ESA turned his face away from the tree, toward the deeper forest.

"You're sure of that?" asked Argus.

"Yes. When I left Tally's tomb I did the same. Not a trace of my database remains in that matrix. John the Murderer would do no less."

Kathryn turned away from the tree and joined Grigory in his surveillance. "The Dead Zone appeared and then disappeared not too far from here."

"Something . . ." said Seesil.

Argus froze. He motioned to the others to be quiet.

"Something," she said again, and began to move. Argus and the rest of the team followed her.

Serina recognized the scene they were approaching. Ayat-ko had shown it to her, the scene of the Zhukovka massacre. Her scalp prickled, but not just from nervousness.

Seesil kept moving, her head and neck stretched in a long line. She did not waver, and only spoke one word. "Something . . ." Serina followed along with the others until they reached a tangled tree that grew out of the side of a hill. "Here," said Seesil, and she walked right into the tree.

And vanished.

Argus followed, then Kathryn and William. Grigory waited for Serina. "You need not follow," he said. "You got us this far."

"I must," she said, and walked exactly where she had seen the others go. She flinched when she got close enough to bruise her nose on the tree, but it blurred before her eyes and she felt an odd tingling on her skin. She kept moving, hoping she would see clearly again soon.

Warmth enveloped her like a blanket, making her pant. Her eyes focused on the faces of her comrades, who watched for her anxiously in the gloom. In another moment, Grigory appeared behind her.

"Might as well take off the costumes," whispered Argus, shrugging out of his coat. Serina noted that his eyes were already expanded into tactical mode. William helped Seesil remove her belled harness—the Gonkha seemed preoccupied, like someone trying to listen to several people at once.

Serina quickly discarded her costume and deployed her helmet, adjusting the vision function so she could see clearly. Once she did, her breath was taken away.

They were in a long passage, obviously deep underground. It was uncomfortably warm, and she had to adjust her suit's temperature control. She heard Argus's voice in her right ear, though his lips did not move.

<Serina, you're up front with me and Seesil. Grigory, Kathryn, William, watch our tails.>

They began to move, still following Seesil's lead. Serina felt utterly calm, but not for lack of fear. The appearance of the long hallway was odd. It teased her senses as if it were somehow twisting space, yet she could not focus on the point at which the twist must be occurring. The walls seemed at first to be plain, but after she had looked at them for a while, she realized that they were covered with intricate lines woven together in complex patterns that made her dizzy when she tried to comprehend their intention.

She stopped looking at them, focusing instead on Seesil, who was not using her eyes to find her way. The ESA blinked as if she were as troubled by the sights as Serina, but she was not influenced by what she saw, listening instead to that sense that wasn't any kind of song a human could hear.

Serina heard nothing but her own breathing. When they passed doorways, she twitched in anticipation of attack. She squinted into the depths of the chambers, saw the dim outline of beautiful furnishings, but no living soul moved there. She both dreaded and hoped that Ayat-ko would suddenly appear in the passage ahead of them.

They walked. She lost track of time. She did not realize she had become hypnotized until Argus suddenly put his hand out to stop her. Seesil had stopped, and was swinging her head back and forth. Serina thought she looked like a mother who had lost sight of her child.

<The song has stopped.> Seesil's voice sounded in Serina's ear.

Serina looked up ahead of them into the darkness. She looked behind and saw the same.

They were lost.

ESA Nesto did not sleep when there was no one to back him up, he stayed in level 2 danger mode. He could stay there for two weeks, if necessary, his senses hyper-alert, his consciousness expanded into the sensor array that used to consist mainly of sprites, but now included a variety of machines, everything from communication and computation devices to weapons. He suspected he would never interface with them as comfortably as he had with the intelligent, resourceful, and infinitely adaptable sprites, but he was adjusting to the new challenges and limitations they presented. He stood in the most defendable room in the house and watched the world, keeping a line open in case Argus called, listening to reports from Archangel Station, and looking for signs of the Dead Zone that would be his only clue to the presence of Enemies.

That was his mistake. The danger suit Lazarus wore employed an entirely different technology.

Nesto had been as ESA for forty-two years. Though never a military ESA, he had worked on many teams whose assignments had placed them in combat situations. Thrust repeatedly into life or death situations, he had developed a sixth sense for danger that had nothing to do with his enhancements.

But this time he sensed it too late.

<INTRUDER AL—>

The ESA got part of a message out, but Lazarus was not afraid of company—he was looking for it. He was covered in Nesto's blood, so he took a minute to wash it off in the shower. When he emerged moments later into the hallway, dripping water this time, he realized no one had responded to the ESA's call. Odd.

Lazarus accessed his mold network. The spores were gone from this house, but they were active in several other places in the world. They had been accumulating information for days. He watched the speeded-up version of recent events, combing for images of Argus Fabricus. While he was doing that he also searched the house.

He found the laptop in the office. He didn't try to get into it, merely grabbed it to look at later. He was on his way to the bedrooms when he suddenly found images of the embassador.

There was the dragon Alexis had mentioned. Lazarus had never seen the life form before. The team moving through the hive wore helmets and danger suits like the dead ESA in the house. Lazarus scanned the rest of the hive and made a decision.

He used his network to activate some sleeping machinery on the Arctic continent.

Then he strolled from the house, walking through the blood and leaving footprints on the floor all the way to the front door.

<Commander.> A technician called Hale on the emergency frequency. <ESA Nesto just attempted to report an intruder at the embassador's house—transmission was abruptly interrupted, sir. No one is answering our calls now.>

Hale did not call Argus Fabricus to warn him. He had ordered a communications blackout with the search team until further notice. ESA Nesto was on his own. And so was Archangel. As soon as the first technician had relayed his message, another came behind it.

<Emergency call from Home Base, sir!>

<Archangel, the Derelicts have jumped! Do you copy?

They started moving less than a minute ago, started coming together—is anyone there? Ready your weapons, they've—>

<Commander, jump gate forming. They're practically on top of us!>

<BATTLE STATIONS!> Hale sent to all stations. <Vasily, better warn the tsar. We're under attack.>

His eyes saw full tactical. He watched the Grinder emerge from the jump gate, its impossible architecture spinning around a center that might have been the gate of hell. For a timeless moment it seemed about to swallow Archangel.

And then it turned its face toward Belarus, and began to descend into the gravity well.

Archangel hit the Grinder with everything they had. It continued to descend, unscathed.

Mother of God. Hale watched it go, helplessly, remembering every detail of what had been recorded the last time the Grinder had attacked. *What now?*

<The Belarusian tsar is asking for details, sir.>

<Ask him if he remembers what happened at the beginning of the Enemy War,> said Hale. <Tell him it's about to happen again. Tell him we're ready to assist—and he'd better start emergency procedures.>

And pray to God, he didn't add, *that they'll do the least bit of good.*

“Mistress, Irina is dead!”

The maid was consumed by tears and panic. Galena gripped her shoulders. “Tell me what has happened.”

“I found her on the floor,” sobbed the girl, “in Duchess Anastasia’s chambers—her head is crushed!”

“When?” demanded Galena.

“Not five minutes ago. I ran here immediately!”

“Good.” Galena released the girl. “Top speed, Tova, alert Mischa. Tell him to bring the fire squad.”

The girl’s eyes widened, but she fled the room as swiftly as a startled deer. Galena was close on her heels, but she turned in the opposite direction and ran to Anastasia’s chambers. She did not go in to view the maid’s body. Her eyes quickly found the trail of blood, which she followed.

It led up to Serina’s floor; Galena found the bloody statuette on the landing, so blood droplets would be much harder to find beyond that point. But Galena didn’t need them. She had already surmised where Ana was going. She couldn’t harm Serina, who was gone, but she could strike at her another way.

Galena moved cautiously. The gaslamps cast a flickering glow in the hallways, creating false movement, so she did not trust her eyes. Instead she used her nose and her ears. She heard nothing, but detected a faint odor: kerosine. She followed it to Serina's library. The door stood open; from inside came the sound of heavy books being dropped on a hard surface.

Galena moved as softly as a cat, crossing the threshold quickly and moving to one side to press her back against the wall. Shadows haunted the corners of the room, but in the center, Serina's study table was piled high with books. A kerosine lamp cast its fitful light from the edge of the table, ready to be knocked over with the slightest vibration.

Anastasia staggered from the depths of the library with another load to add to the pile. Quite the expert, she was working to build a pyre that would make enough heat to shoot the flames high. Once the ceiling caught, the fire would spread much farther. Galena waited for her to go back for another load, then moved quietly around the table. She slid the lamp to a more secure location, but didn't shut it off—that would alert Anastasia. Galena stepped to one side, joining the shadows again. In another moment, the girl appeared with more books. Galena unbuttoned her left cuff and emerged from the darkness.

"Ana," she said.

Anastasia did not pause, but hurled the books onto the pile. She turned to Galena and grinned. "Did you really think you could tell me what to do?" she asked.

"You dare."

Galena's tone made Anastasia frown. Then she showed her teeth, which did not surprise Galena in the least.

Galena walked slowly toward her niece. "You are an animal. We have suffered you long enough. You made your final error when you killed Irina. She was under *my* protection. Now I demand your life for hers."

Anastasia looked pleased. She was not afraid of Galena's proximity. If anything she welcomed it. She balled her hands into fists and lowered her chin.

But Galena did not pause. She moved steadily closer, her

posture regal, betraying no intention other than to close the space between herself and Anastasia.

"You wouldn't dare do a thing to me!" Anastasia sneered. "My mother and Dmitri will put you in your place. They know all about you and your *allies*. They live underground, don't they, Galena? You'll hang in the town square for this. Your time is over!" She threw her head back to laugh, exposing her throat for half a second.

Galena moved swiftly, like a farm wife cutting the throat of a chicken. Her knife was so sharp it severed both the carotid artery and the vein on either side of Anastasia's neck. Blood gushed from the wound, spraying Galena, the pile of books, the table and rug. Ana dropped to her knees, clutching her throat. Her eyes rolled up. And then she fell on her face.

The blood pumped for another minute before it stopped.

Galena stared at the creature who had been her niece. Anastasia's suitors had babbled all sorts of sensitive information to her, which she dutifully regurgitated to her mother. Irina and the other maids had relayed the information back to Galena. She knew who the players were in the game that was afoot to unseat Gyorgy. They would be arrested and executed in due time.

One shadow moved away from the darkness and joined Galena in the pool of light cast by Anastasia's lamp.

"Once again," he said, "you were too hasty, Galena."

But she shook her head. "Not this time. This time the swift kill was best. She was so terribly surprised, Kunum-ko, and that was well worth seeing."

"Surprise is a brief thing," he said. "I have never met anyone who savors it as much as you."

The blood had stopped flowing when Ana's heart ceased. Now it lay in a pool under her cooling body, soaking the rug.

"What a pity," said Kunum-ko, "to ruin such a fine rug. And your dress, Galena."

"They can be washed," she said. "The books are what I value. They will require the attention of a restoration expert."

Ana made such an untidy heap in the middle of her pool of blood. Galena gazed at her with grim satisfaction, as if Anastasia were the symbol of every prejudice and stupid notion that had ever impeded her. Suddenly lavender drops fell into the red. Kunum-ko had cut his palm. He watched his blood flowing with Anastasia's, the stars at the center of his eyes wide with pleasure.

"What are you doing?" asked Galena.

He smiled at her, but the smile wasn't terrible at all. It was almost whimsical. "I want to see what our blood looks like—mixed."

He squatted and stirred the mixture with his finger. The result was a deep red, almost burgundy, like Galena's favorite wine. He stood again and licked the blood from his finger.

"Interesting," he said thoughtfully. "Very interesting." He gazed at her intently for another moment, then withdrew back into the darkness.

Galena walked around Anastasia's body and went into the hall. Voices were approaching. "Here!" she called. "One of you fetch a stretcher, and someone bring some towels. We have a mess to attend to."

But the employees who rushed to greet her were not concerned with what lay on the library floor.

Her steward, Mischa, was the first to reach her, his face white. "We have received a call from the tsar's office," he said. "The Star Men have called an alert. The Grinder has returned, Galena. It's headed straight for our world."

Galena turned in the doorway, searching the shadows between the bookshelves.

What are you up to, my Enemy? Have I read you wrong all these years?

The darkness gave up no secrets, and Galena knew she would have to find out just like everyone else in the world this time.

The hard way.

* * *

Commander Hale relayed few orders once the Grinder descended into Belarus's gravity well, he let his team do what they were trained to do. He watched the Enemy construct in tactical, and pondered its configuration. It was hovering over the main land mass, but for the moment did not seem intent on a particular target. And now that he had a chance to get a good look at it, the thing didn't quite look like a Grinder, either. It's configuration was different this time around.

"I don't think it's attacking the Belarusians," someone said aloud—which made Hale twitch in surprise. A Woov Elder was standing near him. He wasn't sure which one she was.

"What makes you say that?" he asked politely.

"I think it would have finished us off first. Right now we could flee to our various ships and jump, go get backup. I think it was the threat of backup that kept these Enemies from attacking Andrei Mironenko's colony when it was founded."

Hale was only half listening. <Any word from Fabricus yet?> he asked the technician.

<It's like he's not even down there, sir. No life signs, no locator signaling from a dead body—>

Another technician broke in.

<I have a communication from Belarus, sir.>

<Fabricus?> demanded Hale.

<No, sir. This person is calling herself Baba Yaga. She says we need to back off.>

Hale looked at the Woov. She did not seem surprised to hear about Baba Yaga. "We have to stay on alert," he said. "If that thing attacks, we'll respond."

"That seems reasonable," she said graciously.

<Commander—a hot spot is forming on the Arctic continent.>

The tactical screen shifted views. Inside the lines describing the Arctic continent, a red spot began to pulse.>

<What the hell!?> demanded Hale.

"Someone has armed a missile," said the Woov.

* * *

Argus stopped suddenly. The room through which they were moving was furnished identically to one they had already passed through. He didn't think he was imagining it. The throne that dominated the room must certainly be unique.

"We're going in circles," he said, softly.

"Peter has been here recently," said Grigory. "But he's gone now."

"They're jerking us around," Kathryn said, her voice as dry as dead leaves.

"Something . . ." Seesil said.

Everyone froze. The Gonkha stretched her long neck, then suddenly lowered her head almost to the floor and hissed.

"Get down!" shouted Argus, and the team obeyed. He pressed his own face to the floor in time to see the blur of Seesil's massive tail in motion. She lashed it like a giant whip, moving incredibly fast, striking several bodies with a sickening *crunch.*

"Up!" Argus ordered. "Move, Seesil at point!"

They moved fast, stepping on fallen Enemies as they cleared the chamber and fled into a tunnel. But once there, Argus ordered them to stop. He looked behind them. He could see one body from where he stood.

"They were alone," he said.

"Probably just sent to slow us down," agreed Grigory.

"Something . . ." Seesil warned again, but then said, "Something . . . *different.*"

Peter was very hungry, but he ignored it. Of more concern to him was a strong desire to curl up in the darkness and go to sleep. He did not know how long he had wandered; no sound or light had touched him in several eternities, yet he knew they would again. He could not allow himself to meet his fate with his eyes closed, lost in some false dream.

His hand slid along the wall, a sensation that had comforted him at first, then puzzled him as he felt odd patterns and textures. After a time those patterns began to slip into his consciousness and tease him, until he took his hand away to save his sanity. But that didn't work either. That was like floating in a void, and the sensory deprivation did almost as much damage as the intrusions. So finally he settled on the method of letting his hand touch the walls sporadically, just enough to remind himself they were there, but not enough to let the patterns become established.

Then suddenly he reached for the wall and found empty air. He must have entered a chamber, but he could not tell how large it was. He edged toward his left for a time, but found no wall there. He stopped then, fighting the sudden, dreadful certainty that he stood at the edge of some fathomless gulf. He shivered—was the air growing cold? He began to edge back the way he had come when he bumped into someone.

Before Peter could utter a cry, a leathery hand clamped over his mouth. "Keep quiet," a rusty voice hissed in his ear. "Do you want to live? I'm taking you out of here."

The voice did not belong to Kunum-ko, nor, Peter was fairly certain, to any of his clan. So he nodded. The hand left his mouth and gripped his shoulder. He did not resist as it pulled him along. They ran a short distance, and suddenly he bumped into an object.

"Get in," hissed the voice, and he stumbled to obey. He had to take a step up, onto some sort of platform, and then a gate was closed behind him. He reached out and grasped the edges of the thing. It was made of wood. It encircled him up to his waist, he stood hip to hip with someone who seemed to be made of bone and iron.

"Hold on!" she commanded, and he clamped his fingers on the wooden rim. The thing lurched under him, and accelerated until his hair was blowing in a stiff wind. They sped through the darkness like an express train. Peter heard the wind buffeting objects they passed, felt the hot air of the hive cooling around them. A warning bell sounded deep inside him.

What is happening? Where are the Enemies?

And suddenly the dark shattered before his eyes, falling away like shards of glass, and they were speeding through the bright day, the winter wind tearing at them. Peter saw hills ahead, a snowy plain mere feet below, and a blue sky that seemed to grow brighter every second, making him squint. He glanced at his companion and his eyes nearly popped out of his head. She had skin the color of old leather and wore a brightly embroidered jacket. A red silk scarf bound her grey hair close to her head. She gripped the side of the wooden transport with taloned hands, her shiny black eyes fixed on something ahead of them, and the pipe she held in her sharp teeth left a trail of smoke like the stack on a steam locomotive.

The sky grew brighter still, and Peter started to look over his shoulder.

"Don't look behind you!" she snarled. "It will blind you!"

He forced himself to look straight ahead once more, and saw a shiny object. It was lurching toward them on long legs. He squinted, and realized they were chicken legs. A door opened in the thing. They zoomed toward it as if they would crash. Suddenly the light around them was so bright, Peter had to jam his eyes shut.

Then all movement stopped. He felt no g-forces, no thud as they came to a halt. One moment they were hurling through the air like a comet and the next they were standing still. The light that had tormented his eyes had gone out. He opened them cautiously.

She wasn't in the pestle with him anymore. She was standing a few feet away with her arms crossed, watching him with eyes like polished black stones. She puffed on the pipe a few times, then said, "Well? What are you waiting for? Come down from there. We have things to do."

* * *

"Someone is calling me." Seesil was puzzled. The song was like no other she had ever heard. It made the strange lines of this hive seem to dance more coherently, to flow together into comprehensible rhythms. "I can see where we are now. I can see the way out. But the boy isn't here anymore. No one is here but us."

And suddenly the song became a steely voice.

<THIS IS BABA YAGA. I HAVE RESCUED THE BOY! GET OUT OF THERE, YOU FOOLS! FLEE WITH EVERY OUNCE OF STRENGTH YOU HAVE OR YOU ARE DOOMED! NOW!>

Seesil picked Serina up like a cub, tucked her under one arm, and ran with all her might toward the exit she could see in her mind's eye.

❧

Serina could feel powerful muscles moving smoothly inside the great body against which she rested. She realized they must be moving at impossible speed. She looked behind her, down the long length of Seesil's body, and saw the faces of the ESAs who ran just behind them; but their bodies were blurred. She could see Seesil's huge tail stretched out stiffly behind, acting as a counterbalance. The ESA was running on three legs, using the fourth to grasp Serina, yet still managing to carry her without so much as a bump.

In another moment a wave of daylight blinded her; they had left the hive. The helmet adjusted to the light, letting her see the white plain around them and the hill from which they had just emerged—nowhere near the Zhukovka glen through which they had entered the hive. She gazed into the fully dilated eyes of Argus, which reflected light back at her like glass. One moment later his helmet covered his face, and panic twisted in her stomach. Something tore the sky behind him.

Yesus Christos, the sky is raining fire!

A streak of light traced a path down to the spot they had just vacated, a spot that grew smaller as they sped away from it at the speed of the very fastest train, yet not fast enough. Serina watched it touch the earth, whispering a last prayer for all their souls.

She heard an odd crackle, felt a massive shock pass through the ground under Seesil's feet, and the image of the world seemed to shiver like disturbed water. A beautiful light blossomed at the center of the impact, spreading up and down like a column. In that moment Serina recognized what she was seeing from a photograph in one of her books. An instant later, another shock wave began to spread out from the explosion, pulverizing everything in its path. It began to eat the ground behind them.

Then the world tilted; she and Seesil were tumbling over a bluff. The ESA broke her fall; she felt almost nothing of the impact when they hit the ground fifteen feet below. Before she could utter a word, the other ESAs had scrambled down beside her, and Seesil was covering them all with her enormous body, like a hen protecting her brood.

"No, my friend!" cried Serina. "My poor friend!"

She could see one patch of sky. Something shiny and metallic suddenly eclipsed that view. She waited for the force that would burn them all to ashes—but it didn't come.

Seesil's great heart pounded against Serina. Then the big ESA cautiously lifted her head, giving Serina a better view of the metal thing. It perched over them, its giant chicken legs splayed out on either side. Around it flowed the chaos of the explosion.

"Why aren't we dead?" she asked Seesil.

"She has cast some sort of protective field around us," replied the ESA. "We're in a kind of—bubble you might call it. We're safe, for now."

Serina sat up and looked at her companions. She could not tell if they were as dazed as she, because their helmets were still in place. Even Seesil's face was covered. She looked up at the metal object. Its body was completely seamless. Its chicken legs were attached to the bottom as if they had grown there.

"Who is *she?*" asked Serina, knowing the answer but wanting to hear it spoken by sane persons.

"Baba Yaga," replied Seesil. "For some reason, she felt compelled to save our lives."

Argus lowered his helmet. Underneath, his face was calm. In fact, he looked almost happy. "She sent a message just before we fled. She said she had Peter."

Kathryn had lowered her helmet too, and from the look on her face she harbored some doubts. A lot of hope, as well.

Grigory's red eyes shone in the dim light. "We can only wait and see. We'll know soon enough if she was telling the truth."

Peter and Baba Yaga watched the explosion from a round window in her kitchen. He felt as if he were standing inside a farmhouse, waiting for Armageddon to sweep the wooden structure away like so much straw. But no harm touched them. He saw the light at the heart of the explosion; apparently the simple-looking window contained some sort of protective filter. He watched the shock wave spread from the center, and it was as if God had slammed a hammer down upon the world.

"Magnificent," he said. "And so monstrous. Who has done this thing, and why?"

Baba Yaga tapped more tobacco into her pipe. "John the Murderer has done this thing," she replied. "Who knows why."

"He is dead," said Peter.

"Really?" she asked.

Peter thought hard before he spoke again. "Strange things have happened here before. I suppose they must happen again."

"Certainly they must," she said.

Commander Hale and the Woov Elder watched the Grinder hovering over the skies of Moscow. It stayed there just long enough to give the inhabitants a good scare, then moved away at Mach 9, going directly north—toward the Arctic continent.

"What do you want to bet it's headed for the point where that missile originated?" remarked the Woov.

Commander Hale did not comment. The missile had detonated in an uninhabited area of Siberia, and it had originated from an area that was *supposed* to be uninhabited. But obviously people had been to both places, and he had a terrible hunch who they were.

Serina wondered if they were in Siberia. At the moment it looked more like hell.

Seesil arranged herself so the others could lean against her, and together they watched the storm pass. Fifteen minutes later, the wind died completely. The world that was revealed had turned brown and grey, and ashes rained gently from the sky.

The others had abstract expressions on their faces, and Serina knew they must be conversing.

"Will there be radiation?" she finally asked.

"Nothing harmful," Argus informed her. "It was noisy and destructive, but it wasn't dirty. Thank God it was so remote—anyone within fifty miles of this would have been killed."

"Except for us," she remarked.

"Thanks to Baba Yaga," he reminded her. "Otherwise, I promise you, even with these danger suits—we would be an unhappy collection of ashes."

Serina looked up. The hut remained perched over them. The force field kept debris from falling on them.

Grandmother witch, she thought, *I hope we are clever enough to escape your help unscathed.*

"They surprised you," guessed Peter.

Baba Yaga fixed her shiny black eyes on him and blew pipe smoke. "The Enemies have never surprised me," she said irritably.

"No," he said, "I didn't mean the Enemies. I don't suppose they have surprised you for thousands of years."

"Boy, if it is clever to suppose such things, it is even more clever to keep them to yourself."

"Yes, Grandmother," Peter said respectfully.

"Since you're so clever," she went on, "I'll ask *you* a question. Do you know why the Star Men came here?"

"Yes, Grandmother. They wanted to talk to the Enemies."

"They wanted to talk," she agreed. "And it's a damn good thing they didn't know what you and I know, eh?"

Peter understood that he was being invited to express another opinion. "That our Enemies are a dying clan," he said.

"Because if they had known that, they might have felt compelled to tell the Enemies that they knew it. That they could help, maybe make a deal. And what would have happened then?"

"Our Enemies would have felt such contempt for them they would have killed them. Possibly us too. Possibly not."

She laughed, a sound like grinding metal. "Don't let the possibilities get you down, boy. Here's some advice for you. Let the ESAs take you in. They'll be good for you, and you'll be good for them."

To his astonishment, Peter felt a wave of relief. "Thank you, Grandmother," he said softly. "I'll take your advice."

"Of course you will—you're not a fool. Now come with me. It's time for you to join your friends."

Argus stood. "The shuttle is coming."

He had begun to wonder if communications would ever work on or near Belarus again. He was certain either the Enemies, or Baba Yaga, or God knew who, had decided that people should only talk the old-fashioned way inside that gravity well.

A hatch opened in the bottom of the metal hut that still perched over them. The legs bent further, bringing the small square of darkness within ten feet of the ground. And then a boy fell out of it.

He landed in a heap, looking very surprised, but otherwise unhurt. The hut stood up, and lurched away. They watched it run across the blasted landscape, kicking up ashes as it went.

"Peter," Kathryn said softly.

He got to his feet. "I lived," he said wonderingly. "I have been to hell and back."

She ran to him and hugged him so hard it was a wonder the boy could breathe. "There, there," he managed to say. Then he opened his eyes wide and stared at Seesil.

Argus turned to see the shuttle approaching from the south. He resisted the urge to wave. Serina came to stand beside him. He ventured a question.

"Did the Enemies bring us here just so they could blow us up?"

"I doubt it," she said.

So did he. "Where do you suppose they went?"

She didn't answer. Either she was thinking about it, or she was tired of saying *I don't know.*

The shuttle landed softly nearby, and the team greeted the technicians inside. Argus boarded last, taking one final look at the burned landscape that should have been their grave site. Then he hauled himself into the shuttle. Squeezing into the passenger section, he discovered the only empty seat was between Serina—and Vasily Burakov.

The ex-embassador gave him a faint smile. "It would appear I'm no longer persona non grata with this regime."

"A lot has happened since we were away," said Argus, strapping himself in.

Vasily lost his smile. "A lot has happened. And I'll tell you all of it. But first, my friend, some terrible news about ESA Nesto."

Commander Hale got the news that Argus and his team were picked up unharmed. He was surprised to hear it. He was equally surprised when the Grinder destroyed a small piece of the Arctic continent, then stopped.

"I wonder how it shall affect weather patterns," mused the Woov.

"I wonder what was so important there, the Enemies thought they had to take out twenty square miles of ice and rock to get rid of it," said Hale.

"Part of Loki's old arsenal, I suspect," she offered.

"I was just thinking of that old saying," he mused. "The enemy of my enemy—no, I can't quite bring myself to say it."

"How odd if it were true," she agreed.

Together, they watched the Grinder lift itself from the gravity well. Hale half expected it to burp. Instead, it established a synchronous orbit and maintained a position that kept it constantly on the opposite side of Belarus from Archangel. Once there, it did not become four pieces again, but it seemed to shut down in all other respects.

"Our wait is over," said the Woov. "For better or worse, these Enemies have ended their long silence."

"Right," said Commander Hale. "Let's just hope we can stand to hear what they've got to say."

The local police had sealed off the street in both directions. Star Men and Kremlin police filed in and out of the embassador's house. Every inch of the crime scene was thoroughly documented, but ESAs were the ones who removed what was left of Nesto. It took several containers.

Argus Fabricus was sorely grieved, but he remained the steady professional throughout the ordeal. Grigory admired his self-control. His own emotions were running much hotter than that.

Details hovered like sprites. Evidence had been left all over the crime scene. This was not John the Murderer's old modus operandi, but John had stolen the body of Ivan the Mystic. Word on the street was this chimera now called itself Lazarus. ESA Elders believed that Lazarus had lobbed a missile at Fabricus's rescue team eleven minutes after he killed ESA Nesto.

Grigory stood in the night air, listening to the noise of men trying to make sense of chaos. One thing became clear to him immediately. The Belarusian officers took Nesto's murder very personally. One officer sought Grigory out and introduced himself as Evgeny Rostropovich.

"Nesto thought like a policeman, a soldier," he said. "He died on the job."

"All ESAs do the same, eventually," said Grigory.

"You look like a man who needs to go for a walk," said the officer. "Me, I have to stay and write reports. I have to organize the evidence, make sure it's properly handled and stored. I have to file away a man I loved like a brother."

"I'll walk for both of us, then," said Grigory.

"Good," said Evgeny. "And since you're going to get thirsty with all that walking, here's the name of a certain tavern . . ."

Winter was taking over the streets of Moscow, not creeping like a cat, but blowing in like someone had left the doors of a frozen hell wide open. Grigory did not adjust the controls of his suit. He knew that as long as he kept moving he would not freeze. Other Muscovites knew it too. They thronged the street as if it were a pleasant spring evening. He heard talk on all sides of the Grinder that had hovered over the city, and people asking if they were on the brink of another Enemy War.

"Star Man!" Vodka fumes blew into his face and a huge hand closed on his shoulder. "What do you see with those red eyes? Hell itself?"

"Not hell," Grigory replied gently. "At least, not yet." He slipped out from under the hand and kept walking. The air smelled of snow, of smoke and urine and horse manure; he heard the clatter of hooves, singing, cursing, shouting, and laughing. And then he heard something that made him stop.

"Watcher."

Grigory had never heard his secret name spoken aloud before, and had never heard this voice that had just spoken it. He smelled a woman who carried the lingering odor of a hospital with her.

"You have something to tell me?" he asked.

"Don't kill John the Murderer," she said. She stood less than a foot from him, the crowd on the sidewalk jostled both of them as it flowed around. He did not wish to stay there, but the quality of her voice transfixed him.

"Who are you?" he asked.

"Mimi. As soon as I saw you, I knew I must deliver the message."

"From whom does this message come?" he asked.

"The voices tell me everything, and sometimes I can tell the right people about it. John is Lazarus now. He must live because he has a part to play our salvation."

"Mimi—" Grigory could hear the sincerity in her voice, and the odd combination of wisdom and innocence. "He is evil. He will do nothing but harm."

"He is Lazarus," she insisted. "He has not yet become everything he will be. For one thousand years he was John the Murderer, and he slept with the dead. He slept, and we fought the Enemies, our oldest and worst enemies, until after centuries of fighting and hating we have come to know them and they to know us as well as our two species can manage."

Grigory had heard this before. Andrei confided it to him, the message Baba Yaga gave him centuries ago, the warning.

"And now," he said, "what truth have your voices learned, little mother?"

"That the Enemies are not our worst enemies."

"Who is, then?"

"ME is."

The answer sounded comical. But Grigory felt as if someone had just touched the back of his neck with icy fingers.

"I only say what the voices have said." Mimi spoke softly. No one else could have heard her. "I know you have vengeance in your heart. The voices say you must deny it, that you must wait for Lazarus to turn his genius to our advantage. Be more patient than you have ever been in your life."

The rage that had him driven him into the streets still tore at his self-control. Yet he also knew the truth when he heard it, even from a perfect stranger, and he spoke gently to her. "Do your voices have a name?"

"Yes," she replied.

"Is one of them named Tally?"

"Sometimes," she said. "But not this time."

"Who is it this time?"

"Nefra."

Grigory had never heard the name before.

"Nefer-ra is the long version," said Mimi. "It means, *beautiful in the eyes of Ra.* I can see her in my mind. She is like her name. She won't know until she sees you, and you won't know until you find Spritemind, and Spritemind won't know until it hears the Doomsday Song. None of it will make sense now, except to Lazarus."

"Mimi," said Grigory, feeling his anger turning into ashes, "do you know what he did to the girls?"

"I know," she said sadly. "I know better than anyone except the dead." She touched him with a small, cold hand. "When you see Lazarus, speak to him as another Russian. He will understand you as John the Murderer never could."

The little hand slipped away, and Mimi was washed away with the flow of the crowd. Grigory could have caught up with her in an instant, but he stayed where he was. His resolve had vanished, and he merely stood in the street and felt the cold wind, smelled the smoke, the people and their animals, and the scent of an impending snow storm. He heard the same laughter, the curses, singing and crying, shouting and simple conversation—and those bells, which Tsarevich Peter had hated so much.

Moscow has all of those blasted bells! I don't know why they have to ring them all the time. Day and night . . .

Tradition. One thousand years after Andrei Mironenko founded his colony, Belarus wasn't perfect. But it was strong. It had survived Enemies, and John the Murderer in two incarnations, and Grigory supposed it would even survive him.

Someone stopped just behind him, and he recognized another scent.

"ESA Grigory," said Argus.

Grigory turned. "You've come to bring me back," he said.

"I suppose," said Argus. "Or to help you. I'm not sure which. But we both know we can't just go wring the man's neck."

"I've heard he might prove useful someday."

"Baba Yaga said something like that."

"The notion strains faith to the limit."

Argus clapped him on the shoulder. "Shall we walk home again?"

"Might as well. I don't know how this new body handles vodka, or I'd invite you for a drink." Grigory fell in beside the embassador, and they made their way through the crowd. No matter which way he went, Grigory seemed to be going against the flow of traffic.

"We've got booze at home," said Argus. "And now there are only two of us to drink it. I sent Kathryn and Peter up to Archangel with the others."

"Glad to hear it," said Grigory. "So now it's you and me against the world."

"Vasily is still sequestered with the tsar. Pretty soon, he may be on his own here."

"And what of your mission, Argus? Are they giving up on these Enemies of Belarus?"

"I don't know." Argus was low-key, as always. He was very different from Andrei Mironenko, yet he had the same courage, the same calm in the face of trouble. "It was hard losing Nesto. But I confess I thought we might all be killed when we were assigned here. Now things are changing, and what saddens me the most is that I may never find out why."

"Maybe it's worse to find out," suggested Grigory.

"Maybe. For now I've been told to hold down the fort at the house. Everyone is still on holiday, unless the Grinder decides to come back and eat Moscow."

"I don't think it will," said Grigory.

"I don't either. But beyond that—"

They walked in silence for several minutes. The cold air felt good, but Grigory's senses were beginning to tease him again, like they did the day Seesil danced in St. Petersburg.

"I have also spoken with a Woov Elder this evening," Argus said at last, then gave a short laugh. "She called on the telephone. She warned me about a new menace on the horizon. She seemed to think you might know something about it."

"Did she mention a name?" asked Grigory.

"The name she mentioned," said Argus, "was actually a pronoun."

"Understood."

"Tell me, ESA Grigory, have you ever seen a hellhound?"

"Never."

Argus sighed. "No, you never see them until they strike. But it's good to know who they are, even if you can't see them yet."

"Good to know," said Grigory, suddenly looking forward to a good, stiff drink very much.

After the Enemy device destroyed the installation and its nine remaining missiles on the Arctic continent, and before police raided the hidey-hole outside Zhukovka, Loki would have gone into hiding, possibly even left Belarus. But Lazarus went home to his humble apartment and went to sleep. Once he woke, thinking an inhumanly slender woman was standing near his bed. She evaporated like a dream when he opened his eyes. But he did not think she was a figment of his imagination.

He washed his face and felt refreshed. His reflection in the mirror revealed no sign of strain or worry. He was only mildly surprised to discover that Enemy defenses were stronger than Loki had assessed them. The complexity of their technology tickled his imagination.

If Argus Fabricus was truly a man, he would come to settle accounts with Lazarus. And he had no doubt the Enemies did not like the way he aimed his missiles. So when he heard a rap on his door an hour after sunset, he thought it could be just about anyone. He consulted his sensors, then let Nikita Mironenko into his humble apartment. Nikita was carrying a bottle of vodka.

"Sit." Lazarus offered one of two chairs that flanked a

small, battered table. He fetched two chipped glasses and sat in the other chair. Nikita poured vodka into the two glasses. They drank.

"So," said Nikita, "this is where the Mystic lived when he was Ivan."

"It suited me," said Lazarus.

Nikita filled the glasses again. "Does it still? I can arrange for something better."

"So can I." Lazarus studied his old associate openly. "I have better things to do just now. But what about you, Nikita? I doubt you're just sightseeing here. Has Tsar Gyorgy promised to give you any of the Fabergé eggs?"

"No." Nikita's expression remained placid. "I have made my offer, a variety of useful devices and services that the Union won't make available until the pesky issues of repatriation are resolved. He made his counteroffer. I shall soon reply. But for now I wish to become reacquainted with old friends. Tell me what happened to you after the Civil War."

John never would have held Nikita's gaze the way Lazarus did. It would have seemed too intimate to him. Besides, one was very likely to give away secrets with the merest flicker of a glance. But Lazarus gave away only what he wanted. "You know what happened."

"I've seen the records," admitted Nikita. "I wanted to hear your side."

"My side would make you sick."

"No. It would make me less ignorant."

"I amused myself with worthless pursuits," said Lazarus. "They got me killed."

"Did you really hang yourself, or did you have help?" Nikita drank his second glass as if its flavor were something to savor.

"I don't know," said Lazarus. "I wasn't there. But I intend to find out, someday. I'll let you know."

Nikita shrugged. "This world has more secrets than most. I've done some research. I've been allowed access to some private libraries, but not the one I really needed. And I've been back to Natalia Korsakova's tomb, but that wasn't very helpful."

"Did you access her database?" asked Lazarus casually.

"Frankly, I might have been tempted to do so if I could. But she was gone."

Lazarus felt his soul become very still. "Gone," he said.

"Her body has been taken from the tomb," said Nikita. "I wondered if you might have been responsible. But seeing your expression now, I doubt it. I've had a good deal of time to go over the records, especially those compiled by Emily Kizheh. I discovered an interesting tidbit. ESA Grigory had an Avatar."

Lazarus did not speak, because he could not. The name filled him with too many emotions.

"I queried my contacts on Archangel and discovered that a new body was constructed for him, and he has returned—"

Nikita paused when Lazarus seized his arm.

"To Belarus," finished Nikita. "He would have good reason to access Tally's database, don't you think?"

"He has her," said Lazarus. "He took Tally."

"Tally?" asked Nikita, cocking an eyebrow.

Lazarus was almost startled into a laugh. He let go of Nikita's arm and downed his glass of vodka instead, to clear his head. Once he was steadier, he said, "I loved her."

Nikita poured another glass for both of them. "Well. Who would not? Such a face. And such a mind to go with it. It's a rare person who can create worlds. Most of us can only destroy them."

"I honor her memory," said Lazarus.

"Yet you tried to kill her."

Lazarus was steady again. "Loki tried to kill her. *I* am God's servant."

They drank quietly for a time. The bottle became half empty, but neither of them lost his faculties.

"My sons were killed," Nikita said at last. "My family decimated. The Republic fell and none of us could stop it. We have lost most of our influence, but not all of it. We still care about what is rightfully ours. I want the eggs back, and I think I'll get them. But things are changing. New threats have arisen. Enemies are everywhere, my friend."

The word did not seem to have been generically used. "Go on," said Lazarus.

"You were the first to see them. You could have killed them with that missile, if you had chosen to fire it earlier. And you could ferret them out now, if you wanted. They only destroyed one of your caches, true? Many of your weapons still exist, I suspect."

Lazarus thought about his surveillance of the Enemies, and how much Loki had admired them. He would have left them alone if Argus and his team hadn't invaded the hive. But he never wondered *why* he felt that way. "They are Godless," he mused.

"Yes," agreed Nikita. "And as I said, they are *everywhere*. Not just on Belarus, my friend."

Again, Lazarus was surprised.

"The first ship to encounter them was the Union ship *Sojourn*," said Nikita. "Since then, seventeen space stations and twice that many ships have been savaged. Two small colonies vanished without a trace. I've seen the records concerning the atrocities committed here on Belarus, and I assure you they have been comparable elsewhere. The Union has fought back, of course, but it's been expensive, especially in lives.

"That's what the Union is really doing here, Lazarus. Embassador Fabricus was commander of a special force that successfully destroyed a large Enemy base before he was assigned here. He is the only commander who has returned from a mission alive, so they think he can find a way to negotiate with the monsters. Belarusians have survived with Enemies for a thousand years, and the Union hopes to learn something from them. But I wonder if they are making a mistake. It's very possible that Enemies can and should be wiped out."

"No," Lazarus said flatly.

"You're so sure of that?"

"Yes."

"You have weapons that could do it, Lazarus."

Lazarus downed another glass of vodka. "Maybe," he admitted.

Nikita smiled gently and poured two more glasses. "I hoped you might see it," he said. "I don't pretend to know anything about Ivan Sergeivich Khabalov, but I knew Loki. He was a master of weapons technology."

Lazarus did not preen under the praise, though it was true. Nikita had enlightened him far more than he had thought he would, but Lazarus did not return the favor. He knew many things about the Enemies he had not seen fit to share. He knew that the band who lived on Belarus could not simply be colonists.

They must be refugees, or they would have called upon their kin to aid them in the Enemy War. If they died, no one would come to avenge them. He wondered how ESA Grigory would feel about that. Would he be pleased to see them dead, or frustrated that his beloved Union had been thwarted? And would that please God?

"Where is ESA Grigory living these days?" he asked.

"With Embassador Fabricus," said Nikita, who watched him through hooded eyes.

Lazarus recalled the images he had seen of Argus Fabricus and his team of ESAs inside the hive. They had all worn danger suits, and he had not looked closely at any of them.

If Nikita knew he had surprised Lazarus again, he betrayed no sign of it. "You're not feeling vengeful, are you—my friend?"

"No," said Lazarus. "Merely curious."

And that was the simple truth. Argus Fabricus had not pursued vengeance yet, and neither had ESA Grigory. "Have you wondered," he asked, "why the Enemies have allowed me to live, though I have twice almost killed them?"

Nikita drank the glass of vodka as if it were his first of the evening. "I assumed you would not let them," he said.

Lazarus smiled. "I have done nothing to stop it," he said.

"Nothing?"

"I wanted to see what they would do. I confess, I didn't expect Fabricus to escape my missile. I'm impressed with his resourcefulness. And now suddenly all my enemies are exercising extraordinary restraint. That's interesting, don't you think?"

"That's as good a word as any, I suppose," Nikita said mildly.

"They should have killed me," Lazarus told him. "And they could have done it, Nikita, I admit it. There's only one reason not to kill a man as dangerous as I am. It's the same reason you have."

He studied Nikita's neutral expression and laughed. The bottle of vodka was almost gone. They would have to buy another. He would take Nikita to his favorite tavern and show him what real vodka should taste like. But first he had to make something clear.

"You don't kill someone," he said, "when you think he may be useful to you someday. That's what you hope. That's what they hope. And you want to know what's funny, Nikita?"

Mironenko did not ask. But Lazarus told him anyway.

"You may both be right," he said, and winked with his blue eye.

Yuri of the *okrana* stood on the Union embassador's doorstep and rang the bell. He was not surprised when a blind man answered.

"The Eye of Grigory," said Yuri. "The legend has come to life."

"Some would argue I never died in the first place," said the blind ESA.

Yuri gestured with his cigar. "Would *you* claim that?"

"Never," replied Grigory.

"The eye is in your head," said Yuri. "Which one? The right?"

"The left."

"It is the property of Tsar Gyorgy and the government of Belarus."

"It was never the property of anyone but myself," said Grigory.

"You can argue that. But I must take you into custody. I have questions. You can answer them or not, but you're coming with me."

"Very well," said Grigory. He did not seem alarmed; nor was there a trace of threat in his demeanor. Yuri had not expected him to consent. He was pleased. He knew where he wanted to take the Star Man.

Yuri's car was one of the few motor vehicles that could be found in Moscow, and he drove it carefully. The Star Man rode with him to Gorky Park, asking no questions along the way. Yuri imagined he knew where they were going and why, and he was impressed.

"So." Yuri puffed on his cigar as if it were some apparatus he needed to breathe. "You put your memories inside a red gem."

"My mind was stored," said Grigory, "not just my memories."

"Where did they put your soul?"

The blind ESA grinned. "No one has devised a way to store the soul, save God."

"Essentially you could be soulless. I don't know if I can trust a man with no soul."

"Do you trust any man?" asked Grigory.

"A few." Yuri parked the car near the curb. Passersby stared at it, but they saw who got out of it, so they left it alone. "Let's walk a bit," said Yuri. "You're not cold, are you?"

"No," said Grigory, who walked as if he could see.

"Those suits you wear must be well made. Me, I don't feel the cold. I'm bred to it."

A light snow fell as they walked. But the paths were

clear, and they had no trouble reaching their destination, a playground for children. Grigory stopped precisely where Yuri had thought he would.

"Tell me about it," said Yuri.

"It's a matter of record," said the Star Man. "We left nothing out. Some schoolchildren found the head of Sophia Fetisova on this spot at 7:15 A.M. No other evidence was left at the scene. No one saw anything suspicious prior to the discovery."

"How do you think he moved the bodies without being seen?"

"He designed a danger suit with stealth functions unlike anything we had seen before," said Grigory.

"He still has it," said Yuri. He studied the ESA, who did not attempt to hide his feelings about the subject they were discussing. "I have read everything I could find about the case of John the Murderer. I am a great admirer of Emily Kizheh's, and of her associate, Special Agent Bullman. Good police work is very instructive. We use their example to train cadets at our academies."

"You could find no better model," said Grigory.

"Everyone has an opinion about John the Murderer, our most notorious monster. But I wish to know your opinion, ESA Grigory. You knew the man. Why did he dismember his victims and display their pieces at these various scenes?"

"Two reasons," said Grigory. "First, because they were clues he left for us to decipher. John was such a strange mix of brilliance and infantile urges, it amused him to play a puzzle game with us. The other reason is typical of serial killers. He took his victims apart to turn them into *things,* to destroy their personhood. He displayed them to demonstrate that he owned them and to express his contempt."

"Yet his weapon, Bug Spray, saved our world," said Yuri.

"We used Bug Spray to kill Enemies. It killed Tsar Andrei too. We paid a heavy price for our association with John."

Yuri puffed thoughtfully on his cigar. The opinion Grigory expressed mirrored his own, but it was worth hearing anyway. "I first heard about you in the academy," he said. "The Eye of Grigory, one thousand years old. It still sees the world. It knows everything that really happened in the old times."

"Not everything," said Grigory. "Never everything."

"When you locked the Tomb, I knew you were not happy. You did not approve of the new government, which I was sworn to uphold."

"I neither approve or disapprove. But I knew my time here was ending. I had a life before I was the Eye, and now I am leaving Belarus. Argus Fabricus is being reassigned, and Vasily Burakov is returning as embassador. But you know all that. What else did you wish to ask me?"

"Probably there is much I could ask if I had the time. But I know you must leave. I know there is nothing I can do to stop it. And it's not within the law for me to hold you, despite what I said to you earlier. I wanted to hear some things from the man who knew them best. And now I have something to show you. But it's in St. Petersburg. One last trip, ESA Grigory. Will you come?"

"My curiosity has always been my downfall," said Grigory. "We can take an airship, if you don't mind."

"Even better," said Yuri. He took one last look at the playground equipment and felt a chill, which was rare for him. But he supposed the place warranted it. He offered a silent prayer for Sophia Fetisova, and as he turned away could have sworn he saw movement from the corner of his eye, near an old teeter-totter.

But it was just cigar smoke on the breeze, surely nothing more.

Grigory did not tell Yuri he had been present when the foundation stones were laid for the St. Petersburg Public Library, they had much more to catch up on during the trip over. Grigory heard a great deal about Andrei Mironenko's uncle Nikita, and a certain mystic who had gone through a sea change. But the smell of the library evoked many memories. They entered just as it was closing for the evening, but no one questioned or tried to deter them. Their footsteps echoed on the floors, and Grigory smelled books and the people who read them.

"Yuri," said a woman, who sounded pleased.

"Martha," said Yuri, "this is ESA Grigory. He has come to see some rare books."

"Of course." Martha smelled of soap, but also very faintly of something else, something exotically spicy and familiar. It was an odor that belonged in another place and another time. "Please come this way."

They rode an elevator down to the fortified lower levels. No one spoke on the way down, or in the hallway outside the security door. Grigory smelled the odor again when they entered the rare document vault, faint but distinct. Martha sealed the door behind them; then Grigory heard the sound of a drawer opening, and the smell of incense and old spices became stronger. He joined her by the drawer and reached in, felt the touch of several small, cold metal points, a nest of questing snake heads. He grasped them, and they coiled benignly around his hand. He followed them to their source and touched a skull wrapped in fine, dry linen.

"Tally," he breathed.

"Nikita Mironenko mentioned a database that must be imprisoned within those metal snakes," said Yuri. "Emily Kizheh also mentioned it in her journals. I can't hook up to it myself, so . . ."

"I saw Peter put Tally in her tomb," said Grigory. "Back then I was still being moved from one patched-together system to another. Peter had Tam build my final matrix as he was fortifying the tomb. He was a grandfather by then. He had laid Emily to rest a few years before. He would live another twenty without his two most beloved advisors."

Grigory had not been capable of grief back then. He made up for it now.

"These rasta-links," he said softly, "were remnants of an

older technology. I can interface with them, but I cannot guarantee that I will have access to all the information they contain."

"But you're curious," said Yuri.

"Yes."

"Martha and I shall put our faith in you—that you will share information critical to the survival of the citizens of this world."

Grigory singled a tendril out from the bunch and drew it to his right eye. It was the new one, not the eye in which his Avatar still rested, still recorded his essence. The new eye dilated and the tendril slipped in.

His skull filled with golden light, and then Grigory did something he had not done for centuries. He *saw.*

"What is it?" asked Martha with awe. "What do you see?"

"I am standing on a wide avenue," said Grigory. "It is lined on either side by double rows of Sphinxes. I count two thousand of them, so I estimate the far end is ten thousand feet away."

"You can see the Sunset Gate," said Martha, excitement straining her voice.

"Yes. Two colossal Sphinxes face each other on either side of it, and their king's beards jut toward its apex. A beetle is perched there."

"Amun-Ra," said Martha. "The celestial dung beetle. He pushes the sun across the sky."

Grigory heard Yuri's voice then. "Can you walk toward the gate? Can you touch the things you can see?"

"Probably not touch," said Grigory. "But I think I can walk—"

He took a few experimental steps forward, careful not to execute the moves in real time. But when he had gone two steps, two people suddenly appeared. Like the Sphinxes, they faced each other.

"What happened?" asked Martha. "Something surprised you?"

"Tally Korsakova and Andrei Mironenko are here," he said. "Or I should say that their images are. I think I have entered her directory. She chose an image she liked to dwell on."

"So they were lovers," said Yuri. "I've always suspected it."

Grigory had seen them gaze this way at each other many times. He studied Andrei's image. Tally preserved it perfectly, the mild expression, hazel eyes that showed laughter or anger when the rest of his face was perfectly still. He looked at Tally, and was humbled by her beauty. It surpassed anything he had imagined.

"May you dwell in this heaven together," he said, "forever."

Tally looked at him. "Do you have a query?" she said.

Grigory was momentarily speechless.

He heard Yuri say, "Can you talk to them?"

"Tally just spoke to me," said Grigory. "She asked if I had a query."

"You said it aloud!" said Martha. "She is speaking with your voice. Ask her if she can hear me."

"I hear you," said Tally.

"Are you Natalia Korsakova?" asked Martha.

"I am the directory," said Tally.

"Directory," said Yuri, "do you contain the recorded memories of the engineer?'

"Engineer," said Tally, and blinked, then said, "Initiating Imhotep program." She blinked again, so fast her eyes became blurred.

"Oops," said Grigory.

"What's wrong?" Yuri and Martha asked together.

"You said something that seems to have initiated a program. Now the image has developed a glitch. I may have to disengage and—"

Suddenly Tally's image steadied. She looked at him. "Grigory? What time is it?"

"It is four-fifteen in the evening," he said.

She gave him a half smile. "That's nice. Now what *day* is it?"

Grigory hesitated.

"It is Tuesday," offered Martha. "December twentieth."

Tally looked around the Avenue of the Sphinxes. "Who is speaking?"

"Two people are in the room with me," said Grigory. "Yuri of the secret police and Martha, head librarian of the St. Petersburg Public Library."

"The *secret police?* Tally put her hands on her hips. "Grigory, what's going on?"

He thought he'd better answer before Yuri or Martha did. "One thousand years have passed since your death, Tally. I didn't know you had an Avatar."

She studied him for a long moment. Apparently her Avatar was capable of more emotion than his had been. "My death," she said.

"Forgive me, Tally," he said. "I thought you knew."

"How could I know anything," she asked, "if I'm dead?"

"You are an Avatar," he began, but no comprehension dawned in her expression. He decided to start again. "Just now, we were speaking to a recording that identified itself as your directory. I interfaced with your rasta-links."

"Even though I'm dead," she said skeptically.

"Peter did what he promised," said Grigory. "He mummified your body and converted your quarters into a tomb."

"Peter," she said, her expression growing blank, but not from lack of feeling. She looked at Andrei's image. "One thousand years. Everyone is dead. Including me."

She gazed at the face of her beloved, and Grigory was glad that no one felt it necessary to break her silence. At last she looked at him again.

"But *you're* still alive. Except I remember you got killed. Your memories were stored in your left eye, we had to keep hooking it up to stuff ESA Tam cobbled together."

"I have a body now," said Grigory.

She raised an eyebrow. "I guess they learned a lot in one

thousand years. Did the Republic reestablish contact, or did we finally get rid of the Enemies and do it on our own?"

"The Enemies remain," said Grigory. "But the Republic is gone. It was replaced by the Union and the Bill of Rights."

"That would make Andrei very happy," said Tally, but she kept her eyes on Grigory's image. "So now I know why you're still here, but why am I? I didn't have an Avatar in my eye, or anywhere else."

"Your rasta-links," said Grigory. "They could store an enormous amount of data. And I suspect someone may have tampered with them."

"Who?" she demanded.

"Imhotep," said Grigory.

Understanding dawned on her face. "That old rascal. Why did he do that?"

"I was hoping you could tell me," said Grigory. "But I can hazard a guess. He was very fond of you. He thought your talents were valuable. Perhaps he was trying to preserve your genius."

"But *Jesus,*" said Tally, "a damned Avatar? And my body is a mummy! That's too weird. And why didn't you come to talk to me before, Grigory?"

"Because I didn't know I could," he said. "And we have many problems to deal with, Tally, just as we always did. Yuri rescued your mummy from Andrei's uncle Nikita and . . . from John the Murderer, who now calls himself Lazarus."

"He's dead," she said flatly.

"Tally—"

"No. Don't tell me he had an Avatar. Tam searched every inch of his stinking body. We destroyed every atom."

"His Avatar was not stored inside his body," said Grigory.

"That *bastard.*"

Yes, she was capable of more emotion than he had been. But it was not the passion she would have felt in a living body. He could see she was still thinking.

Yuri spoke up. "It is I who wished to speak with you, Engineer. John the Murderer walks again, but he has stolen another man's body. I don't know how it works, but their personalities have merged. The man is named Ivan; he was known as the Mystic."

"Mystic," said Tally, shaking her head. "I can't seem to get away from them."

"Someday I hope I can ask you what that means," said Yuri. "But right now I have to be practical. I have read Emily Kizheh's journals concerning John's crimes, but I need to know more about him."

"I'll tell you the only thing you need to know about John," said Tally. And then she recounted for them every interaction with John she ever had, including his attack against her. "That's the man you're dealing with," she said. "That's the guy who stole the Mystic's body. We found him dead in his cell. But I don't think he killed himself. I don't think he would ever do that."

"Who killed him?" asked Yuri.

"The ghosts," said Tally. "It was their vengeance. They drove him mad. They tricked him into it."

Grigory thought it was a pity the others couldn't see Tally just then. She looked like an avenging angel.

"Please tell me," she said, "you're going to kill the son of a bitch, right?"

"We can't," said Grigory.

"So—he's free to kill again. How many girls have disappeared?"

"None," said Grigory, then surprised himself by saying, "He is not the same man."

"That's hard to believe," she said grimly.

"Grigory is right," said Yuri. "I have been watching Ivan. He is very dangerous, much too dangerous to attack. But he seems to have lost his taste for the sort of killings John the Murderer enjoyed."

"For now," warned Tally. "Grigory, he has those dreadful weapons. We never found them all."

"And we never shall," he said.

"Then what now? Why wake me from my sleep?" She looked at Andrei again, and Grigory thought she would have cried if she could. "My loved ones and my friends are gone. My worst enemy is still walking the world. And now people want my advice, and I don't have any to give. Why did George think I should survive my own death?"

"I don't know," said Grigory. "But I think we should ask him."

She seemed startled. She turned and regarded the Sunset Gate. "Go back to Canopus?"

"He is still there, I think."

"Have you heard from that world in all this time?"

"Once," said Grigory. "Recently I exchanged a message with a person or a system called *Medusa.*"

"Never heard the name," said Tally. "Except for the mythological version. But it's been a thousand years. How that place must have changed! They've been cut off like us, right?"

"Yes. But George was a master engineer. His worlds were built to last. And I cannot help but wonder if he didn't make the same provisions for himself that he made for you."

She looked over her shoulder at him, her rasta-links slowly undulating. Grigory knew their real-time counterparts were doing the same, though the body they were attached to was long dead.

"Do you think our souls moved on?" she asked. "Or are they clinging to our Avatars?"

Grigory knew the answer. Tally herself had told him, in a dream. *You have another chance at life. Make the best of it. You won't see us again on this side of the Veil.*

"The souls we were born with have moved on," he said. "But who can say that we don't have new souls? The great mystery is still intact. We exist, Tally. No one should throw a life away because they're afraid to live it. I'm going to Canopus. Will you come with me?"

"I'll come," she said. "Where else have I got to go? Can

you rig something for me like Tam used to do for you? Will I be able to see the real universe again?"

"Yes," said Grigory. He did not add that it might be possible to do far more than that. He would not bring it up until he consulted with experts.

"I have so much to ask you," she said. "But I'll be damned if I can think of one question right now."

Martha said, "I know the feeling. Engineer, forgive me for intruding. I wish that we could meet under better circumstances. I am a librarian. I have read your books. I want you to know, your work has survived. We have suffered much on this world, but the structures you and Andrei Mironenko put in place still work."

"I'm glad to hear that," said Tally. "Thank you. And Yuri, please don't trust John. Or Ivan, or whatever he's calling himself these days. Don't turn your back on him. You know what he did all those years ago. Watch for signs, and if you see them, contact me. I swear, I'll help you kill him. If it's the last thing I do."

"It's a deal, Engineer," said Yuri. "You have my word."

"I should go now," said Grigory, regretting it. He knew what it was like to be cut off from every other mind, alone in the cosmos. "We need to make preparations."

"I'll be okay," said Tally. "I've got a lot of room to explore in here. Maybe I'll have some good ideas the next time we speak."

"I don't doubt it," he said. "Good-bye, Tally. It's . . . good to see you again."

"I'll be waiting," she promised.

He pulled the link out of his eye. His sight went with it.

"Well," said Yuri.

"You're taking her," Martha said sadly.

"I must," said Grigory.

Martha closed the drawer. "She's safe here until you come and get her. I swear it."

"It should be a matter of hours," said Grigory. He turned

to where he knew Yuri was standing. "Have your questions been answered?"

"Yes," said Yuri. "And no. But I am satisfied. I could not let them touch her, ESA Grigory. Do you understand? She is the engineer. She is the reason I exist."

"Perhaps you will see her again someday," said Grigory. "The universe is strange."

"No argument there," said Yuri. "Come now. Back to Moscow. You must have packing to do."

⁂

Embassador Argus and ESA Grigory entered the St. Petersburg Public Library near sunset, accompanied by Yuri and Martha. They exited carrying a long box. Passersby noted that the box was odd; it had blinking lights on it. Everyone wondered what was inside. But no one would ever know. The Star Men loaded the box into their flying machine. They waved good-bye to the short man with the cigar and the head librarian, and they flew away from Belarus, never to return.

But so much happened after that, hardly anyone noticed.

❦

Serina slept in her quarters on Archangel, but not well. In her dreams, she ran through the endless underground tunnels of the empty hive. Someone pursued her, and in the first days after Peter had been rescued, she thought it was Enemies. But in the dreams that followed, her stalker began to talk to her, and she knew his voice.

You took what was mine. Now you *are mine.*

She wanted to stand her ground. It was shameful to run. But something terrified her beyond reason, something in his voice. It was an echo, as if someone else spoke with him, almost too quietly to hear. It was that other who drove Serina over the edge and kept her running through the darkness. She looked for an exit, and prayed, though it was useless. And then she was aware of a new presence.

Just ahead of her, a small pedestal stood in the center of an alcove. A rose climbed up its base, tiny black flowers bloomed in profusion. And on the pedestal were the head and praying hands of Tatyana Slepak. Serina knelt before the pedestal, overcome with weariness.

Tatyana's eyes opened. Blood poured out of their corners like tears.

Serina was transfixed. The dead girl looked at her as if

she were trying to speak with her eyes. But the voice came from behind her.

"There's a price for my cooperation. You'll pay it, Serina. I want nothing else."

"I'll accept nothing from you," she vowed. "Nothing!"

"Nothing," he said. "When you could have anything . . ."

Tatyana wept blood, and Serina felt dampness on her own cheeks. She wiped them, looked down at her hands, and saw dark smears.

The message alarm woke her. She stumbled out of bed, fumbled for the comm. "I'm awake!" she said.

"It's Argus. Are you all right?"

"Groggy," she said.

"Wake up fast. Tsar Gyorgy is here with Vasily Burakov."

"Yes." She rubbed her face. "I can be ready in ten minutes."

"Serina, better drink some coffee. They brought Ayat-ko."

She opened her eyes. Suddenly coffee did not seem necessary.

Serina met Argus, Commander Hale, and ESA Grigory outside the large door in the docking bay. "We aren't going to a conference room?" she asked.

"They've requested to meet near their ship," said Commander Hale. "We agreed. This is the first meeting we'll have with an Enemy, face-to-face."

She nodded. They opened the door, and a slight breeze rushed past Serina, into the big bay. Grigory and Argus entered first, Serina behind them. They immediately spotted the three people on the other side of the bay, standing near the nose of their shuttle.

Ayat-ko stood in the fore. Gyorgy and Vasily stood just behind, on either side, and Serina had little doubt this meant they would back up anything Ayat-ko had to say. This pricked the scalp at the back of her neck. When they were within ten paces of Ayat-ko's group, Argus and Grigory moved aside so that Ayat-ko and Serina faced each other.

The Enemy woman wasn't smiling yet. "I see the shroud has been cast aside."

"Useless now," said Serina. She studied her Enemy openly. Ayat-ko had discarded the ornate dresses of the human upper classes for her own version of a danger suit. She looked every inch a Witness. Serina looked away briefly to meet glances with Vasily Burakov, whose neutral expression revealed more than it concealed, and then at her uncle Gyorgy. Gyorgy stood fast, but he seemed to have aged years in days. His appearance illustrated better than anything what a dreadful job it was to be tsar.

Serina returned her attention to the woman who stood across from her. "Ayat-ko, why did you kidnap Peter?"

"Because you would not give us a Gift, we had to take one."

"I don't understand." Serina watched for changes in those eyes, but the stars at the center remained small and cold. "A Gift must be given, and Peter was never harmed."

"The concept of the Gift escapes many, even among my own kind," said Ayat-ko. "Peter served to clarify and illuminate many things. He was the Gift that suited the situation, and now we are moving forward again."

"What do you intend to do about John the Murderer?" asked Serina. "He attacked you. Your machine destroyed his missile base, but you have done nothing more to him."

The cold eyes did not waver. "He did not attack us, Serina; he attacked *you.* But you are important to us, and we won't allow him to harm you. He is a wild card, like Peter was. We will watch him. But you are the person who concerns us now. You and the Union." Ayat-ko turned her gaze to Argus Fabricus. "I have a proposition," she said.

"Indeed?" said Argus. "I was given to understand that your kind do not make propositions. You fight or you die; isn't that so?"

"My brothers and I still live," Ayat-ko reminded him.

"One assumes you are still fighting."

At last she smiled. "We could have wiped you and everything you have made from the face of this world. We have the weapons. But what purpose would that serve?"

Serina was overcome by bitterness. "What purpose did it ever serve? You were there, Ayat-ko. You must know why your people attacked us in the first place."

"That was the work of a fool. I could not stop it. Yet I think it was not in vain, because now we have both come to the brink of destruction. Now we can see what we could not have seen under any other circumstances."

"What do you see?" demanded Argus.

The stars at the center of Ayat-ko's eyes expanded and contracted with pleasure. "My clan have spent one thousand years among humans. We have changed Serina's clan—they have changed us. We seek to learn new tactics."

Argus frowned. "Is that all you can think of? Is there nothing more in your imagination?"

"There is something more," she said, losing her smile. "Grope for new concepts, as I do, Argus. After one thousand years, the softness of your kind no longer surprises me. But your strength does. You may have a chance against our mutual . . . *Enemies.*"

"You can offer assistance?" he asked.

"I help myself. My clan is twice conquered. Once the strong clans you have encountered have smashed you, they will kill us too. In their place, I would do the same."

"It must comfort you to hold no doubts," he said.

"Perhaps I can comfort *you,* Argus. I have a suggestion."

"I'd like to hear it."

"Have children with us."

The remark was answered with stunned silence; Serina's ears rang with it. Ayat-ko had uttered a complete non sequitur, yet she seemed to think it was completely plain.

"Ayat-ko," she said numbly, "what in heaven's name are you talking about?"

"Continued existence for both of us," said the Enemy. "And for someone new as well."

"You are serious! Even if we should wish such a thing, after what has passed between us, we are two different species. And how could it possibly help us to survive?"

Ayat-ko slid her gaze back and forth between Serina and Argus. "It is possible, child. Our best minds and yours can achieve it. We are all masters of DNA. Isn't this so, Argus? And as to your second question—remember that I have lived in your household for forty years. It is possible that you and I could negotiate an agreement in some matters. Even though I could kill you anytime I choose, my Serina, I might still feel compelled to listen to you. Do you know how extraordinary that is?"

"Yes."

"Good. But your Star Men can't afford a thousand-year war. Not with *my* kind. Listen to me, you humans. We were outnumbered here in the Dark Veil. We were injured, our technology depleted, and look what we did to you. And now consider what Enemies would do if your numbers were equal and their guns just as big—"

Her gaze slid to Argus again.

"—or bigger—"

"Are they?" he asked.

She shrugged. "I don't know. We have had no contact with other clans for thousands of years. While we have hidden here just trying to keep ourselves alive, they have had time to advance and conquer. Who knows where they are now? Do you care to guess?"

Serina felt numb. She had never considered the concept of an interstellar war with well-armed Enemies. It was too horrifying. "The children," she said. "Why do you want to have children?"

"To bridge the gap," said Ayat-ko. "To understand both sides. They will know, because their blood will know."

Serina was dizzy with the idea. She could not help but think of Anastasia, so beautiful and so cruel. Would this new race be like her? She stared at Ayat-ko and wondered. Ayat-ko was not like Ana. Her ethics were vastly different from Serina's, yet she *had* ethics. Ana could not have even grasped the concept.

"Ayat-ko," she said suddenly, "does the idea frighten you at all? This new race?"

"Yes, it frightens me. But I have better reason for that than you, child."

"How so?"

"These new people," said Ayat-ko, her eyes glittering, "will be half *human.*"

"Interesting." Grigory spoke for the first time, startling Serina. "That is what bothers me as well. They will be half human; they will need affection, consolation, affirmation, and many other things that you cannot even imagine."

"Perhaps not," admitted Ayat-ko, "but Serina can imagine. I will listen to her, ESA, and to you. This brood will be raised most carefully, for they are the future of my people. They will help ensure yours as well. This is so."

Serina's heart beat like a hammer. She looked to Argus, admiring his stony expression. Grigory was also calm, almost intrigued. Once more she turned to Ayat-ko, to find herself watched with that old, cool expression. Once more she remembered a day long ago, standing in the forest with her tutor.

Unveil your eyes. What do you see . . . ?

"Andrei Mironenko argued with your people for so long," Serina said sadly. "He tried to make them see that our fates were intertwined, that we needed each other. Can it really be true that you have only reached this conclusion after a thousand years of war?"

"Yes," said Ayat-ko. "Understand that, if nothing else. I am here now because my clan will not accept extinction. Death holds no honor for us, only oblivion. Andrei Mironenko wanted to talk with us; the Union wanted to talk. Now we have told you what we must have from you, what we will give in return. It remains for you to say yes or no."

"Say yes."

Everyone froze at the sound of the odd, harsh voice. Then a diminutive figure emerged from the shadows behind the shuttle. She walked with the aid of a staff, and in her other hand she gripped a pipe. She moved deliberately, but without a trace of decrepitude, and stopped within a few feet of Grigory. She pointed at him with the stem of her pipe. "Say yes," she repeated, "for this is what must be done."

"Why, Grandmother?" he asked.

Serina stared at the face of a legend. Glittering black eyes looked back at her, but they were not like the eyes of an ESA. They were real, darkened with extreme age, full of a powerful intelligence that would not be ignored or denied. Baba Yaga turned her gaze to Ayat-ko, and Serina thought she saw sparks of bloody red in her scrutiny. "You want to preserve your clan from extinction," said the grandmother witch. "I wish to do the same for mine. This conflict with the Enemies in space can strengthen or weaken us—we must choose to be stronger. Soon we will be fighting a greater enemy than either of our races has ever encountered."

"I have not seen this new enemy," replied Ayat-ko. "But I would not be surprised to. If what you say is true, then we must become allies."

"Your kind have a fatal flaw," said Baba Yaga. "But you may have found a way to fix it. I support your plan, because these strong clans who oppose us now will never be convinced of their error, though they have already been weakened by the conflict. They do not have a thousand years to learn the lessons you have learned." Baba Yaga looked sharply at Argus, Grigory, and finally Commander Hale. "This was the goal of your mission. You have accomplished it. You did not know how your problem could be solved, and you would not have believed me if I had told you."

"How long have you known, Baba Yaga?" asked Commander Hale.

She laughed, a startling sound. "I've known since before Russia was a country, let alone a space colony. You, Grigory"—she pointed her pipe at him again—"you're done here. You know where you need to go next. And you"— this time she indicated Serina—"do what you were raised to do. That's my advice. Everyone here knows their responsibility, yes?"

No one dared to answer.

"Then we have a deal," said Baba Yaga.

Details remained. Ayat-ko would remain on Archangel with Serina. Vasily needed to tie up loose ends for another day, before resuming his duties as embassador. Gyorgy took Serina aside before he departed for Belarus.

"Baba Yaga is right," he said. "You were raised to do this job. I envy you, because I was thrust into my role. I had to adapt to it or die. Your mother and I lived a rough life when we were growing up. We knew how to survive. But I confess, over the last thirty years, I have wondered many times whether I was up to the job."

"You must have wanted it," Serina said softly. "You killed the Mironenkos for it, Uncle."

He looked dreadfully tired, but her accusation did not make him angry. "I didn't want their lives. They died for only one reason, Serina. When Ayat-ko came to them with her proposal, they refused."

She could scarcely believe her ears. "She made this proposal to them?"

"Yes. They would not bargain. They thought they could wait out the Enemies. But Galena and I grew up on the frontier. We knew otherwise. I enjoyed the power at first, I admit. But that pleasure wears thin very fast, Serina, and all that remains is work. I'll do this job until I die. I hope I can die honorably. *You* are the one I must trust now. I believe you're up to it. You must believe it yourself."

He kissed her on the forehead, then climbed into his shuttle. She went to the observation lounge and watched it depart. Then she went in search of her Enemy.

* * *

Sunlight slanted into the room, illuminating the right side of Ayat-ko's slender form. She stood before the giant view window, her back to Serina, like a goddess looking down on the blue-white world. Serina stopped within ten paces, and waited. The Enemy turned her face full into the light and looked at her.

"You stand like a soldier," said Ayat-ko.

Serina stared at her. For thirty years Ayat-ko had been a part of the life she knew, wearing the dresses of an upper-class Belarusian, walking the halls of the great house or the garden, riding in fine carriages. If she imagined her anywhere else, it was in a moonlit glade. But *this* was Ayat-ko's true element, this metal and glass place suspended between heaven and earth. With Belarus turning at her feet, her intentions were crystal clear.

"You don't want to make these hybrid children simply to make peace with the Union," said Serina. "You hope this new race we are creating will kill the other Enemy clans."

"They must decide for themselves what they shall do," Ayat-ko said stonily.

"You know what you *want* them to do."

Ayat-ko smiled, but not in her usual cruel fashion. It was an expression Serina had never seen before.

"Your Star Men are far too merciful," said Ayat-ko. "You know that."

Serina said nothing, though she privately agreed.

"I know my own kind, too," said Ayat-ko. "And now my clan numbers less than one thousand."

Serina was astonished, not only because she didn't know Enemy numbers had fallen so low, but because Ayat-ko had actually revealed this fact to her.

"We can't fight billions," Ayat-ko continued. "And humans think only of peace. Now the time has come when my clan must declare peace with you, but there are conditions, child. Always conditions. You know that. You would never give us a Gift."

"Never," Serina said firmly.

"Now we shall give you one. This will secure your future as well as ours. Now is not the time to be squeamish."

Serina felt herself wanting to agree, and was suspicious of the impulse. "How long?" she demanded.

"How long will it take to fight this clan war? Perhaps a hundred years. Perhaps two."

"And you will live to see it all."

"If I do not die of violence, yes. You will too. I'll see to that."

"You believe I will consent to that," said Serina, astonished.

"I believe you will once you perceive your responsibility. It is your nature to do so, as it was your mother's."

In her mind's eyes Serina could see Galena in her sitting room, drinking tea, her cuff buttoned neatly over the knife with which she had killed to secure her position. "What if these hybrid children turn on us both?" she asked.

"They will not turn on you. You will teach them to love you."

Skepticism and a vague horror warred with each other within Serina. "To *love* us?" she said softly. "Do you know what that means?"

Belarus rotated to present the frozen expanse that linked its North Pole to Siberia. The light shining from the snow was almost too bright to bear; it glistened in the whites of Aya-ko's eyes.

"*They* will," she said. "That shall have to be enough."

"And what will *you* teach them, Ayat-ko? What is your legacy?"

"Strength. The will to survive. And a code by which to live."

The idea made Serina a little ill. "What manner of code? The same that guides you?"

"Not the same," snapped Ayat-ko. "Our code will not serve them. Yours is also inadequate. They will need something new, something absolute. It will guide them through their lives and with the cultures they must encounter. It will teach them to conduct both war *and* peace."

Ayat-ko glided across the floor, closing the distance between them. Serina met her halfway. She gazed into the face of the Enemy, now in shadow while her own was warmed by the light of day.

"Are you beginning to understand?" asked Ayat-ko.

"You and I are to make this code," said Serina.

"You and I."

"That's one hell of a job."

"None are more suited to it." Ayat-ko cocked her head. Suddenly she touched Serina's disfigured jaw. "That is what I saw in you twenty-four years ago, when you looked into the mirror. You and I are each of our kind, yet apart from them. We can see them as they cannot see themselves. We are childless women, yet we will make a race together. They will be strong, beautiful, deadly"—she let her hand fall again—"and ruled by an iron law," she concluded. "That is our contribution to the future. Otherwise there *is* no future."

Serina believed her. Nothing could have surprised her more. And she understood how her mother must have felt when she made her bargain with Kunum-ko, for she was poised to do the same.

"One thousand years ago," said Ayat-ko, "Andrei Mironenko asked us a question. We did not answer, because we do not tell our secrets to enemies. He asked us: *who are you?* No clan would ever have answered. But it was a good question, for it caused me to wonder who might have the right to ask it. And now I know. You have the right, Serina."

Serina was almost moved to tears. Any human would have asked Andrei's question. One thousand years later, her race had finally fought long enough to get the answer. "Who are you?" she said, her voice steady.

"My race is called Ur," said Ayat-ko.

The tears came then, but Serina made no move to stop them. It was Ayat-ko who wiped them away.

"Our children shall weep too, and laugh. And they will Dance, Serina. Do you understand?"

"Maybe not," said Serina. "But I will. And you will. Whatever the consequences, my Enemy."

At last Ayat-ko smiled one of her old smiles. "You *do* understand," she said. "I believe you do!"

Archangel turned, its inhabitants prepared for the future. One of them prepared to leave—forever. Argus walked Baba Yaga to the bay door.

"I have one question that must be answered, Grandmother. If we do what Ayat-ko requests and create these children for her, will there be any need for human beings in this universe once they have reached maturity?"

"Ah—" She puffed on the pipe until its bowl glowed like a hot coal. "Are they going to replace you? Is that what you're asking?"

"Exactly."

She grinned, showing every one of her pointed teeth. "Never. Even with human blood, Ayat-ko's clan will never grow numerous enough to outpace you. And they will be bound to you by bloodlines that will be far more important to them than they ever were to any human clan. They will be dangerous, beautiful, and clever, Argus. You will admire them and pity them, and they will earn both. But they could never replace you, and they will not want to."

He believed her. But it did not comfort him. "I don't think I can overcome my misgivings about . . . making children who never asked to be made."

"Yes." She blew a cloud of smoke past his head. "Good thing it's not up to you. Come on. Give me your arm. Where are your manners?"

Argus offered his arm and she rested her clawed hand on it. She did not lean on him, nor did he need to slow his pace unduly to walk with her. They strolled together down the empty corridor until the lock was in sight.

"One more question," said Argus.

"No," she snapped.

"Grandmother—"

She turned and jabbed her pipe at him. "I said *no*. You have survived longer than any mortal who ever stayed in my company. Don't push your luck, Argus."

"Mortal?" He raised an eyebrow.

"I will live to see the end of this story," said Baba Yaga. "You'll have to watch it from heaven—just as everyone eventually does. Everyone but *me*. Time to go. Open this lock."

Argus obeyed. He escorted her into the lock and stood with her until the door of her hut ship opened. A wind rushed out of the ship, so warm it was almost hot, and Argus glimpsed an interior decorated with carved wood and Persian rugs. It looked nothing like a spaceship.

"Will I hear from you again?" he asked.

"Perhaps. I'm not clairvoyant. There may be a good reason for you to hear from me again. If not, good luck to you, Argus. Find out as much as you can. You'll live longer." She jabbed the pipe at him one last time. "But don't try to find it out from me."

Baba Yaga went into her ship without looking back. The door slid shut behind her. Argus exited the lock and sealed it. He turned to find Vasily standing at the end of the corridor.

"She's gone," said Vasily.

"I'm sure she is."

"No," said Vasily. "I mean from Belarus. She's done with this world. We won't have a Baba Yaga anymore."

"Not that one, anyway."

But Vasily shook his head. "She was the only one, the real one. She was Russia before it was Russia."

Argus walked away from the lock and joined Vasily, weighing his words. Vasily did not look upset, but he was a master at schooling his expression. "Surely," said Argus, "Belarus has enough magic, enough history of its own."

"Enough monsters," Vasily said, and Argus was at last able to see the sadness. "Belarus teaches hard lessons, but some of us learn them too slowly."

"At least you learned something," said Argus. "I'm still in the dark."

"For a century we've been trying to negotiate with the tsars of this world, and with the duma. We thought it was taking a long time. But it was never they who were making the decisions, Argus. It was Ayat-ko. And a century was nothing to her."

Argus thought about that. But it wasn't any memory of Belarus that prompted his answer. It was a thousand memories of endless fields of snow, and of huge, clawed hunters that looked at him over their shoulders.

"Maybe her life spans centuries," he said. "But her death will take seconds. She knows that. And so we have our deal, Vasily. It's the best we can do. You're the best man for this job now, the only man."

"Yes," said Vasily. "But I would be dead if Gyorgy hadn't kicked me off the planet for twenty-three years. He thought I would guess the truth about his deal with Ayat-ko. But I don't compliment myself; if some other embassador was available from the Repatriation Department, he or she would do just as well. They even asked if you should keep the job."

"They didn't ask me," said Argus. "But the answer would still be no."

"So I'm elected. Be careful what you wish. But I have a question for you, Argus. Ayat-ko was the one who told me you could not be embassador anymore. She said you would be too busy chasing hellhounds. What in blazes is a hellhound?"

"Specifically?" said Argus. "A hellhound is a scavenging predator that steals your prey from you after you have already expended every ounce of your energy to catch it."

"Uh-huh," said Vasily. "Sounds like hard work."

"Yes." Argus clapped him on the shoulder. "Civil service. Sometimes it really sucks."

Baba Yaga was gone, and Grigory was going too. Andrei Mironenko's great experiment had succeeded in ways he could not have imagined, but the Eye of Grigory would watch his world no longer. The time he and Kathryn shared together on Archangel was short. Then she had a young ESA recruit to train, and Grigory must take Tally to Canopus to find George, or Spritemind, or both.

As he walked the corridors of Archangel he remembered many things that had been said and done there one thousand years ago. The Star Men had repaired her thoroughly, but she was not the same. She adapted to her time, just like the Star Men. And Grigory too, with his new body, new friends.

And old, old devotion.

<Watcher.>

Grigory could not even smell her. Her body made no sound as she approached him. He felt no displacement of air. But as soon as she communicated he knew who she was, though he had not met with her for a millennium.

<Elder, I am honored.>

<You did not sense me,> she chided.

<No.>

Suddenly her scent came to him, reminding him of herbs. She laid her furry hand on his wrist gently. He did not flinch. <I must make a request of you.>

<Anything,> he promised.

<Your eyes, Grigory.>

He could not answer. His failure to perceive her presence had disturbed him, but eyesight would not necessarily increase his awareness. For over thirteen hundred years he had believed it would do just the opposite.

<Do you remember what it was like to see?> she asked.

He remembered the katerinas in bloom. He remembered three women he had never seen with his eyes, and one of them said *Someday they may offer you another pair . . .*

<A New Age has dawned. We cannot rely heavily on the sprites anymore, Grigory, even if they come back online someday. We have made adjustments. We must all get new eyes. I think you shall find that these are worth having.>

Think twice before you say no . . .

<This goes against my instincts,> he said.

<Does it?> she wondered. <Still?>

For a thousand years he had been incapable of instinct, because he had no body. And now he was in a body that had desires and feelings that sometimes surprised him. His old life was gone. His old pain should not influence him anymore, yet it did. Kathryn had probed some sore spots. Was he afraid that beauty would betray him again? If he were so vulnerable, might not his other senses make him just as foolish?

A New Age . . .

That's all I can get away with telling you.

<All ESAs are to get these new eyes?> he asked.

<All of us,> she confirmed.

<I am still an ESA, Elder.>

<So you are.> She placed his hand on her face, so he could feel her smile. He gave her one of his own.

Argus meant to go to his own quarters and turn in. But to get to them he had to pass Serina's. Even that might not have stopped him, if he hadn't spotted her standing in an observation alcove. He paused.

"Have you ever flown into the Veil?" she asked softly, as if she had expected him.

He looked past her at the view. The Veil obscured half the stars. He joined her in the alcove.

"We've sent probes in there," he said. "None of us have ventured in ourselves. It seemed pointless."

"And dangerous," said Serina. "Something evil is in there."

"I think you're right," he said.

She did not sigh, or take the opportunity to complain of the burden that had been placed on her shoulders. He studied her profile and saw not a trace of sorrow. Like his mother, she would never complain, and he must not speak sympathy for her troubles. But he had something else to offer.

"I'm glad you have decided not to wear your veil," he said. "Or your visor. I want to get to know you as you really are."

"And so you shall," she said. "I'm not ashamed. I haven't been ashamed for years, only . . . cautious."

"I think you will find that Archangel society is far more receptive to your abilities," said Argus.

She was silent, and he debated telling her some of the other things that were on his mind. Yet he didn't feel inclined to rush that. The hunter in him still enjoyed pursuit, and he knew when silence was his best tactic.

"Do you recall my portrait that hangs in the Moscow City Library?" she asked.

"Vividly."

"The artist who painted it was my lover for a short time."

"Ah." He was surprised. He had not imagined that a shrouded woman, even one as privileged as Serina, would be able to steal such freedom for herself. And in her world, the danger of pregnancy was critical.

"There were two others," she said.

"You need not tell me your private matters," he said.

"Why not? You are curious. You wonder how awkward it would be if you were to approach me romantically."

"Yes," he admitted. "I wondered. But I would not have been deterred by . . . awkwardness."

"You thought I might experience physical pain if I were too inexperienced."

He took her hand and kissed it. She did not pull it away

from his grasp, but twined her fingers in his. Her hair, usually wound carefully into formal coils, was loose on her shoulders, and he doubted that was an accident. It was extraordinarily beautiful. He touched it.

"You were right all along," he said. "I'm no embassador. I'm happy to hand that role back to the man who is best suited for it."

"Shall you be leaving soon?" she asked.

"I don't know."

Her breast rose and fell, but still she did not sigh. She seemed, instead, to be drawing energy into herself. "We have more in common than I imagined. We are both the children of savage worlds. And we are both bound by duty, yet free to make choices. Our choices may have heavy consequences. Yet there is one choice we can make that will do only good."

She turned to him and regarded him with eyes the color of the summer sky.

"Shall we?" she asked.

He kissed her. Her lips might be imperfectly shaped, but she used them more skillfully than most. "Take me where you want to go," he said.

Hand in hand, they left the alcove. It grew dark as Archangel turned and sensors dutifully recorded the impenetrable blackness of the Veil. Those who stood on the night side of Belarus watched that edge of oblivion move across the sky. They did not fathom its depths—they did not try. Their lives were changing, but the world remained the same, and some things would never be known.

In Red Square, a woman stood before the statue of Tsar Peter and looked at the boy on his shoulders. She wept a little, but she was happy. "You're where you belong," she said. "But you'll always be my Peter."

Young Peter sat on the stone shoulders of his father and smiled into eternity.